SAILOR TO A SIREN

C000007520

To Catriona

SAILOR TO A SIREN

ZOË SUMRA

Elsewhen Press

Sailor to a Siren
First published in Great Britain by Elsewhen Press, 2015
An imprint of Alnpete Limited

Copyright © Zoë Sumra, 2015. All rights reserved
The right of Zoë Sumra to be identified as the author of this work has
been asserted in accordance with sections 77 and 78 of the Copyright,
Designs and Patents Act 1988. No part of this publication may be
reproduced, stored in a retrieval system or transmitted in any form, or by
any means (electronic, mechanical, telepathic, or otherwise) without the
prior written permission of the copyright owner. All rights reserved.

Elsewhen Press, PO Box 757, Dartford, Kent DA2 7TQ
www.elsewhen.co.uk

British Library Cataloguing in Publication Data.
A catalogue record for this book is available from the British Library.
ISBN 978-1-908168-67-2 Print edition
ISBN 978-1-908168-77-1 eBook edition

Condition of Sale
This book is sold subject to the condition that it shall not, by way of trade
or otherwise, be lent, re-sold, hired out or otherwise circulated in any form
of binding or cover other than that in which it is published and without a
similar condition including this condition being imposed on the
subsequent purchaser.

This book is copyright under the Berne Convention.
Elsewhen Press & Planet-Clock Design are trademarks of Alnpete Limited

Printed and bound by CPI Group (UK) Ltd, Croydon, CR0 4YY

This book is a work of fiction. All names, characters, places, law
enforcement organisations, gangs, inter-galactic agencies and events are
either a product of the author's fertile imagination or are used fictitiously.
Any resemblance to actual events, agencies, policemen (and women),
places or people (living, dead, or mystical) is purely coincidental.

For Lucy and Jay,
because three heads
have always been better than one.

CHAPTER ONE

A gunshot cracked off the tenement roof and cut the Pellite security guard through the throat. He crumpled where he stood, beak-jaw falling open, toes clawing deep into the alley dirt beneath him. As his pectoral muscles relaxed in death, the plasma bursters mounted on his primaries' tips drooped on nerveless wings. One discharged its bolt with a dull thud into the splintering warehouse door behind the guard. The sound, like the gunshot that had killed the bursters' owner, echoed and died in the carnival hum from a few streets away.

Connor Cardwain slammed a fresh plasma pack into his pistol and ran out of the side alley where he'd crouched to watch the door. One shot for the door's lock. A second and third for the gunbird just inside the warehouse. Running feet in heavy boots jarred the alleys to either side, boots belonging to the underside queen Meris Hardblade: up above, he just saw the rooftop sniper skirting the gantry that spanned the street.

Standing over the guard, half in a muddy puddle, he could smell him: feather mites, the oil that the cob had been preening from his breast, burnt flesh and sinew. *You shouldn't have looked up*, he wanted to say, *you made her fire too soon* – but the guard had been doomed from the moment another gang's eye landed on his charge.

Thakar and Zack ran up behind Connor, already breathing hard. As Carm appeared from the opposite direction, Thakar brushed past the others and set his heavy shoulder to the warehouse door. He crouched, then shoved the door wide and rolled into the room beyond in one quick move. Carm slid in after him, dark hair bouncing at his shoulders and jacket buckles clattering: Connor and Zack followed.

Gunfire rang from the other side of the warehouse, and clattering, as shattered pulleys cascaded to the ground. Standing ten feet ahead was a pallet sprayed in the Pellite gang lord Sl'arani's rearing snake logo, twin to the one Thakar was already using as cover. A gunshot burst over

Connor's head close enough to singe his ponytail. He sprinted to the pallet.

Zack hit the ground beside him, still taking a few neat leftward shots. No one could blame him for staying behind the rest: he was much shorter than Connor and much slighter than Thakar."Where's Logan?" Zack called over other men's screams.

"Late," Connor answered.

Over the way, a window shattered, and a second wave of Hardblade's mercs swung in feet first with heavy rifles up. The fight should have been over as soon as they hit dirt. But instead, a plasma volley rocketed back at them, peppered with the warehouse's candleweed stink, scything into them as if they were flowers.

"He's not late," Connor said under his breath. "We're early."

"Late," said Zack. He'd have added more, but a door on the far side opened and he and Connor ducked further into cover. Shots hit their cover-pallet. White powder plumed into the air.

Connor clamped his free hand over his mouth and nose, and ran zigzag for Thakar's pallet, firing backwards as he went. One of the plasma streams gushing at him sputtered and stopped. Lucky shot. Nothing more.

He rolled into cover behind Thakar, who was taking aim at the closest defence team. Zack cannoned into them both, mumbling apologies.

"Where's Logan?" Thakar said over his shoulder.

Connor levelled beside him. "How do I know?"

"He's your bloody brother."

"And I –"

He broke off and, focusing past all the noise, sniffed. Drugs, urine, gun discharge, spicy food-smells coming in from outside.

But –

A tinny acridity boiled on the air, barely sensed or comprehended. Connor grabbed Zack in his free hand and Thakar in the hand that still held his pistol, and dragged them both to the ground. Ionised oxygen zinged. Connor bit his tongue. His gun, in the hand part-full of Thakar's jacket, went off. Thakar swore and squirmed away.

Lightning crackled overhead. Thakar, three feet from Connor, squealed like a dying pig and fell to his knees, dropping his gun. A gunshot just missed him: a second lightning strike cracked into one of the squad who'd come in through the window. She howled, and went down twitching.

"Weaver," the cry went up. "It's a Spellweaver!"

"Stand firm!" Connor shouted. *Think*. A straight hit to the window crew, but a skewed one on his team: if the Weaver could see the former but not the latter, he must be on the far side of the warehouse.

He leant round the pallet, snap-shot towards the far back left and pulled back to cover. His bolt had hit another bale. Weed, this time. Dope-smoke drifted from the hole. Connor closed eyes flash-blinded by his gunshot, and concentrated on what he'd seen in that fraction of a second. The pallets, the target he'd tried to make: the Pellites' main defence barricade right at the back beyond the pallets – and, behind the row of gunbirds defending that barricade, a glowing silver figure.

Connor opened his eyes and, still crouched against his pallet, calculated. Hardblade had sent in three lieutenants to lead the lines: him, Thakar and Mikkson. Mikkson had been cut down with the window crew and Thakar was out of action. That left him.

He snapped fingers at Zack and Carm, and pointed them round opposite sides of their cover pallet, towards the Pellite team at the far left. Instead of following, he pulled Thakar, still shaking uncontrollably, into cover. He squeezed Thakar's shoulder in a meagre farewell, and cut off ahead and right, towards the few left from their window crew, towards the main gun position, and towards the Weaver.

His stomach was roiling hard enough to make him want to vomit. He'd killed a Dalishian once, a ton of web-handed oozing blubber moving so lightly on his feet that Connor'd been wrong-footed by his pace: he'd aimed his shot at a blood sac, and hit lucky. Ditans, the living humanoid robots, were easy – just move in at close quarters with sufficient force to splinter silicon bones and shear their greenish biocrete skin. Absent any reputation they'd gained by murdering their way out of slavery, they were weak. Weaker still were Sapilians, tiny frill-eared swamp-dwellers, saboteurs extraordinaire. As a boy Connor'd been able to skewer a Sapilian, provided he stayed focused, but as a man he'd found it easy to talk them out of his way. He'd never taken on a Kriastan, not at close range – suicidal for one thin-skinned human to go up against their scaly mass – but he'd once cajoled a squad of strongmen high on testosterone and steroids to waylay a would-be turf jumper on her evening stroll. Two of the strongmen had even survived.

But those were adversaries he could outmuscle or outsmart. A Spellweaver? Didn't matter what species they were: when the magic bit them, they all came out one of thirteen lethal variations, raw bright threads spinning from their fingers into a murderer's curtain. Connor spat into the dust. *Fuck all magic.*

Mikkson was sprawled atop a corpse near the window, sightless eyes staring at the ceiling, but a handful from his squad were still crouched in thinning cover keeping up sporadic fire: two senior women and a man little more than a boy. Connor gestured for the women to stay in position and for the youngster to follow him. *Take out the Weaver. Take out the Weaver and the rest will flee.*

One wing strayed over the Pellite gun crew's position. The young merc aimed at it: Connor pulled the boy's weapon down and beckoned him on. It was a rounded crest, not a pointed tip, with real feathers on it: feathers a man could pluck out, instead of an illusion cast in one of a dozen shades of mage-light. A Pellite gunbird, one of the enemies they'd reckoned on meeting here, not a Spellweaver.

Behind them, Carm and Zack's guns bit out, sharp and short. In the half-second's silence before the defence line's barrage restarted, Connor heard the roof hatch creak. He risked a glance upwards. Not one of Sl'arani's crew – that was Galene and her sniper rifle sliding through the door.

If Galene could get a bead on the Weaver, Connor would be a mite happier. He beckoned the boy merc closer behind him. New to Hardblade's gang: maybe seventeen, so he'd lived long enough, but Connor had never bothered learning their names till they survived their first run as men. Right now he wished he'd done otherwise. He wished he knew who the boy was, what had pushed him here, why Hardblade's captains had jumped for him instead of another gun just as cheap, why he'd not yet broken and fled.

He edged to the corner of the next pallet. The youngster, at his back, moved very well – near as damn it to silent on the balls of his feet, free hand holding his nose against the fumes. Connor had breathed in too much weed: the world was starting to quiver. Close enough or not, they'd have to move now. Pellites didn't get high off the same chemicals as humans: Sl'arani's mercs would stay clear-headed, though they might start having trouble breathing soon, and the smoke would wreck their gliding feathers.

And the Weaver? Human and stoned, or Pellite and sane? Connor shivered. Never give a stoned man a gun: a stoned man with supernatural powers didn't bear contemplation.

A casing panel prised off one of the pallets, thick with scribbled delivery diagrams, clunked against Connor's foot. He grabbed it and tossed it high into the air over their pallet, towards the Pellites' position. Ten feet behind him, simultaneous gunshots from Zack and Carm cracked out and past his head, shattering the panel. Molten plastic rained over the Pellites. Amid the squeals, Connor lunged round the pallet, firing.

One Pellite was right in front of him, back arched in a hideous rictus and plastic dripping down his wings. Connor sent two shots through his head. *Keep going.* Guns blazed round the other side, where the boy merc had gone, and now more: Zack and Carm coming up to join in. A quick whistle over Connor's head from Galene, street-speak: *go, go.*

He cleared the pallet. Sl'arani's defence squad was there, behind a barricade in front of the foreman's plasterboard office. A flash of silver incandescence, behind the gun squad – the *Weaver*...

Lightning blossomed over Connor's head. He hit the ground half a second before an electric bolt struck the pallet. The air shook with screams and drug plumes. Overhead, more magical lightning arced around the rafters. Some of that yelling was Carm, maybe the gunboy too.

Connor struggled to his knees. Gun, still in his hand. Couldn't close his fingers. Couldn't move. *I'm dead. Fuck all magic.*

He lifted his head. In the silver-tinged air he saw the Weaver rising, angel-bright. It was a human woman, with a bolt of lightning held in each hand like some pagan goddess from long ago: wings flowed out behind her – glowing wings, silver-blue and unreal. They seemed *holy* wings, a mockery of the pinion-and-feather ichor-stained masses lying splintered on the floor.

But behind the glory-vision, a hell's gate opened.

The back door. It's the fucking back door. Wake up, Cardwain!

– A hell's gate, with a titan barring the way. And the titan raised a pistol and fired it at the Weaver's head.

She turned spirit-fast, lightning scything with her like twin swords. The man in front of her – *Logan, it's Logan* – fired wide right at Sl'arani's squad, tossed his gun to his other hand and shoulder-barged the Weaver, spraying shots left-handed into the Pellite crew. The last bird standing raised a wingtip burster towards him. Galene, above, took the Pellite merc through his skull.

Her second shot hit the Weaver and bounced off. So did Logan's follow-up. Connor staggered to his feet. Weavers – magic – what in eleven hells could a man do?

Logan dropped his gun. He'd a knife out in his right hand already. So had the Weaver. Silver crackles ran up the blade – she'd electrified it.

Connor stared at the office roof behind the two combatants. The portion closest to the Weaver's head was swaying hard. He raised his pistol and squeezed the trigger.

He missed, but someone to his left – Zack, or the gunboy – fired and hit. Debris clattered past the Weaver. She flinched, and glanced sideways.

Logan flung his knife to his right and latched both hands round the Weaver's throat. Lightning strands peppered him. A crack, and the silvery death fell around his feet like rain, first puddling beneath him, then slowly sinking into the concrete floor. The Weaver woman went limp in Logan's hands, and her beautiful, impossible wings faded into her back and vanished.

Connor staggered towards his brother and leant on the

Pellite mercs' barricade. Welcome to Pell Havasi, indeed. He'd throw up any second at this rate. Drug-smoke, and that electric maelstrom.

"You OK?" he said.

Logan dropped the dead woman and nodded. Gold eyes twin to Connor's raked him up and down – predatory eyes, crazy eyes, so the whispers said.

"This all of us?" Logan said, gesturing to Galene making her way down from the rafters, Zack and the gunboy by the pallet, and Carm and Thakar behind.

"There's two alive back there." Connor jerked his head at the shattered window. Nine left. Less than half their team.

Fifteen or more of the Pellite gangsters lay dead, though, with the Weaver in the middle like a fairground prize. Connor leant harder on the barricade, struggling to breathe. Twenty-eight years old: he was aging fast.

Old enough to know the Weaver didn't fit. Connor aimed a shaky finger at the dead woman. The big gangs had cash for such, if they spent it where it counted most, but: "Why stick a Weaver *human* here? This stock's all for the human trade, and you can't risk a Weaver getting high."

"Mistake," Carm said, dropping the block of weed he had been checking for purity marks. "Got to be." He ambled past the gunboy peering at the dead's spilt purses and Zack busy pilfering them, bent over the woman and pulled up her sleeve.

Glistening black on her dull tan skin, a tattoo lurked on her forearm – a ring-shaped lattice, so complex Connor wouldn't have been able to trace the links if he'd just come off eight hours' sleep. The symbol of the Weavers' Circle, the mage-merc cabal.

Zack looked up, clinking coins between his fingertips. "I didn't think Sl'arani rated Circle staff."

"Festival traffic," Thakar slurred from behind him. He was leaning on a slanting pallet, dusted in so much white powder it looked like he'd taken a sand bath. He aimed a finger at Connor. "You shot me."

"Accident."

Galene stopped with her knife still wedged in the office's lock. "You could've done with what she was wearing." She indicated the dead Weaver. "Shields against gunfire –"

Thakar spat. "More magic."

Logan leant over Galene and shoved the office door free from lock and hinges. "Defence magic."

Carm looked up at him, quite a feat. "You been chatting up Weavers?"

Logan tossed a couple of cash bags out of the office to Galene, scooped up a handful of recording rings and data handhelds, and poured them into Connor's unsteady hand. "I can read. Try it sometime." He studied another few recording rings on the office bench, selected one that fit his hand and slid it on. Galene manoeuvred past him to capture the rest.

Connor fumbled at the phone built into his neural jack, and got a connection on the second try. "Cardwain reporting," he said under his breath, just loud enough for the jack to pick up his vocal vibrations. "All clear. Send in transport." He left the phone on just long enough to hear the on-planet captain Tam Coker's acknowledgement from base. God, the trucks had better hurry. He had a powerful urge to go to bed and stay there for a week.

Reports first, to Coker in person, and to Hardblade via quantum tangler. Meris Hardblade, one of the most powerful bosses in the Milky Way's Septième sector, had outlasted a dozen captains and a few score lieutenants: Connor was often surprised she remembered who was alive to serve her at any one time and who had died or left.

Carm stood up and kicked the dead Weaver's arm back across her body. "Fucking menace, these are. Ask me, I'd line 'em all up and make 'em eat their own threads –" He broke off as Logan latched a hand round his throat, picked him up and slammed him back into the wall, hard.

"Hey!" Zack shouted. Logan – nine inches taller than Carm – held him up for another frozen second, then dropped him in a pool of ichor and walked out without a word.

Carm sat up rubbing his throat. The gunboy, who'd lifted a dead Pellite's money belt like he thought the older men would take it straight off him, stood staring at the swinging door with the belt beating time between his hands. Zack stood up, airing uncertain looks at Galene on one side and

Connor on his other. Connor swallowed a few expletives and what felt like a quarter pint of blood.

Killing calmed Logan down. So why would he get riled at the end of a fight?

Screws loose, demons in the soul: Connor had heard all the euphemisms. Crazy men had their uses. The ones who'd do any task, however bloody: the ones who'd run ahead of the line into battle, neither because they were young enough to think they'd live nor old enough to know the score. Any number of reasons to keep them alive.

Just as many to kill them off. Especially the smarter ones. Especially the ones who'd been hellraisers as boys and devil-spawn by twenty. Logan was twenty-three.

In the back, the warehouse door rattled off its remaining hinges, and two armoured cars slid inside, stuttering on overclocked thrusters. Both lowered their bellies to the ground, hydro-jets scorching the concrete: doors marked with Hardblade's mesh-cloaked sword symbol popped open, and a handful of armoured mercs jumped out of each. The closer squad leader gave Connor a truncated salute.

"Load up," Connor called to her, "and check our fallen – I think they're all dead, though."

"Yes, Mister." Two of the mercs peeled off to attend to the bodies on the ground – those bodies with opposable thumbs instead of claws – and a third helped the remaining pair from Mikkson's window squad, both injured, into the closest car.

Connor slid Sl'arani's handhelds into his pocket, hooked Thakar's arm and walked him towards the cars. "If you could have a word with Coker..." he murmured.

"Save it. You'd do better paying Carm to shut up." Wincing, Thakar sat down on the edge of the car's tailgate hard enough to make it bounce. "You want me to help smooth over Logan's crazies, you start by apologising for *shooting* my *arse*."

"Barrel'd been the other way round, it would've been your gun arm's shoulder. You're not Logan: you can only shoot with one hand."

Thakar shifted on his sound arse-cheek and looked up at Connor with over-bright eyes. "If I could tell you to quit him, I would."

"Don't even try." Connor scuffed one boot against the dusty ground. "He has his stable moments –"

"And he's been getting *worse* –"

"Most of three years. I know." Nearly three years since those steady months when Connor'd thought his brother had grown up, when the casually sadistic, adrenaline-soaked, oversized boy had come back from a run wearing a man's maturity. Working harder, drinking less, making his guitar sing instead of scream. Then the guitar'd begun crying, then raging, and the boy Logan had been back again, but bigger and meaner than before. Connor held in a snort. Harder, too. That Weaver girl should have killed him – she'd poleaxed Connor with just a scuffed blow from her spells, yet Logan had walked away after a direct hit.

A pair of Hardblade's crewers manoeuvred a pallet high with blocks of weed towards the car: Connor stepped clear. Now the screaming had stopped, the music a few streets off was all the louder, and the smells of over-spiced meat and fireworks threatened the warehouse's smoke-stink. One week – one ridiculous week when the Pellites welcomed everyone in a thousand light-year radius to cavort on their planet. One week when they fleeced humanity just as hard as they'd once been fleeced in turn. One week when the underside lords – drug barons, slavers, pimps, racketeers, mob kings and queens of every description – hitched up their underwear and joined in.

Connor surveyed the warehouse, increasingly forlorn as it emptied, red and black bloodstains and spilt residue telling a tale on its floor. Making money seemed sickening at times.

Carm was limping towards the cars with one hand over his throat, making the most of his hurts to anyone who'd listen, with Zack and the gunboy ambling behind – the former seemed to be doling out some sage advice, though Connor had no clue whether it would be followed. Galene had dodged all the fuss and was stripping her rifle at the side of one of the cars.

"You had it good, earlier?" Connor said to her, gesturing upwards.

She pushed a few straight dark strands of hair out of her face, back towards her waist-long plait. "No trouble worth speaking of. Where's Logan?"

"Don't know." He grimaced. Logan probably wouldn't reappear any time soon, which was no bad thing under the circumstances. Connor would have time to square things with Carm, and with Tam Coker.

Galene, barrel in one hand and stock in the other, pulled a not-again face. "He's riding for a fall. I wish he wasn't, Connor, but you're losing hold of him."

Connor stared up at rusting roof beams and ran over options in his head. A loose cannon like Logan would never lead a gang, or serve as a captain: make him leave the underside? How and to where? There wasn't a spare scrap of Septième that lacked an underside tentacle prying at its roots.

Off the Septième, he'd find trouble on any planet he hit. Fatal for other people first, sure, but fatal for him in the end. Buy him a ship and tell him to stay in the air? The pirates would gun for him – they'd gun for anyone who flew as well as he did: the better the target the better the tale – but maybe, maybe, he'd have a chance.

Disgorging Logan anywhere and anyhow would mean money. Connor glanced back at the warehouse floor again, dusted with tiny filaments of weed, of unadulterated cash. If only he'd run this operation as a man rather than a lieutenant, he'd have money and a day to shift Logan anywhere he wanted.

"Anywhere he agrees to go," he muttered to himself.

Galene tipped an elderly flash-darkened ioniser out of her rifle, slid a new one into position and started reassembling the gun. "Logan? Maybe he won't want to leave."

"Then I'd better work out what he *does* want."

*

CHAPTER TWO

Lights, glimmering and gaudy, thrashed against heads and faces in time with the music. Logan pushed his half-drunk beer away and stared at the crowd scattered round the bar. Seven species jostling and smiling, even if a smile meant less than nothing to them – smiles dressed in Septième gangland badges, or Huitième merchants' insignias, or logos of the massive trader conglomerates from the Treizième sector: White Canyon, Lionstooth, Cliff Enterprises. Whole thing looked like a target field, one of the ones rigged up by the big bosses or the richest cop squads, 3D pictures of people in the dark. Ten, twenty seconds. No more. Ten, twenty seconds and he could fire off enough shots to take out the lot of them.

Tonight's third girl captured his glass and jigged it back and forth between two fingers. Afraid, like a lot of them were, but she hid it well.

"You want something else?" she said.

"No." He still drank, but he didn't get drunk any more. Ellie'd never got drunk.

She smiled. Paler than him, with olive skin and rich brown hair: the yellow light flashing around her made her look stoned and sick. She dropped the glass and slid half off her plastic bench, bending over him. "Sure?" she said, dangling her right hand to his crotch.

Memory shifted, hard enough to make him sick. He yanked her upright by one wrist and tossed her back onto the bench. "Get out."

Fear won, now. The girl pulled her hand free and bolted, past a few courting couples, a pair of mercs shaking on a deal and two Pellites spitting insults at each other.

Logan grabbed his glass and gulped. As he set it back down he caught sight of his reflection in the lager. For a second he thought he saw Ellie beside him. *'Don't rely on this,'* she'd said in that thick Neuvième accent of hers, looking up from waist level where she'd knelt to work. *'The less you use it, the longer it'll last.'* Odd, serious eyes had met his, another side to a woman he'd no right to say he knew. *'I'm sorry it's so little, but it's all I have for you.'* He'd wanted to say she owed him nothing, she'd paid it off between her legs already and he was desperate for her to stay, but the pale yellow light had shifted round her again: *her* light, rising from her in wing-shapes brighter than her gold hair, and as she'd closed her eyes he'd known there was no point asking. Girls like her didn't stay with fourth-rate ganglanders, hired guns with nothing. Girls like that got whatever they wanted, and damn what their men wanted.

He *remembered*: touching her wings, feeling their threads run through his hands like hot rain he couldn't squeeze and hold – a something built from nothing, just as impossible as watching her kneel in front of him. He'd longed to ask her to bend closer, to put her mouth on him and suck him like a street whore, but he'd just sat, dumb and stupid, while she wrapped her magic threads round him.

'Don't rely on this.' His hand crept to his chest, where that other Weaver girl had pounded her fist on him, first in confusion, then in panic, then in death-flail. Nearly three years, and Ellie's spell had still been working. Likely it was gone now. Did he care? Only in that Ellie'd gone with it.

This sort of shit was meant to stop, when a man bedded another girl. It hadn't. Close to cheating him, this half-dead emptiness, and he'd never taken well to being cheated.

Logan drained his beer, tossed the glass back onto the table and stood, grabbing his jacket. Connor would shit spikes if Logan stayed out all night, like he was some ten-year-old he'd a mind to keep alive. Too decent a man at the wrong times – Connor should be doing a notch better for himself.

Across the bar, the two Pellites who'd been trading curses half-rose into combat crouch, wings spread. Logan fingered the pistol on his left hip, the one the bouncer couldn't see from his angle, and squinted at the marks on the pair's wings. Gangland symbols, as any underside man could see a street away, but neither was Sl'arani's: the pair ran with two other gangs, controlled by Hlarxi and Lt'antis. The bouncer, by the door, just glanced at the quarrelling pair without moving, and looked away. Must have decided those plasma bursters on the Pellites' wings were going to stay powered down.

For a moment Logan watched the fighters, wings contorting to claw at each other, and *tasted* adrenaline. Instead of pulling off his jacket and joining in, he released his pistol and walked across the bar towards the door.

"Pick your bloody feet up," he said to Hlarxi's bird-merc – a lieutenant: by their stripes, both were lieutenants – as he passed. "How're you going to hook his knee if you don't reach for it?" The Pellite didn't answer.

Drinkers dodged him more than they did the bar fight: drifter kids in leather and makeup, merchants and their tail, ganglanders of all stripes – watching his muscles, or Hardblade's badge. So long as he'd the both, he didn't care which they chose to avoid. The bouncer on the door puffed out his breast feathers and nodded to Logan as he passed, as he hadn't nodded to the squad of Lionstooth mercs who'd left moments earlier. Logan had a sudden urge to see what the guy did if he pulled a gun – maybe not to shoot the merchant stalking inside, with her bought yellow hair and her bought gunboys: probably not to kill her, probably just to see her squeal.

He didn't. Instead he headed off left down the street towards Hardblade's base, two miles away.

She'd run this base for longer than Logan had been alive, as carefully as she needed to avoid pissing off the locals, keeping to the human bit of the one open city, following protocol. A bit of trade, a bit of turf, just to prove she could: making contacts, and trucking in the human herbs Pellites smoked to get high. Then, once a year, came carnival.

There'd been a parade along this street earlier, dancers and music and people selling junk on the corners: now the fun had moved on, and Logan walked across the mess it had left behind, smoke wraps and streamer scraps and piss in the gutters. A few drifter kids, kin to the ones he'd seen in the bar, were scavenging for food in corners: the ragged no-hopes, thin and tattered, come not to take their chance but to be taken for a ride. One girl in her mid-teens called after Logan to stop, wait, give her money, she'd do *anything*: he waved her off, and the smaller crowd too, kids not yet ten, who huddled behind. These weren't worth the killing. The older girl, for one, would be dead by morning anyway.

Music jangled from every bar down every sidestreet, with drug-smoke puffing alongside. Glass and metal crunched underfoot from broken bottles and cans. Logan's foot nudged an empty Diakon bottle out from gutter shadow to roll across the wooden pavement, a blur of muddied label colours. A street kid darted out behind him and snatched the bottle.

The Lionstooth string who'd left the bar just ahead of Logan – not all mercs, by the way they walked: four mercs, two men and two women, and a trader who'd never held a gun – cut left down an alleyway. Logan watched them go, fingering one of his guns. He saw no reason for a clean-living pack to head that way: even if they were going slumming for the kick, he'd thought these alleys too dingy for any foreign set. Foreigners could pay for better whores than they'd find in those backstreets.

He kicked a broken pipe down the alley after the Lionstooth crowd. Such as them clung to the city as tight as its stink, in-borne humans tangling with local Pellites and other Septième folk. He'd never seen the use in foreigners. Well, most foreigners.

A few girls – dancers, by their clothes – stumbled out of a door down the alley and past the Lionstooth crew, walking like they were dead tired or dead drunk. One, barely a woman's weight with too great a fondness for blue hair dye, stopped, swaying from foot to foot, to call after the foreign men in a smoke-harsh voice. Another of the girls, skin darker than Logan's with her hair dyed blonde, pulled at the blue-head's arm: the third, pale with hair dyed copper, glared at Logan instead, as if she read him as the greater threat.

Bigger, tougher and meaner than anything out there bar a Kriastan. Angrier than anything on the streets. Hardblade's badge capping him, chainmesh covering a sword: a badge that spoke of power, for as long as she kept the rich people's politicos bribed. It served him well.

"You available, girl?" the trader man said to the blue-head.

"No, she ain't," the fake blonde said, tugging her friend backwards.

The redhead spoke, too quietly for Logan to hear. The trader laughed. "She looks big enough to me."

Behind, in a rustle of wings, a handful of Pellites tumbled out of the dancers' stage door. Drunks gone to peer at human tail, most like. The girls glanced at each other, and bolted down the alley and into a dark doorway.

Prey fled, the leading Pellite shook his head a couple of times and inclined his beak-jaw at the Lionstooth set. "You look like exporters," he said in a high, clipped voice. "I don't like exporters."

As casual as a yawn, all five Pellites stretched their pectorals, and their wings, each tipped with plasma bursters, stretched wide. Five on four, for the trader would surely turn out to be a useless quivering pile of dung. Logan loosened his right-hand pistol. No business of his, if a crowd of out-sector wanderers got taken for a rough night by a planet-grown posse, but stepping in might be fun.

Two humans – men: one tall and heavy, one shorter and slimmer – swam out of the night at the end of the alley. "That's enough," Logan just heard the smaller man say. The bigger one motioned to the Pellites' bursters. From the end of the alley Logan couldn't see much of him, only that he was nearly Logan's height and a good bit heavier.

The Pellite fivesome's wingtips drooped and they strutted off past the humans with feathers fluffing up. The human newcomers murmured smooth-downs to the flustered Lionstooth trader. As Logan turned to go, the smaller man, dark-haired and slim, looked straight down the alley at him, eyes clawing at him from the shadows. For a moment Logan considered shooting the man – for the threat if nothing else – but instead he turned away. He wasn't frightened, and couldn't remember the last time something had frightened him, but as he hardly had in years, he reckoned he didn't want to find out what would happen if he started a fight.

The busker on the next corner, a frizzy-haired human girl with a slim pure voice, had just finished her song. As Logan approached, trying not to feel like he was running away, the girl scooped a few coins from her fiddle case into her pocket.

"Play you something, Mister?" she said as he passed. "I got all the legend ballads. Smugglers cheating the cops, lovers cheating each other, Spellweavers killing for fun and profit. You want a song about Elysium, or the Harlequin?"

If she mentioned another Weaver's street name he'd shoot her, voice or no voice. He spat into the mud next to the girl's open fiddle case. "Legend ballads are for rich folk too far from the streets to see their shit hit dirt. I don't need telling about the underside. I run on the underside."

She smiled past Logan's shoulder, and he realised she was blind in one eye. "The underside's got its legends too. You a pilot?"

"I fly." He did whatever he was told to do, if he felt like it, but he liked flying. Give him a full-time pilot's seat and Ellie by his side, and he'd maybe be happy.

"I sing the Gemstone pilots' tales. You want one of those? Rubies and Emeralds starting wars, or Diamonds and Sapphires stopping them. What's your pick?"

He was set to order her back into the gutter, but remembered Ellie, laughing at a busker's song and whispering her people's rumours about Elearr de Fiorail. Fiorail had died two thousand years back, near the end of the war, but not many people had forgotten her, the fourth pilot called Pearl. "Sing *Spring Charm*," he said. He tossed a half-mark into the girl's fiddle case and walked off with that high perfect voice sketching the song's first verses.

Half a mile down the street, past a drunk rich man being half-carried by his bodyguard and a few drifters and ganglanders queuing up to mug the pair, he skirted too deep a puddle and swung left into a wider avenue free from carnival mess. Edge of the Pellites' own city, the inmost border of the one the human traders had built outside: wide and squat, with a low pitch to the rooftops and spindly gantries bridging each street. Muddier than in the middle of the human city – the birdfolk hated concrete pavements. Bloody pain in the arse for everyone else, or, at least, those who didn't have body servants to clean their boots.

Ahead was Hardblade's office, lamp over the courtyard door, guards outside to clear away trouble, cameras studding the roof and the courtyard's side awnings. Lieutenants clambering down the high doorstep onto planks used to bridge the mud. Lieutenants – Connor, and Thakar behind him, with lamplight glinting off the buckles binding their hair at their collars, and polishing their skin to copper and bronze.

Connor nodded to Logan like he'd expected to see him. "You coming with?"

"Where?"

Thakar jerked his head back towards the human town. "Scout the boss a middleman, before dawn."

Before Sl'arani got pissy about the raid and called in help to sweep them up, he meant. Just like Coker to panic and make them shift the goods before time. Still, Hardblade would be happy if they pulled in the marks.

What in hell did it matter? A year, two years, and Hardblade would decide Connor was too smart to stay a lieutenant and too cocky to play captain, and have him killed. Or she'd end on the wrong side of a gang war, and all of them with her. Who cared if a few million more marks turned up in her bank account – millions they'd see in fractions at a time, doled out to keep them in line?

But then there was Connor – Connor, who'd kept Logan alive this long: Connor, who'd just maybe got a chance of making a break for it if he pulled a few more marks. Didn't matter a snap if Logan got himself killed in a few days or months, but he'd sooner see Connor live past thirty than not.

"I'll run you some interference," he said. "You chosen a line already?"

Connor nodded, and hooked his arm as he sauntered past. "Export."

Logan blinked, and blinked a few more times when he saw that the half-grown gunboy who'd shadowed Connor in the fight was lolloping along behind them like a happy puppy. "Export. When we're in the middle of the biggest party in a few thousand light-years."

"The market here's flooded, and the big deals to shift to the rest of the Septième got signed long since." Connor's face wore that little reflective smile he pinned on for business talk – a smile that meant he wasn't in a mood to be fooled easily. "I reckon we've bigger stashes to build, we look in the right place."

*

CHAPTER THREE

The first two hours after Logan's re-emergence did not go well. Hardblade's best available intel on exporters' current habitats led them to a burnt-out warehouse and a string of abandoned boltholes of decreasing quality, and abandoning said intel failed to produce many more results. At four in the morning the city was still operating, but enquiry after enquiry at every permanent office and temporary shed in the usual export zone produced just one working operation. Connor, though, heard the boss and her gungirl speaking French inside, and retreated. Neuvième women, in his experience, bought weed and weed alone. Suggest they might like anything stronger, and they answered with gunfire.

At that point, he would have willingly shaken down a few street children himself – he'd had three hours' sleep and was in no mood to be gentle. He had his lieutenant's stripes to consider, though, and Thakar opined that their gunboy (Marcello, they had discovered) could stand to do a little work. The first underdressed girl he hauled out of the alleys was too stoned to do more than blather about firebombs and gunmen, but the second pointed them away from the blank spots towards a different area of town. By that time, the four of them had walked seven miles from the base. Rather than hike back or steal a ride, Thakar called for their bikes to be driven over, and set Logan and Marcello to circle him and Connor, taking such guard as they could.

Wise man. Monsters roamed in the darkness: drug-heads gone crazy with the junk they took, men madder than Logan with no brothers to hold their reins, other ganglanders looking to weaken Hardblade, Sl'arani's allies, anyone who wanted a slice of Hardblade's latest truckload. But the little tingle that always leached from Connor's whist cards, telling him which way to play them, now told him that he was, temporarily, safe.

As he stepped over drunks and corpses he let himself entertain possibilities till the sky seemed fuller of plans than of smoke. Sure, there was money to be made on planets like this – the kind of money gained by taking pennies from hordes, shot here and there with greater pickings from merchants, retired ganglanders, petty lordlings and anyone else who'd pulled together a little prestige. Hardblade took a cut from everyone on her turf, rich and poor, and everything, mean and great: racketeering, an armed wing for sky work, and ground runs like Connor's manoeuvre against Sl'arani, combined to tow in enough money to keep her vast organisation running.

But the real money grew in the wider galaxy, far from the Septième sector, the poorest of twenty-four circling the galaxy's uninhabitable core. Travel five, ten, twenty thousand light-years with a haul such as theirs, and the profits would double with every sector they passed, through Huitième, Neuvième, Dixième and beyond.

Hardblade had no direct export arm: decades in the business hadn't been enough for her to break into the tight-locked groups who ran that line. Very few Septième gang lords ever gained that foothold – not with hardmen guarding the keys with blood. So: sell to someone else who could export, and profit thereby.

Such lessons do I learn.

Connor idly watched a small child scamper across the gantry spanning the street above. Two streets away a temple bell chimed for pre-dawn prayers, and closer in, faint sobs carolled on the night, pierced by drifters' whistle-speak. Street names echoed in the whistles, names built from raw reputation: Flash, Blackshift, Lightlifter, names that blossomed every time they were spoken.

The familiar gave an illusion of safety, and its lack made a man more cautious than was warranted. How many times would someone from the Union of Independent Star Systems, the galaxy's most developed quasi-empire, have stood on dirt and treated with an undersider? Standing on grassy banks and drinking expensive wine was more their line, or riding in climate controlled cars over gleaming glass cities. Yes, he'd settle for a foreign exporter: someone he could unnerve.

That sort of manoeuvre might benefit Connor in other ways. He had put his chunk of Hardblade's profits aside for a good number of years: another few runs as top lieutenant, stay in position for a few fat bonuses, and he'd maybe be able to buy a spaceship. Get a ship – take his brother to crew him, as any boss would consider natural – best hope he had enough time to shake the cash loose before Logan threw a fatal temper tantrum.

He waited, while the night shaded from black to iron-grey, making desultory conversation with Thakar over cigarettes while occasional squeals and gurgles heralded amateur muggers coming up against Logan. After ten minutes the bikes arrived, two Nexi models sliding neatly to the street, one Marena from the common pool spluttering behind, and the fourth, a Connaught, sailing a few feet past the others and almost hitting a wall.

"Fucking idiots," Logan muttered, stalking out of the shadows and over to the merc still untangling himself from the overpowered Connaught XR-2 hydrobike. "Can't hold a throttle…" The merc on Connor's Nexi rolled her eyes as she passed it over. She'd known Logan long enough – unlike Marcello, all saucer-eyed – to judge his moods. Though Logan was still swearing at his bike courier while he ran delicate fingers over its controls, he wouldn't spill over.

He'd better not. Carm had not been happy earlier, and he'd made as much abundantly clear. Coker hadn't said much to Connor, but the calculation in his eyes meant Logan was approaching the point where his usefulness was being outweighed by his detriments.

If Logan had tipped over the line already, it was too late for both of them. Hardblade would see it as a personal insult if a merc ran from her judgements, and had feelers all over the sector. There was room to hope Coker would give Connor a word of warning first.

Still pondering, he mounted his bike. Thakar gestured the courier mercs back to base: as Logan threw another too-murderous look at his Connaught's most recent driver, Thakar leant in and murmured, "Who's most likely to get shot next, them or him?"

"Here's hoping neither." Connor felt the retreating mercs' eyes on him as he stared at his brother. "The longer we live the more money we make for ourselves *and for others*. Remember it."

Thakar unhooked the helmet his Nexi's driver had left clipped to the pillion. "You can't sell to corpses."

Connor had no answer to that.

He, Thakar and Marcello fired their bikes' engines and rose in a gentle spiral to rooftop level. The city spread out under them like a dozy stripper: lights lying in strings and spirals, curling round secret havens, with dark holes sinking around the poorest areas. Human city, Pellite city – all seemed one from here, the tall wood-framed arches growing out of the planet's soil and the blocky straggling cubes the humans had brought.

The longer everyone lived, the more money they all made, but not always in the way they'd want. Pellites still sang of what the Earth Federation had done in the war, thousands of years ago, with their Weavers, the Guild, at their side – slavery, dissection, death, and all of it just to bodge an advantage play against the Union and its Circle Weavers. Connor shivered in the night breeze. He fancied he saw Weavers' feathers glittering in each street lamp below. Guild of the Old World, Circle of the New – both were trouble. He wasn't minded to care about the distinction the Weavers themselves drew between their creeds.

A turbocharger squealed below, audible through helmets, and Connor suppressed a squeak as Logan rose vertically into the sky beside him. A bleep, in Connor's helmet phone: "Same again?" Logan said.

"It'll do," Thakar said, tight and hard. "Circle us wide – that thing's loud enough to break glass."

"Price you pay for a decent bit of kit." Logan wrestled his bike into reverse and soared away at an angle, a lazy parabola into the dawn. "Let's get there before the day squads come out." Connor nodded to Thakar and leant on his accelerator.

They drove high over the city with Marcello flitting around them and Logan on the wide circle. At this elevation, when Connor wound up the focal on his helmet visor he could see mountains and forests at the city's outskirts, four hundred miles away. He'd never been the kind of man to pass the borders that non-humans set on human encroachment, but that didn't stop him wondering whether the Pellite-only cities smelt as bad as human-only cities on human majority planets.

Five minutes and the dim streets below smartened by fractions: ten more minutes and they hit the best end of the human city, adjoining a wealthy suburb of the Pellite city, and Connor dropped his bike into a neat wood-cladded pub's back landing patch. He took a long, slow breath. It was light enough to see, now, and all of them were wearing Hardblade's distinctive sword-and-chainmesh badge. Normally it helped: now, it couldn't be helped.

Still. He should be able to drag Hardblade some credit from this anyway.

As he wrestled with the door, which had expanded in the dew, Thakar prodded his back. "What's wrong?" he murmured.

"This all smells far too familiar."

Thakar snorted, nudged him aside and yanked the door open. As the two of them stepped over the threshold, Connor watched him totting up all the little inaccuracies: too few guards, too few signs of presence, even if it hadn't been far too nice a street. Always the *same* inaccuracies, all copied from the same foreign drug-runner's memoir. 'Lord Lighter' must have been an author's fabrication. No one, however unbelievably lucky, could have survived running an operation that sloppy.

As Connor's eyes adjusted from dim street-dawn to half-lit pub, he counted sober mercs in dark, unassuming combat gear sitting between snoozing drunks and the garrulous types still holding up the bar ahead of going to bed. One of the mercs stood out in the gloom: a very young man with a shock of hair so blond it seemed silver, sitting alone in a booth. Connor slid in at his table, opposite him, and the boy jerked in surprise, bright green eyes switching focus away from whatever he'd been illicitly playing down his jack.

"The boss awake?" Connor said in his most neutral tone, swallowing surprise. The boy looked as close as damn it to a pure-blooded New World human, descended from the colonists who had left Earth ten thousand years ago, with no modern Earth blood bred back into him: cheekbones higher than the norm, shoulders broader. Connor'd met a handful of purebloods before. All had been foreign.

"Always." The boy straightened to relaxed attention.

"Who's asking?"

Connor almost bit his lip. Instead he touched his badge. "Meris Hardblade's lieutenant." The boy's voice fitted his face – he spoke with an echo from thirty thousand light-years away, from the Treizième sector, in the heart of the Union.

This, next to a handful of men and women who looked like they could be local.

"I'll fetch him – Mister." The boy rose from the booth and headed for the back staircase. Connor saw him pause at the foot of the stairs as if he wasn't quite sure what to do with them.

Thakar perched on the edge of Connor's seat till Connor slid along the booth to make room for him. "Pretty young thing."

"I was watching his walk, not his arse."

He snorted. "Right, right. I caught just the one gun."

"Same here." Connor leant back and watched the staircase. One gun, one knife, and though the boy had nicely developed muscles – including that arse – he was no strongman like Thakar, and wasn't nearly as tall as Connor. Eighteen years old at the outside, probably seventeen, and not a battle-hardened Septième seventeen.

The staircase creaked, and the blond boy re-emerged, with a man Connor's age behind him. Connor's age, Connor's size, close on Connor's manner of dress: another New World pureblood, but with black hair and mid-brown skin, shades that might be seen on any Septième street. If not for his sharp cheekbones Connor might have mistaken him for a half-blood mix of the Old World and the New, like most humans born between the Cinquième and Dixième. A female merc – a Ditan, emerald-skinned: surely the only one on Pell Havasi – walked behind him, silent and precise. Connor looked her over as her boss reached the booth. She was smaller even than most adult Ditans, and as taut as a jeweller's scales. Connor guessed she was another foreigner. She didn't act like she knew she was in danger.

"Connor Cardwain and Thakar A'syan, I presume?" the boss said, sitting down.

The guy had more intel than an average foreign drug-runner. Connor couldn't place his accent. Neuvième, maybe, and trying to hide it behind a put-on Dixième twang: certainly not Treizième. But his gunboy was definitely Treizième. "You've the advantage of me," Connor said, keeping his tone light. That fair gunboy was staring at him too hard, and Marcello, covering the back door, was maybe not close enough to act till too late.

"Myles Hendrix." Hendrix, assuming that was his real name, gave Connor a polite smile. "You must be selling. Your boss," and he pronounced the word just too carefully, "isn't often the buying type."

"Just as often as she needs to be." Connor mustered a thin smile. "How much freight capacity do you have in dock, and who were your last clients on the Septième?"

"One Ogre-hull freighter and six freight-equipped Hamadryads, their primary role intended as fighter escorts."

When he didn't continue, Thakar, so close to Connor that he could smell him, gave off a sigh. "Mister, my colleague and I've been around the world a while. Not long enough to know every fancy-man comes here from outside." He snorted. "No one lives that long."

"But," Connor continued for him, "their customers are something else. Them, we know."

Hendrix's Ditan gungirl shifted on her feet. Her boss raised a finger towards her, and she quietened.

"I realise," Hendrix said, "that presenting myself as an unknown quantity poses problems –" Connor and Thakar leant back against the booth seat, cocked their heads at each other and sighed. Hendrix's finger flicked to them. "I've worked with Fai Comet and Andrasine Ironbender. Both of them have a presence here and can vouch for me. Two weeks ago I took a shipment via River Sidewind from two farmers on Dalish IV. The price was good."

"I daresay." Thakar pulled a cigarette packet and a plain silver lighter from his pocket. "This is Dalishian-grown," he said, waving the cigarettes. "Not so interesting as some of what you can buy out there – unless you light up side on to a Kriastan's gills – but it's good stuff, for what it is." He flipped open the lighter, lit his cigarette and offered the packet to Hendrix. None for Connor, whose right hand, the one further from Thakar, sat on his gun. Across the pub floor, the barman hissed through his fluted jaw and ruffled his breast feathers, but he said nothing. God knew his wings looked clogged enough with cigarette residue already: a few more puffs couldn't hurt.

"So," Thakar went on, speaking from behind a cloud of smoke like a priest meditating before incense at a shrine. "You're new. Everyone's new sometime. We get that."

"Green, but not under-ripe." Hendrix smiled, laying his cigarette in the ashtray. He slid a deck of cheap playing cards from his pocket, tossed aside their packet and fanned them backs-up across the table in Connor's direction. "Pick a card."

"I don't play cards."

Hendrix's eyebrows went up. "I heard the street calls you Grand Slam."

"I always win. Therefore, I don't play." The cards were staring at him, even with their faces down, staring with pips and eyes together. If Hendrix flipped them over and bared their faces they would start whispering in their half-heard voices: where to go tomorrow, what to do to please the boss, which of their fellows his opponent was going to play next. An echo drifted in from the past, and he thought he saw his mother's hands pulling her one precious deck away from him: *'Don't touch them,'* she'd said, *'and don't trust them'.* She'd never explained why it had been all right for her to touch and trust them, and if they'd told her when she was going to die, she'd ignored the information.

He dragged his eyes away and stared at the packet, discarded near the window. A tiny logo lurked in its corner, two sharp-toothed mountains inside a circle. Whichever Septième factory had printed the cards, whichever slum kid had packaged them up in a draughty dirty warehouse, their manufacturer had made them to order for one of the biggest Union corporations, Cliff Enterprises.

The Union, run by its business conglomerates: the Union, which ruled the Treizième and all the surrounding sectors, and itched at the sight of the Federation's sectors and the independent worlds. Connor glanced at the white-blond boy. He'd seen Union citizens on the Septième before, but never running interference in crowds like this. They tended to have more money and less sense.

He looked up and met Hendrix's eyes. Pale eyes, a pocket of light in his dark face: eyes that seemed to look through Connor rather than at him. "A man with any ambition plays chess instead."

"I thought chess was your brother's game."

OK, *definite* intel. The kind of net he might have loaded to his jack would have carried reams of data on bosses and their captains, but not lieutenants, and definitely not low-rank enforcers like Logan.

"Minutes to learn, decades to master," he said. "But the interesting aspect is learning how the other person's mind works." He snagged five of Hendrix's cards at random: he knew before he turned them over that they were three low-value swords and the two and king of cups. Without looking at their faces he arranged them on the table in an approximation to Sidler's Gambit. "Black has three pawns: White has one, standing between them and the white king. Does White attack, defend or sacrifice?"

"I'd question whether White has to choose at all. It depends where Black's king is."

"Which is its own answer." Connor tapped the table. "All the options are valid. White's trick is to balance his mentality against his firepower. The man who does that has a future. If he can't understand his limits any more than he understands the game he's playing – well."

Hendrix leant forwards and picked up the king of cups. "This game is intricate, I know, and I haven't been playing it long. But over-familiarity is its own weakness."

Connor threw him a humourless smile. "Then let's neither of us underestimate what we're doing. We both have a fortune to make here."

"Based on my contacts."

"And our bleeding," Thakar said. "So, as neither of our teams is likely to get far without the other, we'll take a nice little think, and come back at you *if* we reckon it's worth our time." He stood, collecting his cigarettes.

Hendrix didn't move. "You came here. You'll be back."

"If you offer better than the rest, sure we will," said Connor. "Assuming you like the look of our boss as much as you do your others." Tiny glint in Hendrix's eyes, a reflection of anticipation or shame, and if Connor had needed any more evidence, there it was.

Dawn had broken outside. Connor rose into a patch of sunlight. The world flickered, and for a second he saw mark-signs etched on Hendrix's face.

Thakar's hand fastened on his elbow and Connor jerked back to himself. "Be seeing you, Mister," he said with a half-bow to Hendrix, and he strode to the back door with as much dignity as he could muster.

He pushed open the door and stumbled into the rear courtyard. "Get off," he hissed as Thakar and Marcello reached for him. Marcello withdrew a few steps, looking frightened: Thakar stood, arms folded, watching him. *Damn* it. Connor stabbed fingers at their bikes. "Drive," he said, or croaked. *"Drive."*

Thakar mounted his Nexi before Connor finished speaking. "Logan?" he said, helmet in hand.

"He'll find us."

The three of them drove at low altitude for four or five streets into the Pellite city-space before Connor spied a small landscaped park below them. He gestured downwards and dropped to the grass. The park warden, an aging Pellite with knives mounted on his coverts but no visible firearms, just watched, muttering into his breast feathers, as the three simians settled onto his turf.

"So," said Thakar, pulling off his helmet. "'Be seeing you'?"

Connor took a long slow breath. *Had* to get back into control. "I get the feeling," he said, picking words Thakar would understand, or, hell, words *he'd* understand, "we'll get something out of going his way."

"Come the fuck off it." Thakar snapped two fingers at Marcello. "Brat. What'd you see?"

"Mercs and guns. A foreign businessman playing gang lord." Marcello pulled off his helmet – something else culled from the common pool: it *almost* fitted him – and looked backwards and forwards between Thakar and Connor. "Why not work with him?"

"Because he's a cop," Connor said. The sunlight was

stinging his eyes. Next to no sleep since this time yesterday: he was getting too old for this. "Foreign cop, probably a drug-buster. I knew before we went in."

Marcello's eyes went as wide as conkers. "Then why –"

"Wanted to see his setup," Thakar said. He pulled out his cigarettes again and studied the packet, pale gold foil monogram designed to please richer folk. "Hendrix says he pulled two shipments, but Sidewind's been busy middle-womaning *three* hauls from the Dalish systems: tobacco, weed, and coca. Maa'ee'dis, the coca guy, got hit up last week. A hundred dead workers, another hundred dead mercs, and he's gone bye-bye with his ship and all his records. It was a cop hit." He aimed a finger back towards the pub. "And now we know who pulled it." He glared at Connor. "Except *someone* suddenly don't want us to get any blood money or pickings."

What was Connor meant to say? He'd had these feelings many times before. Half a second, no more. And then he'd be right. He'd always be right.

"You know me." Connor leant back in his saddle and watched the sun rise over park, trees and houses. A few streets and he would be back in the slums: slums so similar to the ones where he and Logan had grown up – them, and Thakar, and presumably Marcello, and myriad others. "I wouldn't have said it if I didn't believe it."

"You've no proof." Thakar prodded Connor's bike with one booted foot, making it teeter. "Sure, I see profit in a vice cop – in ridding ourselves of him. I see no profit in *working with* him." His face creased like he'd tasted vomit. "Except in one way. And I don't do that, and I think you don't either."

"Relax: I haven't had a brain transplant." Connor chewed his lower lip. He'd no answers either. Why did people always want answers? "We go along with him, maybe we'll put ourselves into a position to – I don't know, pinch his contacts. There's a lot of cash in secrets. Don't get me wrong, we need a genuine exporter too: I'm just saying, there's something in him for us."

"Maybe." Thakar pointed to the sky and kicked his throttle. "But if this goes wrong, and it can go wrong in a whole stack of ways including total *mistakes* on that scum's part, we," and he gestured to himself and Marcello, "had nothing to do with it."

"Except for getting killed in the mess, you mean."

"I'm hoping to skip that bit." Thakar paused in the act of replacing his helmet, squinting at the sky. "Where is Logan? He was meant to be riding guard."

Connor bit his lip. Logan was a grown man, and none of his concern. But he couldn't forget the little boy who'd clung to him, shaking, when their mother died. "Likely got bored and went back to base. Or got tired – don't blame him for that."

Thakar grunted. "He didn't spend his nights drinking cheap whisky and bedding whole chorus lines, he'd be in a better state to do more work for us."

"One chorus line." Connor pulled on his helmet and fiddled at its inbuilt phone, looking for Logan's jack number. "*One* chorus line."

"Whatever."

As they rose over the park, scorching a few shrubs, Connor looked back towards the pub. Right or wrong? He didn't know.

Couldn't blame anyone for trying. There was a *lot* of money in export.

*

CHAPTER FOUR

Keep riding the thermals. Logan circled the pub, swooping low and soaring high, watching for movements in each sidestreet. Behind him, his XR-2's six-way engine howled into the morning sky, like a monster without a mate.

A million years ago he'd have shared the sky with the Pellites' ancestors, before they lost the strength to do more than glide from gantry to street. A million years ago he'd have been a grunting ape. *'Still is,'* he imagined Thakar saying.

Movement below caught his eye: a door opening in a plain house opposite the pub, and a string of gunhands sliding into the street. Logan dropped a few dozen feet and bent half out of his saddle to look. Not the export gang Connor'd been going to see – that was Sanctis Merovir's badge on each man's arm, the praying-mantis preparing to strike. Why Merovir's crew, here? Tied in with the exporter? With Sl'arani?

Quarter of the fucking *city* was tied to Sl'arani, and another quarter to Hlarxi. A dormer window in the so-plain house banged open, and a Pellite servant leant out and flung a pot of sticky dung at Logan: instead of shooting her, he pulled away and up. He would have had to shoot the whole house before he was done, and there was no way to tell who the householder was paying. Had to be paying someone, in this good a district.

But whoever the house was paying, it wasn't Merovir, or any foreigner. Logan circled the pub once more, thinking. Merovir had his eye on export. He'd recently made a run that didn't end in disaster, which must mean he'd got himself established behind the scenes. Was he elbowing in on Connor's man?

If so, with the friction between Hardblade and Merovir, it could mean bad news. Not much cause for it – Merovir had fathered five sons: any man should be able to manage with four – but business wasn't yet just business.

He hopped the pub's roof balcony and spiralled down to its garage. A string of bikes huddled inside, all foreign, none of them real class – hells, if you were an exporter, why not buy yourself decent tech? Logan kicked up to roof level. At least he'd not get tempted to steal the help's kit.

The door to the pub's roof balcony banged open just as he drew level with its lintel. His left hand slid back from handlebars to pistol.

"Will you *stop* –" The voice cut out.

Logan's hand froze, dangling limp as a priest's cock over his holster. Familiar voice. Familiar, female, foreign voice: a Neuvième accent so thick a man could bounce on it.

Ellie.

Should have been a vision. Should have been a nightmare. But she was there, standing in the doorway, staring at him with wide green eyes, her golden hair wafting around her shoulders in the dawn wind.

His right hand was still behaving. He bumped his Connaught down onto the balcony and pulled off his helmet. Hair, underneath, slicked to his head with sweat. No sleep last night. Doubtless he was seeing things.

"I wake you up?" he said. *Fuck* his voice. Shaking like a boy's.

"I was trying to concentrate." She reached out a hand, hesitated for a moment and laid it on his bike's handlebars. She looked older. Tiny lines around her eyes, and her wings – opening behind her like an angel's trumpets – were brighter, the way Weavers' wings got when they practised. It'd been nearly three years. He was older too. "You should…" He saw her search for a word. "Make the engine quieter."

"Muffle it? Why'd I do that?" Logan clipped his helmet to his pillion, and instead of grabbing hold of her and pushing her up against the wall, laid his hand on hers. For all he knew, she'd another man. For all he knew, she'd six.

And he didn't give a flying fuck either way. Older, tireder, he *wanted* her.

"Ellie –" *Come with me*, he wanted to say. *Get on my bike and we'll fuck on the next rooftop and you'll stay at my side, as long as you can stand it.* "You're on a job?"

She nodded. "We landed yesterday. I hoped –" Her right hand moved in his and slid up his arm, above his driving gloves. Her Circle tattoo glinted on the back of her hand. Logan shivered. All the tales said never to touch a Weaver, man, woman, child, human or non-human, whatever. He'd touched Ellie before. He would never tire of that feeling, the tingle, magic surging out of her skin against his: a heady buzz that stank of sex beneath. "I hoped you would be here," Ellie whispered, and he couldn't tell why her eyes glittered.

Instead of thinking on it, he pulled off his right driving glove and laid his bare hand on her neck. Oh, yeah. That was the buzz, soaking through her into him, and when she tried to pull away he squeezed her into him. Harder than the roughest moonshine he'd ever drunk, the wood-brew that passed for slum whisky: he'd soak this inside him, and hold it against the night.

Ellie yanked herself free. Red skin, where he'd held her against him. "Don't. It's not safe."

"Since when do I give a shit?" Logan dragged off his other glove and shoved both into his jacket pocket. "That, round you? You think that's why I want you?"

"It's a complication."

"Say that again." Her green eyes widened. "Say it again. Say what in all hells you like. I want to hear your voice." He gripped her wrists, and backed her into the wall just shy of the door: a foot taller than her, and a hundred pounds heavier, he could have held her there forever, till she told him to stop. And she would. Would he care? "I want to hear you, and smell you, and taste you. I want to know you're real."

"Logan." She tugged at his hands, over hers. "*Logan.*" He leant closer, resting more of his weight on her. She reared up snake-like and kissed him.

No shy kiss, no scared girl's fumble intended to get the man away from her as soon as possible: hot and hard, as strong as his hands on hers. He loosened his grip, slid his arms round her and pulled her against him, while his tongue crept into her mouth and his teeth nibbled her lower lip –

– and Ellie pressed down his hands, leant her body against his and spun him round and into the wall.

"I'm what you want?" she said, low and breathily. She laid

a hand on his crotch. If he'd been half-hard before, he was hard now. Her, leaning up against him – he could have snapped her in two, sure as up was up. But that little determined smile on her lips, as her right hand fiddled with his fly, warned him he was stepping close to the line.

Hard? He was *dripping*.

Ellie yanked open his fly and kicked the balcony door shut with her left foot. Logan pulled his hands clear and grabbed for her fly. No buttons: a knot instead. He fumbled at it for half a second before giving up and ripping it. Beneath she didn't wear undershorts, just some fancy embroidered cloth no wider than her thumb, wrapped a few times round her waist and between her legs. He slid his finger beneath, to her slit. She was soaking wet, hot and heady and all his, and damn if he didn't want all of her, all at once.

Ellie yanked off her loincloth and pushed him down to the roof behind his bike. His trousers were still caught round one foot: he wasn't minded to care. She dropped down, straddling him, and he dug his fingers into the coarse gold curls coating her mound. A faint scar, white on her vanilla skin, snaked across her belly. "I'd like to see the man got a cut in on you," he muttered.

"Shut up." She slid down and onto him.

Dear God, she was tight: tight and hot and Logan couldn't stand it. He thrust up into her as she came down to meet him, and gripped her buttocks. He'd have rolled her onto her back but that would have meant pulling out of her and he *couldn't stand not to touch her*. Her magic tingled over her and into him, till he couldn't split it from the heat squeezing his cock, and as she worked up and down on him, flushed and panting, he'd no clue if he was in this world or the next.

He realised he was coming, sooner than he wanted, and tried to warn her, but it didn't work: instead he squeezed her arse down onto him as he bucked up into her, spending himself in a few quick spurts. "Stay hard," Ellie muttered.

"You close?" She didn't answer. He slid his finger to her mound, to the point where she met him. He felt his own seed trickling over his fingers. There was her nub, grinding against him, and he closed his fingers around it.

Her back arched and she bucked on top of him, and fell,

boneless, onto his chest. They'd neither of them taken off their shirts. He ran his arms round her and held her against him – still half inside her, hot and sticky and sublime.

"Ellie –"

"Ssssh. Nothing else now."

He nodded, and buried his nose in her hair, sweat-damp in the cool morning. There was a song about something like this, the moment after the fuck before, when rain tasted of kisses and concrete felt soft. The song didn't last all that long.

The door creaked. Logan froze. Ellie jerked upright, staring over Logan's bike: Logan reared up beside her.

A young man was peering round the door – sixteen years old or so, a foreign sixteen, too young for his years: white-blond, more pretty than handsome. "Have you two finished?" he enquired. "I –"

Ellie grabbed the one boot Logan'd bothered to kick off and flung it, not accurately, at the boy. Though she'd missed him by a long way, he yelped and withdrew, pulling the door most of the way shut behind him.

"*Veux-tu un pantalon?*" he said through the crack.

"*Oui,*" Ellie called. She looked like she wanted to say more, but she let out her breath all at once and looked down at the tiny pool of oil coming off Logan's Connaught.

Logan sat up. His bare arse squeaked on cold roof tiles. There were his undershorts, round his left ankle. "Best find a room next time," he muttered. "There'll be a next time – Ellie?"

"That's what I want." Ellie picked up her ripped trousers and started wiping herself dry. "Everything's difficult."

"Why?" He sat up and grabbed the other end of her trousers to wipe his cock. "*Wanting –*"

"Isn't needing. And what I need –" She shrugged. Gold wings peeping out of her shoulder blades shrugged with her, like she was a butterfly. "What I need may be what I want, if you will it."

"Me?" He worked his undershorts and trousers up his right leg. Something in this didn't hang quite right. Instead of asking questions he didn't know how to ask, he jerked his head at the door. "Who was that?"

Ellie tied her loincloth back round her waist. She'd come outside barefoot. Dust streaked her feet. "My half-brother."

Half-brother? Ellie had an older full brother, she'd said so the last time they met, but she hadn't mentioned this boy. "What is he, fifteen?"

"He's seventeen, and a Spellweaver. Please don't get into a fight with him."

"I'll remember it. Not enough to let him off listening to us fucking, but hey."

Ellie rolled his eyes. "You're such a prude. He could have heard us a mile away: why not listen?"

"Nice of him."

"He's working with me. I would like you to get used to him."

The boy's footsteps approached the door again, and a hand slid through the crack, waving another pair of embroidered trousers. As Ellie wrapped them onto herself, Logan retrieved his right boot, and tried to think.

Almost all Circle Weavers were mercs: same as any others, except for the higher pay. But Circle Weavers didn't do drugs work any more than they did drugs. There was room to guess that the woman in the warehouse hadn't known what she was getting into, or had got so desperate that she ignored all her people's rules. But Ellie, the Ellie he'd held in his heart for years, was so straight-laced she rarely even drank a shot. A woman that hot on prohibition didn't change that quickly.

Here, working, now, she'd be working for: "The guy's set up shop downstairs has you on contract?" The guy Connor had come here to meet.

She blinked. "Yes. He's a police deputy." Logan fought to keep his face straight: *Yep, sugar, I already got that bit.*

"Here to make sure nothing too strong gets posted in your direction?" he said, cool as he could. "Makes sense. A lot of deals go down, carnival time."

"Enough to take all the underside here."

He laid his hand on hers again. "You took this job just to find me? And dragged your kid brother into it?"

"He's seventeen: he needs to start earning."

"That I don't dispute."

Her green eyes held his, clear and pure. "Then – yes, I did. I was sure you'd be here somewhere, unless you were dead."

"The last thing I want to be."

"We don't always get what we want." She slid her hand up to his cheek. "Logan, last time –"

"Was all I'd ever wanted."

"Logan, we have two children."

The wind blew chill breaths around them. Logan exhaled. Children. Sure, girls got knocked up all the time, when they couldn't kick the guy off and hadn't bought a fertility shot. He'd thought Ellie was the type to take her shot. Wasn't like most men bothered.

That perma-tired look in her eyes, like a merc who'd been on assignment for a year already. The scar on her belly. There'd even been extra weight on her hips where he'd held her. Too many fucking clues, and he'd missed the lot.

"Two kids? How the fuck did you not tell me sooner that we had two kids?" He realised he'd gripped her shoulders and was shaking her. "You missed your shot and fucking had *twins* and didn't tell me?" She was nodding, and crying, and he realised he was crying too, and he pulled her against him and rocked her, not sure which of them was the weaker, or was weeping harder.

After a few minutes his grip on her loosened. She'd stopped crying, but her eyes were still red. "Are you sure they're mine?" he said. His voice was shaking. She nodded without speaking. "Boys or girls?"

"One of each." She dashed tear-streaks from her cheeks. "Will you come back home with me?"

"Stay with you, you mean? Be a father?" How did it even *work*? He'd no clue –

"If we can."

"That's what you want?"

For half a moment she looked angry. "I came thousands of light-years to see you: will you at least come back to see them?"

He nodded. What else could he do? But there was Connor, and work, and everything that could come crashing down on them both: "Ellie – there's going to be a problem."

"What problem?"

Logan's jack phone went off. He swore and hit the switch. "What?" Spoke too loudly for jack, loud enough to hurt his caller's ears, but he didn't care.

"Logan?" Damn. Connor. "What's up?"

Excuses, excuses: "Merovir's men're fishing around near you. Be careful." He rang off and looked back down at Ellie. "Now. Let's talk."

*

CHAPTER FIVE

Connor signed off and sat back against his bike saddle, staring into space. The park keeper was burbling ten feet below him, picking over his wounded shrubbery, and the warm sun creeping up the sky felt like a warning beacon.

"What's up?" said Thakar.

What was *up* was that Logan sure as hells hadn't been alone. What was *up* was that the directional tracking on Connor's jack placed him pretty close to the pub where the vice cop had been hanging out. "Merovir's squad's about."

Thakar choked on a laugh. "O*K*. He's smelt our job?"

"I'd guess it's his lieutenants on site, and if they know…"

"…they'll be here for us, via the cop." Thakar's breath whistled through his teeth. "So how's about we talk first." Connor blinked at him. "We call in the big guy, offer him a nice little snatch. Then, when all's done, he'll not know which way's best to move. All we need's a second over him."

All Connor needed was a few hours' sleep and a chat with his brother, but he nodded. "Right now I've no better move."

Thakar cocked his dark head in the pub's vague direction. "You come up with a better, you tell us, 'k?"

"Of course." Connor swallowed an irritated snort. He didn't *want* any more of these damn-annoying half-sights: if he did, he'd pull out a deck of cards.

Marcello sidled his bike a few lengths closer. "Er – where is Mister Merovir?" he said.

Thakar grunted. "Donkey work tells us that."

And donkey work told them, though Connor suspected Marcello hadn't realised beforehand how much of the work would be his. The two lieutenants returned to base and left the young gunhand coordinating Hardblade's string of runners, pages and gadabouts into a search team, while they caught a few hours' sleep.

Half a dream later, Connor woke with someone shaking him. Thakar, he hoped, but he realised almost at once that it was Zack.

"What's up?" Connor slurred. He couldn't see straight, and his head ached. Damn old age.

"We got a line to Merovir. He's holding court in one of the pavilions near the carnival route." Zack grinned. "That gunboy's good. He was already on decent terms with Merovir before Carm got there to oversee."

Connor pushed himself up onto one elbow. His assigned room was barely twice the size of his bed. Zack filled a fair bit of the rest of it. Still, it was private. Rank meant that much.

"Tell me it wasn't you sent a green boy to treat with Merovir," he said.

Zack shrugged. "We can spare him, and I wasn't going to wait for Logan to get back."

Connor sat up in bed and snagged a shirt from his beside cabinet. Over his head, it hid his expression. "Logan still a-patrolling?" he said, muffled through cotton.

"Yep. He called Coker earlier, said he was running surveillance on your cop."

Logan called Coker, and didn't swear at him, threaten him or throw a mood? Connor ran fingers across his stubbled cheeks. He'd have given fortunes to stand face to face with his brother, shake him a few times and ask him what was going on.

Work first. Merovir first. He settled his shirt on his shoulders and nudged Zack to one side so he could pull clean undershorts out of his cabinet. Reminded him of five fallow years when all his undershorts had been stolen from shops, stalls and washer-women's lines. Clothes for him, clothes for Logan, both of them growing all the time: it had been almost as bad as food, for only the sturdy and well-dressed got decent work. Only the ones who could prove they knew how to look after themselves.

"Is Thakar in," he said, "or has he headed?"

"Waking himself up with one of the gungirls. I'd wait till he's done if I were you." He half-nodded to Connor and headed out.

Connor levered himself out of bed and tugged on the rest of his clothing, now there was no point in leaving it off. Thakar shifting to girls wasn't too strange, nowhere near so as Logan heading off into the middle of nowhere and leaving a perfectly civil message, but it did tend to make him absent-minded. Connor'd never quite understood why: he'd always found girls to be very dull bedmates.

But as for Logan's adventures...

He slid on his boots, combed and tied up his hair, and wandered out into the base. The usual handful of off-duty squad mercs had set up a whist school in the mess: he avoided them. A pair of Hardblade's Ditans, new-come from her further holdings with light cargo, sat shivering in the main hall being fed sedatives while Coker debriefed them. Most likely the Pellites on the customs desk had been so excited to see two Ditans running a shipment that they hadn't bothered performing all the searches they should have. Hardblade'd never been the type to worry about expending a few employees' sanity if it bought her an advantage in carnival time.

But what advantage now? Connor itched to ask, itched to get involved, but he knew the rules. He'd brought in Sl'arani's shipment: it was his business to get rid of it before he buried his nose in a side issue.

He waited till Coker'd waved the pair of couriers off to their rest, then said to him, "What exactly did Logan say when he called in?"

Coker's eyebrows went up and he scratched his right temple. Not long back, someone had hacked off the right side of his hair. Connor suspected it had been his squeeze.

"You two start speaking in code," Coker said, "that's not helpful."

"Not my meaning. Anything could be landing he didn't want to say all of it."

Coker grunted. "I see no difference. Anyway." He pursed his lips. "He said, 'Connor's contact's playing Sl'arani's game. I'm keeping a line on his crew.' I just hope it's a useful line."

"It will be." Coker's eyebrows rose again: Connor, torn between explanation and incomprehension, added, "Something about one of his gunboys wasn't right. Logan tells me what, I'll be all the happier."

Coker nodded. Outside, carnival music – this batch some elfin caterwauling from the Sixième nomad stations – filtered down the streets. "Someone shut that door," Coker called. The music cut off, as did the sickly food-smells accompanying it. Connor, light-headed, rested a hand on the wall. He stared at its back. Bones glinted green inside his skin.

Coker's hand landed on his shoulder. "Lunch?"

Connor nodded. Food. Something a little less nauseating than streetside kebabs.

He was polishing off a steak in the canteen – better-done than he liked, but the idiot cook didn't trust Pellite butchers – when Thakar breezed in, thumbs tucked into his belt and looking more than a bit pleased with himself.

"She that good?" Connor enquired as Thakar slid in opposite him.

"She's a byrd: what'd you think was different?" Thakar plucked one of Connor's tiny tomatoes from his plate and tossed it into his mouth. Under the table he hooked one ankle round Connor's, half a reassurance. "Our boy Marcello bears watching. He's pulled Fai Comet's hardmen into security on our chat with Merovir."

Connor snatched his last pepper slice away from Thakar's idle fingers. "Tell me he didn't promise them more than the info they'll overhear."

"If he did, he's paying them. Hasn't told me that'll happen." Thakar leant back and smiled at the ceiling like an oversatisfied priest. "Give us Logan back and I'd be happier, but I've a feeling we'll do."

So had Connor. Not a *feeling*, not one of those green-soaked tingles he couldn't ignore, but a tranquil little centre inside him. It wouldn't last, but he'd take it while it was there. "Logan'll be back – before two of Comet's guys take a slug at one of Merovir's Kriastans and land us in the mix."

Thakar peered at him. "You OK?"

"Just fine."

And he was, he considered as they packed up guns, backup and concealed backup and set off for carnival central. The day was mild, a few native songbirds kept alive for their novelty value were cheeping, and he was fairly sure his brother was doing quite well for them.

So what in hells was about to go wrong?

Wrong started appearing when they hit the busier streets, and a drift kid tried to steal Zack's wallet while he was paying another kid to clear them a way in to Merovir. Two small corpses hitting dirt wasn't the way to start a meet: for one thing, it left them with no path-clearer save their own gunhands, most of whom considered themselves too old and important for such work. So Connor and Thakar took point into the crowd, Hardblade's logo sparkling on their arms above their stripes. Maybe a few of the spivs, candy-apple-sellers, drug-sellers, good time girls and bad time boys who dotted the pavement saw Connor had no intention to lose a tussle.

Besides, he'd tucked his money belt under two layers of clothing. Let younger men spend their pennies here: if Connor had a mind for buying, his choice would cost him more cash than he could conveniently carry.

Ships: men: contracts. *Export.* Whatever he tried to concentrate on, however many dancers and acrobats and strongmen he counted in the crowds around them, he still saw the fake exporter lurking behind, and tried to say to him, *If only you were real.*

Merovir had cleared himself a beer tent two streets off the main carnival route, where the sideshows and food stalls provided enough noise and fuss to hinder his rivals, yet, if he played his cards right, too little to hinder him. He'd paid some seamstress to embroider his praying-mantis logo along the gaudy red awning: it looked like a string of giant insects was preparing to eat the crowd. Connor was still letting Thakar lead them at a saunter towards the tent, watching street brats and trying to figure out how many had been bought for the week by one boss or another, when Marcello strolled out to meet them.

The boy looked a few years older than he had that morning: neither careworn nor cocky, more like he figured himself doing a man's job at last. A sharp memory struck Connor – Myles Hendrix's beautiful white-blond gunboy, not too much younger than Marcello in years, but surely so far from him in experience.

"How's tricks?" Connor said, as off-hand as he could.

"None too bad. Life has its challenges." Marcello's eyes flicked to the tent behind him. "Mister Merovir," he said, with such careful enunciation, "is packing a Spellweaver."

Thakar stopped walking with one foot poised to step on a small boy. "*What*?"

"What colour wings?" Connor said.

"Dark red, with blue streaks."

Dark red: that meant Revelation. "What a good thing we're not planning to jump 'Mister' Merovir."

Connor brushed past Marcello into the tent. Even if he'd wanted to lay a hand on a gun, he couldn't have got away with it. Revealers could see in the dark, round corners, through walls, through clothes, wherever. Damn them. Damn all Weavers.

Merovir was close to the back of the tent, where a sharp knife would take him out of trouble if needed, lounging in an incongruous armchair with two of his four remaining sons flanking him. Both were taller than Connor, and were dressed in not much more than body armour coating their torsos and thighs: bright cotton under-trousers peeped out beneath, all of a piece with their arms – bared to show off their muscles – and the earrings dangling to their shoulders. Neither looked particularly friendly. Merovir was less ostentatiously clad: crisp white tunic and dark trousers, with few rings on his fingers. Several of said fingers were drumming on a side table pulled up beside him – a frightful carnival table covered in pink and orange streamers. Set on the table were a couple of open handhelds and a glass of whisky. The gang lord had another handheld in his lap.

"There are ways," Merovir said to his handheld, "of pulling stunts mid-carnival. Just as there are ways of approaching one's enemies for a business deal." He flicked to a new page.

Connor tucked his thumbs into his pockets. "Ways are changeable."

He flicked an eye over the rest of Merovir's train. A few hulking gunhands and their slinkier female counterparts, the former with a few bored dancers beckoning at them. Two Kriastans, huge scaly hunks of muscle: female by their stature – males were smaller, and were due to enter their musth period soon enough to need confining. The Spellweaver was sitting behind the gunmen: just a nondescript man of Connor's age, with glowing red-blue wings illuminating a disinterested face. In this instance, disinterest likely masked a great interest in something his physical eyes weren't looking at. Connor wondered what else he could cast, in addition to Revelation and Telepathy. Most of them could use most of the threads: just like a Weaver to snare a man with a spell that wasn't forewarned in his wings.

"Changes are unwelcome." Merovir sipped his whisky and glared up at Connor. "Your boss owes me corpses."

Thakar came up behind Connor. "When we speak with her tonight, we'll remind her. In the meantime, do we owe you primacy on a certain deal?"

Merovir grimaced and, with an air of distaste, passed Connor his whisky glass. "That's a question with a complicated answer."

Connor sipped, passed the glass to Thakar and, as Thakar took a swig and handed back the glass to Merovir, glanced around for a seat. There were none, so he rocked back on his heels, almost at ease. His – Hardblade's – squad was behind him, and Comet's spare gunhands dotted the tent. Good enough.

"Mister, were you wanting Myles Hendrix dead or alive?"

Merovir's eyebrows shot up. "That's another complication." He snapped his fingers. Two of the dancers making desultory attempts on the gunmen's virtue withdrew through a gap in the tent and reappeared carrying a couple of stools. The darker one, who'd dyed her brown hair black but had forgotten about the eyebrows, set her stool down for Thakar: the pale one, who'd remembered to dye both her hair and brows red, placed hers by Connor. He sat. How much of anything was a posture?

"Your export operations, Mister –"

"– are, for the moment, proceeding without 'Mister' Hendrix's connivance," Merovir said, setting aside his whisky. "I don't deny he's made me an interesting offer lately. The question is how far I feel like stretching my arm."

"To cover your nuts?" Thakar suggested. "We all know what he is –"

"What he is," Merovir said, leaning forwards and making that little *I'm-a-gang-lord-and-you're-a-flunky* gesture with his whisky glass, "is an opportunity. If you want to sell him for spare parts on Dalish IV when we're done, feel free. For now, we all have moves to make."

"Does he pay?" said Connor.

Up went that eyebrow again. Merovir's expression seemed predatory, an echo of the insect stalking down his team's sleeves. "You're a borderline reckless man, Cardwain."

That sounded more like Logan than him. "That's my affair, and my boss's, and my team's. In your opinion, Mister, does Hendrix sport the cash he says he does?"

"Not cash. Bank funds." Merovir locked his fingers round his glass. "I understand the Dalishians weren't happy when their funds vanished a few days after the balloon went up."

Thakar grunted. "Neuvième hackers on squad." Merovir looked a question at him: Thakar expanded, "Neuvième mercs are hot against drugs. At least a couple of his mercs sounded Neuvième: they'd that throaty accent." He hummed in thought. "Never known whether their hackers were real before. Guess I do now."

Connor drummed his fingers on his thigh. "And that," he said, not sure if it were for Merovir's benefit or that of Hardblade's squad, "affects what I can recommend to my boss." *Or do for myself*, he didn't, couldn't say.

"Counter-hackers," Marcello muttered, behind. "It's got to be possible. Governments –"

"Circle Neuvième mercs hack *into* governments," one of Comet's men said without looking up from the whist hand he'd started with his neighbour. Merovir sent both men a quizzical look.

Thakar waved off the interruptions. "So. Say it ain't possible. Mister, the extent of your involvement in this –"

"My 'involvement' is my business."

Connor half-bowed. "And your business, Mister, is buying and selling. If we sell, are you interested in buying?"

For a moment he saw a glimmer in Merovir's eyes: increased curiosity, or something more menacing. Never trust anyone further than necessary – and Connor knew exactly how far a lieutenant should be able to trust his boss's enemy.

"If you have the nerve to sell, I've the nerve to buy," Merovir said, "subject to the usual oversights, finances, and so on. But Hendrix is not to be my problem. You want my patronage, you get him out of my way."

And getting him out of Merovir's way would pull influence with more than just him, even if Hendrix's were the only foreign vice squad currently on Pell Havasi: fallout from the Dalish IV affair, for a start, and who knew what else. It was tempting. So tempting that a man who wanted to keep breathing couldn't afford to pass it up.

Connor would have time to figure out later which part of the whole thing stank worst.

"As far as we're concerned, Mister, we have agreement," Connor said, rising. "We'll prepare documentation and run it to you by nightfall." He half-bowed again. Never shake on a deal till it was dusted down in blood.

Merovir nodded to him, more than a gesture, less than acknowledgement of rank. "I'll await your docket. My regards to your boss." Thakar rose and bowed beside Connor, and their escorts stepped back to let them lead the way out of the tent.

Afternoon sunshine shone golden on the street outside, and the food-stink blasted ever stronger after the tent's stuffiness. Connor breathed out through his nose, trying to clear his sinuses. Thakar towed him away from the tent flap, past a fire-juggler, her audience and the pickpocket working the crowd, towards the muddy alleys, not even paved in wood. "I think," he murmured, "we need a guard on Mister Merovir's intentions, if we hand over to him. 'Regards', hey?"

"I think there's a few of Comet's still behind us." Connor jerked his head for Marcello, behind them with the other mercs. "A solid shield, as it went," he said as the boy slid in beside them, "though I'll lay you ten that Comet's crew'll get nice and interested in our switchover –"

A touch at his belt, and Connor, on instinct, grabbed the questing fingers in his left hand and snapped his right to his pistol. He knew before he yanked the tiny figure out of the alley that it was another drifter child.

Human – a boy – maybe six years old, maybe nine. Dirty as they all were, the type who lived in gutters: a few gold strands glinted in his grimy hair. Too young to read a lieutenant's stripes for what they were. He was struggling, trying to yank his arm free from Connor's grip, with semiferal fear contorting his face.

Marcello swore under his breath. Connor would have echoed him if he'd had the energy. Stupid kids. *Stupid* kids.

"Hey." Thakar, at his side, was rummaging at his waist. "Where's –" and he peered at the boy, bent and plucked his money pouch from the child's ragged pocket. "You little devil, when'd you take my wallet?"

"Tell me you didn't have that out," Connor said.

"I'm not that daft. Just not as over-cautious as you." Thakar was still staring at the drifter. The little boy glanced back the way Thakar and Connor had come. "Earlier? You lifted it earlier?"

Marcello gestured to Thakar's money pouch. "You weren't wearing that at the meet. I can see it at your belt under your shirt, when you've it on. It wasn't there."

"This," Connor said, dangling the child up by his right arm till he squealed, "pinched your money belt *past* your clothes so neat you didn't notice for ten minutes – and stayed around to follow up with mine?"

"Looks like." Far from acting anywhere near as pissed as Connor felt, Thakar was smiling, and as Connor stared at him he started to laugh. "By God, I've seen it all. Don't shoot him, Connor."

"Why not?"

"I've a fancy you'll regret it." Still smiling like he appreciated a joke nobody else had even glimpsed, Thakar bent closer to the child. "You got a name, brat?"

"Joshua," the boy whispered.

"Well, Joshua –" Thakar captured the child's arm from Connor and lowered him to the ground, though he did not let go. "You come with me, you do as you're told, and I'll give you hot food and a warm bed." The child's gaze slid to Connor, and his gun. "You do as you're told," Thakar added, "and he won't shoot you. You act up, and he will." He shook the boy's shoulder, albeit gently. "Now. You're going to come with me, and behave, yeah?" The little boy nodded, silent.

Connor lowered his gun, but did not holster it. "What if the boss doesn't need another runner?"

"We always lose a few at carnival." Thakar released Joshua's arm, and straightened. The child stood stock still, shivering. "And this one strikes me as quite handy. Joshua, who was listening to us outside the tent?"

"Two byrds," Joshua whispered.

"Two women, huh? Together?" The boy shook his head. "Well, now. There's interesting."

*

CHAPTER SIX

Sometime in the mid-afternoon, with the sun gold in the sky and Ellie's wide-eyed young brother well out of the way, Logan lay back against Ellie's thin pillows, playing and replaying vids of his children. Children. His. No question about that bit: they looked like him, black hair, gold eyes and beaky noses. The little girl seemed fearless, toddling from adult to adult and chattering to anyone or no one in Ellie's native French: the little boy trotted after his sister or snatched at squeaky toys, mini-keyboards, anything that made a noise when he fingered it. Best not take them a kitten.

Ellie shifted against him. She was naked. They'd got naked shortly after holing up in her bedroom, and hadn't remedied it since. "You good?"

"Yeah." And he was. He didn't know what to call it, this soft calm *centred* feeling, but he'd an idea he could pick up the world if he tried. Or steal a government's whole starfleet. Or do *anything*.

Except figure a way round what they were going to do.

Instead of spilling to Ellie, or on her again, he swung his legs off her bed and sat up. Outside the window, white clouds chased each other across a pink-purple sky. They were a way off the carnival route here: hardly any crowd noise. Just them, and their worlds.

"I never met my father." Ellie didn't answer. "Connor won't tell me who the guy was, either. He knows: I think he's planning on calling the guy out, he ever sees him again. Nothing to do with me – he screwed over our mother."

And why not? Women spawned, men left. It was the way things were. Only the big bosses and their captains – only guys with, say, Sanctis Merovir's clout – brought up their kids.

But it wasn't that way among Ellie's people.

"Am I man enough to do what you want?" he muttered.

"I hoped you'd want it." She kissed the back of his shoulder. He felt her wing feathers tangle in his hair and rest against him. "At least, when the job's done, come back to Port Logis with me. Meet them. See what happens."

Port Logis. All the stories. Circle Weavers, Neuvième Weavers, the strangest and most dangerous of them all: fanatics. Deadly fanatics. Streets made of marble, dotted with men and women dressed in silk, treacherous and dangerous. Michael Sinclair d'Aubry, the Circle's greatest ever Weaver, buried at the heart of the people he'd led to glory. "What's it like there?"

"Port Logis?" Her lips didn't leave his skin.

"Mmm."

She tugged him back against her and sideways onto the bed, lying spooned around him, pale legs twining round him. "My family lives in the biggest city. In summer, the sun never sets. Heat pummels the streets till the air shimmers like a hundred mirrors. If you touched the flagstones with your bare feet, you'd burn them, and when you shower yourself in the street, you're dry five minutes later. Women wrap their body shawls around their heads to save themselves from sunstroke. The streets stink of perfume, worse than a hundred temples: everyone bathes in it – it's perfume-scent, or sweat."

She exhaled into his shoulder. "And in winter, the sun never rises. It grows so cold the frost eats into the earth like a living thing. When the aurora flares overhead, you see the world as a shadow of itself: ice crystals the size of roses hanging off every cornice, and snowdrifts as deep as spaceships, burying buildings. For a month, almost no one goes outside – your skin would freeze in under a minute if you tried. We roof over the streets and drive from garage to garage. Only the snowsports idiots go onto the hills. A few hundred die every year." Her arms tightened around him. "It's spring now. The rivers are blue with glacier-melt and the lowland meadows are covered in wildflowers. Fresh bouquets lie on Michael Sinclair d'Aubry's grave, and in every warm breeze it feels as if he walks among us. Children play in every street. Young men and women serenade each other on balconies in the evenings. The world seems built of blossoms and music."

"Sounds like a heaven." Sounded like nothing he'd ever

seen or touched. What did he know but dirty streets, rusting hangars and hunger? Children, his, *theirs* – he couldn't bring them to this, not in a million years, but how was a man like him meant to fit into a vision like that?

Ellie snorted a laugh. "Oh, a heaven. A perfect place, apart from the freezing, the burning, the backbiting – Logan, be serious: there's talk about our people. I've heard it."

He wormed round till they lay face to face. "People talk a lot of shit about a lot of different things. If I hear, all Neuvième Weavers are trouble – if I hear, you can't treat with them, or talk to them, or touch them –" and he drew a hand up her thigh and wound two fingers into the bed of coarse gold curls between her legs – "I know it's just talk."

Her fair cheeks flushed – getting hot for him again – but she said, "It's not all talk." She waggled one wing at him. "This is dangerous."

He ran a hand through her wing feathers, feeling them pulse against his skin. "Where does it come from?"

"The magic?"

"Mmm."

She half-smiled, more reflective than happy, and stretched her shoulders. The wings moved with her, like a dancer's bead-belt. "Think about the last time you went through an E-R Bridge…"

"On the way here. We flew in from Rhyll: Hardblade's based there." He remembered: feeling their ship slowing for the cruise up to the Bridge, going to the cockpit to watch, staring out at the green-black rift in space ahead and daring it to swallow them beyond recall. He'd seen Bridges a thousand times, and piloted ships through them a hundred – set the coordinates, disconnect the AI, fire the singularity engine and steer inside. No matter the number of times, he would never get over looking at them, depthless nothings fighting their anchor points, though whether they wanted to swallow the world or stretch to fill it, he didn't know.

He could happily spend the rest of his life never actually riding a Bridge, though. The stars would vanish and the world would shrink to a black rip of nothing at all, and he would sit with his fingers crossed like a little boy, hoping the ship's shields would hold and the singularity wouldn't crush it to nothing. Bridges whispered, too: terrible half-heard sounds like a giant's curses.

"I swear something lives inside them, and it isn't friendly."

"It does." Ellie's reply made Logan blink: he hadn't meant to speak aloud. "It's the magic," she continued. "Bridges route us through another universe: the magic lives there. It leaks out of the Bridges, and into our heads, and creates the ability to call upon it."

"Another universe? Come the fuck off it." She stared him down, unblinking. *Another universe?* "So when you cast, you're talking to aliens."

"How?"

"If it's alive, and in another universe, it's aliens."

Ellie's closest wingtip curved towards him. She frowned at it. "I don't think it likes the term. Do me a favour and leave it happy for me – when most of what keeps it happy is being used."

"Then it wants something. I never met a man who was happy being used unless he got something out of the deal." He thought, as much as he could think with his naked woman right next to him. "It's the same stuff, used by the Circle and the Guild?"

"Yes. We did some experiments during the war – we're sure."

Experiments like whether dropping acid on a man from Earth still burned him, probably, but Logan passed over it. "What's the chance it wants you guys fighting?"

Ellie sniffed. "We are happy to end our differences with the Guild immediately. They won't meet terms. They've spent the past two thousand years refusing to meet terms. As we aren't driven to illogicality by our powers, I assume they aren't either, and are simply hanging on to the vestiges of their pride for the sake of some half-remembered mystical empire."

It made as much sense as anything else she'd said, and Logan wasn't inclined to push the point. "What about antimagic? It works, I think –"

She shivered. "Yes, it works, and it's very painful, and I'd rather not discuss it."

"OK." What hurt? Logan bit his lip before he could ask

her. "I just wonder what'd happen if you turned on an antimagic generator and dropped it into a Bridge."

"No one'll ever find out, as long as the only installations with antimagic generators stay too big to fit through Bridges – and if that changes, I can name you a few police who'd become very interested."

Cops, poking where they shouldn't: and Ellie's cop boss and Logan's gang queen boss spun together and swam into each other in Logan's mind, with Sl'arani, Sanctis Merovir and the elder pirates dancing a ronde behind, till he couldn't tell which way was up, only that it all bothered him far more than he liked.

"Ellie –" *I want you,* he ached to say. *I want to fly away to Port Logis with you, and play with our kids. Fuck the whole underside.* "What are the exact terms of your job?"

She sat up and tugged the blanket round them both. "To keep any drugs shipments that originate at the Pell Havasi carnival off Circle-controlled worlds."

"Not to wreck them all?"

She snorted. "That's impossible. Too many of them. No: off our worlds we have insufficient jurisdiction, unless the shipment is specifically intended for our people, or unless we're paid to intervene." She wrinkled the blanket between her fingertips. "One shipment here was definitely heading for us. Myles wanted to stop it, but it went missing – I don't know how."

Logan pushed himself half-upright. A shipment gone walkabout? A Weaver involved? *But on the opposite side...* "If you want to know – I might be able to find it for you."

Her fair eyebrows went up. "That would be invaluable. Myles had a specific tip-off about this deal: he'll need to prove destruction if any of us are to get paid."

"Destruction, huh?" Of the shipment? Of the gang that had been running it? Of the gang that had stolen it?

'Destruction' – if the shipment got burned out from under them all, that meant no money into Hardblade's coffers. No cash for the boss and the crew would mean said boss getting more than a little angry with Logan, and Connor through him.

Love was one thing, and if he'd ever guessed what love

was, he'd consider it smelt like this, and like her. But family was one hell of a step beyond that. And if her kids were family, and she was family through them – Connor'd been family for far longer. If there was one thing Logan would never sell for Ellie, he might just have found it.

There was a way out of this, if only he'd see it.

"Keep the money going round," he said. Ellie blinked up at him. "Your Hendrix wants his cash, as do you. So do the folks sitting on your target shipment. And my boss, she does too."

Ellie shook her head. "We don't *pay* drug runners for their shipments: we kill them and take the shipments – and we bill their relatives for the cost of the plasma packs and psi-healing."

"Oh, sure." That really happened? Logan shifted another story from scare-talk to Ellie-confirmed-it status. "But if you hired a few undersiders to do something way other than drug running – something clean – that'd be A-OK."

Ellie's mouth pinched. It must be her business face: Logan'd seen that mark-signs look on other people before. "I see where you're leading, and for now I'll ignore the implications –" Lord, her Neuvième voice caressed that word, the way honey caressed nuts. "How do you believe we should achieve any of this?"

With difficulty. "Is your brother more than just a pretty face?"

Ellie blinked. "He's not entirely stupid, and can fight as well as one would expect of a seventeen-year-old." Out-sector seventeen-year-old, Logan added to himself. Out-sector, and the kind of boy who'd never been desperate, but likely thought he could fight, and that might lead him somewhere. Might lead him dead, but might lead him somewhere first.

"OK," he said. "I think I'm onto something."

*

CHAPTER SEVEN

Logan still wasn't back. Connor rang his jack phone, got no answer and left a message – not that the situation was urgent. Maybe nothing was wrong at all. But at times like this, losing sight of his only known sibling for half a day made a man somewhat nervous.

Thakar's new addition had scrubbed up well: fair, with pale olive skin and dark blond hair that showed a tendency to curl around his ears. The older runners who had held him under the shower didn't come back with many bruises, which surprised Connor more than a little, until they explained he hadn't started hollering till they started combing the tangles out of his hair. After their efforts, the boy looked presentable enough to fetch coffee and whisky while Connor, Thakar and Coker discussed the Merovir situation. Coker, predictably, wasn't happy.

"If he'd a chance of bringing the boss down, he'd do it. And with this cop running around?"

Thakar shrugged. "We're more likely to get killed than anyone, and we're the ones with the biggest cut to lose, save the boss."

Coker mimed a spitting motion. "I got an operation to run here. You *off-planet* fly-by-nights got no clue on what's involved." He waved his coffee mug at Thakar. "Get this office wiped, by Merovir, Sl'arani, this Myles Hendrix, whoever, I'll personally cream your arses."

"Find it tricky if you're dead."

"Then my spirit'll curse you from the hells. Whatever." He stabbed fingers at both lieutenants. "You. Do. Not. Get. This. Place. Trashed."

They escaped from the interview with as much dignity as they could. "He's touchy," Thakar muttered as soon as they were out of earshot.

"He's a man with a lot on his mind."

"Uh-huh." Thakar ran absent eyes over his newly acquired page. "Note that he didn't order us off Merovir."

"I caught that." Oversight or not, Connor was minded to take advantage. Or at least – he would if he could collar Logan for five minutes.

For the city was a tinderbox. It always was, in some ways: the Pellites' wartime sagas spoke of torture and murder, but also retaliation – whole colonies of humans enslaved or executed. A couple of thousand years' passage had dulled the edge of the hatred, closed cities and speciesist murders notwithstanding. But then came carnival. Every year, there came carnival.

God and his angels knew how it had started: maybe some Pellite trader had come across humans dancing amid sex and violence, and had dragged back a few Ditan dancers in chains to head up Pell Havasi's firework-fuelled spectaculars. Over generations they'd made it their own, and the Septième's – and, as shit followed food, every underside lord and lady's strings faced off here with the Pellite gangsters taking their cut from every transaction. And every dance in the open, and every deal in the dark, made the cuts sting that much deeper, till the air smelt of venom, and the underside gangs ratcheted closer and closer to mutual annihilation.

As he and Thakar emerged into the base courtyard, surrounded by roofed verandas and their chipped tiling, Connor's jack phone bleeped. He activated it: "Logan?"

"Yes and no." It was Galene. Guarded tone. Not afraid: trying not to fear? "I'm in *Carapace* –" a bar deep in the Pellite city, neither a regular human drinking spot nor a regular source of carnival trouble – "and so's Logan. You need to come here, now. Don't bring anyone else."

"I'm bringing Thakar."

"I already knew that." She cut the call.

Thakar had stopped in the middle of the courtyard, blocking a car that was trying to manoeuvre out of the garage complex. "What's up?"

"Not sure." Connor jerked his head at the garage. "We drive, now. No gunboys or pages." He pointed at Joshua.

Thakar grimaced, and looked down. "You read and count, kid?" The boy nodded. "If three men stole six marks each, how many do they have altogether?"

Joshua looked at his stubby scarred fingers. "Eighteen," he

said after a moment.

"Good on you." He pointed at the mess. "Go tell Mallison I told you to practise your letters." He gave the child a push in the direction of the closest open door just as the car driver gave up waving at Thakar and leant hard on his horn.

Connor towed Thakar to one side, squeezed past the car into the garage and headed for his bike's clip-rack. Logan, in trouble. When in hells would he stop getting into trouble? When in hells would Connor start letting him get out of it on his own?

When he'd a greater fancy for a corpse than a brother.

He stopped with one leg over his bike, so suddenly that Thakar almost walked into him. "Logan's in *Carapace*."

"I might have guessed he'd found a parcel of trouble in a bar." Thakar pulled on his helmet. "Or started said parcel of trouble."

"Galene didn't say." Connor started his bike and inched it towards the gate. "Why *Carapace*? It's an overpriced moonshine joint, unless you're there for the fruit teas or the blood cocktail. I don't see Logan sampling either."

Thakar's only answer was a perplexed little hum.

It took them fifteen minutes to drive to *Carapace*, and another couple to talk the armed guard into looking after their bikes – a snooty local guard, and Connor hoped the cob wouldn't stand by whistling while the things were stolen. A lot could happen in fifteen minutes, he repeated to himself as he jogged to the front door. A lot could happen in fifteen minutes.

A lot certainly had, judging by the prone bodies on the floor.

Connor stepped over the first – lying with his arms stretched towards the doorway, as if he had been trying to escape – and approached Galene, who was standing on a raised walkway to the left, leaning on its rail and staring at the chaos. Behind her, all around the bar, nervous figures – mostly Pellite, a few Sapilian, two or three human – sipped their drinks, talking among themselves in low voices, eyes down.

The bar was arranged over three cascading levels like a bird in flight, each floor suspended above airy voids.

Wooden tables and chairs dotted each level. Not much broken furniture, Connor noted. A few tables that had been upturned, now being righted one after another by a bar-pen. A couple of smashed chairs. The glasses that had been on the tables. Not Logan's normal level of collateral damage.

"I want to make quite clear," Galene said, "that they started it." She indicated the bodies on the floor: the twitching, the motionless. "They made a number of unprovoked remarks, which were not withdrawn upon request." Sounded more like she was talking to a cop than a friend: as if she were rehearsing for some less than friendly hearing. Her hands – a sniper's hands – were steady, but her tongue kept flicking her lips. "They're all alive. Not by much."

Thakar leant over the rail and squinted at the closest prone man, or at his badge, a rosebud with daggers for thorns. "Holy fuck. Connor, they're Tarsus's crew."

Connor held in a curse. Tarsus? She'd been butting at Hardblade's territory for a decade. Money, ships, men – she'd them all to spare and more. There were a few worse targets Logan could have picked. Merovir, given the current setup. The biggest Pellite crime lords, here on their turf. Hardblade's own crewers. That was about it.

"Has that man got a death wish?" he muttered. Finding a way out of *this* –

"No, no." Galene seized his shoulder and shook it. "Logan didn't do this, Connor. He pulled her off them."

Connor stared her in the eyes. "What?" She nodded, and jerked her head towards the bar's lowest tier. At last Connor saw a shade of primal fear running across her face – her, one of Hardblade's most unflappable mercs – and an edge of the same fear clawed at his stomach, though he'd no idea why.

"Has anyone called Tarsus's base?" Thakar said, behind Connor.

"These came in with a runner: Logan sent him off to find their captain. Connor, you *have* to make her let a medic see them."

"I'll talk to her." Who in hells was 'her'? Connor shook his head. If Logan had got himself into his one-fight-too-many by *accident*, it would be nothing more than cosmic justice.

He squeezed Galene's arm, left her and Thakar on the top tier and walked down and along the bar past the string of shallowly breathing bodies. At the far end from the door was the curving stairway down to the lowest level. He stepped over the last two unconscious men – one of them sporting a junior lieutenant's stripes on his arm – and started down the stairs.

"If I have to deal with one more set of unwashed, uneducated idiots –" The voice was unfamiliar, female, and foreign. Neuvième, by the low, breathy vowels.

"Ellie." That was Logan. A fraction too soft and indulgent, even for the amount of blood spilt upstairs. "Drink your tea and leave them be."

Connor stopped on the bottom step. Logan was there, at the biggest table on the lowest tier, leaning back against the scarlet-cushioned wall with a fond smile on his face. And perched on Logan's lap was a woman. Blonde, athletic – nothing like his usual stick-thin barside pickups – taller than most women, judging by the way her legs were folded up. Vanilla-pale skin, taut and smooth: regular, unblemished features – but her deep green eyes were fixed on Logan, and his hawk-gold eyes, oddly gentle, were fixed on her.

Something unpleasantly close to jealousy churned in Connor's stomach. He cleared his throat. "What's going on?" The two of them started and turned to him as if they'd forgotten where they were.

"Connor?" Logan said, face breaking out in a smile. "Connor, this is Ellie." He indicated the blonde woman. Foreign, and Neuvième, and had Logan spent his day hanging too close to Hendrix's crew? "Ellie, this is my brother Connor."

"Half-brother," Connor clarified. People bowed, on the Neuvième, a shallow movement from the shoulders. He bowed to Logan's woman: she straightened on Logan's lap and bowed back. "Do I understand you had some difficulty with Tarsus's crew?"

She sniffed. "The 'difficulty' will not be repeated."

Thakar jogged down the stairs behind Connor, with Galene on his tail. "You sure of that? Looks like a repeat's walking in the door right now."

"Not again," Logan muttered, but he was smiling. Crazy man. Connor glanced from side to side for the concealed exit he knew was around somewhere. There was always a concealed exit, for bar staff and gang lords.

Thakar and Galene sidestepped off the staircase as heavy boots tramped down it. Connor didn't turn round. "Mister," he said, "good of you to come."

"I wish I could say the same." Tarsus's planetary captain, Mack Filarson, a man Connor knew from a handful of unsatisfactory deals, came up beside him. Short and squat, he didn't quite reach Connor's ear, but he didn't need to, with a gun-string at his back. "I have to ask —"

Ellie slid off Logan's lap and to her feet. She was tall, as Connor had guessed: not as much so as Galene, but a good five feet seven inches – still a foot shorter than Logan.

"I have to ask you, m'sieur," she said, "whether your people were raised by barbarians from the Federation."

Filarson stopped moving, and pulled a face like he'd tasted rotten fruit. Behind, his string of gunboys and gungirls stopped too, and all their hands, Connor realised, were a very long way from their weapons.

"Mistress," Filarson said, "I —"

"My name is Éloise Falavière."

Her fingers went to the single glove she wore on her right hand, and she peeled it back. The air split apart. Connor heard, as if from a long way away, a high vicious humming sound, and yellow light swam out of nowhere behind Ellie – *Éloise* – into the shape of a pair of wings. On her hand, a tattoo lurked at her glove's edge: woven cords, all in a ring, indescribably complex.

Neuvième. Weaver. *Circle.*

"I do not work for your organisation," she said, hard and snippy. "Your masters have no quarrel with mine. I had no private disagreement with your men about matters of business or pleasure. So tell me, Mister —" and she took a light purposeful step forward, ignoring Logan behind her swallowing snickers of laughter – "what right had your men to insult me?"

Filarson's lower jaw stiffened. "None," he said with some difficulty. "Éloise, I apologise —"

"Your men have already apologised." She extended one wing pinion towards the bleeding bodies upstairs. "I will assume you have come to remove them, and to pay for the damage they caused."

Filarson looked like he wanted to slap her, but instead he bowed to her – not the light bob Connor had made earlier, but deep, to his waist, with one knee slightly bent. His dark hair's silver tie glinted in the lamplight. "I will do so."

"Good." Her expression did not change. Yellow wings, floating behind her. Yellow meant the Defence thread. Filarson could empty his gun's whole plasma pack at her without hitting once. "My husband tires of exerting himself on your squad's behalf." Filarson's eyes flicked to Logan as he straightened, but he did not react.

Tarsus's crowd filed back up the stairs. Above, Connor heard mutterings and curses, and heard the injured and unconscious being carried out of *Carapace*.

"We were outnumbered four to one," Thakar whispered, from the side of the staircase. "Why in hells did he run?"

"Because I told him to." Éloise adjusted the elaborate tunic she wore and sat back down, beside Logan this time instead of on top of him. Her wings folded into themselves and vanished. "I'm glad he'd heard of etiquette. Burning through a whole team to find the one person who understands the basic initial mistake becomes tiresome."

Logan's hand slid down from her waist to hover near her arse. "Don't make me keep the peace for you too often. You'll wreck my reputation."

"I won't." She gestured upstairs. "They might."

"Whatever." He towed her against him and rested his lips on her temple. Some of the aggravation-lines faded from her forehead. Connor realised he was staring at the two of them in some stupefaction. Logan, with a woman at his side for longer than the few minutes it took to spend his seed in her? Logan, stopping someone else's bar fight?

Best not wonder if that capacity for violence was part of the attraction.

He slid in to the seat opposite Logan and Éloise. How much did she know? Neuvième Circle Weavers' involvement in drugs work extended to shooting the smugglers. "Logan, I'm glad we caught up with you – we've had an interesting proposition from Sanctis Merovir."

Logan grimaced. "I heard, and there's likely to be a problem with that." He jerked his head at Éloise, who frowned.

"I have a working reputation to protect –"

"And we got heads to keep on our shoulders," Logan cut in. His gesture encompassed Thakar and Galene as well as Connor. "Besides. I have a plan." He glanced up at Connor. "I've worked this all out."

"I bet you have." Without consulting Connor. He wondered whether to feel insulted.

"The details are still a little sketchy."Connor jumped and turned in his seat. Yes, it was Hendrix's white-blond gunboy, jogging down the staircase towards their table. "We've time to iron them out," the boy continued. "Ella, was that what you meant by rude?" He gestured upstairs.

"No, rude is when I've a reason not to hurt them. Scoot up, Logan." Logan shifted left, and Éloise slid round too, leaving room for the gunboy.

"Mais ils n'y en ont –"

"In English." She glanced at Connor and Thakar.

The boy half-bowed to Éloise with some of Filarson's earlier floridity. "As you wish. But why haven't they learnt manners?"

"Sometimes several thousand years' experience isn't enough."

The boy looked unconvinced. "If that's the line you want me to take, I'll –" He stopped. A strange disgusted expression passed over his face, as if he'd smelt effluent running through the bar, and he half-leant forwards, almost sniffing the air.

"What?" Logan and Éloise said in unison.

The boy leant across the table and caught Connor's jacket cuff. He rubbed his fingers on the jacket leather, and lifted his hand and grimaced as if he had vomit on his fingertips.

"Calad," Éloise said, almost a threat.

"Guild." Calad's wide green eyes, more startled than accusing, stared into Connor's. "You *reek* of Guild magic."

The pit fell out of Connor's stomach. The Guild meant the

Federation: no other reason why their pet Weavers – murderers and spies to the bone – would turn up here and now. What in hells were they planning: to restart their millennia-long war with the Union for control of the Septième? An opening salvo of Guild versus Circle on carnival turf?

"Back up." That was Thakar. "We've seen no Guild agents, Circle boy."

"I believe you." The boy – Calad – finally took his seat next to Éloise, but his eyes never left Connor. "Go over everything you've done since I met you earlier today. You were clean then."

"Good of you to tell me."

He snorted. Faint arrogance brushed his face. "Mister, you were in the same room as six Circle Weavers. If you'd come into that meeting with this on you – I would have killed you myself."

Thakar laughed in some disbelief. Connor elbowed him. Why burst the boy's bubble? But the Guild – trouble never hit in small doses. "Talked to Thakar and our muscle. Went back to base and slept –"

"It can't be anything at the base," Galene said. "You'd have shown signs this morning, at the meet with Hendrix."

"True." Connor tried to concentrate. "Went into town. Met with Sanctis Merovir. I take it your people have been 'dealing' with him, and saw no sign?" Both Weavers nodded. "Headed back to base, stopping to allow Thakar to adopt a pickpocket. Came here."

"The pickpocket?" suggested Calad.

"He's seven."

"Not him, then – an adult left this trace." He touched Connor's sleeve again with one finger. "Young adult, human. Male? I think male."

"In the streets, then." Éloise grimaced into her teacup. At least the tea explained why Logan had made the trip to *Carapace*. "Tracking isn't my strong suit. Calad –"

"I'll pull backup later and search." Calad half-bowed across the table to Connor. "Thank you, Mister, for your assistance in tracking down a Guild Weaver. Preliminary stages, but still."

"Not that I intended to give it." Connor studied Calad, and Éloise beside him. The same green eyes, and some of the same bone structure around their eye sockets. Not much else. Éloise's skin was a few shades deeper, and her hair was a honey shade instead of Calad's platinum: she'd some Earth ancestry within the past twenty generations, whereas Calad's high cheekbones and angular features betrayed the New World pureblood. "You two cousins, or half-sibs?"

"Half-siblings," Éloise answered. She glanced sideways at Calad, and smiled. It changed the aspect of her face, from chilly arrogance to springlike sweetness. Again that tiny shaft of jealousy lanced Connor's side, and faded. She was Logan's: that much was clear.

And that much was going to be a problem.

Logan picked up Éloise's teapot and rapped it on the table. "Now. Four of us here," and he gestured to Connor, Thakar and Galene, "have a job to do if we want to live, and the other two," and he gestured to Calad and Éloise, "have their jobs resting on stopping us. Or that's the way it appears." His arm slid round Éloise's waist. "If we shift this on the Septième, and quickly, it never falls into your remit. Huh? And you'll know exactly where it is when you want to pick it up." He turned to Connor. "We profit less than we might, sure, but more than we would if we let things slide till Hendrix next talks to these two."

"Logan." That was Galene. "You're suggesting we deliberately stiff *Sanctis Merovir*." He grinned, and nodded. "That's somewhat unwise."

"There's a word," Thakar said, nodding. "How about *crazy* – and not your usual kind. Dealing fairly with him is one thing, but –" He stabbed a finger towards Calad. "Damn it, the end point of this is to leave us *alive*."

"Exactly," said Logan, with a broad smile. "So we tell Merovir what's going on."

There was a short silence. "He won't bite," Galene said in the end.

"He will. How's he meant to refuse and keep his rep? He wants to get one over on our boss: he doesn't do that by sidestepping. No, he'll take this and do like us – try to shift it as quick as he can. Then either he makes it – in which case

we're all happy and Hendrix's squad stiffs Merovir's buyer –
or he fails, and he's out of Hardblade's hair permanently."

Connor exhaled slowly. This had shifted from a cash grab
to a tightrope walk. "You're betting everything – *everything*
– on Merovir's willingness to defend his reputation."

"He hasn't lacked that in thirty years."

Thirty years. Merovir was getting to be an old, old man.
Old people were cunning, but they could be proud – bent on
defending a name built up over so long that was so, so brittle
if attacked.

"We need to assume interference from every Pellite team
we see," he said. "Lt'antis won't deal with Sl'arani but she'll
set her crews on us for inter-species theft. With Hlarxi's
crews it may be a little more involved –"

"Last I saw *their* lieutenants they were quarrelling," Logan
said with a snort. "Bar fights and team-ups don't go
together." Connor frowned. Lt'antis would be down excess
officers before the week was out, if so: she'd banned
altercations with Hlarxi's crew years ago. A fight, in
carnival season, when they'd humans to attack instead?

"The Guild." He didn't know why he said it. "Would they
interfere?"

Calad wrinkled his nose. "They could have as many
unnatural narcotic-fuelled habits as they wish: I wouldn't
know."

Éloise leant back, teacup nestling between her hands. "One
thing strikes me."

Her brother inclined his head towards her. "Hmm?"

She sipped the tea. "Out of ten thousand shipments
arranged here this week, this was the one Myles was
watching."

Galene leant forward. "Maybe Sl'arani was hired by the
Guild to ship this lot to your systems." Éloise nodded in
agreement. "But he had a Circle Weaver on guard."

"Not incompatible. Desperate people will do desperate
things."

"But it isn't what you'd expect."

Éloise nodded slowly. "It bears further investigation."

Calad shrugged. "The Guild have a thousand ways to
cause trouble. One Circle guard – that part could be

coincidence."

Connor pursed his lips. He disliked coincidence.

"Whatever." Logan tapped a fingernail against the recording ring he'd appropriated from Sl'arani's warehouse. "If we're in agreement to do this, let's shake hands on it now." He touched the ring's button.

The world shaded green. Connor's stomach churned. "Don't!" he shouted, diving for Logan's hand.

Too late. Logan flicked the ring switch. Calad cried out in pain. Éloise gave off a strangled squeak, and fainted.

*

CHAPTER EIGHT

Oh, dear God.

Logan rolled Ellie onto her stomach on the padded bench. Her arms flapped off its side, and her wings, broken light-shards, cascaded around her, slashing into the seat back, her tunic, Logan's clothes. Down the bench's far end, Galene shoved a cushion underneath Ellie's feet, and swore, staring at her lacerated hands.

Behind Galene, Calad was heaving into the bucket the bar staff kept around for less teetotal patrons. Connor was half-supporting him, one hand holding the boy's hair out of his face. "Is that thing off?" he said over his shoulder.

"It's off, and off my hand." Logan stared at the ring, lying on the table. How in hells had something so *small* hurt them this badly?

How had it happened at all?

Thakar scooped the ring off the table and peered at it. "It's a recording ring. I'd swear on my life it's a recording ring. But if it isn't – what *is* it?"

"Antimagic," croaked Calad.

Thakar and Connor looked down at him. "What?"

Calad spat into the bucket. "It's an antimagic generator. Smallest one I ever heard of. Pass me that tea."

Galene handed him Ellie's quarter-full cup: while he swilled his mouth out, Logan studied the ring, still held between Thakar's finger and thumb. He'd seen bases' antimagic generators. They were massive things, made up of ten or twenty coils each as tall as him, radiating a magnetic field powerful enough to knock out all magic – and almost all electric signals, and a good chunk of sentient bioelectricity – over a multi-mile radius. That thing, so small: "Someone redid it on microtech," he said under his breath. "Must be short-range."

Calad held up his left hand. A napkin fluttered down from the bar's upper tier into his grasp – stained with blood: last used on Ellie's etiquette pupils. He wiped his mouth and draped the napkin over the bucket edge. "You want to know its range – let me find that Guild Weaver." Reddened green eyes met Logan's. "We can tie him up, and you can turn that thing on and walk away from him. When he stops screaming, we'll know its range." Calad waved off the hand Connor offered him, levered himself upright, staggered back to the table and collapsed into the seat Connor and Thakar had taken earlier. "Just don't ask me to join in."

Logan watched him, leaning back against seat cushions with pale eyelashes wafting against his cheeks. A very handsome boy: and Logan's woman's brother, and Logan'd bedded his Weaver enough times to know how their magic could fuddle a man's cock. He was the least likely of them all to turn his head at a pretty boy's face, too.

"Nobody else touch me," Calad said without opening his eyes. He stretched, and winced. "I'll stop radiating soon." No one answered. He cracked open one green eye. "Oh, don't get embarrassed. Our aurae always feel like sex unless we're concentrating. How many Weavers have you worked with, anyway?"

"Also-rans like us?" said Galene. A smile glinted round her mouth. She plucked the ring from Thakar's palm. "Is it me, or might you have your Guild angle?"

"I don't know." Calad glared at the ring in her hand as if it might bite him. "I'd thought there were some depths even the Guild wouldn't – Ella?"

Ellie stirred on Logan's lap. The garbled words she part-whispered and part-hissed weren't in English and didn't sound polite. Logan squeezed her hand. He didn't know what else to do.

A woman who could take a gunshot to the head without getting hurt, and he'd knocked her out with a ring?

"Don't pick her up," Calad said. His chin dropped into his hands. "Someone get a waitress. Ask for the special tea. They'll know." Connor, moving like he was trying to hide a semi, was halfway up the stairs before he finished speaking.

"Logan," Ellie croaked.

His hands tightened on her. How he'd ever let her go, he'd no idea. "Ellie?"

"Whoever designed that thing." Bloodshot green eyes

peered up at him through messy gold hair. "Find them. Kill them." He nodded. Someone had shoved a stick down his throat: he couldn't speak.

Connor's careful footsteps descended the stairs, and a few moments later he set a tray on the table – one tray, holding two cups and a steaming pot that reeked of half-fermented wood alcohol and pond water. Calad rotated the teapot, poured out and sipped his cup, grimacing. Connor's lips moved in distaste. "Tell me that tastes better than it smells."

"Not much." He pulled a face. "It works, though."

Ellie levered herself upright and groped for the second cup. Logan held it to her lips. For a moment he thought she'd throw up – he'd seen that look on people's faces before, normally when they'd drunk too much or he'd hit them too hard – but she swallowed and kept her stomach.

"That," she said, aiming a wobbly finger at the ring Galene still held, "changes everything."

Calad rubbed his temples. "Because Myles knew?"

"Or suspected."

Galene cleared her throat. "Circle law bans hard drugs. Does it ban antimagic?" Ellie and Calad blinked up at her: she nodded, looking pleased. "This isn't like cocaine, or murder – to you, it's unthinkable." She jerked her head at the innocent little ring. "But something's different this time. Maybe the portability. Enough to make someone else – maybe someone very big – think the unthinkable." Calad didn't look convinced. Ellie's face was too blank. She believed, Logan realised. She believed.

"Now," Galene went on, "your boss gets wind of what's coming. But – even though your people don't lie – he couldn't tell anyone, because no one would've believed him: even you two wouldn't've believed this unless you saw it."

"So he hired us on the vice run." Calad pulled a face. "It's worse than us not believing him – if Myles had told anyone about this, except someone as thickly shielded as Ella, the whole Neuvième would have heard the story inside a day, and whoever ordered the generator would have gone to ground, or killed him before he could do anything."

Connor grunted. "Whole star systems full of mindreaders – how'd Hendrix keep the secret? Is he a defender too?"

Ellie half-drained her teacup and dropped it back on the table. Tea splashed out and over the tabletop. "No, but he's a *very* good telempath – good enough to hide his knowledge for long enough to get out here, secure the generator and regroup."

Logan slid his arms back round her. Now she'd drunk that tea, the touch of her didn't make him want to throw her onto the table and fuck her in front of everyone else: he didn't bother wishing the feeling would come back, just rested his chin on her hair. Her wings were still half-out. They prickled against his chest. "Regrouping takes *people*, Ellie. That's one thing we've a nice stash of here." He looked up at Connor, who wore a weird constipated expression on his face but didn't interrupt. "We've time and space to deal with this. Shift the shipment to Merovir quick as, then kick back and gather round Hendrix. Whoever's on Port Logis planning this –" he'd tried to copy Ellie's pronunciation of 'Port Logis' and not got it right, he knew, but it was close enough – "doesn't know us. A bit of surprise goes a long way."

Ellie leant back into him. "If this was started by a non-Weaver faction working against the Weaver factions, it may work. If it's a Weaver –"

"It *can't* be," Calad said.

"If it's a Weaver..." She reached up without looking and tapped Logan's forehead. "Mindreading."

He kissed her finger. "And that's where your spells come in." She turned partway to look at him, but grimaced and lay back down against him, eyes closed again. "When your head's up to it," Logan corrected, "that's where your spells'll come in. You can coat us till no one could read our minds."

"It may be enough." Ellie's voice was fainter than it should have been. "One thing doesn't fit."

"The Guild?" Thakar said. Ellie nodded, eyes still shut. "So the tie-up's worse than you thought."

Calad drained his teacup. "All the more reason for Myles to get us out here and cadge that thing before doing anything else." He took the antimagic ring from Galene, tossed it into the air and caught it again – his stomach must have settled – and slid it onto his index finger, the only one it fitted. "I'll take this to Myles now. Get it put away safely –"

"It'd save time," said Thakar, "if we wrecked it right now." He held up his gun. "A plasma round should do it."

"He's a policeman. Policemen like evidence." Calad manoeuvred out of his seat, nodded to Logan, bowed deeply to Ellie and trotted away up the stairs.

Ellie pushed aside the disgusting tea Connor had brought, slid off Logan's lap and wandered off – not quite in a straight line – towards the toilet. With a quick glance at Connor, Galene followed. If she were hoping for girl talk, Logan'd a feeling she'd be disappointed.

Connor sat down beside him on the spell-ripped seat and crooked a finger in the direction Ellie'd gone. "So. Care to explain?"

Logan shrugged. What was a story? Just a few coincidences, nothing more. "It started three years back, when we were shaking out Atildar's nest on Axartes. Ellie'd been slumming it to get some practice. One of Atildar's guys thought we were running Circle, and picked up an anti-Weaver priest and his squad to smoke out all the Circle mercs in his district. Ellie got caught up in it. She ran into me in the *Dog and Rat* and hired me as a bodyguard."

His brother's eyebrows went up. "That's it?"

"That's it." Some *it*. They'd spent a week together, sleeping rough on rooftops, snatching what food and drink they could from markets, staying one breath ahead of the fanatics till a spell-guarded ship had hit the spaceport to pick her up. He remembered: that first night, lying awake beside her as she slept, running fingers down her honey-blonde hair. He'd never thought he would lie beside a woman without fucking her first. The next night, he'd asked her.

"What are you going to do?"

Logan started. "Huh?"

"You. And her." Connor jerked his head upstairs. "Weavers earn a sight more than half the underside's willing to pay. You planning to talk Hardblade into hiring her? It's that, or accept you're going to end up on different sides one day – without this nice cosy fix-up you've got going."

And that didn't work, and it never worked, and Logan knew he'd got to jump on this while he could. "When this job's done, I'm taking a break. Heading to Port Logis with Ellie."

Connor snorted. "Holidays?"

"Uh-huh." Upstairs, Ellie and Galene's voices were becoming audible. More girl talk than he'd guessed. "I got a couple of kids not much more than two years old, I guess I need to pay 'em some attention."

"You have *what*?"

Ellie emerged on the staircase. "I disagree," she said to Galene over her shoulder. "If you have the capacity, a hand to the solar plexus is as effective at stopping a man as a knife to the femoral artery. Killing, no, but stopping, yes." She stopped on the bottom step and sent an enquiring look at Connor and Logan. "What?"

Logan closed his eyes. She belonged with him, didn't she? And the kids – he wanted to see his kids. He *had* to see his kids.

*

CHAPTER NINE

"What do you mean it doesn't work?" Calad tapped his garage token on the guard's desk. "This is from your garage. It's got your logo on it. Let me in to my bike."

The clerk clacked his bill a couple of times and ruffled his wing-feathers. That was a sign of embarrassment, according to the etiquette manual Calad had read before heading to Pell Havasi: embarrassment, and a little nervousness. "Token doesn't work. Nothing more to do."

"You'll – fine, fine." Calad bit down on frustration and retreated past a little queue of aggravated mercs that had built up behind him. What idiots picked a working Weaver's bike to star in a ringers' circle? Just asking for the lot of them to be wiped out – as soon as he collected backup.

Out of the garage he stared up at the sky, at clouds and cars' jets flitting across the violet expanse. What first? Go back to Ella, and the man she'd chosen? He'd come at least two miles from the bar: it would take him twenty minutes to get back. Calad was no soft-soled investment baron to baulk at a stroll, but he couldn't disturb Ella now. She still thought she needed to persuade Logan he wanted to be her husband, and though Calad believed that Logan needed little further persuasion, it would be wrong to deny her her time.

And Calad needed his time too, but with the city. Better to find one of the rickety buses than borrow a bike he couldn't afford to crash. With one hand near his pistol and a fresh trap-spell coating his money belt, he sidestepped a couple of dried meat sellers squawking in over-loud competition, and headed to the corner. The next winding sidestreet bore a signpost to the bus stands, albeit smeared in gangland graffiti and daubed in corporate stickers.

Ella had warned him what it would be like. She'd told him to ignore the child beggars and watch out for the few coins he carried, to respect underside hierarchy and avoid corrupt police. She hadn't told him what the streets smelt like when it rained, and how that differed from the way they smelt when it didn't. She hadn't told him that every other folk song lauded an act of piracy, or that children sang of pilots long dead more than of men and women they could see and touch.

He rolled the garage token around in his hand. A professional Weaver couldn't indulge himself with personal revenge over an incident like this: better to find at least one other victim to pay him to perform the investigation, even if he or she only paid him a mark. His mother wouldn't mind him working without a contract, and neither would his grandparents and his uncles on her side of the family, but his father and his Falavière aunts would be furious. The complications of having one parent from the Treizième and one from the Neuvième: Dominic Falavière and Gisele Delacourte might look so similar to, say, a Pellite, both being pure-blooded descendants of the New World colonists with what their societies considered a privileged upbringing, but Calad had seventeen years' experience of the differences in his parents' mentalities, and still had no idea what had prompted them to come together or stay together with such radically opposing views about almost everything.

Down the next side-alley, dingier than the street along which he walked, a couple of juvenile Pellites – one with a handful of feathers missing – were taunting a human child of ten or twelve years, amid rubbish piles that hadn't been bagged for disposal. Would Calad's niece and nephew come to feel the same way he did, split between two ways of life, the Neuvième and the Septième? They were just toddlers now, playful little buttons with no notion of the world above knee height, but children grew. They learnt.

Calad stopped short, blinking. The street had narrowed and met another at a crossroads. Suddenly there were no more of those bus-stand signs to tell him which one to take: all options looked equally unpromising, with their packed earth beds run to mud, the wooden pavements splintered and the buildings' once-elaborate awnings faded and cracked. Shops had petered out, replaced by unrelieved tenements – built by Pellites, and in the supposedly Pellite-only area of the city, but, Calad guessed, usurped by human poor driven from the enclaves. External stairs that narrow couldn't be used easily by the bird-folk, and those crudely-cut windows were a human touch.

The only activity he could see was straight ahead. Calad started along the pavement towards it, but broke stride as he sensed a familiar mind nearby – somewhere up above him.

He spun a strand of warp thread and fed Telepathy magic into it. *Delia, is that you?* he sent.

Yes: up here. The answering psi-signal was far stronger than his: Telepathy was Delia's specialist thread. Calad looked up. There – that biker circling over the rooftops was her, with a larger male figure perched on her pillion. Millennia ago, Pellites – following humans' lead – had enslaved Ditans as a matter of course, and even now, after several hundred Circle crackdowns, a Ditan walking Pell Havasi's streets alone would be subject to anything between abuse and abduction. Delia, Myles's second-in-command, had her spell-threads as protection, but Calad was relieved she'd brought muscle along too. It did mean he wouldn't be able to hitch a ride on her bike, though.

My bike was stolen by the garage, he sent to her.

The same thing happened "to Marius's," Delia said, settling to the street and pulling off her bike helmet. A couple of passing Pellites, drab respectable folk, squawked to each other and scurried away. Delia ignored them. Marius was the muscle-man perched on the bike behind her, a minor defender Myles had hired as backup for Ella, a human not much smaller than Logan. Two more bikes manoeuvred streetwards after them, each carrying another of Myles's crew. "I'm glad we caught up with you here," Delia continued, with a strange note in her voice.

"What's up?" Calad glanced at the others: small and wiry figures both, Rebekah the human pyrokinetic, Harlek the Ditan telekinetic. They didn't look too happy.

Delia planted both feet firmly in the dirt street. "Calad, we know what you've done. I need you to give the antimagic generator to me."

What? "I'm taking it to Myles now."

"Sure you are," Marius grunted.

Calad stared again at Harlek and Rebekah, then back to Delia. Her arms were folded across her chest, and her fingers tapped a steady rhythm on her elbow. How did she know about the generator? He'd only found out what it was an hour ago. "Who told you?" he whispered. Behind Delia, Rebekah shifted on her feet. Calad glanced back to her. She'd not looked quite certain of herself before. Now, she was.

"There's been a misunderstanding," he said, inching towards the closest side alley. How in eleven heavens had Delia learnt he had the generator? His eyes slid back to her. She'd been suborned. Must have been, to know about this in the first place, and to convince the others – to find time to convince the others, in an hour flat – that Calad was trying to pass it to the Circle's enemies. Had she persuaded Myles to hire her specifically in order to get her hands on the generator?

That so, if he gave it to her, Myles might never hear a word of it. She'd tell the others she was handing it over, and would give it to her real bosses instead, and delay any conversation with Myles till she was away and safe.

"Let's all go back to base," he said, fighting to keep his composure, "and talk about this." Yes. Get back to base, and to Myles and the rest of the squad, the ones Delia couldn't have had time to lie to. Everything would be fine then. Not if he gave it to her here. Damn all telepaths.

"Why did you drag three innocents into this?" he whispered. Too late he realised that the said three innocents might take that as an admission of guilt. "I haven't done anything," he said again, and louder. *Help*, he called inwardly, directing the thought in Ella's direction. No response. He touched Rebekah's mind-shields with a come-in signal, an invitation to her to lower her defences enough to read his mind. She did not.

"If you're so clean, give Delia the generator," said Marius. He raised his hands. Magic swirled around them: his warp thread, spun from the latent nimbus surrounding his mind, ready to receive weft magic channelled from the other world. It would be a Defence spell, strong enough to hold Calad down while Delia stole the antimagic generator. And he wasn't ready to hear the truth: none of them were.

Unless they were all in on it. They couldn't all be in on it, could they?

He had to assume not. He had to *hope* not.

But all of them – *all* of them – had fresh magic rising in their grasp. Calad inched away from Rebekah. "You," he said, pointing at Delia and hoping, praying, that one of the others would *listen*, "have dragged me into conflict with three of my own team-mates. I want that to be remembered."

"We will –"

Calad whipped out a thread, fed Electrokinesis into it and thrust it towards Delia's face.

She dived to one side, but fell awkwardly, and Calad knew he'd hit her. "Stop!" he shouted both aloud and telepathically to the others. Too late. Before he finished the word he saw the threads rear up: yellow Defence threads, red Pyrokinesis, orange Telekinesis.

He dodged, putting Marius between him and Rebekah's hot scarlet threads. Mud boiled up into plumes and arced over his legs, telekinetic and pyrokinetic working in unison. Calad cried out. Marius, his face set and hard, arched his spell out in front of him, hemming Calad against the wall. All the walls were wattle and mud-brick. Calad ducked. The spell slashed through clay and cement, and Marius hesitated as the house-front trembled.

A ghostly hand moved in front of Marius, grasping at Calad.

Calad spun a Healing thread over his legs, and brandished another electrokinetic thread at the ghost-hand.

Rebekah's head clove in two. Sparklebugs and snakes slithered from the gap.

Unclean, unclean. Calad drew another thread and gripped the holy magic, temple magic, divine flame from another world. Gold light burst from his hands and he half-saw, half-sensed Harlek spin a shield. *He's been duped*, Calad told himself. *They've all been duped.*

They are no dupes.

Calad hesitated. Fire licked at his shirt cuffs. He lashed his spell at Rebekah. Marius brought round his shield to interpose and grunted, buckling at the blow: Rebekah cried out.

They are your enemies.

Calad's feet went out from under him. He twisted midair, fighting the grip on his ankles. A flash, a rush, and Harlek hurled him at the earth. He tried to roll. Too slow. His shoulder struck the ground, and he cried out.

They are your enemies.
They are in the right.
You are the enemy.
You stole the generator.
You stole the generator.
Give it back.

Calad rolled to his knees. Mage-light dazzled in the air. His golden threads rained down on him, the others, everything.

Give it back, the voice thundered in his mind. *Give it BACK!*

– and Calad, shaking, thrust Delia out of his mind.

Should have killed her. Should have made that electric strike count and fried her silicate brain inside her exquisitely tiny body, and held off the others until they believed him. But now Rebekah lay moaning in the mud, and Marius was swaying from spell-weight: only Harlek was upright.

Give 'back' the generator.

So Delia wanted it? Fine.

Calad forced himself to his feet. *Help*, he sent, as strongly as he could, but he felt the impulse fizzle out no more than a couple of streets away. OK. On his own. "You want it?" He held up a hand to Marius and turned to Delia, on her knees at the corner. "Here. Have it." His right hand blundered to meet his left index finger.

This'll hurt. This'll hurt.

And he flicked the switch.

Marius shrieked. Rebekah's wails peaked and cut out as if someone had slit her throat. Harlek and Delia gave off twin high-pitched cries, hands scrabbling at their heads at alternate edges of Calad's fading field of vision.

Up. Now. Out, now. He staggered, moaning, past Delia – past her hand limply grasping at his ankle – and into the alley mouth. He slipped, fell against the wall, pushed himself off it.

Too slow. Too slow. *Get away.* Couldn't stand it – the

tearing, screaming pain lashing his head – he had to turn it off. He needed to get out of sight before he turned it off. *No.* His right hand snapped back round his left, and he struggled, fought with the generator, with himself, half of him pleading for respite, half fighting the desperate urge.

A hand closed over his: a smaller, wirier hand. The generator powered down. Calad slumped onto the strong shoulder beneath his, and staggered forwards a few more steps before blacking out.

*

CHAPTER TEN

Connor realised he was trying to chew a fingernail through his helmet and driving gloves, and pulled his hand from his chin. Idiotic. Ridiculous. Not an example for a man of his stature to set. But still, as he meandered along behind the others in the vague direction of Hardblade's base, watching Éloise cuddling up to Logan on the Connaught's pillion and listening to Thakar and Galene chaff each other down their helmet phones, he couldn't shake the sensation that something was wrong.

Nothing he could see. Nothing he could smell or taste. The streets were as they always were: muddy and sewage-ridden, with children scraping in the dirt at each corner and hanging off the gantries overhead like monkeys. The right number of Hardblade's sentries stood posted below them at the right intervals. When he opened his visor, the right sounds carolled in the air: music and shouts and a few cries, tinged with engine whines and interspersed with drifters' whistle-speech. Nothing untoward, except for that green haze on the air.

Green for Augury. He'd learnt it in school: not the free year, when teachers were too busy drilling hungry six-year-olds in their numbers and letters for anything more, but in the later years his mother, Priya, had bought him, mixed up with classes in history and galactography. Thirteen flavours of Weaver magic, with thirteen telltale colours for their thirteen lethal effects. What school hadn't taught him was how a man like him, manifestly not a Spellweaver, could sometimes see a glinting green thread spinning over the world, and why it always meant something when he did.

He watched the others hop over a roof-truss ahead. What for him, in the future? Some Spellweavers were still made from normal men, rather than inheriting the power from their parents: transfigured while ships traversed an E-R Bridge from one planet to another. Drunkards said the magic could contact any man it chose while ships skimmed the singularities. Maybe Éloise would know how it happened.

Did the how matter, when the what was so unpalatable? He'd seen it happen once before, to a woman from Hardblade's gun-string. She'd screamed for two days at the pain in her head, and had never quite recovered, but Hardblade had paid her to cast anyway, till it killed her four years later.

Connor's eyes drifted back to Éloise. Everyone said Neuvième folk lived long lives, from their medicines. Maybe that didn't include their Weavers. It wasn't as if Logan, or Connor, would live particularly long either. Sicknesses, gunfights – only those of Merovir and Hardblade's stamp could expect to escape it, and that with both skill and luck.

But Éloise and Logan had two children.

And that surely had more of a tale to it than Logan had let on. What woman had a quick screw or three with a merc she'd only just met, and *kept the kids*?

He was watching Éloise more closely than maybe he should, so when she slipped in the saddle, he noticed at once. He accelerated and caught up to Logan's bike in seconds, pushing between Thakar and Galene to get there. "What's wrong?"

"My threads twitched. I don't know why." She looked around and about herself as if trying to see something that wasn't there. "I don't know," she repeated.

"Are you any good with Augury?"

Her head tipped to one side and he wondered what she was trying to see inside him. "No – I'm not the most useful Spellweaver you'll meet: I'm weak on all the threads except Defence. Logan tells me you get touches of Augury, at times."

Bugger Logan. "I believe so, at times. Usually inconvenient ones." He ignored Galene's too-mild stare.

"At least an inconsistent dose won't drive you mad." She craned her head at the sky again. "No more twitches. Hmm. If you have one of your *inconvenient* predictions, please tell me."

"I never –"

Connor stopped, swaying, as a greenish glow coruscated across the sky. No, he'd never disbelieved his hunches, for he'd never wanted to admit to himself that they meant anything whether the circumstances were peaceful or martial: he'd just acted on those non-instincts, and always found them hideously accurate. And now. Again. Here.

He was dimly aware that Éloise and Logan had accelerated towards the base, that Galene was swearing behind him, that Thakar had tucked an arm under his shoulder to stop him sliding from the saddle – and of car and bike engines, too many, in the sky. A shake of his head and his eyesight cleared. Logan had landed in the base courtyard: "Get Coker," he shouted at the guard on the street gate.

"She's not cleared," the guard protested, pointing at Éloise with his assault rifle.

"She's with me. Get him!" Half a threatening gesture, and the guard stowed his gun and ran inside. Logan loosened his pistols and stood covering the gate in the guard's place. Galene dumped her bike outside the door between garage and courtyard and ran into the base calling for her juniors and personal servants, but Éloise stayed at Logan's side, squinting at the cars overhead and shielding her eyes with her hand.

Connor wrenched himself from Thakar's hold, landed outside the garage and leant on his handlebars, staring at dust and mud on the courtyard floor. What was coming? Who? Why? But as he looked up at the incoming bike string, he saw feathery wings protruding from the bikers' backs, and the pit of his stomach quivered. A troop like that hadn't come flying overhead to sell pillows. *Sl'arani. Fuck.*

"What's all this?"

Connor turned, pulling off his helmet. Coker, his face a frozen fury-mask, had marched out of the office corridor into the courtyard and was glaring daggers at Logan. "I'm halfway through a contract meet, you oversized half-wit. You want to keep your neck intact –"

Connor climbed off his bike, pushed it towards the little knot of gunboys on parking duty, shoved past Éloise and Thakar and gestured at the sky. "Incoming hostiles." Before Coker could interrupt, he continued, "I suggest, Mister, that you try to stall them. They're your covering fire." He snapped fingers at Logan and Éloise. "I'm first defence wave, Thakar's second."

Thakar elbowed him. "I'll take first. You're the better strategist." Before Connor could argue, or point out in not so many words that a united front against their superior officer would have worked better, he'd jogged away, calling for mercs.

Coker's gimlet eyes swivelled back to Connor. "Why is the blonde byrd here, when I don't recall employing her?"

"My name," said the blonde byrd, "is Éloise Falavière, and this one is on me." She turned her back on Coker and stalked out into the middle of the courtyard.

Logan's left palm crept to his face. "Someone is going to get hurt." He withdrew his hand and jabbed a finger at Coker. "Start praying those really are hostiles and she takes it out on them."

"Who is she?"

"My wife." Logan drew both pistols and held them aloft as a car descended to the courtyard, flanked by the bikers' leaders.

Out of the car stepped a Pellite cob – short, fussy-looking, feathers limp with age, but with a sharp look in his beady black eyes. He clacked his bill a couple of times, and two more bikers dropped in beside him. "You," he said in English to Coker, "I have an accounting. You will pay. Now." He gestured up and around, to his attack team, to the extras Connor could hear over the back of the building, out of sight.

Coker held his ground. "In coin? Or blood?"

"Both."

The elderly Pellite gestured with one wingtip. The gunbird on his left spread coverts and fired point-blank at Logan. The shot ricocheted off him and rebounded into the old Pellite's breast.

"Hold," Coker called to the rest of the Pellite squad, before they had chance to react. "*Hold.* In Meris Hardblade's name I claim this ground." Logan rubbed at his chest with a surprised expression on his face. Éloise hadn't moved. The Pellites started chattering and singing in their own languages, feathers puffed out in mounting anger. Behind Connor, that new clattering meant a defence team, Thakar's crowd. "I demand to know why you attacked my man in a base of peaceful operation!"

Guns shoved into the courtyard, and Pellites' wings opened with plasma bursters mounted on every pinion. Connor ducked back into the base and ran. He heard himself shout to the designated second defence team to assemble: one unit already in the halls to stand by as the first team's backup, two units to go the garage's entrance, two more to the back door. None of the squad's few snipers answered muster. Galene must have succeeded in hiving them to the roof.

Connor pulled open the closest store cupboard door, and found it already emptied of heavy weapons and spare plasma packs. The next was along the corridor. He shoved it wide. No rifles, but he pulled out three fresh packs the right size for his pistol. A pistol, when he was in the middle of a *response raid* – but on a planetary HQ? Had Sl'arani or his captains decided their home turf advantage meant they could get away with it?

Connor realised the base's comms chief was jogging past him towards the back door, and grabbed his arm. "Gabbler, call offworld, now. I want a backup ship. Don't give a shit when it'll arrive, I want backup."

Gabbler pulled his arm free. "We've no off-planet lines."

"*What?*"

He nodded his dark head. "Not getting a peep from the tangler. Can't phone the spaceport crew either." He grimaced. "I've sent a boy to Comet's to ask 'f we can use his."

Connor stared at him, feeling his stomach quiver. "Phone the 'port crew's neural jacks."

"Jack connections are down."

Oh, dear God. No tangler, no phones – no help: not even a chance to alert Hardblade that she would have to avenge their deaths. Internal sabotage? External?

Gabbler grimaced again at Connor and moved off. Blamed him, maybe, making a connection to the warehouse raid the day before. Damning, if so. If Connor lived out the day, he would need the crew on side.

More voices echoed down the corridor, including Zack and Carm's, both of them assigned to the second defence string, both shouting contradictory orders to their mini-squads. Connor hurried up to them. "Sexton, go to the garage: head the team there," he said to Zack. "Carmichael, take charge of the second wave at the front. Mistress Prialova has the rooftop sniper squad. I'll take the back door." No man could be in three places at once. The others nodded, and backed away.

More men and women skittered past in all directions. Sounds of firing were coming from the back door now, as well as the front. Damn. Connor recognised Marcello just as the boy headed past him, face set hard, towards the front door reserves. "You come with me," he said loudly enough for Carm, down the corridor, to hear him.

"Yes, Mister," Marcello said, changing direction with some relief on his face.

Connor hadn't the heart to tell him that the front door, with Éloise and her magic on guard, was the safest spot available. Instead he lowered his voice and said, "Go to the garage. Tell Zack Sexton I sent you. Prep as many bikes as you can, but make sure the first you do is Logan's. Get mine ready if you've time." He'd spent a couple of hundred on his own bike, as had Zack and Thakar, but that was nothing compared to the amount Logan had spent on his.

Marcello's eyebrows went up. "What's going down, Mister?" he said in the same undertone.

"Anything or nothing. *Move.* If Zack has a reply, bring it: otherwise, stay on his shoulder till I see you again." He clapped Marcello's shoulder and made for the back door.

A day's difference, he thought as he came up behind the back door defenders. A day since he had led his team into Sl'arani's warehouse. And now, as he jogged down the line inspecting weapons and patting fighters' arms, he felt the mirroring, and shrank from it.

Some God-awful noise broke out in the front courtyard, and bike engines roared, receding. Connor relaxed for half a second before their high whines crescendoed, closer to him. "Stand ready," he called.

The world erupted. Connor threw his left hand over his head as the building shivered. Gunshots rattled out of the door and windows, into high walls and mounted bodies. A bike, two bikes, crashed to the street. The barrage eased – had the bikers withdrawn? Yes! But the engine sounds restarted: *second wave, second wave*, before Connor had time to breathe.

"Runner!" he shouted into the base. All the runners would surely have run already – but a small figure, Thakar's new boy Joshua, peeked round the corner from the offices. "Go to the front door," Connor called. "Tell A'syan I need reinforcements." The boy nodded and scampered off.

He would probably manage to deliver the message before he got killed. Connor surveyed the corridor mouth from which Joshua had come. Some squeakings and wails back there. Coker had been in a meeting. His clients?

More gunshots, from front, rear and garage, and ricochets from the roof spaces. Connor shuddered. Serious assaults, feints, were all in a tangle.

He *had* to stay where he was. He yanked one of the men out of the line: Iguana, he called himself, a tall gangly boy with a red bandanna tied over his left sleeve to cover a hole. "Go into the office space," Connor yelled in his ear. "Any admin staff, cooks, runners, pages – and *especially* any clients – get 'em into the bunker, or get 'em out via the garage. My authority." He gave Iguana's shoulder a shove in the right direction and turned back to the firefight at the door.

Via some magic born not of Spellweaving but of combat, the chaos resolved itself before Connor's eyes into patterns, sustainable, comprehensible – *predictable*. And he saw everything, now, without a shadow of doubt, impossible to halt. Even as he heard himself scream orders to the men facing the rear yard, the women at the left edge, the boys on the right, *fire, reload, reinforce, watch those new bikers bearing eighty-five degrees*, he knew they couldn't win. Even as he heard extra boots running up the corridor behind him, felt new guns push wounded, dying or dead squadmates aside and take their places, he didn't need a green shadow or a deck of cards to tell him they were still too few against too many.

Sl'arani'd *sent* too many, more than he could have mounted without notice. Connor swallowed the implications. Get as many as he could out of this. Get himself out of this. Watch the patterns. *Predict, predict.*

If they couldn't win…

He grabbed the arm closest to him – a gunwoman. "Re-check the office corridors," he bawled. If they were clear now, *if*, he had a move to make. These were flimsy buildings. Best he ensured this one fell in on his terms and not Sl'arani's.

The woman darted off and returned twenty seconds later. Sl'arani's gunbirds were still dropping from the sky: left, right, giving fire, taking fire. "Office corridor's clear, Mister," the gunwoman yelled in Connor's ear.

Great. Connor leant outside for half a second, checking the damage to the rear wall's frontage. One glance was enough. Cracks ran all the way up it. "You five," he called to the closest little group, "back into that corridor. Second rank, give covering fire. First rank, withdraw to behind second rank." Slowly, Hardblade's squad began to rearrange, to draw back on itself like a turtle. "Rest of you, take up position in –"

A tearing, screaming crash echoed through the base, behind and right. The walls shook. Connor stood frozen in shock for too many seconds. Behind and right was the garage area. Behind and right was their only escape. He found his voice. "All but those five of you," he said, gesturing, "withdraw to the front door."

Wager his people's safety on the skills of a woman he'd met only today and whose powers he couldn't comprehend? Hope that this renewed attack wasn't intended to drive the rest of them to the front courtyard and oblivion? Too late to second-guess, for twenty men and women were already running past him.

Connor knelt between the closest two remaining guns. "On my mark," he said as quietly as he dared, "take two steps back and fire into the right hand window's lintel." He clapped the man and woman's shoulders and went to the furthest pair, to whom he gave a similar order.

Bikers were landing in the alley outside the back door, some taking cover behind their machines, others advancing. Connor inched backwards and came up beside the last merc, a woman: dark, short and a trifle rotund. "We do the door lintel, huh?" she said.

"That obvious, was it?"

She shrugged. "Nothing else left."

Connor glanced at Hardblade's dead – his dead – in the corridor. "Keep hoping," he grunted. If he habitually carried two pistols, like Logan, he could have done this with them, but not with just one. He holstered his pistol, picked up a dead man's rifle, and half-knelt beside the gunwoman. The gunbirds outside crept closer, their wings spread, plasma-webs fixed round each flight feather. Closer, closer – they'd stopped firing on the building, just aiming at the humans – "*Now*, and run!" he roared, and as he spoke he emptied his rifle into the door lintel above.

The frontage shuddered. Connor vaguely realised the four gunhands at the windows had fled and the gunwoman who'd helped him take down the door was yanking his arm. Shaking – dust descending – he kicked his limbs into motion and staggered into the office corridor with the gunwoman towing him.

With an almighty crack, the base's back wall caved in. Pain blossomed in Connor's ear, down the backs of his legs, along his temple. He staggered, choked, spat out a mouthful of dust. *Keep going.* His vision was swimming. The front door. Logan. *Keep going.*

All was quiet, deathly quiet, for too long, and then all became noise again, controlled shouting more than panicking, order instead of chaos. Hands, not the gunwoman's but someone taller's, slid under Connor's arms and eased him to the ground. Noises became comprehensible: gunshots' patterns, the whine of approaching and receding bikes, orders flowing across the courtyard. A raised Neuvième voice instructing someone else to get behind her and stay there.

Thakar's face swam into view. "You OK?" he seemed to be saying.

Connor waved a hand in Éloise's direction. "Whoever she's ordering around," he said in a thick voice, "make him do it." Neurones, thoughts, plans: "Tell Coker –"

"He's dead."

Shouldn't have been a surprise, shouldn't have worried him two pins, but Connor's stomach lurched. Coker, the base captain. Coker and too many others. The collapsed garage – Zack and Marcello – and the fucking *clients*.

Get up. He had to stand, and see, and think. He clamped a hand on Thakar's forearm and levered himself partway upright.

Tell Coker. Not now. Tell the top lieutenant, tell *himself*, what to do, how to do it.

He looked up, down, around. Dead bikers littered the street: Sl'arani's. The base was a bulwark at their backs. So: "Down the alleys," he said, or croaked. "Make for the Beaverden lockup." Hardblade's closest spare bolthole, through a lot of tiny sidestreets that would block effective bike pursuit, and in among a lot of other undersiders' square footage – too many to offend. "Thakar, you and Carm take the lead. Éloise and Logan, rearguards."

"Carm went to reinforce the garage just before it collapsed," Thakar said.

Damn it. *Damn* it. "Did Galene get down from the roof?"

"Yes," Galene said, behind him.

Connor swallowed an exclamation of relief. "Good. You and him take the lead."

Thakar leant away from Connor. "Go via the tent walls," he called to the junior lieutenants – men with *just* too much to lose to defect – who would help marshal the others through the alleys. Yes. Tents. Carnival tents. All the more meat shields.

Connor let go of Thakar's arm. The street shivered: gunfire, he hoped. A strong hand shook his shoulder. Logan's. "You need to lie low," he heard his brother say down his ear. "You won't make it to the bolthole."

For a moment he longed to rip away the fingers. He squeezed Logan's hand instead and nodded up at his fuzzy, confused face. "I can. I will. Take rearguard." Éloise, at Logan's shoulder, nodded. If her expression were comprehensible Connor couldn't read it.

He turned away and jogged after Thakar into the alleys, heading in the straightest line possible for carnival central. *Think. Plan.* The Pellite city was split between five kingpins, each of whom ran alliance with different non-Pellite gangs. Alliances, boundaries – *trouble*. Maybe Beaverden adjoined one of Sl'arani's current allies. Maybe he would flatten the place and kill them all regardless of collateral damage.

Hells, if Sl'arani just wanted the shipment back Connor was inclined to let him have it. The expensive part wasn't even inside any longer. But he was fairly sure that the shipment was no longer the point.

The line of mercs snaked right and then left, into a tent-filled plaza. Men and women of all species stared, cried out, fled from them: hauliers on their break, tradesmen with their wares, dancers out of costume. Frightened faces swam in Connor's field of vision, framed by hair natural or dyed, black, brown, purple and copper. For a moment he stared straight into a red-haired woman's wide blue eyes, and wondered how many guns were on his tail, and whether this woman would be the first bystander killed.

Revenge, this, now, nothing more. Connor swallowed a mouthful of blood. In front of him, a drifter woman dolled up as a fortune-teller pulled her child from his path, and for a second he saw a similar woman, twenty years ago, push her two sons behind the soothsayer's skirts she wore when she needed money, hiding them from gangland enforcers and her angry clients alike.

No matter how much revenge a man – or a cob – took, it was *never enough*. He'd learnt that, when his mother died: in what she'd done and left undone, in what he'd done when he grew to be a man. Sure, in Logan he could put it down to pure blood-lust. Not in him.

He skidded on a patch of oil. The jolt shook him back to himself. Get to the bolthole. Fire enough shots into the air to make Sl'arani pull back. Make him *think* – he might rid himself of all Hardblade's on-planet crew, but off-planet she had fifty times his forces. Hope no other crew attacked them in the meantime. Then start thinking about the whys and wherefores.

Because this didn't add up. Raid and counter-raid, dance as old as time – the pattern was malformed. Connor dashed blood from his chin, dashed a child's hand from his pocket's vicinity. One foot in front of the other. One fact in front of the other, till he saw them all, till the world made sense.

And floating in front of everything, he saw the antimagic generator. Enough to destabilise the Neuvième. Worth enough for Sl'arani to panic at its loss. Worth so much Sl'arani *had* to get it back.

He ducked a trailing awning, rounded the corner into the alley leading to Beaverden, and stopped. Hardblade's mercs lined the alley walls, guns loose in their hands, an audience or an honour guard. All down the alley before them lay feathered bodies.

He felt Logan's breathing over his head, and heard the crackle of Éloise's open wings. He lifted his hand from his gun and walked between the massed mercs, down the alley, over the corpses. Thakar was at the head, he realised: arms folded, staring at a crunched-up tangle of limbs on the ground.

Sl'arani's snake mark lunged from each piece of tattered clothing. Another set of enemies dead: the triumph tasted like vomit. Play meant counter. "Who the fuck perpetrated this without my permission?"

Thakar gestured at the skyline. Connor looked up. Snipers, on the roof, guns at ease, looked down at him with incurious expressions. A nasty weight settled in Connor's stomach. "I want it to be known that this was not our team's doing," he said to the purpling sky.

A hydrobike's high-pitched engine whined on the descent. One bike, two occupants. "I'll tell Sl'arani," Sanctis Merovir said as he pulled off his helmet. "I wouldn't want my team to kill unrewarded." The chauffeur-bodyguard at the bike's controls snorted.

Connor took a deep breath, then another. The city still swam around him. "Mister Merovir. I'm aware that I owe you some contract documentation. Circumstances beyond my control have delayed its delivery."

"The whole city noticed." Merovir stepped over the closest dead Pellite, light on his feet, just another graceful killer savouring his prey. Connor didn't move. "Give my condolences to your boss."

Was that the phrasing Hardblade had used when his son

had been killed? "Regarding the contract –"

"I see no reason to change anything."

Connor felt Thakar's hand touch his arm. Was this a trick? He fumbled an empty handheld from his pocket and loaded one of Hardblade's standard contract forms. "Fine. Shipment details…" He inputted them. "Delivery to where, Mister?"

"Hangar O-28. I reserve the right to collect from you." Merovir stared over Connor's shoulder at someone, or something. God alone knew what. "I require delivery in forty-eight hours."

End of the carnival. "Fine." Connor added the date and time. One shipment, in one of ten or so spaceport warehouses, storage details uncertain without access to Coker's files, several hundred miles away, through a city teeming with Sl'arani's gunbirds. Who gave a fuck, with six snipers on the roof? It didn't matter now what Merovir wanted. Drugs, gems, data, sexual favours. Connor's hand shook again. He squeezed the stylus tight, made one more adjustment to the contract form and signed it. "Here," he said, pushing the handheld at Merovir. The gang lord scanned it briefly, signed his name and gestured for another of his bikers to fly down and serve as witness.

"Will you oblige us, Mistress?" he said past Connor's shoulder.

"It's Éloise." Éloise walked past Connor and took handheld and stylus from Merovir. Connor blinked a few times to clear blood from his vision. That was Merovir's Weaver coming to countersign: he looked nothing so much as a plain brown sparrow without his bright plumage. That saturnine expression was unmistakeable, though.

Two Spellweavers as witnesses. Did Merovir think Connor was planning to cheat him, even now? Connor stifled a laugh. He wished he could explain how far that was from his mind.

Merovir reread the documentation, snorted in some secret amusement, and froze the handheld. "Nice to do business with you, Mister." He copied the data from Connor's handheld to a second, froze that one too, tossed the copy to Connor and slid the original into his pocket. His jack must have been down too, or he would have used that for his copying. "Forty-eight hours." He nodded to his men on the rooftops, who dispersed, then mounted up behind his chauffeur and drove away. The Weaver followed.

Beaverden's triple-reinforced door creaked open, and its three permanent members of staff poked their beaks outside, ruffle-feathered with nerves. Connor rested one hand on the closest wall and gestured to the others to get inside. He felt very sick.

"Connor –" he heard Thakar saying.

"Leave him," Galene said, a dozen miles away.

"But –" Thakar's voice cut off in a squeak.

"Staff," Logan said in what definitely wasn't a whisper.

Connor stared up at the sky. "What the fuck matters now?" They were staring at him, he realised: incredulity from Thakar, chilly calculation from Éloise and Galene, concern from Logan. "Cold shipment, hot shipment – whatever."

"But what if," and Thakar's voice sank to an exaggerated whisper, "the pallets aren't what he wants?"

"It doesn't matter," Connor repeated.

"Why not?" Thakar half-advanced on him, but stopped at Éloise's touch on his arm.

"Because," Connor said, so softly that the simian and avian mercs preening each other a few steps away didn't hear, "I took out the capacity rider." Thakar's eyes widened. "It's not Hardblade who's promised handover, it's me. Now I need to sit down." Logan's hands slid under his arms from behind. "Or fall down," he thought he said, but the words took so much effort and he'd had too little sleep lately and he just needed to rest. Just for a moment.

*

CHAPTER ELEVEN

"I'm fine," Connor slurred for the fortieth time. "I'm fine."

"Sure you are," Logan said. He nodded to the grizzled medic still taping up the shrapnel wound in Connor's temple, and backed out of the sick room.

Ellie was in the corridor outside, pacing around with her arms folded and her wings fluttering. A handful of runners and gungirls hovered in the background staring at her in God knew what mix of awe and fear. She stopped moving when she saw Logan. "How is he?"

"Just needs a rest." He hooked her arm and walked her down the corridor away from the kids. "Concussed," he said under his breath. "Don't let them hear." She pulled a face like she didn't understand. Logan searched for words: "Connor's in charge now," he whispered, eyes on the corridor, on the hard-bitten gunhands passing them. "Top man standing mustn't be seen lying down."

Ellie rolled her eyes, but didn't argue. "Is any part of this place outside comms blockers?"

It was Logan's turn to blink. "Nothing's blocked."

She tapped her neural jack. "I can't get a signal."

"Did it short on your spells?"

Ellie grimaced. "Maybe. I tried to call Calad when everything started earlier – I thought I'd fumbled the connection, but maybe it had already broken then." She looked around, at their warren of steel built inside a brick shell. "Where are we going?"

"Conference." Logan rubbed the skin under his left ear. Strange. His jack was working – he'd saved those vids of the twins to it, and he could play them back just fine – but it wouldn't connect to the nets, or the phone, or Hardblade's private network. "I can't get a signal either – and I hear the comms crew couldn't get the phones or tangler going earlier." He palmed open the door at the end of the corridor. A metal table with a few screen points embedded in it, several canvas-and-steel chairs, Thakar slumped in a seat staring at the rubber floor tiles, Galene standing at the back staring at a city map with her hands tucked into her trouser pockets. A galactic map glowed beside the city map, numbers one to twenty-four marching clockwise from Earth along the galaxy's spiral arms: an open ring surrounding the core, echoing the Circle knot on Ellie's hand.

Logan dropped into the closest chair. It creaked under his weight. He flexed one forearm, feeling muscles move beneath leather. Whatever they'd lost back there, he still had the strength to hold what was his.

What was his. He looked up at Ellie, drawn and wary. Did that include her? Their kids?

Thakar jabbed a button on the table, and the door lock clicked. "We're down Coker, Carm and Zack," he said without preamble. "Mikkson too, from the other day. Annasdottir won't live: neither will Gabbler." He jerked his head at Logan. "If you can keep your shit together, you're getting a promotion to junior lieutenant. We've not the line staff to hold, not in all this."

Not in carnival season, with every other crew here, when any man or woman might jump to a rival team just for the sake of a clean slate. "I hear you," Logan said. "You want me to play mean, I can do it on the inside as well as the outside."

"I hope we don't need it," Galene said from the far side of the table. Thakar gestured her towards a chair: she sat, like it hurt her. Maybe she'd had some shrapnel pulled out of her arse while Logan wasn't paying attention. "Merovir," continued Galene. "He knew what was happening quick enough to step in. Any number of ways *how* – but *why*?"

"The contract," Ellie said.

"He'd signed nothing," said Thakar. "He'd lose nothing if we died before we completed. Will you sit down and stop glowing at my eyeball –"

"Sorry about the glow." She retracted her wings. Logan watched her, golden long-limbed sacrosanctity behind him, and wondered how the wings had become such a part of the way he pictured her that he didn't notice whether they were in or out. "If I sit, I'll splinter the chair. I don't have control of my spells. Now, Merovir."

"Something got him interested," Logan said. As he spoke, the chess pieces moved around his mind, till he began to see a pattern. Was it like this for Connor, when he touched a deck of cards? "Sl'arani shouldn't have gone in on us that hard. Merovir'll have heard the shipment came from him, and he'll understand the payback was too much. So he knows there's something more to that shipment. He's intrigued enough to want it, and that means keeping Connor alive long enough to sign and deliver – Sl'arani would go straight after him if he just stole it from us."

Thakar snorted. "He'll be disappointed when he checks the crates and doesn't find anything special."

"Doesn't matter," Galene said. "We'll give him exactly what we promised him. No more, no less."

"With the minor snag," and Thakar waved at the wall, "that we're stuck in here."

Logan shook his head. "We'll get comms back. We can get off-planet backup here inside a day."

"What if we need to get out to establish comms?"

Maybe a runner kid could get out unrecognised. Maybe a smart man could avoid Sl'arani's teams. Maybe a messenger could use another gang as a shield.

"There's nothing to stop me leaving." Logan blinked and looked up at Ellie. She shrugged. "I'm not one of Hardblade's hires. All gangs treat passive Circle as neutral: if they don't, we refuse their descendants the opportunity to hire us. Besides…" She looked down at her bare pale arms. "Gunshots bounce off me. Now, what do you need me to do?"

"How about," Thakar said, voice rising, "forget the fact that *you're a fucking cop*?"

Ellie's face didn't change. Its stillness wrote paragraphs."Language, Thakar," Galene said. "She's a hireling, not an ideologue."

Logan found his voice. "She's not a fucking cop, she's fucking me. Thakar, you're the one needs to get your shit together."

"No, no." Thakar waved a finger half at Logan, half at Ellie. "This is *relevant*. I don't give a toss where you run or with who, unless – *unless* – this bloody complication of yours just shoved us into a tie-up."

"Myles has no arrangement with any gang that runs drugs," Ellie said, too patient. "He's a Neuvième policeman, and a Circle lord. He can't do that."

"You didn't know about the generator," said Galene. "The generator, which I'm guessing has just killed a stack of our people. I don't blame you for not knowing –"

"Thank you."

"– but you need to accept that a lot of people haven't been straight with you."

"I know." Ellie's hand rested on the back of Logan's chair. He heard the metal crackle. "So I'm going to ask Myles to tell me the truth. I can't read minds, but no one can read mine: he has no reason not to share that truth with me." Her fingers crept to Logan's shoulder. Warm tingles slid down his back like sweat. "Now. What do you want me to transmit to whom?"

Thakar clenched one fist, raised it and studied it. Some of the same self-reflection that Logan had felt earlier? "Hardblade's main offices are on Rhyll. See whoever the duty comms officer is now Gabbler's dying: he'll give you today's ident codes. Assuming you can get a signal anywhere in this Godforsaken city, tell the captains we need ten ships sent here immediately."

"Will ten be enough?" said Galene.

"Enough to keep us alive, sure. More and we'll spark a clash with Hlarxi, or even Tarsus." He shook his head. "It won't be enough to gain us much. Even if Merovir buys, this won't have been a profitable carnival."

And Logan spent a few seconds wondering how mad Hardblade would be with Connor for losing her a packet of money, before remembering Connor had taken the Merovir contract on himself. Deflecting blame from Hardblade when something went wrong for Merovir? Would ten ships be too few to protect Connor from the flak? If not, Connor would just need to steal a ship, and Logan could fly him away in it too neatly for any pilot in the Septième to match. He tried to remember the times when all he'd wanted to do was fly.

"Ten it is." Ellie squeezed Logan's shoulder once more and moved to the door. "Assuming your comms stay down,

I'll come back as soon as I have a return message."

Logan watched the door close on her. With her gone, he might be able to keep his mind on business. The image of his kids playing on those vids crossed his mind. They seemed further away than ever.

"One thing she can't do for us," said Galene.

Logan blinked. "Huh?"

"Lay hands on that shipment Connor now owes Merovir."

Thakar looked up at her – she'd risen, and was swaying slightly from foot to foot. Definitely backside injuries. "What in hells are you on about? It's Hardblade's: it's warehoused: it's safe."

"Do you know which warehouse it's in?" He stared at her. "Neither do I – one of eight or nine, sure, but not which one." She spread her arms out to each side. "By now there'll be several teams in the way on the strength of the drugs alone, plus whoever was smuggling that antimagic generator and thinks it's still inside."

"Then that's Connor's problem," Logan said, "and mine. Not yours."

Her eyes on him were bright. "You planning on moving up now? Be serious."

"I'm *planning*," he said, rising, "on protecting my brother. As I ought." She was nearly six feet tall, used to looking down at people. He glared down at her from his additional inches. "I run with Connor. Always have, no matter the boss. Now – I'm backing his scheme. No, I don't know which way it'll land: Hardblade's new bright boy, or high in some other gang's lights, or dead in the ground. Makes no difference. I stand with him." He poked her bony chest with one heavy finger. "You got an issue with that? You stand up to me and tell me. Or you take it to Connor – last I looked, he outranked you."

"In Hardblade's hierarchy." Her face stayed steady. Her arse, though, twitched like she wanted to back away. "How long he *stays* there is the question."

"Hey." Thakar had risen too and was standing a foot away from them, hands raised, almost begging. "Guys, leave it." Slowly, his hands lowered onto their shoulders, Galene's right, Logan's left. "You got some valid points, Galene, but we need Connor to answer them. He'll be out of it for hours. Leave this for now – pick it up again later – and help me calm this place. Both of you." He gave Logan's shoulder a little shake.

"OK," Galene said after a quiet half minute. "Later." Logan relaxed and stepped away from her.

"Good." Thakar reached back to the table and opened a screen. "Stores list. Logan, go check this is accurate, and look over our security – door guards, access points, the lot. Galene..." He brought up a plan of the city streets around the bolthole. "We'll draw up a plan to evacuate to the spaceport."

"Ten shiploads coming to break us out."

"It'll take them at least eighteen hours to get here. Assume we need out before they land." She nodded, and sat down beside him.

With his jack still not picking up signals, Logan typed up each line manually and went off in search of the quartermaster. The check didn't take long – as close to right as he'd expected, and it wasn't much: this was a bolthole designed for ten at most, but which now had fifty crammed into it.

He told the surviving cook to work out how to make the stores feed them for twenty-four hours, checked up on the door guards – tense behind their foot of steel, for Sl'arani's squads were roaming the alleys – and was rooting around the cellar walls, wondering how many bulldozers it would take to dig into them and which gang lords owned the land to each side, when the penny dropped. It dropped so far and so hard that he stood staring at the rear sewer's brickwork for far too long, listening to water trickle around him, feeling the stink seep into his clothes.

Connor taking the shipment sale on his own account diverted blame from Hardblade if anything went wrong with the transaction, for sure. But she wouldn't let him divert any profits.

Connor wasn't suicidal. He must think he'd a chance of pulling the trade to Merovir, never mind that he was in a sickbed, never mind that they were stuck in a feather-strewn foreign port with death on their every side.

So, if he'd no intention to do anything other than profit by this – he had to be planning to make a jump. And not to one of Hardblade's competitors: a rebellious lieutenant might be taken on, but a treacherous lieutenant would never get promotion. No – he must be planning to set up for himself.

"He's twenty-eight," Logan said to the dark sewer walls. Past thirty was when captains usually decided their apprenticeship was over and they knew as much as, and as many people as, they needed in order to survive alone. But Connor was smart. Understood people, understood business. Good head for taking some accounts and seeing what could be done with them. Strongarm brother, who was also a quality pilot, to watch over him.

Logan, head spinning, backed out of the sewerage outlet and took a deep, hard breath. He wanted to talk to Connor. He wanted to pick him up and shake him till he spilt what he was planning. Did he, Logan, want in on it? *'I run with Connor'* – what if Connor was the boss?

Galene knew, he realised. All her what-ifs – she knew Connor was planning to stiff not only Sanctis Merovir and Myles Hendrix, but Meris Hardblade, his boss and hers. And Thakar? Did he realise, or was he waiting for Connor to wake up – so he could confirm whether he'd gone totally crazy?

Logan half-laughed into the cellar's quiet hum. Crazy, or very, very clever? If he jumped far enough and strutted brazenly enough, could Hardblade do much more than accept him as a new competitor?

Feet pattered down the stairs. "Mister," a runner girl called to him – one of the few runners who'd survived to make it here. "Mister, you're wanted upstairs."

"Coming." It'd wait, at least till Connor was awake and they could talk.

Upstairs, comms were still offline. Logan threaded his way through bedlam. Thakar, marshalling three strange runners: sent by the dead clients' employers. Galene, despatching a handful of toughs to fire on one of Sl'arani's nests a few blocks away, and ordering another of Hardblade's runners off to the crews at the spaceport, whether it took theft or hitchhiking to get there.

And Ellie. Ellie in a back corner, silent and withdrawn: Ellie, staring at the floor like half her world had fallen in. As she looked up at him, and he saw the devastation running through her, he realised something terrible had happened.

*

CHAPTER TWELVE

After Éloise had finished talking, the curtained bay went quiet. Connor leant back against his pillows and watched, not her, but Logan. He seemed grim, but bewildered with it – not as if he didn't understand what was happening, but as if he didn't know how to react to Éloise's distress.

"This Delia." Thakar's voice was steadier than Éloise's had been. "You considered her trustworthy –"

Éloise made an impatient brush at the curtain closest to her. "She's a Circle Spellweaver. That means maintaining certain standards of behaviour, on pain of – well, on pain of living in penury on some ha'penny backworld, or running crooked shipments for poor pay like that girl Logan killed at Sl'arani's warehouse. We all *have* to maintain trust."

And she believed that: and she was so, so unlikely ever to see the gaps in her own logic that Connor didn't bother to point out the inconsistencies. He rubbed his temple. Swelling was still tangible under bandages. He'd lost seven hours to this. He couldn't afford to lose too much more.

"You said yourself," he said, "that Hendrix must have been tracking this against someone else's machinations. Well, either your friend's been hired by the other side –"

"She can't afford to be caught in a lie. I *told* you."

"– or she honestly believes Calad's on the other side."

Éloise gave off a weary sigh. "She's a specialist telepath, better than anyone in our squad at reading minds. No one could lie to her."

"So she's the one who's lying," Galene said, from behind Logan's shoulder. "If she's that good, she couldn't have been honestly mistaken in Calad. She's lying, and she's trying to betray you all." Éloise didn't answer, which must mean she agreed.

Logan was shaking his head. "Still doesn't make sense. Not her, but the others. There's no reason for the others to go along with her." Still nothing from Éloise, and this time, the nothing sounded ominous. "Ellie?"

"He's my half-brother."

"We all know *that* –"

"He's the son of my father's second wife."

Logan rolled his eyes. "A lot of men have a dozen wives. So?"

"They don't all marry them!" Her head dropped, and her voice dropped, till nobody beyond the bay could hear if they'd tried, till Connor could barely hear her. "My parents didn't just call each other husband and wife, they were *married*."

A few tiny things started making sense. Her edge of arrogance. The way she held herself, the way she spoke. Connor had met few married people, or children of married parents. Most had been paying him for something.

And subsequently, Calad: "So how –"

She batted a wingtip at him. "My mother died. Magic overdose, which surprised no one: she was powerful. She wasn't even forty, though. *That* was a surprise – we usually live till fifty, at least." She didn't speak for a moment, lost in some private moment of grief, but continued, "My father completed his mourning, went out to the Union for work – and married again."

Connor felt his mouth drop open. He *what*? "What the fuck?" Thakar whispered.

"I know." Something far from a smile twisted Éloise's lips. "Out there, they see nothing strange in a second marriage. You – you understand."

Galene cleared her throat. "How long did it take for her to get called a whore and chased off Port Logis?"

"My father's the head of our family, and was a married man. Both of those things give him a few privileges. I'm sure that when he dies – and he's a powerful Weaver, and twenty years older than she is – she *will* get called a whore and chased off Port Logis, possibly still in her mourning veil, but for now, she's safe enough." Éloise shook her head slowly. "She only ever had the one child. I don't think she realised that having eight in ten years would have been the only way to rehabilitate herself to my aunts – or maybe she was just being stubborn. I don't know. I've never been close enough to her to ask her. She flits backwards and forwards between the Neuvième and Treizième, taking Calad with her, pretending they belong in both places, till I'm not sure where they belong."

Connor leant back against his headboard and closed his eyes. Maybe Neuvième and Septième people were more similar than he'd thought. A child of a second wife – a very long way down the hierarchy, below children of parents who'd never attempted to get married, children who had never met their fathers, and convicted fraudsters. With that, some of the suspicion began to make sense.

He took a deep breath. *Don't distrust him. Don't point to that background and that Treizième accent, or the inexperience, the incredible inexperience, which means he utterly does not belong on a run like this. Think about that wide-eyed innocence.* "Hendrix is looking for him. Yes?" Éloise nodded without looking up. "We piggyback on his work. You tell me where he's looking, and I'll make sure we get to the places he doesn't think to look before he or anyone else does."

Thakar snorted. "A man in a medic's care, acting chief lieutenant –" did Connor imagine he stressed the title? "– of a decimated crew stuck in a sealed bolthole."

"We'll be out of here by tomorrow at the absolute latest." Assuming Hardblade felt they were worth the saving. Assuming her captains didn't hear enough snippets to figure out what Connor was planning, and stop him.

And how much harder would doing *anything* be when he had another few shipments of loyal staff underfoot?

Too late for that kind of worry. Connor half-closed his eyes. Better to worry about his present inability to walk in a straight line.

"Where's the generator?" he said.

Éloise blinked. At last he saw her begin to *think*. "Delia said Calad still has it."

"'Delia said, Delia said'…" mimicked Galene.

Éloise shook her head. "She's either the exporter's rep or the importer's rep. If she had taken it, she wouldn't still be squeaking about it. And from what the other survivor said, Calad walked away still holding it."

"Survivor?" said Thakar.

Her head dipped. "Calad killed two of our team trying to get away. It's – caused bad feelings."

Connor wondered whether to doubt the quality of Hendrix's squad, but decided against it. Logan had incapacitated Éloise and seriously impeded Calad with the antimagic generator. If Calad had used it on his erstwhile team-mates, it explained how a raw spoilt seventeen-year-old had killed experienced mercs.

Logan squeezed Éloise's shoulder like she was made of explosives. "Wherever Calad is, he's got a bargaining chip." Neatly left out the fact that *they* could have made good use of said bargaining chip, given that Hendrix wasn't to get it as planned, but Connor said nothing. He'd find other leverage. "Connor's right. Our people know the city better than Hendrix – we'll find him."

Thakar cleared his throat. "And then what?" Logan and Éloise stared at him. "Trot him out for Hendrix to decide whether some raw kid or *his second-in-command* has been lying to him?"

Éloise shook her head. "That's why Delia can't afford to let anyone else, including us and Myles, find Calad before she does. She must be giving Myles false readings." Her wings fluttered. "That's conceptually possible. She's good. Calad *isn't* good enough at that kind of magic to lie to a man like Myles – he'll see Calad's innocent."

And if anything were that easy, Connor would retire to a seminary, but he didn't fancy the task of convincing her. "Go sit down with our on-planet staff – or what's left of our off-planet staff – and let them work out the likeliest boltholes based on Hendrix's search patterns. Logan, take her."

"Would if I could. We need to talk about our situation."

Again, too much stress on the last two words: and before Connor could ask questions he might regret, Galene hooked Éloise's arm and led her through the curtains and away.

Thakar hadn't moved. He just sat there swinging one leg under his chair, a parishioner in a dull temple."I got something private I want to discuss," Logan said, not quite threatening.

Thakar squinted up at him with one eye shut. "I've known your brother since before you were *born*, brat."

Logan raised a finger. "I don't give a fuck, any more than I give a fuck what you are to each other. Husbands, whatever, I don't care. You aren't blood kin. This is private stuff."

Connor took a careful breath. Whatever he was capable of right now, a shouting match with Logan wasn't on the list. "If you mean what I think you do, it's not going to stay a private matter for many more days."

Logan exhaled hard through his teeth. "Have you gone nuts?" he asked, low and gruff. "Or are you being the smartest bastard I ever met? You're sometimes that." He pulled out his hair tie and ran fingernails through his sweaty black curls. "I'm not too stupid. I don't know all that much, but when I learn it, I learn it good. You're different. Smart enough to do well for yourself. I always knew it." He leant in close to Connor. This was what it felt like to pass over the core of an active volcano. "But why now? Why like this?"

Thakar kicked back in his chair and rested one boot-toe on the frame of Connor's bed. "I'll agree, I was a mite confused about how we were meant to get away with this."

"We?"

Thakar grinned. "Think I'd watch you scoot off on your own? I want my excitement too."

Connor relaxed, inside. A strange type of trust Thakar had given him, but it was trust nonetheless. "Hardblade –" He had to stop thinking of her as 'the boss'. "She's chasing one profit chunk from one narcotics shipment. Set aside revenge for the base: she'll get that later on her own account." He spread out one hand on his coverlet. "So. One set of cash, from one buyer. But we also have…" He laid out his other hand. "A second chunk, from a second buyer. That's profit one." He crossed his hands. "Profit two comes when we play them off against each other, something that won't displease Hardblade whether it's her old enemy or the interfering foreign cop who loses."

Thakar laid a finger on Connor's interlocked hands. "That was the old assumption that Merovir would pay extra, either because of the hype or because we were going to push Hendrix out of his way, and Hendrix would pay at all. But he only ever wanted to pay to get the generator. Éloise wants to clear Calad with her boss, he'll get the generator then, and he won't even pretend to pay us later. That's leaving out the difficulty of getting his bank funds to turn into hard cash."

And he already knew Calad had it because of all the noise Delia had made, damn it. "Hendrix may be playing whatever game he chooses, but his crew signed contracts to say they were on a drugs bust. He has to let them go at it." He shook off Thakar's hand. "And you're disregarding Sl'arani. He wants that generator, to give back to the exporter or hand over to the importer. Otherwise he would never have attacked us this hard."

"So how do we play it?"

Connor half-smiled. "We make Merovir think Hendrix is out of the way, contract to Hendrix to hand over the shipment with payment in advance, sell the generator to Sl'arani, sell the drugs to Merovir, then stand back and let Hendrix's crew in to grab the drugs on one hand and the generator on the other. If Merovir lives he'll not shake down Hardblade for it, he'll blame me instead, and I seriously doubt Sl'arani'll survive an attack by Neuvième Circle Weavers that angry. Meanwhile, we'll have grabbed all the cash and run."

Logan barked a laugh. "Hells, we could end up selling the damned shipment to someone totally different while we're waiting for the noise to stop… Connor."

"Hmm?"

"Where do you think Calad is?"

"I haven't a clue." Connor lay back and half-closed his eyes. Too bloody tired, however long he'd been asleep. "We need to find that generator, Logan. Before Delia does, before any other gang does, preferably before Éloise does – or you'll have to explain why you're taking it from her."

"You mean we need to find Calad."

"One of the big assumptions running round is that he's still got it. Could have been stolen from him by now. He could be dead by now – trying to go to ground in a city like this isn't the same as succeeding."

There was silence for a few moments, and not a comfortable one. Connor stifled a sigh. What was the point of undue hope? Sure, they needed to find Calad if only to give Éloise peace of mind, but if he turned out to be alive at the time of finding, Connor would take it as a welcome extra.

But the manner of Calad's disappearance troubled him, and for more than the one reason. Since Logan had first turned on the generator they'd considered themselves to be working against some faceless conspiracy. Suddenly the conspiracy had gained a face – and a thus-far unblemished reputation. It necessitated a change of tack.

"Logan, get Éloise to run over this Delia's past history: family, friends, old employers, political views, anything. If I know Circle Weavers, nothing will be hidden. Also..." He grimaced. That other possibility, the one line he didn't want to think, never wanted to think, and here it was hitting him. Maybe this was what it was like to be a gang boss – forced to contemplate the unpalatable. "Calad sensed a Guild Weaver hanging around. Ask Éloise if she's told Hendrix about that bit – and whether any of his team are looking into whether the Guild operative's already killed Calad and walked off with the generator. She isn't the right kind of Weaver to do the looking: Hendrix'll have to send someone else."

Logan nodded, unnaturally solemn, and rose. "We'll assume the Guild guy isn't in league with Delia, or, putting it the other way, she isn't working for them."

Thakar snorted. "Guild and Circle is as likely as priestesses and pox."

"I've met a few priestesses." Logan nodded to Connor and headed out.

Alone at last with Thakar, Connor was suddenly lost for words: apologies, excuses, reasons, all of them queued up on his tongue and evaporated. They'd shared dreams, when they were boys, dreams of independence. Maybe the years had dimmed them: but from Connor's perspective, his choice from now on was to dream or to die.

He picked up a discarded bandage packet from his bedside table, and flipped it over till the tiny maker's logo instead of the huge brand name was uppermost. Lionstooth's, either fake or real. Did Treizième rich folk dress in clothing by Kaijin, eat Aunt Millie chips and mix their Diakon with Marks Label vodka, the way the Septième middle classes aped? "What do you think it's really like out there?"

"The Union?" Thakar snorted. "Clean cities. Politicians who think they're better than ganglanders. Cops who arrest you, unless your bribes are enormous or your doings too big to see. Ask Calad, if we find him, or Éloise: he's her half-brother – she must have visited his family."

"I like your 'if'." He stared at the roaring sabre-tooth logo. A world where a man could run a business, a *clean* business with no link to the underside. A world where, if a man's business got big enough, it would get bought by another man, and again and again till four or five conglomerates ran them all, their doings as intricate and interlinked as any diagram of the underside. And the conglomerates controlled the government: so, in that respect, it was no different from the Septième...

"Huh?"

"Éloise would have said 'when', and I suspect Logan might have done so too. Consider also that we might need to sell his death to Hardblade as an apology for this string of fuck-ups, on the grounds that he had the generator last."

"She'll still be pissed at both of us," Thakar said softly.

"We'll need to steal ships, if we can't open our accounts to buy them." One light freighter each: enough to get away. Enough to start. "And – I'll swing this round till she comes out well from it. She can't get that angry. It happens to them all. It's happened to her before now."

"Not too often." But Thakar was smiling. "Grab some money, eh?"

Connor nodded. "Grab some money."

"And we'll make it –" Thakar planted a rough kiss on his lips and pulled him into an embrace, and Connor relaxed. No, not husbands, but they'd been close as damn it. "We'll make it," Thakar said into Connor's left ear, "because we'll watch each other's backs."

He nodded. Thakar's hair drifted into his mouth. "We'll make it."

*

CHAPTER THIRTEEN

Logan stepped over two young gunwomen huddled together on the corridor floor, and leant round the comms room doorframe. "Ellie?"

"In here." She was behind a stack of boxes, sitting on the comms crewer's stool, wearing a woeful expression. "This room's useless: I figured that made it private." She waved a hand at the desk's silent light-screens. Her lower lip quivered: more anger than grief, he thought. "I can't understand – Myles doesn't even seem to want to find him. He sent out our team, and posted a reward, but he's not looking himself, and he's good at that kind of work."

If he'd needed proof she was too upset to think, there it was. "Right answer, wrong angle." No other seat. He perched on the edge of the desk. It smelt of lavender deodorant and gun oil. Galene's scents: where had she gone? "Sure, Hendrix doesn't want to find him, and I don't blame him." She was silent. He laid a hand on hers, and felt her tremble. Steer her, like a misfiring spaceplane, till her course steadied: "Think. Hendrix knows one of them's a mole – Calad, or Delia. Maybe he can't crack Delia's head. I reckon he wants to put off finding Calad till he's got backup on hand, just in case – I'm saying this from his angle – just in case it's his oh-so-skilful right-hand-woman who needs taking down. And we know he's right to be worried." She was still shaking. He squeezed her fingers. "I said, *think*. All your team-mates reckon Calad's the bad guy – you reckon Hendrix, with all those doubts, wants them to find Calad till he's got proof he's clean?"

"No." She lifted his hand to her lips. "I called my brother, earlier."

Michel, he remembered. Another boy named after Michael Sinclair d'Aubry. "Thought he was military."

"He is. A presumed-dead half-brother qualifies him for compassionate leave. He'll get here as soon as he can, and help us look."

"Nice if you can swing it. Team of bosses who don't mind you running off –"

"He has a duty to his family, as do I."

She stood up and leant into him, head tucked in beneath his, breathing into his chest. Logan stroked her hair. He hadn't thought she knew how to get this upset. "I've not had time to wash since it went down," he said instead of trying to reassure her. "I must stink –"

"I don't care." She held him tighter, like one of them was going to drift away. Logan wished he knew which. "There'll be more trouble later, when Connor sells Merovir the shipment –"

"There will." More than she knew. "We'll be lucky if a dozen gangs don't jump in."

"And if the Guild Weaver finds Calad, that's more trouble we'll need to help him out of. So…" She released him. Her wings sprouted from her shoulder blades, yellow-and-gold feathers cascading behind her. "This time I'll make sure you're protected before we go in."

"Anyone'd think you cared."

She paused with her hands on his biceps. "I care more than I can conveniently tell you. When that gun-pen shot at you earlier…" Her green eyes clouded. "Well. I have reflexes. But I prefer not to rely on them."

"I didn't notice it was a female." Her hands on him, her scent in his nostrils, her magic tingling up and down his limbs: it was sending him hard again.

"That's your parochialism showing."

"Hmm?" She was doing it again, kneeling down in front of him. Any second he would tow her head to his cock. Any second.

"Assuming that because someone's trying to kill you, it must be a male. Violence isn't gender-restricted in any species."

"Kriastan males aren't so hot at it."

"That's a social construct." Her hands slid to his hips and her forehead rested on his belly, tantalisingly close. "If it were biological it would carry to their warrior clans too." Magic tendrils fluttered over his feet, around his arse, along his balls. It felt like her hands stroking him, teasing, tantalising. "Male Kriastans who become Weavers lose their inhibitions quite quickly. Something about realising they're finally as powerful as their females, and more so than any other species. They just conflate comparative physical strength with permission to be violent: that hasn't been true since the invention of the projectile weapon." She opened her eyes and stood up. Her hand went to his crotch and closed over his erection. "I don't think the relation between males and females is that simple."

"Relation, huh?" He gripped her arms. Still in her foreign bright clothes, not Septième ones. That'd mean tie-waist trousers again. He'd wean her onto button flies if it killed him. "You want to know the list of ways I *relate* to you, start with this." He backed her up into the wall. Over his left shoulder, he heard someone open and then swiftly close the comms room door. "I want you, every inch. Your hair, your breasts, your arse, your wings – your *mind*." He cupped her chin in his right hand. His left went to the knot at her belt. Expecting it this time: he undid it instead of tearing it, staring into her eyes the whole time. "I never met a woman I wanted to own before, Ellie. Plenty I could have owned. None I'd wanted to – and none I'm bloody sure would never let me own 'em." He tugged off her loincloth. "You could say you were mine a million and one times, and you might think you meant it, but it wouldn't be true." He rubbed a finger round her nub. She shuddered against him and rocked into his hand. "Even when I do this –" He slid a finger inside her, watching her squirm, listening to her harsh breathing. "I don't think you will ever, ever give in to me."

He shook his cock free from his trousers and drove into her, hard and fast, shoving her off the floor. She cried out and gripped his shoulders. Her fingernails dug into him. The pain-jolt just aroused him all the more, and he lifted her, held her straddling his waist and wailing against him till he didn't know which of them was which, only that she was coming hard as a freighter under him and the sight and sound of her pleasure was tipping him over the edge too.

Seconds or hours later, he pulled out of her and sat back hard on the comms stool. Plastic pinched his bare arse. Ellie, shivering, leant against the wall. She looked drained and lost.

Logan scooped up his undershorts, wiped himself and tossed them to Ellie. "Here. Fix yourself up. There's a shower down the way, you want it."

She took the shorts and made some attempt at wiping off his semen, still with that glazed expression, like their coupling had sucked the last energy out of her. She dropped the shorts, staggered to him and leant on him, one arm round his neck. "I know I'm doing the right thing," she said into his chest.

He kissed her hair. "Good. That's good."

After what seemed like an age he released her. She was still trembling. He kissed her cheek, pulled on his trousers and slid out into the corridor. The gunwomen were still sitting on the floor outside. He glared them out of his way.

In the shower cubicle he washed quickly – the bolthole was too hot with all of them inside, but the wash water was cold – and stared too long at his hands before dressing. Ellie'd been shaking, when he left her: he was still shaking now. *Damn* it.

Her – everything he'd ever wanted – and that tiny tantalising glimpse of a future that she'd shown him: he didn't know where to place it or what to do with it. Somewhere inside he'd gone numb, he realised, as if he didn't want to think. He didn't give a toss how difficult it would be to raise kids. Living was difficult. Dying in this brick box would be easy.

And if they got out, only for Connor to lead him onto Hardblade's guns on the way out of her employ?

He sleepwalked back towards the entrance hall. Three junior mercs had just slipped back inside, flushed and panting as hard as he'd been earlier, but from a different reason. Galene was stalking around the hall, watch officer: "Raiding parties?" Logan asked her.

She nodded. "We're keeping Sl'arani's crew scared away from the door, at least – but they can definitely communicate, unlike us."

"I'll go out, see if I can figure what's going on with that." For a moment he thought she'd argue, but then remembered the new stripe taped onto his sleeve and realised she wouldn't break a lieutenants' consensus now.

"We've had no reply from the spaceport," she said as he fastened his flak jacket. "The ships'll have gone, or been destroyed, and I don't like to calculate the boss's reaction to either."

His boss was likely to be Connor before too long, but he didn't quibble. "It's not our problem: it's Sl'arani's, or the captains'."

She made a noncommittal sound. "On the off-chance Sl'arani hasn't noticed, I don't think we should give him any clues."

"I'll be careful." As the door closed on him he heard her snort a laugh.

Logan leant on the door for a minute or two, listening to the streets, smelling them, drowning himself in the night. He hadn't checked the time for hours, stuck in their windowless box. If his jack's clock was still right, it was four in the morning.

Inhaling the reek of stagnant water and rotten dung, he set off down the alley to his left, heading back the way they'd all run earlier. Broken glass and plastic crunched underfoot, but he didn't care: he wasn't aiming for silence, just to be quiet enough to hear any approach, and loud enough for his patrol to be heard. He half-laughed into the darkness. Ellie's spells lay thick-wound on him – and at least some of Sl'arani's team who'd seen plasma rounds bounce off him earlier must have lived to report. The Incredible Gun-Proof Merc. Didn't matter how many of them shot at him now.

And the same magic blocked Weavers' spells. If only Ellie'd set shields over Calad!

Discarded cans and metal scraps clinked against his feet. Down the next wynd, a cat meowed. Logan cocked his right-hand pistol and fired just past the sound. In the scintillating afterimage he saw a youngish Pellite running away, clawed wingtips flailing.

He quietened his steps and walked to the Pellite's hiding spot. The gunshot had killed his night vision: he waited for thirty seconds, then another thirty, and at last the tiny alley swam back into view, cast in faint lamplight reflected from several streets away. Logan looked down. Sure enough, the youngster'd dropped something, in among the mud and rubbish: a dark scrap of plastic, wing-clip designed. He retrieved it and scooted back into the main alley.

Round the corner, out of the kid's sightline had he decided to come back for his toy, Logan rubbed off the mud and studied it. The Deltacorp logo stared up at him, alongside a tiny winking light: as he watched, the light shifted from green to red, and cut out. He laughed softly. A radio transceiver. Sl'arani had gone back to good old-fashioned radio waves for his people's on-planet comm system. Sure, they could be interfered with and overheard, but if nobody else had known this was coming, nobody would have been able to cobble together the tech yet to overhear or interfere.

Again, his brain caught up with itself, and he took a deep breath. *Nobody*, he'd thought, *nobody*: and the more he considered it, the more he wondered. Phones and tanglers worked off open satellite relays. If theirs had gone down, were anyone else's up?

He could buy Sl'arani having done something to their comms before attacking – any leader would do it under the circumstances, if he could – but knocking out relay satellites? He'd have pissed off every team on planet, and not a few gang lords…

Slowly, trying to think, Logan walked back to Beaverden's iron door without further incident. Even at the dead of night he could hear the city move: bakers stoking ovens, whorehouses throwing out drunkards, hauliers making deliveries. Nothing but him in this alley, still smeared in black blood.

No one would sing of this night decades or centuries down the line: no one would grant tonight's dead their immortality. Gemstone pilots like Aelin Carrow and Chastity Matin had their names sung every generation, till they seemed more like gods than men and women who'd bled and died here, and even priests spoke of the greatest Spellweavers as if they had had a special link to heaven. Would anyone name himself after Zack Sexton, or Tam Coker, or any of the rest of them, the way boys did after Jack Ellenson or Michael Sinclair d'Aubry? Fairness was a toy for rich children, but it still grated, till Logan felt he was bleeding: or that he wanted to make someone else bleed, which was usually better.

Past Beaverden's door he stared down towards the far end of the alley. Black-purple darkness in the main, with a single light's flicker breaking it. Still with one gun up, Logan strode down the alley. More debris clinked underfoot, and moulds born of Pell Havasi and more distant worlds fought for space on the walls. Fewer corpse-remnants, though. He fired an experimental bolt up and right, and listened. No sound, no whimper from a hidden watcher.

And if he walked all the way back to Hardblade's base – former base – now? Maybe the vultures, of all species, would have come and gone already, picking over possessions, stealing data. Coker'd paid a few good techs to keep it all encrypted, but any crypt could be broken, assuming the drives had survived. Logan spared a few melancholy thoughts for his Connaught XR-2, stuck under the wreckage. He'd left good men and women under that wreckage too, but the bike had been his, as had his guitar.

Could Calad have gone to hide there? It'd figure on anyone's list of unlikely boltholes. Best he checked, after backup had landed.

From the smell, some baker no more than a street away'd burnt a batch of bread. Logan waited, listening. The bakery boy throwing away the burnt loaves. A few drift kids pulling them out of the bins and running away. Silence again.

Logan walked on a few more paces. Another, sharper smell wafted out of the gloom. Incense.

He stopped at the door at the end of the alley. A wooden door, carved with the symbols for all eleven angels and the three aspects of God. A human temple, here? Sure, the Pellites permitted non-Pellite places of worship in their city, but Logan hadn't expected one down a dung-stained alley too small for cars.

The faint light he'd seen was a candle set into the door. On impulse he pushed it open. The shoe rack was just inside, beside a pail of water. Logan eased off his boots, rinsed his feet and slid past the sanctuary curtain.

He'd been in temples, big and small, a few hundred times before: this was the smallest he'd seen, one room no more than ten feet wide and fifteen long. No space for shrines to each angel, with screens and votive pedestals – instead, five icon plaques stood mounted on each side wall with a prayer-shelf beneath each, and the angel of Transcendence's icon was glued to the back wall, lonely and lost. Three tiny altars stood in front of it, in a rough triangle. Traditional trignoscite priests here, not the modern monotarian lot.

Logan sat down on one of the rough benches bisecting the room. Candles flickered next to his head, on the shelf in front of the angel of Mercy's icon. Mercy was male, he remembered. He'd never thought that made sense. He stared at the trio of altars, at incense smoke streaming off them. That numb feeling was sliding back into him, however hard he wanted to make it stop.

Just a day ago, he'd known where his life stood. A brother, a boss, a base, a job: his biggest dreams aloft, of piloting spaceships through starscapes the Diamond and the Sapphire had once flown. Now he had a woman, two kids, no base, and a brother planning to drag him into a betrayal.

He'd called Ellie his wife earlier, no matter that he'd said it to a man now dead. If so, that made Calad his stepbrother. And *that* meant he had to find him, dead or alive, with that generator or without it, just as he would have had to find Connor under the same circumstances.

A door creaked at the back, by the angel of Understanding's icon. Logan looked up. A priest, dressed in crumpled blue robes, stood peering round the shadowy doorway. "Can I help you?" he said.

"Probably not." Logan looked back at the cluster of candles on the angel of Mercy's shelf. "I've sinned."

"All men have."

"I'll probably sin some more tomorrow." The candlelight shimmered, tinged with green, and Logan tried to see a pattern in the glare. "It's been the way of things, these years."

"Well, recognising one's failings is important," the priest said carefully.

Logan half-laughed. "A man can't move in carnival season without sinning. You're selling a tough message – tough as old meat." He rose. Had the priest winced? They didn't eat meat, not if they were devout.

He dug into his money belt, teased out a handful of pennies

and dropped them on the angel of Mercy's prayer-shelf. "What would you do," he said over his shoulder, "if someone you... cared for was going to rest too much on too tight a chance?"

"That would depend on what would happen if the chance were not taken at all."

Did it? Logan ran his eyes along the wall, right from Mercy, to the angel of Victory's icon. A man *had* to take his chance in this world. The alternative was living slow and dying young at someone else's whim.

Maybe Connor'd found the best path he could. Logan bowed to the angel of Victory, nodded to the priest, and headed out to find his boots.

*

CHAPTER FOURTEEN

Perched high on a gantry overlooking Hardblade's old base, a Pellite chick squawked to his fellows, and a little crowd pattered along after him, flapping unfledged wings and calling to the mercs below. One of the men levelled a gun at the chicks. "Put that away," Connor called, dropping the crowbar he had been using to lever roof struts off rubble. "Do you want a mob after us sooner rather than later?"

The merc, Packer – one of the relief crew, heavily armed and armoured – stared at Connor, not lowering his rifle. "We don't need scum on our tail."

"They're not drifters, they're locals." Connor shook his head. Dust from the rubble blew up his nose, threatening to make him sneeze. He was coated in it already, as were almost all the squad, and had blisters building beneath his gloves. "They have protection. Imagine what we'd do if someone shot your kid."

"I don't have a kid, unless the last dozy bitch didn't get herself fixed."

Logan tossed a hundred-pound cross-brace off the pile, marched to Packer and yanked the gun from his hand. "Then make it simpler. You do as he says."

Packer glowered and adjusted his jacket – no holes in it, unlike the threadbare crew who had been attacked – but said nothing. Connor swallowed a sigh. Stupid men, making stupid moves on planets they didn't understand, and if he were any judge, the bosses were normally the ones who had to deal with it, if only because the stupid ones were dead. Sure, they'd needed rescuing, but by this lot? He'd seen most of them once or twice, and once or twice had been too many times.

He glanced across the street at the one figure among them not covered in muck, a businesslike woman in reinforced leather armour, working at her bike's data centre – Marika Kylesdottir, the captain Hardblade had sent in charge of the only four ships she could spare. Connor had wondered at the number, at first, and still wondered what move Hardblade was trying to cover, but at least four ships – with three already gone, evacuating wounded – had a chance of running under the radar.

Kylesdottir beckoned, and he abandoned a move to pick up the crowbar again and went over to her. "Any luck getting an upload, Mistress?"

"Comms are still down and I'm not getting the backups' distress signal, which is a 'no'." She retracted her screen with a grimace. "Under several tons of brick the signal might be blocked. We keep digging."

Until Sl'arani's squads attacked, she meant. Until Sl'arani's spies heard cheeping from those innocent, protected, garrulous little chicks on the gantry, and sent a radio message to his gunhands to come and finish what they had started. But Hardblade's newcomers had found corpses amidst the rubble, and were angry enough to put up a stiff fight.

"I'm building an outline for what to do next," she continued. "Anything we can retrieve from the backups, I'll want as ammunition."

Reprisals, she meant, and Connor swallowed his misgivings. Attack, counter, remise: "I'm in a position to give you my opinion, if you'll class that as data."

She cocked her head at him. "What makes you think I wouldn't?"

"Well –"

She laughed. "Don't get caught up on titles now. You'll be made captain as soon as you get back to Rhyll. I wouldn't worry about small stuff, when you've held the crew together like this."

"Thank you." It didn't feel like he'd done much, just woken up at the right time to relieve Thakar with a plan already in place, then stalk around giving people orders till they thought of him as a figurehead. He glanced back at the string of mercs following them along. The only ones from the original city squad were those who had insisted – Logan, Thakar, Galene and a couple of the squad mercs, including the woman who had helped him bring down the base's back wall. Her name, he'd since learnt, was Pritie Mayasdottir.

All the rest had been driven considerably over the speed limit to the 'port, and slipped out in Hardblade's freighters before Sl'arani's bribees in among the traffic control staff had realised they were running false IDs.

The thought of promotion seemed inane, or maybe the conversation he'd had with Thakar the night before had been inane: built on not much more than coincidence and opportunity and painkillers, like a house of straw built upon sand. Kylesdottir and her crew, or their physical reality, had blown it away.

He risked a glance at Logan, back on digging duty, still trading a few insults with Packer and the other new-come mercs. Éloise had headed back to her boss's base. No one had found Calad yet, neither her team nor anyone else's. How Connor was meant to explain to Kylesdottir that he needed to divert a few smart heads to look for the half-brother of a woman not one of their squad, he didn't know. Maybe Éloise would offer to hire them to help.

Family mattered. Kylesdottir knew more of her antecedents than many did, for she bore a parent's name as her surname, but she didn't necessarily know more than that. Connor's great-grandmother had known nothing of her family, but since her there had been two more Cardwain women, and now two Cardwain brothers. Logan was his family, and Éloise and Calad were connected in their turn: that, above even a loyal man's duty to his boss, should be his priority.

"I've negotiated a sale of goods to Sanctis Merovir," he said. His stomach quivered. Merovir, with a son dead at Hardblade's hands. Family mattered: and if Merovir were any kind of man, wouldn't he plot to double-cross Hardblade's lieutenant, contracts be damned? "If the plan was to evacuate as soon as we've concluded our search, I'd welcome a delay till we've handed over." Maybe that wasn't even true – but he *had* to stay. He *had* to take the risk, whatever it cost him, for the chance of gain.

"When's the handover scheduled?"

"Sunset tomorrow."

She squinted at the sky. Connor looked up after her. It was a couple of hours till sunset. "We'll have to bring it forward. When we're done here, go tell him the situation's changed."

"The last thing I want to do is get left here on my own to make the trade." In reality, getting left behind wasn't anywhere near the top of his list: the second to last thing he wanted was to lose the sale, and the last thing he wanted to do was to leave this planet without finding the generator, preferably with Calad attached to it.

He could always tell her what was really happening, and how valuable that antimagic generator was, but the endgame there would be Hardblade getting her hands on it. That wouldn't please Éloise, or her boss, or Sl'arani, or anyone else who had half a stake in it.

The searchers levered aside a larger area of roof, revealing part of the entrance hall and another pile of day-old bodies. Connor shook his head. "Such a fucking waste of lives," he muttered. By the time Sl'arani sent in his squads they had already lost the thing he was looking for!

Assumptions, assumptions. For all he knew the Pellite gang boss might not have had a clue about the extra package piggybacking on his shipment, and the vicious reprisal had landed because Connor's crew had unwittingly killed one of Sl'arani's clutch-mates in the warehouse assault. Somehow, Connor doubted it.

Kylesdottir would have answered, but the scanner on her bike beeped. "Run a D-cam routine," she called to the team's tech, who pulled out a portable version of the kit Kylesdottir had on her bike, and climbed as far up the rubble as she could, scanner held out before her. Across the courtyard, Logan had joined the squad excavating the garage's wreckage, but was staring at a lump of twisted metal protruding from a pile of bricks. Connor nodded to Kylesdottir, walked to his brother and patted his upper arm.

Think of this as your cosmic reward for being such an arsehole, he almost wanted to say, but couldn't. Severed limbs poked out of the wreckage too, and a blood-stained red bandanna half-protruded from a pile of rubble: he had no right to say much to anyone now. "With this week's bonus you can get another one."

"Kids grow out of their clothes every time you stop looking

at 'em."

"I didn't think you'd noticed." It had been him who'd had to worry about buying or stealing their clothes, not Logan: Logan had just acted, or acted up, while he thought. He glanced at Galene, also poking around the garage, maybe looking for the bodies of the crew who had been with her on the roof. "Get her up high and set her looking for one you can steal –" That was too sharp a grimace on Logan's lips, and too sudden. "What?"

"Her eyesight's going."

"*What*?"

"Flashes and dust in the fight. Her vision's blurred. Not so you or I would notice, but she lives by her eyes, and she can tell the difference."

Connor exhaled. A sniper with fading eyesight was out of time. "Why didn't she tell me?"

"By the time she realised it wasn't getting better, you were sitting in Mistress Kylesdottir's pocket." He grimaced. "And what's Hardblade going to want to hear from her new golden boy?"

Connor glanced towards the others. "I don't know what's going to happen –"

"I know you've a captain watching you."

Which did he resent more, Logan throwing Galene's wellbeing at his head or Galene not talking about it to him from the outset?

Logan prodded the buried XR-2 with one toe. "What gets me about this – my clip was on the far wall. Not like I parked it, the last time – but the boy would have put it on my clip."

"My fault." Connor stared at the wreckage and wondered what he was admitting to whom. "I told Marcello to prep it in case we needed a getaway." Then the garage had fallen in before anyone had had time to get away. Damn it. *Damn* it.

"Right." Logan bent, picked up a few fallen roof tiles and shoved them under the Connaught's handlebars. "Strikes me this landed damned near to the bunker door." A brick flew down from the courtyard rubble and bounced off his head. "Hey!" he shouted, turning, pistol already in his left hand. Two of the new-come mercs glared down at him.

"Stop fucking around," one said, "and give us a hand."

"I'll give you your fucking hand up your arse!" Logan gestured with the gun. "Leave me to it or you'll end up –"

"Cardwain."

Logan stopped mid-rant and turned: Connor stopped trying to reach his brother's gun hand and looked round. Kylesdottir was three feet away, eyebrows raised like a disappointed schoolteacher. "Cardwain," she said, looking at Connor, "a word." Connor nodded, squeezed Logan's shoulder and walked away, leaving him trying to fit a crowbar under the Connaught.

As soon as they were out of earshot, Kylesdottir said, "How would you assess your brother's attitude?"

Connor wondered who had been working on his superior in the brief time when his back had been turned. "Erratic. At his best when someone points him at a problem, at his worst when he's got nothing to do. Too bright to make a good grunt, too hasty to make a good captain. He'll stay mid-ranker all his life."

"Mmm." Kylesdottir's lips were pursed. "I'm aware he's historically worked with you, due to his violent tendencies."

"Yes."

"I was *not* aware that those tendencies spilt in our team's direction."

Carm must have had a squeeze somewhere in the base, and damn it if he hadn't noticed. "Violent men are useful."

"That I don't dispute." She looked up at Connor again, and he saw the steel inside the velvet glove. "It cannot be allowed to compromise team stability. Not under *any* circumstances."

"I understand." Connor forced himself to *feel* her dispassionate mindset. He'd need it wherever his future led. "He wants an out for a while – to spend some time with his wife. It's a compromise that might mollify the people he's upset."

Her eyebrows shot up again. "Wife? A merc?"

"Yes."

"Attached to whose team?"

"None at the moment –" no Septième team, at any rate – "she's for hire."

She half-laughed. "What makes you think Mistress Hardblade's going to be particularly happy to see one of her mercs, a man in a position to know secrets he shouldn't, going off with someone who is likely to associate herself with a rival at any moment?"

It was what Connor had said to Logan days ago, but from another angle. The more Connor thought about it, the more impossible it seemed. How could any two mercs stay in a relationship unless both were already embedded on the same side? Words, compromises, froze on his lips. Pay Éloise's fees himself?

"Hey," Thakar called from the direction of the garage. "Mistress, Mister, you want to get here."

Connor looked up. Logan had been joined at the crowbar by two other mercs, and another pair were gripping the bike, stopping it from sliding. "Hey down there," Logan called.

Hands pulled bricks and tiles off the bike. More dust cascaded and pipework creaked. Connor realised he had crossed his fingers.

The debris pile slid. Logan dodged sideways and threw a hand over his mouth. Dust settled, and the bike sat free of debris, jammed half in and half out of the bunker hatch.

"Nice of you to remember us," a familiar voice called from the basement. "We were starting to think we'd have to dig ourselves out."

"Wait for jacks to start working again, and you could have called." Logan shifted the bike, leant down into the hatch and towed Zack up into the garage's ruins. A cheer broke out among the mercs. Hands reached past Logan to slap Zack on the back.

Connor embraced him – gently: his left arm was in a makeshift sling, and he must have climbed the bunker ladder one-handed – and said, "How many are down there?"

"Eight of ours, and four clients." He nodded to Kylesdottir. "Some of the priorities worked out OK." She grinned, granted him a nod and descended the ladder. Connor heard her talking in Pellite cityspeak to the marooned clients.

He looked Zack over again. Grubby, for sure, but no apparent injuries other than the arm. "Been having a nice party down there?" he said, more gruffly than he had meant.

Zack grinned. "Hey, stuff to do, you know? Keeping the others happy and that." He inclined his head at Logan. "I hoped you'd come back for your bike."

"Don't tell me you jammed the hatch with it on purpose," Logan said: half a threat lurked in his voice, but he was grinning.

"I wish I'd thought that hard. No, it was just the biggest hunk of junk I could see –" He broke off, laughing, as Logan mock-tackled him. "Mind the arm!"

Logan set him gently on his feet. "Sorry."

"No biggie. Your bloody bike hit it already: I'd rather you didn't join in." He squinted at Logan. "You taken a nice pill or something?"

He snorted. "Hardly. It's been a weird few days, though."

A tiny figure poked up from the bunker – the little runner, Joshua. He looked to either side, spotted Thakar, and glared at him.

"Not my idea to stick you down there," Thakar said in placatory tones. Joshua didn't stop glaring, but he nodded.

Down below, Connor heard more voices: Carm, Marcello, Lorasdottir, Waltzer. He realised the muscles in his shoulders were relaxing. More alive than he could have ever hoped when he limped away from the base the night before. Every man and woman around him was smiling, even the tech.

A perfect moment, or what should have been a perfect moment. But the clouds overhead would not go away. Sl'arani and his quest for vengeance. Calad, missing. The antimagic generator, missing with him, and behind that, whoever had wanted to buy it. Connor shook his head. Enjoy the moment, shift the shipment to Merovir, then worry about Calad. A man had to navigate each storm as it came.

He reached for his jack to check the contract form, but the subcutaneous buzz brought him up short. *Damn* such reliance on physical documentation. He pulled off his right glove, slid his copy of the contract from his pocket and thumbed down it. No, he hadn't phrased it so the handover had to be at that precise time: from that respect they were good to close the deal now and worry about Calad afterwards.

"Problem?" Thakar enquired, one hand extended to help Carm out of the bunker.

"Not the one I feared we had. Just the minor snag that we don't quite know where that shipment is. I'm sure we can find it."

"Your sale goods?" Kylesdottir said, emerging from the shaft behind Carm, helping up a wounded client.

"Yes. But we can close the deal early." He waved the contract form. "And if we can get into the base's hard records, we're sorted on the location. Coker had it on file."

"I bet he did." Carm, slightly less dishevelled than Zack, captured the contract and flicked down it. Connor watched, misgivings mounting. "In the money on this, aren't you? While the rest of us did the bleeding."

"I don't recall you getting shot the other day," Connor said, as coolly as he could.

"I don't recall you getting stuffed underground for twenty-four hours because your squad-mate, the top lieutenant, pissed off some feathery prick." Connor glanced at the client, who was still chirruping away in Pellite cityspeak and didn't appear to have noticed. Kylesdottir, beside him, waved for four mercs to chauffeur the four emerging clients to offices or hospitals. Her eyes kept flicking to Connor. Carm flipped down another page, made to toss the contract back to Connor but stopped mid-movement. "Oh-ho. Now I see it."

"See what?" Kylesdottir said, emerging from the departing bikes' tails.

"See that your boy there's been cooking the books. Can't trust the smart ones. I wondered what he'd get up to when he'd no one staring at him."

"What the fuck are you on?" Zack shouted, pulling away from the mercs ushering him onto a bike.

"He's off his head," Connor said. A nasty cold feeling was spreading across his stomach. "How much water did you have down there?"

"Not much."

"Men can't think straight when they don't have enough to drink."

"I can still fucking *read*," Carm spluttered.

Logan made a threatening move towards him. Kylesdottir interposed between the pair. "Give me that." She took the contract from Carm. "Carmichael, you need to sit down and pull yourself the fuck together. You're still alive, thanks to him. Remember it."

She walked away towards the bunker door running idle eyes down the contract. Thakar hooked Logan's arm and yanked him away from Carm: Carm righted Logan's ruined bike and sat down on it, a picture of wronged innocence.

That cold feeling in Connor's stomach was spreading, and not from one cause. Kylesdottir, reading and rereading the contract, looking for something she knew must be there: and Carm, sitting shivering on the bike, as he had sat shivering on a truck's tailgate two days ago, in Sl'arani's warehouse.

Legs moving almost of their own volition, Connor walked to Carm's side and whispered, "Bad move. I've a counter-play."

"How long do you have to make it?"

"How long have you been in Sl'arani's pay?" Connor countered.

"Not long, and I'm not staying there. He fucks over humans, or just fucks them." A nasty grin spread over his face. "Like you're fucking over the boss."

"That's not what I'm doing."

"That contract tells me you're a liar."

"And you?" Connor jerked a head at the base. "Sl'arani hit the wrong place. I can see that: Kylesdottir'll see it too. He should have hit our warehousing – all of it – not the base. But someone lied, and told him the shipment was here." His belly was quivering: repressed anger as much as fear. "I wondered why you'd gone to the garage."

"How about," Carm whispered, "because I'm not quite as stupid as –"

"Cardwain," Kylesdottir said, an odd note in her voice, "how many contracts have you drawn up?"

"Some," Connor said. "What's wrong?"

"He's drawn up dozens," Carm said. "Enough to put a capacity rider in the right place – if he was planning on working for the boss instead of, I don't know, Sl'arani or someone."

Sixteen heads turned towards Connor. "He's bluffing because he invited Sl'arani to pay us a visit," Connor said, throat drying. "Decided he didn't like putting himself in the way of gunshots for the pay he was getting."

Carm shrugged. "He's lying. Does this brick still work?" He kicked the Connaught's starter motor. It coughed twice and spluttered into life. Carm grinned. "Huh, guess those navvies make better kit than I thought."

"Get off my bike," Logan said with a threat in his voice, "and quit badmouthing my brother."

Packer loosened his rifle in its sling. "Sounds like your brother's asked for it. Mistress?"

Kylesdottir was nodding. "Cardwain, do you have any foundation for your accusation? Because I'm looking straight at the foundation for his."

"He just admitted it." It sounded lame even to him. He glanced around the ruins. Twenty mercs, all staring at him, all armed, and maybe six or seven looked vaguely friendly.

"He's lying," Carm said again, and revved the Connaught's engine.

Kylesdottir sighed. "Nickel, A'syan, Packer, I need you to take Cardwain back to the bolthole –"

Twenty mercs all staring at Connor and none staring at Logan.

Twin gunshots thunked into Carm's torso. He collapsed, falling away from the Connaught. Logan sprinted the ten feet to the bike and scrambled on. One of the new-come mercs snapped up his gun and fired: the shot bounced off Logan's head. Someone screamed. It sounded like breaking futures.

Logan kicked the bike into reverse and slid in beside Connor. "Get on!" he shouted. Before Connor could protest he bundled him onto the pillion seat and pulled away.

*

CHAPTER FIFTEEN

The XR-2's engine casing was punctured. As Logan drove, head low and left hand shielding his eyes, he felt the back end swaying and coughing underneath him, trying to die. Airlock in the pipe, fuel leak: didn't matter which, when he couldn't stop to fix it. He kicked the throttle again, trying, hoping for more power, but still the splutters continued, and still the bike crawled along at seventy miles an hour.

Behind, other engines began to whine. Pursuit. "Hang on," he shouted over his shoulder to Connor, and dropped the bike down thirty feet. As he hauled it back into line, the engine cut out. For fractions of a second Logan saw the alley below coming up at them, saw the echo of their bodies splayed in the gutter. He kicked the starter, and again and again, and on the third try, it caught. He hit the accelerator and drove hard into the closest maze of streets, not much caring where.

Here, below rooftop level, gantries criss-crossed each street at hundred-foot intervals, scored by sharp toes where Pellites had gripped them to push off into a glide. Logan cut back to forty-five, took a ninety-degree bend and accelerated down the next street. They were surely still being followed, though he could no longer tell the squad's engine noises from the others in the sky around them.

The engine cut out again, and they fell another ten feet. Logan ducked, and felt Connor move with him. A gantry just missed their heads.

Connor yanked on Logan's arm. "This is crazy," he bawled in his ear. "We have to land."

Instead of answering, Logan looked down at the street below them. Residential backroad, close to a high street. Carnival vendors' trucks were lined up outside each house, most with parking tickets glued to the windscreens: another few suppliers' trucks were inching along the street, looking for a spot to land. One had stopped in the centre of the road, with its tailgate open and bakery boys dashing down a nearby alley to the main street carrying trays of pies and cakes for human carnival-goers. Logan slowed down, drove inside the van and dumped his XR-2 onto a pallet of cakes. He rolled off the bike, guns already in his hands, as he had a thousand times. It had never been quite like this.

The man in the driver's seat turned, scrabbling for a handgun: Logan levelled two barrels at his head before his hand got halfway. "Drive," he said, and the courier dropped the gun and took the van out of neutral.

"W-where to, Mister?"

I don't care, Logan nearly answered. "Get six streets away. North or east – *not* south-west." The van accelerated. Logan forced himself to relax, forced his heavy breathing to slow. Never mind gangland bravado: for once in his life, he had to *think*. "Don't break the fucking speed limit, you dumb prick. Drive casual."

"With your gun at his head?" Connor said in the background. He'd figured the not being noticed part, and had closed the tailgate.

"It's called an incentive." He itched to turn round. Connor didn't sound normal. Stifled, in spirit more than body. "You OK?"

"I'm not hurt."

That's not what I asked – but that was another thing he couldn't say. Not now, not here, not with a terrified stranger in the front seat: treat Connor as the boss, even if they were down to two of them.

Two. He thought about his two children, the only ones any woman had admitted bearing him. It would even the odds a mite if they had more than two gunhands.

He stared out of the windscreen. The driver'd obeyed instructions, and was swinging them round the backstreets that supplied the carnival, avoiding major thoroughfares, staying low. Logan tapped him on the shoulder with one gun. Dodge Hardblade's crew, dodge Sl'arani's: "Drop us by the back door to the *Governor's Head*."

"On Hooper Street?"

"The back door, I said. Straw Wynd."

Three minutes later the van thumped to a halt outside the pub, in an alley so criss-crossed with gantries, wiring and washing lines that the sky was invisible. Connor pushed open the back door. "Sorry about the cakes," Logan said, backing away, holstering one gun and grabbing the XR-2 in his newly freed hand. The driver floored the accelerator. Connor, Logan, the bike and a couple of trays of pastries cartwheeled back out of the open door and hit the street hard.

Logan flexed muscles in his back and legs, decided he'd picked up no injuries worse than bruises, and sat up. "Should have shot him," he muttered. Another bit of casing had fallen off the XR-2. He picked himself up – harder than it should have been – and checked the bike for fresh fuel leaks. When he found none, he unlatched the pub's peat cellar door and shoved it inside. Connor'd sat up, though hadn't yet stood up. Logan helped him upright and ushered him through the pub's back door.

He glanced back into the street. A few children had crept out of nearby alleys to pick up the spilt pastries, both sweet and savoury. Logan delved into his money belt, and called to the oldest girl in the pint-sized crowd, "Hey. You want marks? I want a messenger."

The girl, halfway through stuffing a cheese roll into her mouth, straightened up. Without taking her eyes off Logan she shoved a meat pie into one pocket of her ragged dress and a chocolate pastry into the other. "Where d'you want me, Mister?" she said round the roll.

Logan beckoned her away from the others. A young boy tried to follow, but Logan patted his left gun, and the child withdrew. He tossed the little girl tenpence: she caught it in one sticky hand. "That's for now. You want more?" He opened his hand far enough to show the girl a five-mark piece. "Take my message, this is yours."

She shifted from one bare foot to the other. "What message?"

"Get to the *Heather's Frank* on Michael Mark Street. There's a woman staying there called Ellie. She's foreign. Got yellow hair."

"Ellie, with yellow hair."

He nodded. "Tell her Logan wants to see her. Bring her back here, and the money's yours." The little girl nodded, grabbed another two pies from the street and scampered off to find a ride. Logan nodded to himself and withdrew into the pub.

Connor had secured a seat at a cramped corner table. An underdressed barmaid was glaring at him from behind a stack of empty glasses, or more accurately at the lack of drink in front of him, but he hadn't noticed: he was staring at a puddle of spilt beer, looking lost. Logan shouldered through the crowd at the bar, bought two shots of cheap whisky to mollify the bar staff, and returned to his brother's table.

Keep thinking. "Here." He plonked one of the shots in front of Connor. "It's shit enough to wake you up. Drink it."

Connor grabbed the glass and downed it in one. "Satisfied?" His voice was hoarse. "What in hells you're doing I don't know –"

"Getting us moving." He kept his voice low. "Getting us *doing.*"

Connor laughed, like nails grating on concrete. "We are fucked, Logan, totally *fucked*, with no comeback. What do we have, three guns and a broken bike?"

"And one set of Defence shielding, and our brains." Logan sipped his whisky instead of downing it. It burned his tongue: no wonder Connor's voice wasn't working. The pub was packed – every pub in the city centre was packed – but they were off Sl'arani's turf and into Hlarxi's, and all the little rosebuds dotted along the sleeves around him meant they were in a hangout frequented by Tarsus's crew, not Hardblade's or her allies'.

Them on one side: all of Sl'arani and Hardblade's organisations on the other. Maybe add Merovir too. It didn't look good in any respect. But that was no reason to panic. Carnival season: there'd be a way to run and hide, unless Hardblade put up a ridiculous reward for their delivery to Kylesdottir, and even that would be a kind of leverage.

But maybe that wasn't what was on Connor's mind. Logan stared at him, his lowered eyes, his heavy expression. They'd just high-tailed it out of everything he'd been working towards in the fifteen years since their mother died. He'd taken his responsibilities seriously. He'd been *good* at his job. He would have made a very good leader.

"We're alive," he said. "As long as we're alive, we've a

move to make."

"What move?" Connor gripped his empty shot glass like he was set to fling it at Logan's head. "I could have talked us out of that, you fool! But you had to go and shoot him –"

Logan laughed. "How the fuck were we meant to get out of it? He was *right*, Connor, or as right as damn it. We'd have ended locked up with no guns, no bike and no friends, and shot as soon as not. That's not a good place."

"This is good?" Connor waved a hand at the crowded bar.

"You've talked more to Tarsus's top brass in the past five years than any other of Hardblade's captains or lieutenants. They're not likely to shoot you, any more than they are to help her crew."

"Neither are they likely to help us, thanks to your homicidal girlfriend."

"A good chunk of them'll be *frightened* of my homicidal girlfriend. Besides, we needn't stay here if it doesn't suit us." Logan glanced at the back door. Outside, the day was dimming. At night, in carnival, anyone could hide anything.

And news here couldn't spread fast. If his jack phone had been working he wouldn't have called Ellie anyway – Hardblade's scanners would have monitored the conversation – but from the undercurrents here, the curses under the breath of every fourth drinker, nobody had working phones. Boys with spiked hair adding a foot to their height, trying to get net access for music pages – girls with six-inch skirts and four-inch shirts paging through newssheets' job listings instead of nets' – no phones, nets, anything. He'd been right about the relays.

Logan drained his whisky, returned to the bar and, still staring round the room, bought a half of dark ale for himself and a bottle of Diakon for Connor. Sure, there were a lot of people in here just enjoying themselves, and a few conducting business face to face – but that percentage who were getting increasingly pissed off, as opposed to increasingly pissed, spoke of a lot of confusion they could use as a smokescreen.

As he sat back down, Connor glared at the juice bottle. "I'm not six years old."

"I need you conscious. *We* need you conscious." He

sipped the beer – a nicer experience than the whisky. "We need a bit of logic."

Logic said they needed to get off-planet, alive, with as many of their problems fixed as possible. Sl'arani after them for the shipment? Hardblade after them for betrayal? Merovir after them for contract breach? Even if Kylesdottir traded with him, *Connor* would still owe him a sale.

He glanced at Connor. Drinking his juice, muttering into it, not in a helpful mood. OK: his turn to continue the logic.

Connor was fucked with Hardblade for some years to come, and would be fucked with Sl'arani till one of them was dead – which wouldn't take long if the antimagic generator's seller or buyer found out that the bird-lord had lost it. Merovir, then, was the best problem to solve, and if Connor owed him a shipment, it was best to give him the one they already had.

He fingered his money belt. A day ago, when he and Ellie'd gone drinking without a care in the world, he'd taken the risk of drawing a hundred marks from his account. Less the five he owed the drifter kid, he had seventy-odd left. It would get them somewhere, but not very far.

"Connor?"

"What?"

"Does banking need comms satellites?"

"How the fuck do I know?" Connor caught his breath and, with what looked like reluctance, met Logan's eyes. "Banks can work a manual transaction from on-site records. Credit chips need comms."

"I wouldn't know." He'd never expected to rate a credit chip. Jack transfers he'd done, mainly to bike mechanics, but that definitely needed comms. "There'll be a lot of queues at banks, and a lot of angry rich folk in those queues, and a lot of people walking round with too much cash in their pockets."

His brain caught up with itself. Hang *on*. Earlier, Ellie'd found a working tangler. Whatever block Sl'arani'd set up must not have been able to stop Neuvième equipment. "We've an advantage," he muttered.

"What advantage?"

"Never mind. I've no clue how we can use it."

The shipment: in one of Hardblade's warehouses in the industrial park next to the spaceport. She had ten 'port warehouses, of which one was out of action thanks to a burst sewage pipe. Sl'arani would be able to access records showing which were hers, but might not know in which one the drugs had been stashed, any more than Logan and Connor did. He'd be ready to root through each in turn to find it... unless one of his compatriots, Tx'lnia or Hlarxi or Dxarnl or Lt'antis, slapped him down because of the risk it posed to their long-term business. The four of them'd be far happier with him if he worked out which warehouse held the stuff, and just hit that one. Stay on his shoulder till he did it...

"Logan?"

His first thought, as he swung round, was that he'd expected Ellie in more like two hours than twenty minutes. His second, as he saw her, was that every time she was out of the room he forgot quite how beautiful she was.

She wasn't the only white woman in the room, or the only foreigner, or the only blonde, but to him she had an aura all her own that had nothing to do with magic. He'd seen her in Septième clothes before: had seen her in a bar in Septième clothes, for that matter. He'd never seen her dressed for nightclubs.

She was wearing a sheer gold-and-pink mesh shirt, over a gold cropped top that cupped her breasts as neatly as his hands ached to do. Her golden hair, bound into a few thin braids, caught the light and scattered it, setting her aglow like wings would: and if the trousers she wore under the gold flared miniskirt didn't fit the picture – black snakeskin, too conservative – a casual watcher wouldn't care.

The grubby drifter girl poked her head round Ellie's hip, pointed at Logan and held out her hand. He tossed her the five-mark coin. "Here. Now, beat it." He touched Ellie's hand. He wanted to touch her body. "How'd you get here so soon?"

"I already had my bike out when she met me. We drove straight here."

"Straight?" She might have been followed – and Logan crushed the thought. What was done was done. "Didn't think you could drive in a straight line."

She wrinkled her nose. "OK, so I've never been a professional driver."

"Just a professional busybody." He held her at arm's length and looked her up and down. "You were going to look for him." She nodded. "Dressed like that."

"Dressed like half the women in the city."

"They don't wear trousers with skirts."

She flushed. "Dancers and whores bare their legs: I'm neither." She lifted his hands from her shoulders and kissed their palms. "I thought you were safe. I thought everything had settled for you, and I could concentrate on him."

"It *had* settled."

Too many mercs were staring at them. He pulled her into the back door's shadow, and in as few words as possible ran her down what had happened. She listened in silence, occasionally glancing at Connor hunching over his table, as if she wondered why he'd left such a big flaw in such a crucial plan.

"We need to get the shipment to Merovir," he finished. "I figure Sl'arani's going to hijack it. We want to get it off him when he does that, or off Hardblade's crew beforehand."

She nodded. "Where is it?"

"In one of nine or so warehouses, and we'll get shot if we go knocking on their doors to ask."

"Shot *at*, in your case."

"I don't want you to have to hold off every squad on the planet. I want as little mess as possible."

Ellie nodded. "I see the sense in that. What do we need?"

"Intel. Firepower. A plan for a smooth in and out. I think…" He looked her over. He'd her to back him up, but: "I think we need to go over the area Calad went missing. We find him, we have another gun. We don't – well, we need to try."

"Thank you."

He smiled, though he didn't feel like it. "Besides, two search better than one, and I know that's where you'd go next anyway. Then. With or without him, we stake out the warehousing and find the right one, then…" He hesitated. A merc couldn't afford sentiment. "I don't want to shoot guys I've worked with for years. OK, I just shot one, but he was a dick. But me, killing Galene, or Zack? No."

Ellie's mouth set in a hard line. "Then you're putting yourself in a position of letting Sl'arani's crew do it – if you're so certain he'll jump, that is."

"I *am* certain. Look at all those people out there." He waved a hand at the crowds around the pub's main bar and near its front door. "No comms, any of them. That pair, there?" He gestured to a man and woman in captains' stripes in the corner by the front door, immersed in intense, angry conversation. The man, he knew: the woman, he could identify by the shooting star on her sleeve. "Your friend Filarson from the other day – Tarsus's bright boy – and one of Fai Comet's top women. No one pisses off people like them just for the sake of it, nor any of the other major players here right now. Sl'arani's panicking. Everything he's done in the past day smacks of arse-covering. Of *course* he'll attack, just as soon as he works out where to hit – he's the staff to find it and the forces to pull it off."

"And your Kylesdottir knows it too. She'll move the shipment first."

"She doesn't know where it is, any more than I do. I was with the team tech: she couldn't pick up anything from the old server. Besides, Kylesdottir thinks she owes it to Merovir."

She frowned. "Merovir may use this to snag two shipments for the price of one – one from Kylesdottir on Hardblade's behalf, and one from Connor."

Laughing all the way to the bank. "Which'll piss off Hardblade even if she doesn't have to pay for the second load. Connor and I need to get this shipment into Merovir's hands. Then you can arrest him, and everyone's happy."

"I will be if we find Calad. Michel'll be here this time tomorrow at the latest."

Another gun if they needed one. Guns. "Guns."

She blinked. "Not my speciality. I can't shoot from inside these shields."

"I'm thinking we need something very big. I can fire a rocket launcher: Connor's not strong enough, but one's plenty, and we can get him something nice and interesting too – or we could, if we had more than seventy marks plus

Connor's loose change. We need more money, in cash."

"If Sl'arani has any sense, he'll have ensured his people still have banking access."

Logan grinned. He knew he'd found the right girl. "Perfect. How did you get hold of Michel, and Hardblade's teams?"

"Myles's staff tangler."

"I thought it was your fancy tech. Well, if we can think of any more help to call for, we can use it again. Right now I'm just glad Kylesdottir can't get backup." The moody barmaid appeared behind Ellie's shoulder, still frowning. "OK, OK: we're spending." He shouldered through the crowd to the closest edge of bar and waved at the nearest server, a pen Pellite. "Three bottles of Diakon."

"Three?" Ellie enquired.

"We need clear heads. I've had enough and Connor's had too much." He tossed the bar-pen her money, backed out of the crowd and snapped the top of one bottle for Ellie as they returned to Connor's table. She sipped it as she sat, and grimaced.

"This is bootleg."

"No, it isn't," Connor said in a weary voice. "Your people prefer sweeter drinks to us, so White Canyon changes the recipe for you." He took the third bottle from Logan and said, "I hope you don't want me to run too far tonight, because my arse is thumping as hard as my head."

It wasn't an apology, but Logan pretended it counted as such. "Not if you don't want. We're safest in this kind of crowd: no one could find us –"

Connor looked past his shoulder and gestured with one finger. "Not quite."

Logan turned. Thakar's little blond pickpocket was standing two feet away, with a look of mulish triumph on his face. He inched round Logan and passed Connor a slip of paper.

"How'd you find us, kid?" Logan said in an undertone. Not just finding them, but this *quickly* –

"I looked." Joshua's eyes hadn't left Connor. "Answer, Mister?"

"Come to me again at exactly eight-o-clock tonight. I'll

have an answer then. In the meantime, say you couldn't find me." Joshua nodded, and slipped back into the crowd. He was still wearing the dirty clothes he'd been trapped in. Thakar must have been as frantic as Sl'arani.

Logan turned back to his brother and gestured to the note. "Offer of support?"

Connor nodded, and started ripping the note into tiny fragments. "One insider, secured. How many more he can smooth down for us he doesn't know. Now, what have you two decided we should do?"

Logan shrugged. "Get cash. Buy guns. Ambush Sl'arani just after he ambushes the shipment. Sell it to Merovir. Run away."

"It makes sense," Ellie said when Connor's frown deepened.

"Why am I not surprised two combat mercs would think that way?" Connor took a swig of his juice. "This is what we're going to do. Logan, go find me a deck of cards."

"What?" Connor, volunteering to play cards?

"You heard me. Éloise – see Tarsus's captain, Filarson? You go and tell him why comms are down. Make sure Comet's woman hears you. That's our start."

*

CHAPTER SIXTEEN

Strobe lights and neon danced patterns in the carnival night, now and then kaleidoscoped by flurries of rain. Music blared from every bar on every street, a Septième symphony of cacophonic sound, and waves of people washed into and out of tents, clubs and bars as the rain advanced and retreated.

A solitary security camera, half-dangling from a ruined wall outside Hardblade's old base, circled to follow Logan Cardwain's unmistakeable dark figure down the street. It rotated one last time, flashed a warning light and died.

Six bike mercs in Hardblade's badge, hovering over the ruins, gestured one to the other and dropped to the concrete with guns raised. Logan wasn't there. As the mercs stared around, searching for a shadow, a noise in the next street startled them. Five swung towards the sound: the other inched backwards.

A string of Sl'arani's mercs came roaring round the corner, wings spread and plasma bursters glittering. "Wait!" the leader of Hardblade's team called. The rest, bar the man at the back, were already firing.

The rearmost man swerved and peeled away. "Run!" he shouted. Too late: plasma bolts were hitting sinew, muscle and feathers. In the seconds it took the biker to reach the corner, his whole team, and all but one of Sl'arani's team, had fallen to the muddy ground, dead or dying.

Sl'arani's last gun-cob glanced backwards and forwards, considering his move, and finally tucked back his wings and drove away. Hardblade's last man inched into the darkest alleyway leading off the street. "Here," he said softly.

"Zack, good to see you." Logan emerged from the shadow behind a peat-shed. "You OK?"

"Hale and happy." He embraced him. "Want a lift anywhere?"

"Let's not risk it. Some street kid somewhere'll see you and tattle, even if we manage to wipe all the cameras before they get to transmit." Logan grinned, teeth just visible in the dark. "Go home and explain your tragic losses. I'll see you tomorrow."

"Tomorrow it is."

Connor, tucked into an overhang beneath a silent bakery's eaves, slid off his glasses. His left hand fell to the deck of cards in his pocket, and he fingered their cold edges. Just – cards. Coated paper and ink, nothing more. If they were a conduit for something he could not understand, so was he.

A simple finesse that left two sets of enemies dead: and if these were small fry, individuals with whom Connor had no quarrel, it created confusion, and contributed to paranoia. Write one note to Thakar, and wait. Nothing easier.

Logan, in the alley, retrieved the least badly damaged bike Hardblade's team had let fall, and drove up to Connor's shadowed hidey-hole. "You could have picked up a couple of helmets," Connor murmured.

"They still had heads in them." Logan stopped for just long enough to let him get on the pillion before driving away. Enough bikes already littered the sky to swallow their engine noise. A tiny few were Hardblade's, desperate men and women looking for Logan and Connor, but far more belonged to other ganglanders, whether natives or, like them, aliens. Connor's hand sneaked back to the cards in his pocket. He'd a feeling the bikers' mood was going to change, and soon.

Twenty minutes took them to Sl'arani's most run-down casino complex, at its busiest at this time of night, many hours past sundown. The frazzled young Pellites on the door were no longer taking biometric records, just running visual checks on the hundreds of incomers, and they had so much trouble telling humans apart that Connor entertained no fear that they would be recognised. They had taken Hardblade's badge off their jackets before setting out from the *Governor's Head*. It had felt like peeling off a scab.

"Plasma packs out of guns," the chief doorman said as they pushed past in the middle of a crowd. "Declare all playing cards, Olympus markers, racer-shot paddles and other gaming equipment. Plasma packs out of guns…"

Connor had already unclipped his plasma pack from his gun: while Logan disassembled his, Connor walked through the crowd with his cards aloft. One-handed, he shuffled and cut. Seven swords danced in a ring across his upcard, and the world changed in a greenish shimmer. "Females' lavatory," he murmured to Logan, who peeled off without another word. Shorn of his backup, Connor swung left to an oval chemin-de-fer table, handed his cards to the house banker for safe keeping, and sat down.

There was such a freedom in letting go of one's inhibitions. He'd seen it before, in abstemious men getting drunk or stoned for the first time: not just the action itself, but the thrill of the forbidden – not forbidden by society, but by one's own rules. And now, as the banker turned over a page and two of cups on the table in front of him and he tapped the green cloth for a third card, he felt that secret rush of glee, and wondered if he would have the strength to leave this as a once-only, or if he would return to it again and again, as hooked as any junkie.

As the cards turned, as the banker dealt and redealt to him and the six other players, the whispers in his mind slowly became whispers in the air, snaking around the casino like influenza. Twenty-four hours since anyone but Sl'arani's team had had communications: the rumour mill was running at full pace, barely comprehensible. Sure, the whole underside had already been angry, but till now, the anger had been formless. It was beginning to mutate.

One whisper from Éloise to Filarson, a man who'd been trained to respect Weavers. One echo to a posse of senior lieutenants who had no reason to distrust Filarson. Talk upon talk, while those lieutenants were distracted: talk that was beginning to spiral out of control.

The banker dealt him a king and five of wands. He saw himself, in cleaner clothes and with a few white strands in his hair, talking to a mining corp rep above a massive open-cast dig on Thiela. That was no good. "Another," he said, and the banker turned over a card. Eight of coins. Pell Havasi's main strip flitted across the card, with children running from warring men. He tried not to smile: he'd worsened his hand.

As the banker shovelled chips to the winning player and collected the cards, three of his fellow players rose, abandoning the game. A glimmering gold figure slid in next to Connor and sat down. "I'm just watching," Éloise said to the banker.

"Glad to hear it," Connor said. A page of coins peeked from between the banker's claws as she tucked the used cards away, and the casino shifted, an image of the banker collecting stakes.

"In, Mister?" the banker said, glancing from Connor to Éloise.

"Not this hand."

Éloise waited till the other players had received their cards, then said in a low voice, "Filarson's gone to Hlarxi's offices. Tell me he won't be shot."

"Not if he took the backup I suspect he did."

The Pellite merchant who had won the previous hand tossed in his cards with an aggrieved whistle. His Kriastan neighbours and the human beside Éloise pushed hands towards the banker: a pair of fours, a king and eight, and an ace and seven. The banker smiled politely, and flipped over her six and three with one wingtip. All three players sat back with a range of disappointed expressions on their faces: Connor nodded in to the next hand.

"Where's Logan?" Éloise breathed.

He glanced at the banker. "I'll explain later. Look over at the bar and tell me who you see."

She swung round. "A lot of people I don't know. Merchants, bodyguards, mercs, two cops. That's the biggest Kriastan I've ever seen – who is she?"

"Her name's Haartisi. She's one of the Huitième's richest merchants." The banker dealt: Connor peered at his cards' corners, trying not to see the faces. Ace and knight: he tapped the table for another card. "Go and ask her what Mertia is doing at carnival. Tell her she's just coming out of the *Wildstaff's Leg* – go see for yourself if you want to sound like you mean it: it's across the street."

"Explain."

"Later. Timing is critical." Éloise stared at him for a few seconds, then slid off the stool and marched away towards the bar.

The banker turned a seven of wands up in front of Connor. He smiled politely, waited for the deal to finish and, in unison with the other players, turned over his cards. Two totalling seven, another six, and the rest down at four or five. The banker pushed the chip pile towards Connor, as the world swam again: Pell Havasi, him here and now, watching the sun set from the spaceport warehousing, and the sun rising on him older and elsewhere, in a high city tower with a distant sea visible out of the window, and a black-haired young woman he didn't know haranguing him about something he couldn't understand. He closed his eyes to clear the images.

Over at the bar, a Kriastan snarled in anger, echoed by three others: a battle cry born thousands of parsecs away, anachronistic beyond words or thought. The banker's claws jerked and the cards spilt from her grip: she swept them up, mumbling apologies in six languages. Connor turned round in his seat, with men and women of all species around him doing the same, and watched Haartisi and her bodyguards shoving their way to the door.

The fuss slowly died into a generalised background hum. Connor turned back to the gaming table, and the banker, bowing Pellite bows of contrition, dealt another hand. Connor checked his cards: five and two of wands. *Take another*, they whispered. Against all sense or reason he tapped for another card.

Éloise sat back down beside him. "Now. Explain."

He lowered his voice. "Haartisi and Mertia are in the same clan – Haartisi's rank is far higher. Last time the males went into musth, she expected the melee winner to mate with her. He chose Mertia instead. Mertia's been keeping away from her ever since."

"How many species' sexual hangups do you intend to exploit tonight?"

The banker dealt the two of swords face up in front of Connor. A woman grasping two blades, both hands bleeding, unable to drop either weapon. "As many as I have to. I've little choice." All seven players flipped over their cards, and the other six sighed. The banker shovelled another pile of chips towards Connor. He calculated. Enough for an assault rifle, a rocket launcher and a few grenades? Looked like. "I'm done," he said, rising. "I'll take my own cards, thanks."

The banker, with an air of bad grace, pulled Connor's deck out from under the table and passed it over. Connor nodded a Pellite thank-you bob and gestured for Éloise to collect the gambling chips.

"As soon as Logan joins us," he murmured as they walked across the floor, "you head out and start bar-hopping. Listen to what people are saying – feel the anger, find out whether it's directed at Sl'arani, Hardblade or someone else – and try to make it worse. I want the suspicious to become angry, and I want the angry to attack. It doesn't matter who."

The teller's office, in the centre of the casino, was walled in shatterproof, fire-resistant glass six inches thick. Éloise poured Connor's chips into the slot and stood back, watching the young female Pellite inside tot up the proceeds. "Is this a risk," she said, "or is it a certainty?"

"Call it a calculated gamble." The teller poured a clawful of marks into the dispenser. Connor extracted the coins – mostly hundred-mark and fifty-mark coins, each one a fortune to most on these streets – and slid them into his jacket's inner pocket. Éloise's wings started glowing, a faint yellow outline, and she slid her arm into his as they walked to the door. The small smear of hangers-on and bullyboys crowding up near the doorway edged back from them.

Outside, the street was stained with dark blue Kriastan blood. The two merchants were still sparring outside the *Wildstaff's Leg*, teeth bared and tails crunching together like meat being tenderised, with their bodyguards dead or dying around them. In the background, more squeals and battle screams heralded more fighting Kriastans, drawn in by loyalty to one or the other, or taking advantage of their seniors' quarrel to settle a few personal scores. Connor and Éloise headed in the opposite direction, towards the garage.

Logan caught them up just as they reached the door. "Got my rocket launcher?" he said, and he dropped a kiss on Éloise's cheek.

"Wrecked my information?"

A grin spread across Logan's face. His hooked nose cast a shadow across his face, semi-demonic. "I never saw an outlet hidden in a toilet roll cupboard before. No matter – I scrambled every one of the records for what was in each warehouse and whose warehouse was which. Sl'arani's guys can look all month and they'll not find the shipment."

"Unless they took a hard record," Éloise said.

"Why would they take one, when they can use comms? Unless a team's walking up to the warehouse now, they'll never find it – but we will." Connor poured the marks into Logan's hand: Logan dropped them into his belt. "I'm off to a gun shop. Do we head over now, or at dawn?"

"Neither. Trust me on the timing. Logan, hurry up. I want to be sure we get our arsenal while the shops are still open."

"They never shut."

"They will tonight. Éloise, head out. You know what to do." She nodded, and embraced Logan. The two of them headed into the garage with tokens in hand.

Connor waited on the steps, dark-clad in the dark night, listening to the city. An edge of panic was starting to invade the evening, beneath the carnival's euphoria, and he wondered how many would die tonight. He slid a card from his pocket, looked at it, and saw Sl'arani's teams fanning through the night to ransack warehouses and boltholes, with not a single holding warehouse or industrial hangar's ownership certificates or stock inventory accurate. Invasions, murders, destruction of any and every piece of inventory, smuggling cartels being left with nothing to smuggle, trader gangs losing their trades – every gang lord on the Septième would field thousands more armed guards at the next carnival, if carnival's reputation were capable of being rebuilt. It didn't matter, at least for tonight.

Logan reemerged, hauling his stolen bike. "Where do you want me to drop you?" he said.

"Main strip, not far from the city hall. Pick a pub Ironbender or Baker's teams use."

"Sure." Éloise, behind Logan, came out of the garage already buckling on her helmet, and headed up and off to the east: Logan waited for Connor to mount and then swung his bike north-east, over the street brawl, and over carnival tents and stalls, occasionally snapping a string of bunting. Connor stared down as they drove, watching people, seeing opportunities. Midway, they passed Hlarxi's headquarters, and Logan dipped to first floor height and hovered outside the window: within, Filarson was haranguing Hlarxi's duty captain fit to make her feathers fall out, with underside lieutenants pressing up against the rosebuds on his back, a united front that would last until they left the office.

Logan dropped him by a pub two notches up from a dive, grubby and none too fragrant, with three of Ironbender's captains drinking outside. He greeted them with brief nods – they grinned in return: must have heard he was no longer persona grata to Hardblade's team – and headed in. A guitar band was playing in one corner near the front door, driving out as many drinkers as it enticed inside: Connor bought two bottles of Calypso lemon, waved off the vodka shot the barmaid tried to sell him alongside, and headed to a table near the back door, out of sight of the front door and the band. His pocket felt heavy, almost itching at his skin. He cracked the top of the first juice bottle, and drew out his cards.

Carnival stayed peaceful because too many big names wanted it to stay peaceful. Stick any four or five merc strings together in one place, add drink and drugs, and each little fight that had threatened all year would blossom. At every nearly moment, with every false step, a lieutenant or captain would stamp on the spark, and it would wink out.

Now, with the top people distracted, the flames would rise.

He separated his pack into court cards, jokers and pip cards, and started to deal the court cards into the bases for a hand of Chimaera, but paused with fingers brushing the king of swords at a tiny unfamiliar noise behind him. "Back again?" he said softly.

"I slept." Joshua's little pale fingers slid a recording ring across the table to Connor, who passed him a full Calypso bottle in return. Children needed feeding.

As he thumbed through Thakar's security forms, Connor watched Joshua sipping the juice with a mixture of suspicion and pleasure flitting over his face. He remembered: sleeping for no more than a couple of hours at a time, hyper-aware of every little sound. The street bred nervous men. Maybe Joshua was young enough to grow out of it, once he had spent long enough in the relative safety of a gangland base.

"When you've finished," he said, "go back and tell Thakar

I'm in a casino off Mount M'xynn Street, talking to Merovir's lieutenants."

Joshua drained the bottle, licked his lips and wiped his mouth with his sleeve. "What d'you want me to tell him when we're not being listened to?"

Connor allowed himself a brief smile. "Tell him to find it and wait. He'll know what I mean." The little boy nodded, and pattered back out of the door. Connor flicked on the ring.

Beaverden's meeting room swam into view, looking almost as it had looked a day earlier when Connor had risen from his bed to inspect the base. The wobbly table, the recycled chairs, the city map on the wall, now flanked by a detailed plan of the spaceport warehousing. No men in view, just two women: Galene, and Kylesdottir, the latter bending over a cumbersome old radio set. Connor lifted the ring closer to his face. The sound stream was faint, but he could just hear it over bar conversation and increasingly loud comments from Pellites on the city streets outside.

"*My interest in your future activities is solely altruistic,*" said a voice from the radio. It was Myles Hendrix.

"*Really?*" Galene, still standing awkwardly, gestured to the city map. "*You've feelers out all over the export zone and you expect us to believe that?*" She indicated a swathe of city streets around the pub where Connor had met Hendrix, a corner of the Neuvième afloat in a Septième storm. "*I know Connor couldn't find another exporter for love nor money. So, who's sponsoring you? An active cop squad, here, needs sponsorship. If you didn't have it you'd already be sunk in the sea in your own ships.*" She tossed the pointer onto the table. It skittered towards the camera, which darted outwards – Thakar's hand, wearing the recording ring, stopping the pointer's roll.

"*Mistress Kylesdottir,*" Hendrix said, "*I suggest you ask your woman to stand down.*"

"*My lieutenant guards my interests, and my boss's,*" Kylesdottir said. "*She's right: you can't be trusted – and until you can, I'm not in danger of disturbing your rest.*"

"*I have more influence than you suspect. I could make your lives significantly less comfortable if I chose.*"

Galene laughed and made a crude gesture at the radio. *"You think? The Pellite gang lords, Hlarxi, Dxarnl, Lt'antis, Sl'arani, they could shut you down. We off-planet guys could do it if we worked together – we've enough clout across the sector, and you're one team. The only reason you have the nerve to say that to us is that we're alone, with no way to talk to our allies or enemies."* She dropped into a canvas chair, squinted at the light strip overhead and aimed a finger at Kylesdottir. *"He's taking you for a ride, Mistress."*

Kylesdottir stroked her chin as if she had a hair ingrowing. *"My only question is which of his arms I cut off first when I meet him face to face."*

Hendrix laughed, just audible on the tinny recording. *"Mistress, do you want me to arrest you for smuggling?"*

"Me and the rest of the sector."

"Ah, but you interest me – or rather, your sale goods interest me, much more than anything else I've seen."

"I'm not trying to ship to your worlds. We have an arrangement, the Circle and the underside – your squads haven't troubled us in centuries, for we haven't troubled you."

"Maybe I think you're being less than frank."

Kylesdottir rose and started pacing around the tiny room. *"And I fail to see how your tactics will assist either of us. You have no way of finding our shipment. I have no way of handing it to you, given our current position."*

"And as I've said from the start, my help could be invaluable." Hendrix sounded like he was smiling. *"Visit your bolthole, escort you to the spaceport –"*

Galene scowled. *"If we admit to doing what you see as a crime? I've no desire to die here, and neither has my captain."*

Connor paused the recording and slid the ring into his money belt. That was enough for him to be sure Thakar had passed the hint to Galene, and enough to be sure Hendrix was just as distracted as could be hoped for. He felt like a spider, spinning a web across the city, built of lies, misinformation, and just enough truth to frighten. It was more than a smokescreen, more than a shield: like smoke, it could be funnelled, and it could kill.

Moving slowly, fighting to clear his mind, he retrieved the rest of his cards and finished dealing the Chimaera bases. Midway through his second attempt to make the pip cards come out, two pale hands deposited a cup of tea on top of the cards. "Hlarxi's fourth in command is duelling Sl'arani's fifth in command outside the public records office," Éloise said.

"I thought there'd been an extra dose of squawking." He understood the common Pellite languages when they were spoken at a normal tone, but not when they were shouted – the inflection changed, and so did the tense structure. "When the seniors turn up, tell me who and how many." He sipped the tea. It made a change from fruit juice. "Calad?"

"No sign."

"Keep looking."

"You knew I would."

He half-smiled. This was the benefit of using people's prejudices *for* them as often as against them. "Start dropping the word there's a Guild Weaver in town. A few of the other gangs run Circle teams: let them spearhead the search. If I understand anything about the Circle, your crew'll join in so hard they're unlikely to get to Calad before you do – and it creates one more dose of confusion for me." And it diverted Hendrix's attention. Merovir had wanted him out of the way, after all.

Éloise nodded, and retreated to the pub's back door. The casual drinkers in the front bar ignored her, for they were all watching the fuss on the main street, dancers and rioters and good-time girls jostling for space.

Connor dealt another set of four cards across his discard heap. The last one glinted, mutated, and he saw from far away an image of himself scooping up the cards for yet another attempt. If this deal wasn't going to work, it wasn't going to work: instead of bothering to lay the sixth row, he dug through his pockets. Handhelds, delivery dockets, but nothing on which he could handwrite. At least he could plan on a handheld. He activated his emptiest, and started drafting.

The back door creaked again, and Connor glanced up in time to see Logan slip inside. He was grinning like a little boy who'd just stolen his first bike: rocket launcher and automatic rifle slung across his back, pistol warm in his hand. "Can this night just not stop?" he said.

"It won't for a while. Get me a piece of paper and a pen. Pellite makes, not human." Logan's eyebrows went up, but he headed off into the pub crowd, threading towards the front door. Connor collected all his cards bar the jokers, shuffled, and started laying a Queen Topsy-Turvy.

Five minutes later with a frustrating half of the cards resolved, Logan dropped back into the chair opposite, and set a pad of straw-paper and an ink pen in front of him. Connor picked up the pen and scrutinised it. Black blobs streaked its shaft. "Is that blood or ink?"

"Who cares? Plant juice or Pellite juice, it's all the same." Logan poked the cards on the table. "Seen Ellie?"

"Ten minutes ago. She's bar-hopping."

Logan picked up Connor's joker deck and started thumbing through it. The glee faded from him as if a cloud had crossed the sun. "She needs to find Calad, Connor. If she doesn't, it'll eat her mind up for years."

Connor remembered a shock of startlingly fair hair and an innocent smile. "We need to find him, for a whole host of reasons. In the meantime, busier is better."

Logan fidgeted in his seat, cards slipping in his hands. "I could follow her, see how she's doing –"

"I need you to do something else." Pellites used three alphabets, but two were restricted to rarer languages mainly used by the southern mountain tribes. Connor tore off the pad's top page, practised a few letter combinations in the more common alphabet, and when he was happy that his muscle memory was accurate, pulled off a second page and started writing. Mimicking the right kind of bad English was difficult, but he persevered, concentrating on the nuances of common cityspeak, the imperfect way each phrase translated into English and the problems a Pellite would encounter when transliterating his bad English into his own alphabet. "Take this to Beaverden. Find a suitably dramatic way to deliver it, and make sure you aren't seen doing so – and pull yourself a posse of Pellite drifters to torch the door as soon as whoever's got the message inside."

"Torching an iron door doesn't work."

Connor rolled his eyes. "Do I look like I want to burn Thakar and Galene to death?"

"I guess not." Logan studied the note, while Connor dealt again. The queens seemed more interested in cavorting with the pages and sixes than with the knights and kings. "A challenge from Hlarxi to Kylesdottir?" Logan said after three minutes' concentration.

Connor scattered his cards across the table. The knight of swords was a human blond: ink glinted up at him, a shadow of gold leaf. "Hlarxi could pressure Sl'arani back into line if he wanted: Sl'arani must be paying him a *lot* for the inconvenience. That doesn't get the other leaders off his back – but blaming Hardblade just might. My main worry right now is that Kylesdottir'll get a genuine challenge from his team straight after you deliver the fake."

"I'll hijack any of his I see going that way." Logan folded the note up, zipped it into a jacket pocket, nodded to Connor as if to a gang lord, and headed back out.

Connor picked up the knight and queen of swords, leant them against each other, and palmed a card from the top of his joker deck. It was the Emperor. He balanced it delicately on top of the two swords, cornerstone of a house of cards. Fifty major underside gangs, Septième-wide players. Five thousand smaller ones, active on one or two planets. Five hundred thousand one- or two-man freelancers. Too many people.

He swept up his cards, tucked them into his jacket pocket, drained his last juice bottle, and headed back out into the street. Still none of Hardblade's people, and only two of Sl'arani's, losing a fight fifty feet away, surrounded by baying drunkards. More carnival revellers, some still singing, some sobbing, ran along the street with Pellites pursuing them bent on blood.

Carapace had been the starting point, so he began from there, and worked outwards. The first three pubs he passed, along a spiral away from *Carapace*, all had fights spilling out of their doors. The fourth was still quiet. Connor nodded to the bouncer and wandered in.

Strobe lights glittered overhead, and the neon adorning the

bar was as bright as a Weaver's wings. Éloise was sitting in a corner seat, left hand on a bottle of grapefruit juice, eyes on the dancers on the tiny makeshift stage in the centre of the bar. Around her, in front of the writhing girls and near-nude boys on stage, other people laughed and shouted: six human languages, two Kriastan languages and eight Pellite ones, delivered by the idly overdressed.

Working his way round the room towards the inevitable back door, Connor watched her: leaning back in her seat, dropping an idle word to the man whose head was closest to hers, then staying motionless as he hurried away from his date as if her gold eyeshadow had turned toxic. The woman, in turn, said a few angry words to Éloise, who whispered enough idle confidences to make her sit up straight and stare.

Glass crackled in the corner near the front door, and a drifter girl screamed as the first bottle flew across the bar. Half the dancing girls and all the boys scattered. Three girls kept dancing, slender waifs each with her hair or skin dyed: purple hair on brown skin, copper hair on white skin, black hair on blue skin. The copper-head was one of the two who'd been hanging around Merovir's tent the other day. Éloise never took her eyes from the trio, their pattern of limbs as much suggested as seen, sinuous in motion as chaos erupted around them. Connor, for his part, never took his eyes from Éloise.

Was she thinking about Calad? Even dead men found it hard to stay hidden. No matter who found that generator, it would come to light. When it did, she would have her answer, and, if Connor had ever met a Circle Weaver, her revenge.

The dancers sashayed together on the tiny stage and drew apart, skimming the stage's edge, their bosoms beckoning for tips. The copper-head was closest to Éloise, who teased a coin from her belt and tossed it to her. She spoke, too quietly for Connor to hear: the copper-head answered just as quietly. Before Éloise could speak again, the girl shimmied off towards the opposite end of the stage. Éloise frowned after her, but did not follow.

Unremarked and unremarkable, Connor opened the pub's back door. A wooden ladder, fire escape, snaked up the exterior wall beside the peat-shed: he pulled on it, testing its strength, and when it neither moved nor creaked, he began to climb.

Thirty seconds took him to the roof. Up here, in the chimney's shadow, the city's streets seemed alive with light, pulsing through it like blood in arteries: carnival lamps, flares, fires. Cries and songs and all kinds of sound drifted up to him on the breeze, and he smelt life and death spiralling together in the night air, beneath the reek of burning peat.

Every detail of the street below him was so sharp and clear: revellers, brawlers, killers in deadly earnest, rich folk trying to escape, street children trying to hide, all spilling out together along a row of splintered shop fronts with blood running in the gutters around them. The city smelt of a death far more final than any he had seen in years. Now and then he saw a man or woman he knew, and understood what fight had brought them outside, but for the most part, he couldn't know.

It didn't matter. The effect was what mattered.

Fifty miles to the south, well into the richest area, fires and flares ignited the night, and when he pulled on his glasses he saw wealthy respectable Pellites and their bodyguards brawling with ganglanders in the street. Old slights, current injustices: hells, even revenge for the cancellation of a host of live-HV dramas. It didn't matter. None of the details mattered. Not when men and women of six species were killing over contract failures, sexual peccadillos, any reason or none. In the background, drunken revellers sang and danced in an orgiastic chorus. Every temple's door was bolted, and Connor did not need to peer through windows to know that the priests inside were praying: the eleven devils were here, made flesh, and given form.

No beleaguered team trapped in a tiny bolthole could possibly force an early shipment sale now. No major boss, even on his own turf, could reposition himself enough to destroy an enemy in the middle of all this. The night had turned in on itself, like a snake eating its tail, and no one embedded within it could possibly see how it would end.

He could see it. Above the night, floating in the sky, he could see patterns extending in front of him from the deck of cards that lay in his pocket. He could not know what sequel would come, but the night was his, and he held it to him like a last warm coal.

But somewhere out in that night was Calad. Where was Calad?

*

CHAPTER SEVENTEEN

Darkness caked Calad like a living thing, an animal set to suffocate him more from carelessness than design. Now hot, now cold, it pulsated around him and into him, a universal heartbeat. He could see nothing, hear nothing, feel nothing.

Is this death?

Flashes of lightning snaked across the sky, first far away, then approaching step by step. With each strike, with every accompanying boom of thunder, pain shook into him, increasing each time till he wished he remembered how to scream.

Cool rain pattered onto his forehead, and the pain eased, just far enough. He slept.

A long while later, he opened his eyes. At first he thought his vision was damaged, for everything he could see was grey – grey ceiling overhead, grey pipes snaking along it, grey sky outside the little room's little window, grey blanket tucked around him. Then he spied a fruit grower's gaudy logo on the makeshift chair by the window – a couple of crates with dingy cushions atop them – and he realised that it was dawn.

Dawn. He'd left Ella… in the late afternoon? But the rash of stubble on his cheek felt like he'd gone more than a day without shaving, and when he moved his legs and arms, it felt as if he hadn't moved them in a long time.

He sat up. The room swam: that only made it look bigger than it was. He was lying on a pallet tucked into one corner: the only other furniture was the 'chair', a small table with one mismatched leg, and a tiny chest of drawers. A shard of broken mirror was propped up on the chest, near the window. Nothing else. Even the light fittings in the ceiling were gone, with trailing wires their proxy.

Not Myles's base in the pub. Not a hospital. Didn't look like an underside den.

Images swam in his head: Delia and the others, their attack, Delia's threads seeping into his head. Calad shivered. He hadn't killed her: now she would have poisoned Myles against him… but Myles was a telempath. Could a telempath see through a telepath's lies?

He swung his legs off the bed, and stopped halfway as pain shot through his left leg. As he bent to examine it, another sharp jolt in his right shoulder halted him, and he sat shivering for a few moments, trying to focus.

His secondary power was Healing: he had studied some anatomy. He coiled half a spell-thread in his fingers and, with some difficulty, probed his right shoulder with his left hand. Bruises, a trapped nerve, a tiny stress fracture. Could have been worse, given the velocity at which he'd hit the ground, but whoever had tucked him into bed had done nothing for the injury bar propping an extra pillow under his arm.

Sure, only a doctor or a Weaver skilled in Healing could have treated the stress fracture: maybe no Weaver other than a healer would have even noticed it. But when he'd passed out, it hadn't been due to his aching shoulder or the sharp agony of burning skin on his calves: it had been due to the agonising, searing pain in his skull from the antimagic.

Antimagic. He felt his left hand for the antimagic ring: it was gone. His rescuer had taken it.

He ran fingers over his cheeks again. No more than three mornings' stubble and probably only two. The kind of psi-pain he'd inflicted on himself with that generator should have taken weeks to heal. So – his rescuer must be a psi-healer, a specialist in managing the damage Weavers caused themselves with their spells.

Calad ran Healing strands through his shoulder, thrice by thrice, till the fracture was sealed enough not to crack more severely when he moved it, and till he felt it safe to free the nerve. All the time he kept thinking. A psi-healer. Rarest of all the magical disciplines – even Augury appeared more often, though it drove its Weavers insane so quickly that few experienced practitioners remained at any one time. Maybe Michael Sinclair d'Aubry had been as mad as any other man with green bands in his wings: only insanity could have driven anyone to reform the Circle.

He released his shoulder, let his arm fall back into his lap – even that little spell had tired him – and looked around the room again, at crumbling plaster and cracked windows. This must be a slum Weaver's lair, home of one of the mendicants who wandered the Septième in search of casual work, either from choice, for penance, or for experience, as Ella had once done.

But why would a *psi-healer* turn slum wizard? They relied on other Weavers as their clientèle, and there weren't enough out here to pay anyone's way.

Shoulder patched up, he looked down at his legs, and tried not to gag. Seeing suppurating burns on someone else's skin was bad enough. But his unknown rescuer had cleaned off the mud, and dressed the wounds in transparent gel. He sank a couple of tendrils into his legs and *concentrated*, knitting flesh back together, repairing nerve endings, blocking pain signals.

Not blocking them well enough, and after a couple of passes he could no longer stand to regrow any more neurones. He stopped, and stood, wavering. After a minute he lurched over to the chest of drawers and peered at himself in the mirror fragment, with the rising dawn his only illumination.

Definitely two mornings' stubble. Ella always joked she couldn't see it well enough to tell, but he knew. Bloodshot eyes, tangled hair: he was naked, and the bruising on his injured shoulder was as colourful as a spell-loom. He almost wanted to prod it again in sick fascination. He'd never caught himself that badly in training.

His stomach gurgled, and he realised with another shiver that he was hungry, thirsty and in need of a lavatory: a quarter-full bottle of water tucked beside the chair made some headway towards one of the problems, but only one. His clothes weren't on or in the furniture, but he found his money belt in the back of the middle drawer, tucked beneath some undergarments. He buckled it on, and also pulled on the light dressing gown that inhabited the top drawer.

Its sleeves came halfway up his forearms. He checked the middle drawer again: he'd never seen Septième human undergarments of either sex, but they looked a little small to be a man's, and the bottom drawer was half-full of items from a female dancer's outfit. Definitely a slum witch rather than a slum wizard.

The sky was lightening. Calad stared out of the window at the dawning day: people scurrying about the alleys, carting loads, clutching tools or carrying nothing but a furtive expression. A day and a half. Ella might have been told any amount of nonsense about what had happened to him. He half-drew another thread – but stopped, twitching, as a familiar sickly sensation bumped against his Telepathy weft.

Spell-threads: not his. Spell-threads: not Circle.

The Guild. Guild-woven magic, acrid and bitter, was snaking all around the garret room. He'd been captured by the Guild squad.

He sat back on the pallet, ignoring the squeal from his right shoulder. The Guild, arriving just when he'd turned on the antimagic generator – and the generator was missing –

Delia, in league with the Guild? He couldn't buy that.

Light, stealthy footsteps hit the landing outside. Calad tensed, looking for a weapon. The broken mirror?

The door creaked. Calad turned, coiling a thin thread in his hands. Guild Weavers never trained as hard as Circle ones: some of them even wore three or four threads in their wings into adult life, never bothering to develop their best two to maximum extent. He'd surely have the odd useful trick this woman hadn't seen – but as the door opened he stopped halfway, unable to move.

It was the Guild Weaver – a woman no older than Calad. She was dressed for dancing, in a leotard, brief over-dress coated in sequins and a hat made solely of feathers. Deep copper hair sprang from her brow and rippled down her head: copper, *red*, shining like raw wire from shaft to tip. That kind of red hair only ever grew on pureblooded Old World humans. The gene had died out millennia ago among the few who had left to colonise Terra Nova, and had not yet re-established itself among the mixed, halfblood population – people like Logan, and Connor, and Ella's mother, and almost all the humans from the Cinquième to the Dixième – who had been bred since the two strands of humanity were reunited.

The woman's deep blue eyes looked Calad up and down in some disapproval. "Should I assume you didn't realise it was me?" She spoke in English, but with an Earth accent – humans spoke so many languages on Earth, and in so many ways. Calad had once tried to learn what all the different accents signified, when he'd toyed with working for the military or the diplomatic services. He couldn't remember this one. "Or had you decided to be particularly ungrateful?"

"Ungrateful?" Calad re-coiled his threads. "You *kidnapped* me –"

She rolled her eyes. "Oh. A stupid one." While Calad was still spluttering, she tossed a bundle at him – his trousers and loincloth. "Your shirt was unsalvageable. You can buy a new one for a few pence outside, if you don't get stabbed first. Now, get out of my dressing gown and out of my room."

Calad didn't move to pick up his clothes. "Where's the ring?"

She pulled open her bottom drawer and tossed her hat into it. "In your money belt. Out."

If she'd abducted him, why tell him to leave? There must be a dozen of her mates downstairs...

... but the absence of other Weavers' threads on the room, an absence that Calad wouldn't have been able to distinguish if *someone*, presumably someone a few feet from him, hadn't healed his psychic injuries while he was asleep, told him that they were alone.

He sat back down on the pallet. Delia, attacking him. Delia must be in league with whoever slipped that generator into the shipment Logan and Connor stole. So was the Guild's involvement secondary? Or had the Guild instigated it, and was Delia the opportunist?

Might the Guild not be involved at all?

He fingered his money belt, and the ring inside it. "What is going on?" he muttered.

"What's going on is you're still in my bedroom and still in my clothing." The Guild woman tossed her over-dress into the top drawer and held out one pale hand. "Change, and leave, and go get yourself killed – anything to keep you out of my hair."

Nice hair, Calad thought. He'd seen many different kinds of women's hair before, at his mother's house on Terra Nova and his father's home on Port Logis – lustrous black curls, tight cornrows and majestic afros, thin blonde strands, tumbling brown waterfalls. He'd never seen red hair on a white woman before, except in pictures. "But I won't be. Out of your way, I mean, if I get killed. You psi-healed me…"

So her thread-traces were on him. So, if Delia came back to finish what she had started, she would see the Guild tracing, and would call in the rest of Myles's squad to find and kill Calad's rescuer. Never mind what else was happening – Circle would *always* kill a lone Guild Weaver in their territory, just as Guild would always kill Circle. Unless there really was a tie-up – no, he didn't believe that. Circle wouldn't work with Guild.

He pulled off the dressing gown and tossed it to the Guild redhead, who slid off her leotard with a grimace that told Calad she had come to the same conclusions that he had and was now regretting her charity. Calad wound on his loincloth and slowly pulled on his trousers – Septième trousers with a button fly, not the Treizième slick seals or Neuvième wrap-ons he usually wore. His gun belt, with his pistol buckled into it, was still attached to the trousers, as if the Guild woman had disdained even touching it.

He knew – *knew* – Ella wasn't working with Delia, no matter whoever else in the squad might be doing so. She could protect him for long enough to prove his innocence. But how was he to get to her? She was no kind of telepath, for her Defence shields were far too strong: a call loud enough to reach her would be overheard by every other Weaver on the planet, including Delia. Delia had oversight of the team's phone frequencies too. No chance of phoning from his neural jack, or to Ella's, even if his jack hadn't been buzzing like it was dead.

"Are you leaving?"

Calad looked at the Guild woman. She was standing a foot from him, wrapped in the thin dressing gown, hugging it to her. Maybe her people had a nudity taboo: lots of Earth populations did. Maybe she'd been too angry with him to mind, a few minutes ago, and was regretting it.

"I can't leave. I'll be killed." Maybe even by the rest of

Myles's squad. Delia had asked for the generator in front of the others: they *must* have been innocent, or she wouldn't have bothered. But he had hurt three of them, and that would be enough to make it personal.

"This doesn't explain why I should care."

"You cared when you healed me." A few more things clicked into place. "You leave a trace, when you touch things, or people." Connor's jacket. "But you're still alive, so you must have put a scatter on this place – or on yourself – to keep Circle from finding you here."

She shrugged. "It's a basic trick."

It didn't seem that way. "I need to stay."

The woman tossed back her glorious hair and laughed. "The wealthy, pampered Circle Spellweaver, in a bedsit with mice and cockroaches – and me."

"This is my first job. I've no more money in my account than – than you have." Actually, he would have more, for his mother and her parents couldn't resist spoiling him whenever they thought his father wasn't paying attention, and there had been a lot of distractions lately. "Please let me stay. I can pay you –"

"Not quite so impecunious, then –"

"– on account. I'm due a lot of money for my current job, some of which I owe you anyway."

She gestured with one foot for him to get away from the bed. "Owe nothing. Our people decide when to do something: we don't expect to be paid for heroism." She clambered into the bed Calad had so recently vacated.

"Think you're so civilised, don't you? Here I thought all Guild Weavers only breathed when Council ordered them to do so."

"Oh, shut up." She wriggled down into the none-too-comfy pallet. "I had three hours' sleep yesterday thanks to you. Go away and maybe I'll die well-rested." She closed her eyes.

Calad backed away. "OK, OK." But he'd no intention of leaving. Not till he'd worked out what was going on. "What's your name?"

"Atalanta," she said, not opening her eyes.

"I'm Calad." She didn't answer. Maybe she was already

asleep.

His boots were tucked beside the makeshift chair, on the opposite side from where he had found the water bottle. He picked them up and stared at them. Leave this room and he was dead – so...

More footsteps pattered on the stairs outside: someone trying to be quiet, someone light and small. A child?

If Atalanta had the sense that Calad suspected she had, she would have put her trail-scattering spell on the stairwell as well as her room and herself. He pushed open the door, and almost hit the small girl just outside. She took in his height, and pressed herself back into the wall, set to run up to the roof hatch, the way she had come in.

Cajole her? Threaten her? The former wouldn't work, and Calad, no matter what he'd seen other men do here to poor children, couldn't bring himself to do the latter. Instead he patted his money belt. The girl's eyes narrowed. "Half a mark if you bring me some food," Calad said, "and another mark if you bring me a shirt." She nodded twice, and scurried back up the stairs to the roof.

As the hatch swung open and shut, Calad leant against Atalanta's bedsit door. He was shivering: nothing to do with the temperature, or being stuck in a Guild Weaver's power, but more to do with what had happened the day before yesterday.

And he still hadn't found a lavatory. The stairwell had been used for that purpose in the recent past: instead, Calad opened its door onto the rusty fire escape and urinated into the street, another procedure he'd seen several times this week. Maybe women used a bucket. Why were there no drains? Another question Ella would have told him not to ask...

After he had adjusted his loincloth and fly, he dug into his money belt for coins to give the little girl. His fingers brushed the antimagic generator. Such a tiny, unassuming thing. But Calad harboured fewer and fewer doubts that this scrap of metal was why he and eight other Spellweavers had crossed thousands of light-years – in his case, quarter of the galaxy – to this seething, stinking, all-betraying, all-alive alien planet. He braced both hands on the fire escape's doorjambs and stared at the city. Smoke plumes rose in the distance, behind wood-and-wattle roof pitches. This was the native part, probably no more than a few streets from where Delia attacked him: he and Atalanta resembled two parasites in a place that wasn't theirs and never could be, on a planet that tolerated their incursion for just as long as was necessary. Maybe that was why non-Pellites organised so many shady deals here.

But why had Atalanta come here?

The roof hatch creaked again, and the little girl clambered back inside, with a grey shirt tied round her neck and a hot bun balanced in one hand. Calad relieved her of both, tossed her the coins – scraps of adulterated metal that passed for money here – and said, with one finger pointing at his belt, "There's more for you if you help me. More than if you *mention* me. Got it?" She nodded again, and he gestured to her to be off.

He'd eaten the bun and was putting on the shirt before he realised he'd withdrawn into Atalanta's room to do so. She was definitely asleep now, despite him. Despite the fact that he should have killed her. Despite the fact that she was in enemy territory. Too tired not to sleep? Too sure of herself and her protections?

His hand brushed his pistol's butt. Why hadn't he considered killing her since she first came in? She might have saved his life, but even bad people did an occasional good deed. She was a *Guild Weaver*. They'd murdered millions during the war, and had refused to atone: they'd spied on and sabotaged peaceful Circle missions in the years since. They devoted their lives to supporting a brutal dictatorship, for God's sake!

Yet some prickle of conscience told Calad that he'd seen none of that, and had seen a Guild Weaver save his life without being asked.

He wanted advice. He wanted to talk to Ella and Michel, or to their father: he wanted to visit a temple, or even a wayside shrine to one of the eleven angels, and pray amid clouds of incense for whatever guidance the heavens chose to give him. But he was alone, with no guidance at hand save Atalanta's, and she wasn't likely to assist him with this.

Instead of pondering the conundrum any further, he buttoned the shirt – too big for him, and not quite fresh – and sat on Atalanta's crate-chair, watching the day outside, and trying to think about the somewhat more pressing mystery of what he was meant to do. It hung on too many things – ifs, buts and especially whys – and within half an hour he had thoroughly confused himself. He snagged a notepad and stylus from Atalanta's bottom drawer, resisted the temptation to translate the letter draft on the pad's top page, and started jotting notes of what had happened already and what would be the probable outcome of each move he could make from his present position. The sun climbed in the sky. Sirens wailed, for any reason or none, and a few gunshots echoed in the distance. When a police truck rumbled out of a nearby alley at such a steep angle that the pile of dead bodies in its bed almost flew out, he wondered what had happened during the previous night. Once, a small boy clambering gecko-style along the outside wall surprised him: he paid the child to fetch him a bottle of Diakon, and hoped he would keep quiet about it.

Atalanta woke seven hours later, with Calad staring out of the window, stylus forgotten, and two more hot buns on the table, courtesy of the little girl who'd brought Calad his shirt. She sat up quickly, suspicion wrinkling her face. Instead of apologising – why apologise to Guild? – Calad passed her a bun. "They're not bad," he said.

She took a cautious bite. "Why are you still here?"

"To give you a chance to take your spells off me so they won't lead back to you. Why are you here at all?"

She sat up, tugging the dressing-gown around herself. "On assignment. And you?"

"On assignment. How many of our people did you come here to kill?"

"As few or as many as necessary. Why were you keeping company with a woman who was exporting a weapon to be used against my people?"

Part of him wanted to declare verbal truce: part wanted to shake her till she gave him some straight answers. He could do that at any time. Any time. "I'm not sure she wants it to use against your people," he said, finally voicing the fears

Galene had seeded in him the other afternoon. "I think it's part of an internal Circle power-play. At least at the moment. I'm sure the winners would use it against the Guild afterwards – and if Delia could be made to admit she wanted it, doubtless she'd say it was an anti-Guild weapon – but not yet."

Atalanta swallowed the last of her bread. "You're very quick to assume you weren't working with a fanatic."

"Fanaticism doesn't smell like that. I'm sure –" His brain caught up with his voice. "That's twice."

"Huh?"

"Twice you said – *admitted* – you knew that Delia and I were on the same squad."

"I have eyes, ears and a brain." She squinted at the sky. "It's been almost two days now. Rumours run thick. Your boss has put out a reward for your capture, alive only – he must want your side of the story."

A little knot of tension in Calad's belly lifted. That was one thing going his way. "My sister? Her name's Éloise –"

"Your half-sister," and there she went again with things Calad had never said, "is caught up in one of those *charming* underside fracas, but is keeping in with Myles Hendrix at the same time. She also wants to know where you are. I almost wish I could tell her just to offer more money than Hendrix did: in this city, it's a reasonable tactic." Outside, a trumpet squawked in discordant accent.

Accent: and Calad's old tuition finally clicked. Her accent was upper-class. Faking it? She couldn't have known he could tell different Earth-English accents apart, and a few of her mannerisms sat so well with the voice that Calad was sure it was genuine.

"Do your parents know you're here?" She blinked. "You were born to money and power. I know that." He leant towards her. Both of them were still seated, she on the bed, he on the 'chair': they were a few inches apart. "Why are you traipsing through our territory pretending to be a dancer? What does it get you?"

If she'd had any of her bun left she might have thrown it at him: instead she straightened, staring at him like he was an insect. "What you *mercenaries* fail to understand is that someone may do what she does for the good of her people rather than for her *own, selfish* good." She relaxed the spell-thread that bound her visual aura, and her wings fluttered out behind her. Calad looked, expecting to see Psi-healing's lavender strands paired with God knew what else to denote her second most powerful thread. Instead he stared in growing disbelief at three, six, eleven, *thirteen* colours snaking and undulating behind her. "I have a gift," she went on, "and I intend to use it to better *my people's* position – whatever the tasks they set me."

"You're a Harlequin," Calad breathed, one hand stretching out towards her wings. That must have been why they'd sent her! A thousand years ago, another Guild Weaver with all thirteen threads visible in his wings had come here and worked wonders in the gutters, and had survived as a hero, rather than being slaughtered as an enemy. Calad had heard street children singing about the Harlequin, when they weren't singing about pilots, pirates and other local heroes. One flash of those wings and she'd have far more friends than enemies.

So why the backstreet hovel? Why the dancing outfit?

Atalanta struck his hand away. "And what of you? An over-paid flunky chasing profit around the galaxy, with no care for who your employers are and what they do? You people," and she drew in a harsh breath, "are not *Spellweavers*. You're parasites: mindless killers who never evolved."

"Rather a parasite than a drone!" His voice had risen. He didn't care. "Our people at least *think*. We don't run off at our superiors' connivance to conquer worlds beyond our borders – our soldiers have ethics. Yours don't!"

"Ethics?" Her voice was as loud as his. They couldn't be shouting. She would have realised. "I could name you whole *families* wiped out by your death squads!"

"And in every case there'll have been a blood debt. Why did your people assassinate – I don't know – Tisha Mawfrey, and thousands of other people, and raze half Ransomvale, and occupy Reeman's Point?"

"There was no blood debt when one of your people razed three quarters of Ilamena – which, as I recall, was one of your own planets at the time!"

Calad caught a breath. His throat hurt. "The Union ran it, not the Circle," he corrected. "The Circle has always kept itself at arms' length from the Union, unlike the Federation and the Mage-Guild. And there was a reason for Ilamena, a blood debt of a sort, though I doubt the inhabitants cared."

"There are reasons for everything," Atalanta said in a calmer tone, "and if not for your thrice-damned war –"

"*Our* war?"

"– the Guild would have more autonomy than it currently does."

For a minute or so they were quiet. The trumpet outside squawked again, this time attempting a tune, and Calad thought he heard another band strike up in a different direction. So many people outside. So many looking for him.

"Do you know where Ella is?" he said.

She shook her head. "I know where she'll be in a few hours, though. And if I'm wrong, that magic cloud she leaves behind her isn't subtle. That could work against you – if you go to her, all that your Delia'll need to do to find you is follow her trace." More of a mushroom cloud than a trace, and its size made it imprecise in a tightly packed city, but Calad nodded.

"I need to risk finding her anyway – maybe even to call my brother, though Logan and Connor's contacts might be enough: and you, if you'll help me." He held up the notepad. "I didn't translate your letter –"

"As it isn't in plain language any more than it is in English, translating wouldn't have helped you much."

"Without doubt," he answered in Gallic, the Old World's closest analogue to French. "While you were asleep I had time to work through the available data and come to a number of conclusions."

For the first time he spied a gleam of interest in her eye. "What were your conclusions?" she said in careful New World French. He drew in a breath, and began.

*

CHAPTER EIGHTEEN

Logan slid his glasses off and blinked a few times to clear his eyes. "We hit it. Nice little stream of mercs heading inside now." He twisted round to look down at Connor, in the alley below the warehouse Logan had climbed for a vantage. "I could get to like your timing trick."

"You and no one else." Connor was sitting on the ground with his head in his hands, his new heavy rifle lying forgotten across his back. He'd slept for nine hours, all of it after dawn. Logan would have worried, if Connor hadn't told him before falling asleep exactly when they had to hit the warehouse. He hadn't doubted, exactly, any more than he'd really doubted that Galene would keep Kylesdottir off-balance or that Thakar would stall proceedings till the timing was close to being too tight, but it was nice to have confirmation.

He stared back out over the spaceport warehouse complex. Permanent holdings, rented hangars, municipal docking facilities, all spread out like a map of corporate interest, scarred where the night had eaten into it. Local Pellite kingpins and queenpins, major undersiders like Meris Hardblade, the pure traders who sold out-sector and the factory owners who supplied them, foreign merchants, reps for the biggest trading conglomerates in the galaxy – they'd all had a bad night.

It was a pattern, like an engine's wiring had a pattern: not a powerful one, not a well-maintained one, but it worked. Belting Connor on the end had felt logical, like adding a new circuit extension. Even last night – the city had exploded underneath them because Connor wanted it to happen. But now, looking at twenty thousand square miles of other people's power, however tarnished, Logan felt a tiny shaft of doubt.

He didn't have time to doubt. Not now, when he'd the hardest part of the sequence to fit together, and the riskiest, even though the thing he risked most was other people's lives. Only when it was over would he have time to worry whether Connor's wits would be enough to keep them going without a big boss at their back –

– and worry about that bloody antimagic generator.

Logan dropped his glasses back into his pocket. Without them he couldn't see the warehouse, which was around ninety miles away, but only a glasses-wearer on the roof would be able to see him and Connor, and the person on the roof was bound to be Galene. He dropped into the alley and poked at his half-repaired Connaught. "It'll do for another ninety miles," he muttered. Connor had inherited the bike Logan had stolen the previous evening, though he'd wobbled so much while driving over that Logan had been tempted to synch the two bikes and fly them in convoy. That wouldn't have needed a comms link.

Muttering obscenities under his breath, Connor hauled himself to his feet and onto his bike, and Logan kicked the XR-2 into life. It still spluttered like a pneumonia patient, but the spluttering didn't seem to herald imminent failure any longer. At some point the previous evening they'd 'borrowed' two helmets, though Logan had had to rip all the padding out of the bigger one to make it squeeze over his head, but they had only one driving glove between them, and Connor's right hand had been almost numb by the time they stopped for a recon bout. Logan's weren't doing too badly. It was probably Ellie's shielding: since the first time they'd met, back on Axartes, he'd never got too cold or too hot.

They drove off into the warehousing, below roof height. Logan glanced at insignias on battered doors and broken windows as they passed: Hlarxi's, Merton Albert's, Comet's, more of Hlarxi's, a few belonging to Cliff Enterprises with an army of pro guards on duty. Cliff ran the odd Weaver, from what Logan had seen. Maybe they ran enough Weavers to help dig out the rogue Guild agent. Logan nursed a private, shameful hope that they wouldn't: as long as the Guild guy stayed un-caught, he'd stay a distraction for Hendrix's crew when they all went looking for Calad again.

Past the Cliff warehouses came a handful of Sl'arani's – even one of those had had its door battered in – and then a whole string with so many crossed-out gangland symbols on them that it was anyone's guess who bunked inside. These ones had taken a real pounding overnight. Logan grinned inside his helmet. Never say graffiti wasn't useful.

He counted plasma packs tucked into his belt. Sixteen for his pistols, plus two for Connor's rifle, plus that special little load of smoke bombs. All set.

Fifteen minutes later, with the sun warming his back, Logan finally slowed and settled into an alleyway half a mile from the warehouse where the shipment was stored. "OK," he said, pulling off his helmet, "cards time. Pull them out."

"Not doing it."

Logan blinked. "Come *on*. You said you'd do it. We need to know when Sl'arani's about to turn up –"

"And I'm *not doing it*." Connor dropped his helmet onto the clip on his pillion and sat back, halfway between a boss and a child. "I am *never* having a night like that again, and I'm not starting that never by carrying on with it today."

"Then how the fuck are we meant to pull this bit? You got us this far – OK, OK." He looked his brother up and down, trying to see past the stubbornness. "It can't be *that* bad."

"It is that bad." Connor met his eyes for half a second and looked away. "I was starting to see everything – I'd look at a man and would see how he was going to die – and the dreams I had last night were something I cannot repeat. I tell you, I *cannot*." His hands were shaking. "Sure, waking up with what feels like the worst fucking hangover I have ever feared getting is not helping my mood – but that's not what puts me off."

Logan clenched his fists till his shoulders shook, then released them. If they lived past the day they could have this out then. "What do we do instead?" he said. "We need to *know*, Connor."

"We use our eyes. Yours, for preference: your glasses have a better focal." He gestured back towards the city. "Start watching. The moment you see a move, tell me."

You can't punch the boss. Swearing inside his head instead, Logan backtracked down the alley till he hit a warehouse with an elevated skylight, and hauled himself up onto its roof. Skylight between him and Hardblade's warehouse, he pulled his glasses back on, and looked.

Afternoon was settling in the north. Ships were beating in from the Bridge high overhead, Ogres, Hamadryads and Cyclopes, and Logan wondered who was bringing in ships in what numbers and whether he should start worrying. He liked to know how people were getting on in the world. Not being able to access the 'port landing lists – however many IDs on there were fake – was making him itch.

He dropped his eyes from the sky and started scanning the warehouses in front of him, long slow arc, watching for any movement. He'd caused enough problems of this kind for other people, for year on year: he tried to concentrate on what he'd do if he were in charge of an attack on this warehouse – but he wasn't a kingpin and, specifically, wasn't a *local* kingpin, working on home turf.

A flicker, at a warehouse in the distance, and Logan zoomed in. Praying-mantis logo – Merovir's warehouse, and Merovir's team, preparing for collection. He wondered about the guy's late son, and whether he'd figured to pay Hardblade for the shipment with Connor and Kylesdottir's dead bodies, and what moves he'd factored Sl'arani making.

More movement, closer in, flicking over the lenses. Logan blinked a couple of times and altered his zoom. Another warehouse, untouched by the previous night, with Lionstooth's familiar logo of a roaring sabre-tooth dotting every door and every guard's uniform: and with too many of those guards darting around, talking, unbolting doors.

Logan frowned. Lionstooth? They manufactured, they traded: all that action meant a ship was landing or leaving, most likely, at this time of year, to trade. He'd never liked seeing the Union big boys in town. The governments pretended to govern when Union ships were in, and the police were more likely to fight and less likely to run.

He scratched his chin. With all the mess going on, he hadn't shaved for two days: his face was itching. Sure, Pell Havasi manufactured, and it was a prime place to drop trade goods that were a-OK on human planets, such as basil and marjoram, because if Pellites bothered to put them in food, it'd be for a very special party. But a good few of the big manufacturing bosses from this planet weren't happy about selling to humans, and were less happy about selling to humans based off the Septième.

Carnival sales, those made and closed at carnival as opposed to ones made there and closed later, often meant drugs. It wouldn't surprise Logan if every single warehouse in this complex held something narcotic, just as it hadn't surprised him or anyone else when Connor and Mikkson had announced to their favourite combat squads that they were about to take a walk to one of Sl'arani's in-city holding centres and clear it out of something interesting. But Union planets, with police and governments and lawyers and all the little things that didn't quite work on the Septième, had nice stiff anti-drug laws that actually got enforced. Sure, the places were full of drugs, from what Logan had heard from the mercs who'd taken a tour that way. But the people who *ran* drugs there were outlaws, smugglers, scruffy types from the Septième or Huitième working at Union gangs' say-so: outsiders, who weren't missed when they got caught. A big Septième trade corps running drugs wasn't surprising. A big Treizième trade corps running drugs made no sense.

He zoomed his glasses out, and saw trailers clustering at a few small warehouses full of carnival goods and stalls: minor traders leaving earlier than scheduled, not willing to risk another night like the last. It wasn't fair, maybe, and another day Logan – at least, the part of him who'd thought about Ellie's notion of fairness – might have driven over to tell them they'd be OK tonight, that it wouldn't happen again. He couldn't. Flecks of cloud were clumping overhead, speaking of drizzle later: the air smelt urgent.

Over to the west, a few more small gangs' warehouse doors were opening and closing, but no Pellite crews, nobody who might be tied to Sl'arani. One of them had a pair of wings as its logo: angels' wings, or Weavers'. Maybe Ellie would be able to get away from Hendrix's crew, or tear herself away from looking for Calad, and join them. He'd feel happier with her at his back. He'd feel happier when this was over.

Play the one enemy's plan against the other: basic, or so Connor said, a simple switch in card games. Logan preferred chess to cards. Maybe neither of them fitted in a world where lieutenants played cards and captains played chess, but Logan'd never figured he'd make a good lieutenant, and

Connor's ambitions had gone beyond becoming a captain.

He slowly rotated his field of vision, watching for *changes* – and hit it. Bearing north, a string of bikers was winding out of the city, far too purposeful for normal carnival travel. Logan zoomed in. Sl'arani's logo, a snake rearing to bite, was blazoned on every bike.

Moving quickly, trusting to Galene, he wormed off the roof and dropped into the alley. "We hit it," he called to Connor, who mounted his bike and hit the starter. Logan vaulted onto his Connaught, and ruined the effect by having to kick it three times before its engine caught.

They slid back into the air, still below roof height, and accelerated as much as they dared, as if they were driving in from much further away. As they cleared the last corner and braked hard to drop in to the warehouse, Logan glanced at the roof. Galene, watching with rifle in hand, making no move to stop them.

The warehouse had picked up a dose of graffiti surrounding Hardblade's chain-fence and sword logo. Whoever'd started to paint over it had abandoned the job, but no one had broken into the place during the night. First try, down. As Connor buckled his bike to the rack outside – most gangland warehouses held goods too delicate to permit indoor garages – the side door creaked open and a trio of gun barrels poked out. Logan moved in front of Connor. "Glad you could join us." One of the guns spat. He held his ground. The bolt bounced off him and ricocheted into the wall. "Put those things the fuck away: you'll get yourselves hurt." He strode up to the three gunhands – staring at him like he was a ghost – and, one by one, shoved their rifles down.

"Thank you," Connor said behind him, dry half-amused tones, like Merovir or Hardblade would say it. Logan picked up the closest merc by his jacket lapels – Packer, the hardhead who'd tried to shoot the Pellite chicks the day before – and moved him out of the doorway. Connor sauntered past him and into the warehouse, inspecting crates and bales like a buyer or an owner: Logan followed, as close to Connor as he could manage. The rocket launcher on his back dug into his shoulder blades. He ignored it.

"You've a nerve."

Connor stopped in the middle of the packing area and half-bowed to Kylesdottir, who'd emerged from between two crate-filled pallets with a merc on either side of her. The one on the left was Pritie. Her gun barrel was a lot lower than that of the man on Kylesdottir's far side. Logan itched to interpose, but he couldn't risk moving out from between Connor and the door guards. "Mistress Kylesdottir: it's a surprise to see you," Connor said. "I'd have thought you'd be setting defences by now."

"Against more than you?"

"Against the string of Sl'arani's mercs flying in to kill you."

"Hey." Logan glanced to his left just as Thakar shoved his way through a little crowd of motionless mercs. All, including Thakar, were a lot more heavily armed than they had been the day before. "Connor – Sl'arani?"

"Please don't tell me you didn't expect him."

Thakar gestured to the warehouse, the activity, the pallet sitting motionless on the forklift, the bales already removed from storage bays and sitting on the loading floor. "We were trying to get out ahead of him."

"It didn't work."

Kylesdottir contemplated the purity markings on a bale of weed. "A'syan, pick up the physical transit dockets for all this." Thakar retreated towards the stock controller's office on the far wall to the left.

"You don't need to distrust him," Connor said.

"I don't need to do very much of anything."

Connor exhaled. "Except one thing. You need to listen quite carefully to what I'm saying, because while you were sitting snugly in a locked-up bolthole last night I was out in that city, and *you are in danger*. Tell me any other reason why I would have come anywhere near Hardblade's crew!"

She looked him up and down. "From your perspective –"

"From my perspective, I see a panicking Pellite gang lord who's under fire from every angle at once. Currently verbal, but it'll get physical within hours, unless he gets this shipment back and tells the comms channel staff to get the satellites working again: there's a lot of rich folk here annoyed enough to get the police or the defence squads involved, and if there's one thing Hlarxi and Dxarnl don't want, it's that."

"The day I see Septième cops interfering in underside business –"

"Is today, unless Sl'arani plays his game well. But now he's found his target, and you, and insofar as I angered him in the first place, I have to help you defend."

"When I see the slightest shred of evidence –"

"Hostiles," Galene called from the roof hatch. "Bearing east, thirty seconds out."

"I told you," Connor said, voice calm amid the sudden frightened rumble. "I told you they were coming. You should have believed me – you'd have had another ninety seconds to plan."

Logan bit his tongue. Bearing *east*? That wasn't the set he'd spotted...

He stared around the warehouse. If this was the path they'd chosen, best make sure they rode it the best they could. They'd all but invited this attack.

"If there's cover up there, get into it," Connor called, "and keep us posted." He turned to Kylesdottir. "Twenty-eight of us here," he said before she could speak. "God knows how many of his. I've a mind we should make them commit and hit them from the flanks with whatever we can."

She hesitated, but nodded. "We've no better alternative." She nodded to Logan, who hauled the lever to drop the main door down to the floor and pulled across the bars on the pedestrian side door. Thakar, with a string of assorted perplexed and angry mercs behind him, was standing just outside the stock controller's office, dockets in hand. Kylesdottir beckoned to him: he tossed the paperwork back into the office and trotted over. She said, "Pull the squads in and sort out first wave and standby."

Thakar nodded. Connor was staring at the roof-space: Logan followed his line of sight. The hatch from roof-space to roof? "Joshua," Connor called. Thakar's page peered round the crate closest to Thakar's legs. "Get up top. Run us down a message as soon as all the bikers are in sight." The little boy looked at Thakar, who nodded a confirmation.

Logan stared round the warehouse. Open loading area:

storage bays, some holding other cargo, some still holding part of the shipment and some empty: stock controller's office, leading to the secure back rooms: roof space. If he'd learnt one thing over these years, it was that the man on the defensive had to take his choice of geography, and use it.

They'd seen the flip side of that a few days back, when Sl'arani's team had tried to defend their warehouse and had lost.

Connor gestured to a pair of junior mercs hovering behind Thakar. One was Marcello. How in hells was the kid still alive? One more Logan had a mind to keep that way, if he could. "Set up an info chain from here to the roof," Connor said. "I want numbers and weaponry, before it hits us." The older merc bridled at the order – it was menial – but Marcello towed her away.

"They'll want the shipment," Thakar said. "They won't burn the warehouse till they've got it."

"So we need to keep them outside." Connor gestured up at the high row of windows along the warehouse's broadest wall, at right angles to the office, with storage bays dotted along it. Each was too small for a human or Pellite to use as entrance or exit. Several were over empty bays, but three were over full bays, with just enough space for a body to fit between the top of one pallet and the bottom of another. "Three of you," he said, "get up there and use the windows as firing points."

Kylesdottir nodded, and waved an arm at the rows of crates already removed from storage bays ready to go out. "Four rows of crates: four of you, take position prone on top. I want them to think before shooting at you." As Zack led three others off to take position, she continued to Logan, "Cardwain, how long to batter through that door?"

"With this?" He hefted his rocket launcher. "Not long." Overhead, the roof space team opened the windows. Bike engines seeped inside, an echo of the attack on the base. "Assuming standard guns, two minutes, maybe three."

"Two minutes, exposed and under fire, and needing to reload afterwards. I like it."

"Back door," Connor said. "That's thinner."

"So you and I go to lead its defence." She threw Connor a

humourless smile. He nodded as if he'd expected it. Maybe he had.

"Forty incoming," Marcello yelled from the rafters. Logan looked up. The boy merc was wrapped round the roof ladder like it was a baby. Maybe he was scared of heights. Joshua's tiny head poked back inside the hatch, saying something too softly to be heard on the main floor: Marcello nodded and shouted down, "More behind."

"Get into cover if you can," Connor shouted back up to him. "Maintain that chain." What cover he was meant to find on an exposed ladder, Logan didn't know, but it was the right thing for Connor to have said, for *a leader* to have said. "Logan," Connor said, turning, "you and eight others get ready to mount a rolling line of fire when they bust in. You're shielded: you have to stay in front."

Kylesdottir started towards the stock controller's office, gesturing for the remainder to follow her. Connor trotted past her, quickly enough to duck into the office in the lead, and headed to the right towards the office's side door, the fastest route to the warehouse's back door. Kylesdottir, Thakar and a string of mercs vanished behind him. Logan nodded to the rest. Time to get exactly as many of them killed as he needed.

*

CHAPTER NINETEEN

Atalanta dropped the Revelation thread and, still horizontal on her bed, stared at the ceiling, her face a study in sculpture. "Well?" Calad said.

"It's from Ransomvale."

"What is?"

"The ship on its way to join in. It's an Ogre, more than halfway down the Highway." She glanced at him. "Oh, come on. Didn't you realise someone would come to sweep up?"

"I'm not stupid: I'm just not prone to making that kind of mental leap without any evidence." Calad looked over at the window. It had been a little way past midday when his landlady had woken up. How long he'd been talking to, or at, her, he wasn't sure, but the sun had moved perceptibly, and the buskers outside had run through quite a bevy of tinny trumpet tunes.

"It's not exactly that big a leap, even if you've not missed anything else."

"Now you're making excuses."

"For what?" She sat up and leant back against the wall, head positioned between two questionable stains. "I didn't say I would come with you, so I have no reason to give an excuse for not so doing."

Calad bit his lip. She'd already run risks on his behalf: he'd no justification to ask her to do so again with his need the sole reason. But ask he had to do: "You're just about the only person I can trust right now."

"Oh, the irony."

"You, and Ella."

"If 'Ella' is back with your boss's team –"

"Well, then. I need to get there."

He wasn't certain what he feared most. But if he was right – about the generator, about Delia's deeper motives, about everything that was happening – a lot more people, including Connor and Logan, were in line to get hurt, and he didn't want that.

Atalanta swung her legs out of bed, padded to the drawers and pulled out some clothes. "The 'port warehousing begins three hundred miles away, and is several thousand miles square," she said over her shoulder. "I'll drive you there."

"I didn't realise how deep in the city we were." His brain caught up with his mouth. "You've a bike? Where?"

She pulled undergarment and trousers up to her waist. Stark white thigh skin peeped from under her dressing gown's tail, marred by a black tattoo of the ancient letter psi: the Guild's symbol. "Elsewhere." She gestured round the bedsit.

"Obvious, obvious." She frowned at him, and kept frowning with her hands on her dressing gown's tie till he turned his back. "Thank you for your help," he said, staring out of the window and trying not to watch her reflection. She wouldn't like it.

He heard elastic snap into place. "The best thanks you can give me is to melt away into thin air before anyone uses you to find me. I may have thirteen threads at my back but I'm not a miracle-worker."

"I wondered whether you were really any *good* with any of them." He'd spent half his life on Port Logis, where women bared their breasts in summer in favour of veiling their faces. Asking him not to look was what made him want to look. He quashed the thought: his aunts didn't need another reason to criticise him, and admiring a Guild woman's figure would definitely give them cause. Better to count the people outside instead. Street children, itinerant food sellers on their way to better stall spots, wandering mercs of all species, working-class Pellites with their feathers fluffed and their beaks in the air.

"Better with some of them than you are," Atalanta said, voice muffled by clothing. "Call me a cynic, but your constant criticism –"

"What?" Calad said when she didn't continue. He glanced round. She was standing quite still, her thin jumper ruckled over her breasts, head cocked at the door, listening. "What is it?"

"Some strangers just came into the stairwell. I think three."

Calad looked out of the window again. "There were a few mercs outside a minute ago: they've gone. It must be them."

"And how many explanations can you concoct for a merc string to come poking around here now?"

He stared into her eyes. Deep blue, but they seemed icy. "Just two."

Outside, he heard a voice in the stairwell, and he hauled on his boots. Fight or run? Atalanta pulled on jacket, boots and gun belt, and yanked two handhelds from under her mattress, sliding them into her pocket. "Window," she whispered, and pointed past Calad's shoulder. Calad hauled up the sash, clambered halfway out and stopped, staring down.

"*Move*!" Atalanta hissed.

Calad dropped onto the gantry. "Want to guess who *he*'s looking for?" he said, gesturing downwards.

Meandering along the street with a contented smile on his face and both hands tucked into his side pockets was a Circle Spellweaver. Dark red wings speckled the daylight at his shoulders. A speculative child ambled up to him and slid a hand towards his back pocket: "There's nothing in it," Calad heard him say.

"Fuck," Atalanta breathed, still halfway in and halfway out of the window, staring down in something close to horror.

"He's not with Myles –"

She poked his shoulder with one boot toe. "He's in Sanctis Merovir's train. He saw me two days ago. I thought he didn't realise."

Behind her, the bedsit door rattled. "Are you staying or coming?" Calad whispered. Stay, and she'd be able to bluff it out if the mercs wanted him rather than her, but not if they too were tied to Merovir.

Dark red wings meant a revealer. He'd be able to see her red hair through walls. The bedsit's shields were designed to keep Circle Weavers from noticing anything was there: they offered minimal protection once a Circle Weaver realised what they were for. Maybe the man had come here because he realised his view of the city included a big black hole where a room should be.

Atalanta clambered out onto the gantry and pulled the window shut behind her. Calad pussyfooted to his right till he reached the closest corner, and slid round it to the right, off the main street. Atalanta'd headed in the opposite direction. Splitting the searchers, or halving her risk of being found? Was there a difference?

Back in the street, the window rattled. Calad stared ahead. Unbroken alleyway for fifty yards: suitably abandoned, but offering nowhere to hide. He looked at the gantry beneath his feet – a flat steel girder most of a foot deep – and bent to peer over the edge. Struts supported the girder every dozen feet or so, linked by cross-beams: solid steel bars the width of his wrists.

He darted to the closest strut, leant over the edge and gripped the cross-beam. Round the corner, booted feet hit the gantry. Calad swung off the edge and dangled from the gantry frame.

There was a gantry on just about every floor: the next one down was ten feet below his hands and about two feet below his toes. Easy drop. One that any searcher might expect him to make. Instead, Calad swung up his legs and braced himself underneath the gantry.

Between his legs, looking backwards down the alley, he could see a junction fifty yards ahead. Get there without being spotted, and he'd have a good chance of hiding in the backstreets. Slowly, feeling his way, he inched hand over hand down the alley. Just like an overhang, just as simple, and with more handholds: but on an overhang he'd have his father on one end of the rope and one of his siblings on the other end, and nobody would be idling nearby ready to shoot at him if his grip faltered, and he wouldn't risk exacerbating a major gangland conflict if he killed anyone who did take a pot-shot at him.

'Don't use your knees,' he thought he heard his father saying. *'Climb with your hands and feet. Keep your weight supported.'* Would Ella think of calling their father, or would she want to fight this battle herself? She couldn't know how deep the rot went. She couldn't know how badly they needed backup. Suppressing curses, suppressing any sound, Calad crept on. His arms were already burning.

Voices became audible overhead. Grumbles, muted argument. Couldn't listen. Keep going. That was all.

That's an interesting position to be in.

Calad froze for too many seconds, then shook himself, hooked a knee and an elbow into the gantry framework, and looked backwards and down. Merovir's Weaver, still with that knowing smile on his face, was standing in the alley staring straight up at him. For a moment Calad forgot to breathe. A revealer – he'd be fighting blind.

But the man hadn't spoken aloud, or drawn a gun. Calad steadied and sent, *What are you doing here?*

Not looking for you. The reward isn't worth my trouble. I find your red-headed friend more interesting.

Calad gripped the gantry frame. Atalanta? He'd had the same reaction...

Now, the revealer pursued, *what interests me is why you haven't killed those three thugs on your tail yet. A proud boy of Port Logis, avoiding a fight?* He smiled, not pleasantly. Another couple of street children hovered behind him, each daring the other via tiny exchanged nudges to try to mug this incautious target. The Weaver ignored them. *I can think of two explanations*, he sent. *First, you're guilty as sin and are having compunctions about killing to protect yourself. Second, you're trying to protect the Guild bitch. Which is it?*

You said there's a reward out for me.

And?

How many thousand people do I not want chasing me? Calad worked his leg free and hauled himself a few more feet down the gantry. *My problem's not killing these three. It's killing the ones who would come after them, and then more, and then more again. It's not wanting to spark a gang war. Do you understand?*

You're already involved in a gang war, boy. The revealer folded his arms. *Your sister and her husband have catapulted you into just that situation irrespective of anything you can do to get out of it.*

Calad's sweat-soaked palms almost skidded, but he kept hold. Why did everyone else poke their noses into his business? *Then I don't need a second.*

Oh, everyone'll be queuing up for a slice no matter whether these ones live or die. You're the hottest property in the sector right now.

Calad swung round and looked back. It hardly seemed he'd covered any distance at all. Still the Weaver was standing in the alley, watching with that smile on his face and sewage running around his shoes. *And yet the money isn't good enough for you?*

I'm not stupid, and I know how to read a rumour. You're a very dangerous man.

You have no idea –

He released the Telepathy thread and froze as one of the mercs above him half-leant over the gantry edge. But he didn't look Calad's way, just glanced about and called, "Nothing."

Calad looked down. He could drop onto the gantry and run, now. The other Weaver's dry laugh echoed in his mind. *Stupid men. For all they know you could have turned yourself invisible – not a good illusionist, I take it?*

No.

Which does keep things interesting. Now. His smile widened. *Shall I tell the three Misters Expendable that you're here? Or will you help me find the Guild girl?*

For a moment the city seemed quiet, motionless in the mid-afternoon, waiting like a concert hall waited for the conductor to open her score and raise her baton. Then Calad dropped onto the gantry a floor down and fled.

Behind him, he heard the mercs calling to each other, first in uncertainty and then in growing anger. Corner, just ahead: Calad flung himself round it, skidded and fell hard onto the gantry. For half a second he saw the alley floor coming up at him, but he flung out an arm on automatic and grabbed the edge. His full weight thunked onto his wrist, but his grip held.

Still twenty feet above ground, dangling over alley dirt: he let go and swung himself onto the bottom-most gantry. Out of sight – but the mercs were following. They'd heard.

Too late to second-guess. He ran on along the foot-wide girder, chest already beginning to burn. Two days of no exercise shouldn't have done this. He must be more badly hurt than he'd thought. Trouser fabric rubbed against his bad leg like sandpaper.

A few tiny alleys, too narrow for gantry access, yawned

away to his left. Calad counted two, then jumped off the gantry, down to the street. Mud splashed his boots. The mercs were at the corner. Calad darted down the third alley.

Tall houses reared up on each side, narrowing the daylight to a lilac strip overhead. Calad could have touched both walls at once. While he tried to keep his eyes on the alley floor, he kept glancing up at the buildings: spirally and circuitous, some topped by broken gantry pieces, a ghost suburb of the original city. Were a few Pellites still living here? There wasn't a feathered household in the city that didn't pay one or other of their gang lords. Ella had told him to ignore the graft, the backhanders, the oppressive edge of an entire sector on the take, but when he had to avoid sparking a gang war, he couldn't exactly forget it.

And they didn't like humans in their places, and they definitely didn't like humans from Earth or Terra Nova...

He cut to the right down another tiny alley. Improvised gantries made from rickety ladders soared overhead, mocking the rest of the city. Ahead, the dead-straight streets began to meander where houses had fallen down and been rebuilt jerry-fashion. Calad vaulted a part-collapsed wall, squeezed against the right hand side of the street – the shadowed side – and kept going.

Atalanta couldn't be far off his trajectory, unless she'd doubled back to her bedsit for the sake of its protective screen. Maybe he would be able to sense her location through those scatter-shields, now that he knew they were there. He half-closed his eyes and, still running, touched the Telepathy thread. Earlier, before he'd met her and understood, he'd seen the barest glimpse of her in her infinitesimal contact with Connor. Everything else had faded when he tried to touch it, like the bloom on a peach.

Faintest glimmer, very close, and he cut left and immediately right, deeper into the alleys. Behind, in the architectural tangle, he heard voices, raised and querulous. The mercs: they'd lost him. Trying to find him, or hoping they wouldn't? Whatever story Myles had put out, it would have contained part of the truth: he was a Circle Weaver, after all. But not the whole truth...

He rounded another corner and with no warning almost

collided with Atalanta. She backpedalled, glared up at him – not far: she was barely two inches shorter than he was – and whispered, "Why in hells are you leading him my way?"

"I'm not –"

"Yes, you are!" She grabbed his hand and yanked him down the next alley. Magic trickled down her fingers and up his arm, winding round him like a snake. Calad shivered. He'd known magic all his life, but this –

"Stop complaining." Atalanta slowed down and stared from side to side, all but sniffing the air, cat-like. "I'm not sure where we are. You could always go and lead them off, you know."

They were at a crossroads in the alleys. Eerily quiet, it lacked the omnipresent organic stink that wreathed the city even two streets away: it smelt more of decay and death. Mould and rot crept up walls. No, the Pellites weren't still here. Nobody was.

"I want out of this." His voice wasn't loud, but it seemed so, in this strange stillness. "I want to end this, and drive to the spaceport, and fly away without a whole sector chasing me. Fighting and killing doesn't gain me that. It doesn't gain me anything."

She swung round, hands on her hips. "What in eleven hells do you think *I* want?"

He stared at her, blue eyes and shallow freckled cheekbones and flying red hair, and every time he thought he had something to say, he realised he hadn't. Even apologies felt too paltry. He opened his mouth to stutter the least feeble of those, but as he drew in a breath, he realised they were being watched.

He slid his eyes up the wall behind Atalanta's right shoulder. A little pair of eyes stared back at him, wide and solemn. Calad glanced left, then right. More eyes. Little fingers clutching broken brick walls. Little heads emerging one after the other: little faces staring down silently at Calad and Atalanta.

Children. Pellites, humans, and amazingly one or two Ditans. The youngest was maybe three, the oldest eight or nine. Healthy, sick, hale, disabled: every possible phenotype: and all of them dirty and thin. From the top of the highest remaining wall, the girl who'd sold Calad buns earlier stared down at him, one grubby finger in her mouth. He'd thought her tiny, before, and had wondered how any parent could abandon such a young child. Here, she was one of the oldest.

Atalanta's head jerked towards a new little crowd that had popped out of another alley – including a tiny Kriastan: since when did they misplace their nestlings? One cob chick poked his beak against Calad's wounded leg. He winced. "Beat it," Atalanta hissed at a little girl eyeing her money belt.

Calad glanced back the way they'd come. How long till that Weaver, or those three mercs, caught up? The kids were starting to whisper among themselves. Next would be talking, then shouting or crying.

"Where're you going?" one of the boys said, startlingly loud in this abandoned street.

"Are you going to the sick house?" a girl piped up.

"They're running away," another girl confided to her neighbour, a Pellite chick with more down than feathers. "They're running from scary men."

"That's a little gun. Why don't you have a big gun?"

"Have you got knives?"

"Have you got bikes?"

Atalanta sidestepped towards the next alley but stopped, confronted by a wall of inquisitive faces. Calad dislodged the baby Kriastan's tail and teeth from his right wrist and caught Atalanta's hand. Her spells prickled his palm.

He hadn't spoken to her telepathically before. He'd never heard of Guild and Circle Weavers using the Telepathy weft for communication as opposed to hostilities. Her shields were still contorting in their scatter-pattern: Calad waited till he saw a regularity in the undulation, and flicked a Telepathy thread underneath. It sizzled, a shock rippling up and down the thread, and he could only hope it hurt her less than him.

She grabbed the thread from his tentative hold and anchored it. The sizzle subsided. *Why won't they move?* she sent, exasperation flooding the cast. *Every drift child I met before ran from me!*

That was on adult turf. This is their turf. Calad looked round the circle of waist-high faces. "Yes, we're running away," he said, "so you need to let us go."

Three children squealed in delight and another six started jumping up and down. "Are you going to have a fight?" one said. "Can we watch?"

"I like watching fights," the Kriastan nestling burbled. "There's lots of blood, and no one shoots at us."

"They do sometimes," a human boy corrected. "When they get cross."

Atalanta picked up another child and set her down a distance from her money belt, risking fleas. "We need to go *now*," she said. More ecstatic squeaks. She stared at the sky. "Seriously. Now!"

Calad glanced upwards too. The sun was dropping, and if he was lucky, he had till it set. Maybe that would be less than two hours. And he *wouldn't* hurt these inquisitive little vagrants. No matter the number of dead children he'd seen in these alleys this week, he *wouldn't*.

A warning shot, Atalanta sent. Calad shook his head. He never fired a warning shot unless he was prepared to shoot for real.

Snatch at that thinnest strand of mythology? "You need to let us go," he said, trying to make his voice carry to all the children, trying not to worry that it might carry to their pursuers, "because – because she's the Harlequin." He pointed at Atalanta.

The children looked her up and down. "She's not got wings," a little boy objected.

"And she's a lady," added another, "not a man. The Harlequin was a man."

"The Sapphire was a man, and then a woman, and then a man again," Calad said. "There's only been one Harlequin. There hasn't been time for the Harlequin to be a woman." He bent down, smacking the latest little hand away from his pocket. "There's nothing that says *only the second* Harlequin can't be a woman."

"But *wings*," a pen Pellite chick insisted.

Calad looked over his shoulder at Atalanta. Her expression could have frozen lava. "You can show us all your wings," he said, half to her, half to the children. "Not hard."

I could light up a bloody great bonfire for that insect

following me. Besides – this is obscene: you're playing on their beliefs.

Failing to contradict their beliefs, you mean. "Please," he said quietly, and this time it was all to her.

I hate you, she sent, and Calad tasted venom behind the words. He waited.

The air began to hum behind her head, and the children around Atalanta's legs backpedalled. As the impossibility sprang up around her, all magic's thirteen glories in the alley dirt, Calad thought of the ten years he'd spent learning to tame a tiny fragment of that power, and wondered, no matter her comparative weakness in any individual discipline, how hard she must have trained and how much it must have hurt to learn to use every single spell-thread.

It hurt. Satisfied? Atalanta surveyed the awed faces around her waist. "Now we are going to go," she said, and the children moved back to let the two of them pass.

"Will you come back and tell us stories later?" a little girl ventured. "We want some of your stories. We don't know them."

"Later," Calad said. That was a sound, back down the alleys in the direction of the living city: a voice, or a step. "Maybe quite a lot later."

His eyes flicked up to the girl he'd met earlier in the day. She hadn't moved or spoken, just stayed on her high perch, watching. He nodded to her, and hurried into the alleys after Atalanta.

After, and a way after: Atalanta had almost reached the next corner already. *Slow down*, Calad projected. *I can't run that fast.*

I should leave you here.

Why? If someone asks that little lot who went past them, they'll talk about the Harlequin, not about two fugitives.

Because it's wrong! She stopped at the corner with her hands braced on the alley walls, wedged between mould patches. "I am not some – some figure out of fairy tales! I'm a working Guild Weaver from a multidisciplinary school, nothing more." She spoke at a whisper, magic forgotten, but her wings still pulsed at her shoulders, seething with life. "Don't tell me you believe in reincarnation."

"It's not orthodox theology." Calad took a breath, steadying himself. "It doesn't matter whether it's orthodox. They believe in it: that's what matters." He wasn't sure it shouldn't matter, didn't know why it didn't... and he sighed. He was overdue a visit to a confessor. "I know you didn't like it, but it worked, didn't it?"

"Circle expediency given tongue." She turned her back on him and stalked into the next alley. Calad trailed after her.

"You're just upset because you didn't realise this part of the city was inhabited," he said to her retreating back.

She stopped so abruptly that he almost walked into her. "I'm upset," she said quietly, "because they're children."

Calad swallowed. "It's not nice, and I don't think it's nice. But didn't you know, before you came?"

"I didn't believe it."

He touched her shoulder. "Me neither."

For a moment the city stilled again, till Calad could believe they were alone, but then he heard footsteps back behind them, and Atalanta pulled away from him and jogged off. She beckoned for him to follow, but he was already doing so. He had no idea what else to do.

Round one more corner Atalanta stopped and prised open a door dangling on one rusty hinge. This building was sturdier, less ruinous, but no less abandoned. Inside, it smelt strongly of several species' guano. Calad tiptoed in after Atalanta, feeling his way.

Her wings retreated up a banisterless staircase. "Up here." She spoke at a normal volume: must have decided there was no longer any sense in fear. "The floorboards are missing. Hurry."

Calad padded up the staircase and stopped. Atalanta was on the far side of the room, pulling a tarpaulin off a bike. There was no intervening floor, just a couple of beams.

As she righted the bike and grabbed the little case that had hidden beneath it, Calad wobbled his way across the closest beam. It should have been easy. It was far from easy. "Take that," Atalanta said as he reached her, and she shoved the case into his hands, almost pushing him off the beam in the process.

"They must be close –"

"And if they come in, we're sitting ducks, until we get into the air." She mounted the bike and kicked its throttle. "Jump on." Calad edged across the last few inches of floor beam and swung onto the pillion seat, still clutching the case.

"What's in here?" he said.

"More guns, explosives, wire. Useful stuff." The bike rose into the air. Atalanta reached up into the rafters overhead and lifted out a helmet. "We'll make do."

"We?"

She pulled on the helmet, aimed for the patch of sky visible through the ruined roof, and accelerated. "I'm starting to dislike this situation almost as much as you do. That being so, I've a mind to stay around."

*

CHAPTER TWENTY

"Stay away from the plant," Kylesdottir's flunky Packer shouted from the back of the string.

"What in hells is in there to help us?" Connor pressed on, past the plant room entrance, leftwards into the passage leading to the washrooms. Black mould traced patterns on the right hand wall, the internal one between corridor and shower block. On the left was the external wall to the alleyway behind the warehouse. Its tiny high windows rattled with engine noises.

"Six, too close," Thakar said behind him.

"I agree." The back door was just ahead, opposite the washroom entrance. Connor hefted his automatic rifle, and ran.

As he reached the door he heard a bike's brakes squeal outside, and half-heard something that could be a Pellite gliding on feathery wings from a bike to an elevated window. He flung open the door and fired outside without looking. A strangled avian squeal answered him. He yanked the door back shut and clicked its bar into place.

Thakar and Kylesdottir skidded up behind him. Connor glanced past them. Five mercs were puffing along behind: Pritie leading three gunhands ten years her junior, with Packer bringing up the rear. Eight, versus whatever proportion of his troops Sl'arani chose to throw at the back door. He'd hoped the odds would be better, but they could have been worse. He could have been shot as soon as he drove up to the warehouse.

He glanced from side to side. The corridor down which they'd come, back and around into the main warehouse and snaking away in the other direction to the secure stores. The washrooms, off the wall at his back. The corridor to the left, winding along the outer wall to the quartermaster's stores. Quartermaster's and washrooms were both dead ends. Dead ends were bad news. At least here, Logan and the rest of the mercs were covering their backs, albeit from a long way away.

"How many?" Kylesdottir said, gesturing to the door and the new raft of engine noises.

"One less than there was." A familiar rifle cracked outside, and a bike and rider crashed to the floor with a metal scream. More gunshots volleyed towards the roof. *Damn* Galene – he'd wanted her out of the worst danger. "Two less."

"*Fewer.*" Thakar shouldered Connor aside and pressed the bar down. The door swung open again. He leant out, aimed three quick shots into the air and withdrew, pulling the bar up again. "I see eight up there plus some shadows. At least twelve overall."

Eight defenders facing twelve attackers was decent odds. Connor crushed thoughts of Zack, back in the main warehouse with the rest of Sl'arani's squad heading at him. No way to tell how long Logan's shields would last, either. Instead of worrying, he gestured at the windows high in the passage. "Cover and a firing point." The mercs at the back were short: too little food when they were young. "Packer, Thakar, you're tall. Take shots."

Packer rolled onto the balls of his feet and rested his gun on the closer windowsill. "Enjoying yourself?" he said without looking at Connor.

"I'm feeling more sanguine than I was two minutes ago." Connor set his back to the door.

"I bet. None of us's shot you yet."

"You won't want to do that by the time I'm done." Connor opened the door and fired upwards, just missing the tailpipe of a biker who would have been in his sights had he taken his shot half a second earlier. Kylesdottir and Pritie leant past him, shooting round the door. A second's delay, if that, and shots hammered into the door's far side. Connor shoved the two women back inside and yanked the door shut again. This time the, the gunshots didn't stop hitting it. Tight angle, from high up: it would take Sl'arani's squad time to hammer inside, unless they landed.

"If you don't think we all know what you've been doing," Packer continued, still firing out of the window, "you're wrong."

"Same as ever." Some Pellite smart-shot had scored a few

hits on the same spot on the door. It wasn't glowing yet, but was warm against Connor's cheek. He moved a step back and tried his jack. Still nothing.

Kylesdottir too was fiddling with her jack. "Someone's going to have to run to the 'port," she said. "I won't have this guy wiping us out without the boss knowing."

A nasty judder started up in Connor's stomach. "Get to the 'port under fire, get *through* the 'port staffed with people who answer to our attacker, get up the Highway and into the Bridge without being shot down –"

"Your optimism is touching."

It had little to do with optimism or its lack, and everything to do with needing to stop any of Hardblade's crew talking to her about him. Stack up all the hassles of having no comms – beginning with an inability to access a single remote document, including the blasted contract he owed Merovir – and at the end of it he might wind up happy he'd traded that gross inconvenience for the chance to stall Hardblade. "Sl'arani's responding to weakness with strength. It's a decent tactic to avert any retaliation for the base."

True, insofar as it went, but there was so much more to it than that. And in all the fuss of the previous night, Éloise hadn't found Calad, so Connor had had no opportunity to snatch the generator from his finger or his corpse and demand that Sl'arani, or anyone in the whole Septième, told him what in hells' names it had been doing alongside a perfectly ordinary drugs shipment.

That ordinary shipment had had a Circle Weaver on tap…

Glass shattered at the windows. Thakar leapt backwards, arm thrown up to protect his face. An incendiary flew through the window beside his head, missing him by a hand's width.

"Extinguisher!" Kylesdottir shouted. Gunfire, sickening yellow plasma bolts, cannoned through the window. The young merc who had jumped to obey her captain's call staggered and fell. A second jumped over her and ran off towards the plant room. Connor could only hope he'd gone for an extinguisher and not gone to hide.

"Fall back!" he called. Thakar stumbled sideways into the shower block: Connor hesitated. Never get trapped in a dead end.

The back door was glowing dull red now. As the merc who had run down the passage reemerged with an extinguisher and started spraying a thick patch of foam on the incendiary, Connor backed away from the door with his rifle levelled on it. He would get a minimum of one shot.

At his left, the junior merc had the incendiary fire under control: it had dug itself into the floor flags but hadn't had time to spread. One of Sl'arani's bikers dropped into view through the window that had had its glass blown out. Connor fired. Hit or miss? Miss. The biker evaded but didn't crash.

Mistake to show his hand. Gunfire poured in through the window again, striking the remaining two junior mercs. Connor snatched the foam extinguisher from the closest boy's dead hands and flung it at the door. "What are you doing?" yelled Kylesdottir.

"Trying to kill us all," Packer shouted back.

The door flew open, outwards. Two gunshots hit the extinguisher. It exploded. Shards of its canister metal blasted into the air, and high-pitched Pellite squeals punctuated the gunfire. For the first time Connor heard shooting from the main warehouse, behind them, punctuated by orders blasted out in whistle-speak: *<Move left>*, *<Beware above>*, *<Withdraw>*. Logan's street name, Checkmate, echoed loudest: *<Fire at Checkmate's target>*, *<Take cover behind Checkmate>*. He had no time to think about the implications. Instead he dived to the ground, gun above his head, firing at an angle out of the door. The incoming fire stopped.

"What's going on?" Kylesdottir said. She was staring at Packer, not Connor.

"If we die –"

Another volley exploded through the window. Connor yanked Kylesdottir into his shadow. She fell awkwardly, with no attempt to protect herself, and before she landed he knew she was dead.

She hit Connor's back hard. He struggled to his knees, levering her off him. *Had* to keep firing – and he stopped, halfway up, as he saw Packer's rifle barrel pointing at his head.

His stomach quivered. He fought not to back into the wall, just to stare at the gun, oily and menacing, a foot from his forehead. "We need him," Pritie said in the background.

"No, we don't. We *fucking* don't. Because if he kills us all, there's nothing to stop him giving the boss his version of what happened here. Stay where you are, A'syan." He smiled, a rictus more than a grin. "I'm going to enjoy this."

"Listen," Thakar said from the washroom entrance, "we can –"

A shot cracked over Connor's head. He dived sideways again. Packer crumpled, and his gun spat in a dying burst, just missing Connor. From the door, another cannon of plasma fire rippled into Packer's falling body. Connor's rifle was trapped under his torso: he clutched his pistol and forced up his hand, firing at the door, and counted gunfire streams heading in the door's direction. Four.

The incoming shots stopped. Thakar stumbled to the door and peered outside. "All down," he called. Connor struggled to his knees and looked up and round, expecting to see Logan. Instead, Marcello's uncertain brown eyes stared down at him.

"Are you OK?" he said.

"Unhurt." Connor pulled himself upright using the wall as a prop. "What's happening?"

"Their second wave's coming. They'll get into the warehouse." His eyes strayed to Kylesdottir's corpse, but he said nothing more.

"Not this way," Thakar said, and he hauled the buckled rear door to. "You two, go to the secure store, and get me a couple of chains and a padlock. Down the corridor, there." He waved back and round the corner.

Marcello and Pritie departed at a trot. Thakar hauled Connor off the wall and embraced him. He smelt of sweat and smoke. "Hold hard," he whispered.

"I will." He stared down at Kylesdottir's dead body. Her comms links had been as useless as anyone's, so if she'd held the contract so important... he bent and started rooting in her pockets. "Help me." Thakar knelt beside him and, as Connor worked round her pockets clockwise, started working round anticlockwise. Gunshots sang, back in the warehouse, punctuated by the rocket launcher's boom. A frantic thirty seconds later, Connor slid a hand into Kylesdottir's inside trouser pocket and grabbed the handheld onto which Merovir had copied the contract.

Thakar stood up, blocking the sightline between Kylesdottir's body and the corridor, and Connor rose to his feet just as the other two reemerged toting a heavy chain between them. While Pritie and Thakar secured the door as best they could, Connor asked Marcello, "Who's alive?"

"Maybe half of ours, maybe less. Mistress Prialova's still on the roof. Your brother's leading the line."

"Sounds like Logan," Thakar said. He clipped on the padlock and moved past Connor. "I'll take point."

Connor was glad of it. His hands were a breath from shaking. Partly Packer's gun in his face, but he'd been prepared for that ever since he and Logan had driven up to the warehouse, and at least he'd got through this part of the fight unscathed. Seeing Kylesdottir killed in front of him, though, had hammered home exactly how fast he was going to have to talk to Hardblade to get out of this mess permanently. Taking a run after delivering her a windfall would have been easier than doing so after delivering a pile of corpses. *Damn* Carm and his interference.

Blame Sl'arani? He couldn't. Connor'd started this, breaking into that city centre warehouse in a bright afternoon that felt so long ago. Sure, he'd cleared the run first with Coker. It was still his responsibility.

Blame the buyer Sl'arani had lined up for not the drugs, but the generator? That would involve admitting he'd known for days that the generator existed…

Ahead, Thakar clicked open the door to the stock controller's office. "Clear," a soft voice said from inside, and Thakar ducked low and slid in. Pritie, Marcello and Connor followed.

A desk hugged the office's left wall, and above it a single window faced onto the warehouse floor so the supervisory staff could keep tabs on how much was being skimmed from the top. One young merc, not much more than a runner, was peering over the desk out of the window. "Can't see anything," she whispered.

"Good," Logan said from the door into the main warehouse, past the window. "Three of you, follow me out. I mean *follow*." He glanced at Connor and nodded a greeting. "Rest of you, hole up here." The window was blast-resistant, though the plywood door wasn't.

Connor counted heads. Zack. Two mercs who'd been on Logan's team. Him and his three companions. Nobody left who'd complain when he signed the shipment over to Merovir. He'd *won*, as long as he stayed alive now: no need to resort to the stun grenades or smoke bombs to stage an escape – just open the door and walk out.

"How many in the second wave?" he said.

"Fewer than the last one. Maybe only ten." Logan made to open the door.

"Wait." The world was moving too quickly, making too much sense. Impossibilities became certainties. "How many of the first wave are left?"

He shrugged. "Five or so. We can mop them up before the second wave hits." He eased open the door and slid out. Zack and two mercs followed him.

Thakar shook Connor's shoulder. "What's up?"

"Ten's a tiny squad."

He stared at him. "Yeah. Either they're armed for Armageddon or they expect us to be dead before they hit."

"Could be." Or they could represent the sum total of captains and top lieutenants whom Sl'arani trusted totally – trusted enough to go in with him and find the generator. But the generator wasn't with the shipment...

"I'll talk to him," he muttered, and he realised he was at the door with the rest all staring at him. "What?"

Thakar shoved past the rest and grabbed Connor's arm. "Have you gone mad?"

"He –" Connor stopped as he realised the others present didn't know about the generator. "This is personal now. Feels that way, doesn't it?" Thakar nodded. "But Sl'arani doesn't have all the information – he thinks he does, but he's wrong. If I talk him off, no one else dies." He pushed the door open and hurried into the warehouse proper.

Gun-rattles greeted him – Logan and his team 'mopping up' the last of the first wave. For a moment doubt gripped his stomach. Was there a possibility, however slight, that Sl'arani hadn't known what his shipment was coating?

No. The Weaver woman had given it away from the start.

Blood, ichor and urine blotted the floor. Connor jogged towards the loading door, reopened by some brave or suicidal Pellite. Liquid splashed his boots.

"Hey!" He turned. Logan was staring at him from down a row of pallets, pistol in hand, standing over a couple of corpses: one human, one Pellite.

"Are you finished?"

"Unless we missed one." Logan glanced up to the roof walkways and maintenance ladder, which Galene was descending, and slung the rocket launcher off his shoulder. "I think that means we didn't. I'm down two." He grimaced. "Damn it, I told them to stay behind me. Stupid kids wanted to be brave."

"Put your guns away. I'm going to talk to him."

"*Talk*? After all this?"

Connor picked up a fragment of broken wing and pinion, and waved it at Logan. "He killed ours, and we killed his. Turnabout's fair game. Now, I want him off our backs and onto other parties' backs." The sky felt like it was clearing in front of him. Merovir, Hardblade, Sl'arani. He'd a path clear to settle with Merovir and just had to talk fast enough to Hardblade. Smoothing out his situation with Sl'arani would finish it.

Logan didn't answer immediately. Outside, bike engines whined their high notes in the approach. "I'd considered him a willing participant," Logan finally said. "Not his mercs, sure, but we all get screwed over by our bosses. How could he *not* know?"

"Know what?" Zack said, coming up behind him.

"I think he knows what was going on," Connor said, "but I don't think anyone explained the implications." He jerked his head at the door and the whole 'port complex beyond. "If we're to get off this planet alive, we need a boss's backing. A boss is driving right up to our door, now. I see this as a pleasant coincidence."

"He won't play," Galene said in the background.

Zack reached out to pluck Logan's sleeve, but stopped with

his hand partway out as if he were reconsidering. "What's going on?" Connor turned away towards the door.

The packing area was strewn with burnt body parts, mostly Pellite. Blood and fluids streaked the forklifts, pallets, storage bays, everything. It sickened him, not just the carnage but the thought of what lay behind it: if he didn't know much, he was becoming more and more certain that Sl'arani knew even less.

An image of Calad snaked across his mind – Calad with the generator on one finger, the last time anyone had seen it. With a reward on offer, half the city would start looking for him as soon as it had outgrown the chaos Connor had started the previous night. Sl'arani's help, if it could be obtained, would be invaluable there. Tell him the boy Weaver had his prize, on condition he returned Calad alive? Maybe he should have tried that angle the moment he heard Calad had gone missing, rather than getting Éloise to call for help from Kylesdottir on the one hand and her elder brother on the other. If he'd been able to conduct a conversation then in something quieter than gunshots, none of today's dead need have died, and he could have already been away and safe with a start-up fund in his back pocket.

He drew up at the edge of the last pallet, and tried and failed to synch his jack to the warehouse's systems. Still nothing, more was the pity – he could have done with intercom access.

In edged the first bikers, cobs and pens in lieutenants' stripes playing no-account bodyguards, each one with plasma bursters mounted on his or her wings. Connor stayed still. He could only hope Logan wouldn't shoot.

A row of captains slid in next, and at the back in an armoured bubble-bike, Sl'arani. He was as small as Connor remembered. A clutch runt who had risen as high as anyone could go. Why had he decided to run the generator? Just out of greed, or had he been blackmailed?

//Stand down,// Connor called in Pellite cityspeak. Hooked beaks and wingtip bursters turned towards him. //We need to talk.//

One of the captains fanned her wings. Sl'arani said something to her in a language Connor didn't understand,

and the pen lowered her coverts.

"I don't feel we have anything to discuss," Sl'arani said. In English his voice was high and just a fraction off tuneful, with a few clipped edges. "We trade corpses. That is all."

"But you were trading something else, and every one of your team knows it." Two of the Pellites glanced at their boss. He extended one wing in a gesture to wait. Alone among them, he was unarmed: the type of leader who ordered others to kill for him. "We need to talk," Connor pursued, "about whoever it was who's fucked you over – because that's the way it's turned out, even if you thought it was going to go well for you. I don't think you were lied to, but I definitely think you were dumped in the sewer when things got interesting, and I suspect it was always intended to go that way.

"It's not here, Mister Sl'arani, any more than it was at our base." Time to risk it. He walked into the Pellites' full view, right hand casually close to his pistol, and pointed with his left hand to the corpses near the door, some Hardblade's, mostly Sl'arani's. "These, here? They died for *nothing*." He stopped ten feet from the row of lieutenants. Logan probably had a bead on the one who was fidgeting. For now he wouldn't protest. "It's gone missing. We can find it, together, but I need to know I can trust you before I start working with you."

Sl'arani's breast feathers puffed out. "You ask a lot."

Green mist stirred around the warehouse floor. "Who hired you?"

His beak clacked. "You now ask for proof that you *cannot* trust me."

"On the contrary: I like your answer. I can find out who was behind this in other ways. It'll be easy to narrow it down by the amount they paid you – that Weaver'll have cost you."

He cawed a snort. "I didn't hire her."

"You didn't?" Logan said, from behind.

Sl'arani spat. "All my Weavers have real feathers to bolster the insubstantial ones –" Pellite Weavers, he meant, with two sets of wings jutting from their backs – "it's as well I choose that way. The girl was foisted onto me, and she did badly."

"She did well till she ran into another Weaver's shield," Connor said.

Sl'arani hissed, a sound from the gutter, and his captains' beaks clacked as one. "Which Weaver?"

Boom.

Sonic burst, a faster-than-sound craft passing overhead: but *no*, and Connor dived back behind the closest pallet, roaring to his squad to take cover. That wasn't FTS, but was rebound sound: sound that had bent back in on itself in an attempt to conceal a craft's approach for as long as possible.

Gunfire rattled again from the door. This time it ceased in seconds. Connor counted to ten, lifted his rifle and peered round the pallet.

Dead gunbirds scattered the floor, Sl'arani and all his seniors, a power trip arrived at its ultimate terminus – on Hardblade's turf: if Connor ran to the Vingtième he wouldn't be far enough away from her. Four newcomers stood in the doorway. One was the female Ditan whom Hendrix had packed as backup in their meeting three days ago, and the rest were three of the human mercs who'd been lazing round that pub: a slim woman and two men, one slender, one massive. All had wings out: pale blue outlines for the Ditan, yellow, white and royal blue for the humans.

The world smelt very, very wrong. Connor waved for the others to retreat. Thakar shrugged a query: Logan ignored Connor's signal and pushed past him, out into the packing area, towards the final two figures standing at the door – Hendrix, and Éloise.

That guilty glint in Éloise's eye, that tiny droop in her shoulders. She'd told Hendrix where to find the shipment.

Logan swung his rocket launcher to his shoulder before anyone, Hardblade's crew or Hendrix's, could speak, and he fired full at Éloise. She flung up one hand. Light sprung from her palm into a shield-shape. The rocket cannoned into the shield and imploded. Connor flung his hands over his ears, waiting for aftershocks to level half the warehouse and him with it: but though the concrete floor at Éloise's feet buckled, the walls stayed standing. Logan made as if to fire again: Éloise twisted her hand, and the rocket launcher twisted with it, bending out of shape into a useless hunk of steel.

He threw the useless rocket launcher to one side, drew his left-hand pistol, and broke into a run. Shots spat from his pistol in a long burst straight down the string of Hendrix's Weavers. Amid ricochets caught by the massive male defender, he drove all his weight into Éloise. The Ditan Weaver drew and fired at him, heedless of Éloise, but her bolts too flew wide, and she lowered her weapon.

Éloise rolled as Logan barrelled into her, taking him along too before he had a chance to crush her. Still rolling, she kicked out hard at his stomach, a trained fighter's kick: he caught her leg in his, dragged it round almost hard enough to break her knee, but again she went with the move, minimising it. He threw a punch at her, catching her cheekbone, knocking her head back against the floor: she blocked the next blow and kicked up at him with both legs, thrusting him away.

"Stop!" the big male Weaver called. Neither acted as if they'd heard. Logan rolled to his feet, kicked the door release and dodged as it came crashing down: Éloise moved just slower, and the hundred-pound door bounced off her shoulder. She hissed, in something less than pain, and shrugged off the weight as if it were nothing. Again he moved in on her, with feet and fists flying. She blocked the first punch, kicked away his ankle, spun and kicked him in the face. He swayed backwards, grabbed her ankle and pulled her off balance. She landed hard on the floor, but launched herself up and at him again.

Connor glanced backwards. Why hadn't he led the lot of them to the back door? Too far now, no way out: and he shuddered at the sheer magnitude of his stupidity.

"Enough."

Hendrix, pale pink wings extended, pushed to the front of the little knot of Weavers, a grenade in his hand. "You're shielded," he said to Logan, "but the others aren't. Stand down."

Logan didn't react. He was bleeding, Connor realised, and Éloise was too: maybe the sight had shocked her teammates into immobility, just as the sight of a woman half Logan's body weight going toe to toe with him on his terms had stunned Hardblade's mercs.

"Logan," Thakar called, "stop. You'll get us all killed."

Hendrix nodded in some satisfaction. Connor measured the distance between them. Out of even Logan's reach – surely gun-resistant, given he was toting two defenders around – no handy suspended pallet ready to drop on him – "You're all under arrest." He smiled at Connor from too many yards away. "Endplay."

*

CHAPTER TWENTY-ONE

Atalanta elbowed Calad's ribs. He ducked back beneath parapet level. "What was that for?" he whispered.

"You're as blond as a floodlight."

"It's almost sundown: anyone who looks up here'll be squinting." He peered again over the parapet and down at the warehouse opposite, with Neuvième bikes lined up outside it. Damn. *Damn.* "We were on time. I'm sure we were."

"Not if we ran into someone else's plan," Atalanta said, below him. Calad glanced back down. She'd spun a Revelation thread, and was scowling at it, or past it. "That Ogre just landed."

"See? On time." He twisted up onto his knees and counted the Weaver crew's bikes lined up outside. Somewhere in all his calculating, he'd missed a step, and in it, he'd lost the initiative. He'd *needed* Connor and Logan's guns at that vital moment when the Ogre's crew came calling. When he found the person responsible for this, he'd have quite a lot to say.

He wriggled backwards off the roof's highest pitch and down beside Atalanta on the lower level. "Does the Ogre have takeoff clearance?"

She shook her head. A little frustrated expression played over her lips, possibly aimed at the out-of-tune busker somewhere in the alleys. "I don't know, but it doesn't matter: from here we've no chance of causing a delay. If we get to an anchored 'port terminal, it'll be different."

"Or to its hangar. All we need to do is get the customs officials interested." Whether said officials would expect a bonanza of bribes or arrests, Calad neither knew nor cared. He was sick of the whole business.

Atalanta coiled her threads and leant round the corner. Sunset licked her copper hair. "It's nothing without guns." She stiffened for a few seconds, silent, then pulled back into cover. "False alarm," she said to Calad's raised eyebrows. "I got distracted."

Distractions. Calad lay on his back and stared at the sky.

Atalanta had seen thirty crewers on the Ogre: that definitely warranted a distraction. A few stars were beginning to prickle through sunset and smog: strange stars. Was that busker playing ballads of those who had died amid these stars? Legends of pilots with names like Emerald and Diamond, and Weavers with names like Stormbringer and Harlequin. He glanced at Atalanta. The Septième's second Harlequin. Was there really no such thing as reincarnation?

"We need to move now," Atalanta said, "if we're going to get our guns at all. We can set up a blind on the other side of the warehousing –

"We haven't time. I've a quicker play."

Liquid blue eyes stared down at him. "What's the catch?"

"It's dangerous, especially for you." She shrugged. "I'll take that as a you-don't-care. Now, are you just pretending to be a dancer or can you dance?"

She rolled her eyes. "If I couldn't dance, how could I pretend to be a dancer?"

"Fine: stupid question."

"Yes, it was."

Calad didn't rise to that. Instead he gestured to her bike, behind them on the roof, and said, "We need to get that into the alley, and warm the engine."

"We'll have thirty seconds before it gets stolen."

"We only need thirty seconds." Keeping low, he clambered onto the hydrobike, and reversed off the roof and down to the alley floor between warehouses. Atalanta climbed down after him, staying close, as the bike would only remain running if in proximity to her ring-key.

As she reached the ground, Calad dismounted and left the bike idling. "Push off," he said to the small child whose head had poked out of a ground floor window. Ring-key activation could be overridden in minutes by someone who knew how. He hoped the child didn't know how.

Just Delia, Harlek, Rebekah and Marius? Or the rest of the crew? By now Delia could easily have pulled everyone except Ella onto her side. He had to assume he had all of them to tackle.

Best to concentrate on Delia. It was the quickest way to get this finished.

There. Delia was walking out of the warehousing, hands tucked into her pockets, staring at the sky as if she expected company. For a moment Calad contemplated asking Atalanta to do this part alone, but he rejected the idea. His problem. His plan. His involvement.

The busker ended his song. Two, three seconds while he tipped liquid out of his valves, and then he struck up another tune, jauntier, celebrating great deeds done rather than great lives ended. That'd do nicely. Three-part time, too. Calad bowed to Atalanta. "May I have this dance?"

Her eyes widened, but she lifted her hands to his. Folk waltz hold, he realised, not ballroom waltz. He could keep it up for long enough.

He slid his right arm under her left and swung her out onto the street. Her right hand was light in his left and her feet moved lightly, unerringly, delicately with his. For a few seconds, as she turned on her heels within the circle of his arms, he forgot where they were and what they had to do, forgot everything but the pleasure of dancing with a woman as skilled as this. But someone shouted from the far warehouse, and Calad felt Delia pull a spell-thread.

He dropped Atalanta's hands and sprinted off, away from the alley where he'd parked. Behind him, he heard Atalanta jump onto the bike and kick it into life. Another alley opened ahead, twisting its lengthy way towards the hangars sixty miles away. He ducked, still running, as a spell tingled on the air. Smelt of Electrokinesis. A crackle, and he dodged. Delia – but she wasn't good with pure attack magic: the bolt flashed past Calad and into a wall.

Atalanta had dropped her scatter-shields: her magic snaked in the air, tangy and tantalising. Calad hit the corner and risked a glance backwards. She'd doubled back and was riding at Delia, a lightning bolt of her own held captive in her hand, like a charging knight. Guild magic's after-scent wasn't too bad, when a man had time to get used to it. Different, like spiced meat was different, but not unpleasant.

She swung out of her saddle and thrust her spell at Delia, who flung herself prostrate on the floor. The spell missed her by inches.

"Marius!" Delia called. She fiddled with the ring-key on

her hand. Atalanta must have seen the movement too, for she hit reverse and arced away, bait waiting to be taken.

Calad turned and ran deeper into the warehousing. Behind him he heard Delia's bike swoop in and away, following Atalanta. If either of them survived, Calad hoped it was Atalanta, though his opinion of Delia had risen slightly in the past few hours.

Someone was following him: chasing on foot – and his leg wouldn't stand running for more than a couple of miles. Granted, he didn't *want* to run two miles, he wanted to be right here: but how in hells' names was he meant to lose his pursuer in this condition? The Ogre had been on the ground for six minutes now. He had to be in position by the time its occupants drove over: he'd no time for this.

Left, then left again. Now he was running back towards Hardblade's warehouse. He half-closed his eyes, blotting out mud beneath his boots, graffiti-stained walls and cracked, barred windows to each side, and drew a Revelation thread.

The alleyway faded to grey, and the greyness began to glitter. Around Calad rose 3D images of the streets, truth beneath lies: cracked bricks beneath neat plasterwork, weak locks inside impressive iron surrounds. He could see for miles, all the tiny details, all the people moving around inside. And down the side of Hardblade's warehouse, one broken window.

Calad dismissed his spell and ran faster. So close, so damnably close. He skidded round another corner. There was the window: small and forgotten. His.

"Stop!"

Too high. Jump for it? Instead Calad grabbed a discarded crate and dumped it under the window.

An invisible hand yanked at his right foot, pinning it to the floor. He tried to turn, failed, and twisted round with his upper body instead. Marius, panting hard, was leaning against the warehouse at the corner. He looked sick. Calad smiled. "You've spent too long off the Neuvième. You're out of condition."

"I want," Marius said, waving an unsteady finger, "two words from you before I break your neck."

Calad gave up dragging on his ankle and levered a spell-thread under his foot. The only snag was that he couldn't use the Defence thread half as well as Marius. He should have known it was a defender on his tail when no gunshots flew at him – and Marius had no combat magic. "Try these two. I'm innocent."

Marius spat. "You're a bloody murderer."

"No murderer – and no traitor either, unlike others present." Break the spell? With what? Enough concentrated waves of magic might be able to erode it. He called into the other world, to the Telekinesis thread.

"Traitor?" Marius laughed. It sounded like a grave-wail. "Harlek and Rebekah are *dead*, Calad, *dead* – you killed them!"

Calad dropped the thread. Its trailing end clapped the side of his head, and he saw stars. Dead? The generator *killed*?

"Delia's doing," he choked. Not even he believed that anymore: why should Marius? "She shouldn't have brought them." That was true, at least. "She's a traitor, Marius, a traitor to our people!"

"'Our'?" He advanced on Calad with one finger raised, still breathing hard. No combat magic, poor cardiovascular fitness, but a hefty personal best in classical weightlifting. "Call yourself a pureblood? You're a *half-breed*, a relic from an age we outgrew long ago. You are not one of us!"

"Half." Half Treizième. Half Neuvième. Half effete, half superman. "And all of me Circle. She's betraying the *Circle*, Marius!"

Marius's eyes widened. The grip on Calad's ankle vanished.

Calad shoved the little window wide and launched through it head first. Broken glass grazed his shoulders, but he landed, rolling, on a bare concrete floor in a back corridor, just missing a couple of corpses. Outside he heard Marius step onto the crate, and heard it give way under his weight. He was too big to fit through that window anyway.

The buckled door down the corridor was heavily chained: no way in for Marius there, but surely he'd just walk round. That would take him two minutes at most – which was two minutes more than Calad might have had. He closed his eyes and clutched the Revelation strands he'd used earlier. Back and into the Ransomvale Ogre's hangar, pinpointing it. That'd do. He withdrew the Revelation weft from his warp frame, and called to Pyrokinesis.

Not enough to burn the ship. He didn't want to burn the ship. But from what he'd seen of Septième spaceport hangars, they always harboured a little junk, and some of it was always flammable.

Many miles away he felt a couple of paint cans explode. Outside, he heard the spaceport and warehousing's linked fire alarm go off. He clambered to his feet and headed off, away from the barricaded door.

If he used too much more magic he'd attract attention. Instead he moved quietly, listening to every sound that penetrated the alarm's wail: clanks, engine noises, words spoken too far away for comprehension. All the time, he calculated, or recalculated. *Get Logan and Connor* became *Find Logan and Connor*. *Tell them about the Ogre* became *Move them into position before anyone else can get here*. *Avoid Delia* became *Hope Atalanta deals with Delia*. And Ella? He'd never told her what to do, at least not in circumstances where he needed her to listen.

A scuffling noise in the next corridor alerted him half a second too late, and a white hand clamped round his wrist and yanked him to one side. "Where the *devil* were you?" Ella hissed in a furious undertone. "We were worried sick!"

He stared at her too-pale face, her wild hair, the red marks on her face and arms. Only Logan could hurt her – and that meant: "You did this," he breathed, speaking as quietly as she had, but in Dixième Catalan instead of French. "You – why? You've wrecked my plan – I needed their help – where are they?"

He made to push past her. She caught his arm again, less fiercely this time, and to more purpose. "Don't worry." Her accent was strong: she'd always been bad at languages. "I've made arrangements for that. The guns will be there. You – do whatever you must." She stared at him for another few seconds, then pulled him into her arms. She was shaking. He squeezed her tight and breathed in the scent of her hair: perfume, sweat and blood.

"Why did you do it?" he whispered again.

"You were too slow. There's a ship in from Ransomvale –
an Ogre –"

"I know."

"I had to get that in place too."

He would have asked her more, but a noise behind her
stopped him. Instead, he just kissed her. She wriggled out of
his arms and gave him a little push down the next corridor.
"Get into position."

*

CHAPTER TWENTY-TWO

In the fifteen minutes since they'd been locked up in the secure store, Logan had visualised how best to kill Ellie exactly forty-four times. Closing on forty-five, now. Stupid woman, making him immune to her magic. Didn't matter how many times – he'd strangle her, make sure he *hurt* her before she died, if only so she learnt, in the seconds she had left, just how badly she'd hurt him.

He'd been so close. The life she'd made him want, the escape he'd come to crave: it could have been his, theirs, inside a day. Instead, the emptiness stank like rotten eggs.

Someone nudged him with one toe: Pritie, he realised, looking up. "What?"

"Stop mumbling. It's not helping."

"I'm not mumbling."

"You were," Thakar said without looking up from the door's lock. "It's driving me up the spout. Connor, your turn."

Connor stopped pacing around for long enough to gesture Marcello to try the lock instead. Not that it was likely to work: Hardblade had always bought good locksmiths.

Logan clenched his fists, feeling fingernails score his skin. If he had a guitar now he'd hold off braining Ellie with it for long enough to make the world hear what she'd done. There were times when a woman called a man to her and he would go, no matter how deadly her trap, snared by her siren song till she chose to drop him. If he'd been unable to resist her before – she'd given him the weapons to do so now. And he was good at using weapons.

It was none of Ellie's doing that they weren't all dead with Kylesdottir. Blood spoke for blood – well, there'd be a fountain running through this 'port before he was done. He was sick of playing nice.

Zack was lying flat on his back in one corner, staring at the ceiling, ignoring the others as much as he did the alarm going off outside. Connor paused his pacing in front of him. "Tell me you're listening for what's going on."

"Nope."

"Only damned excuse I can think of for you to be sitting around."

"I'm thinking, *Mister*." Zack glanced at Thakar. "What happened to your shadow?"

"Hid," Thakar said, "and not without cause."

"I wonder *where*. But, no matter." Zack touched the skin under his left ear. "Great things, neural jacks. I downloaded a whole encyclopaedia to mine a while back. Never get stuck with nothing to read."

One of Connor's eyebrows went up. "You found the lock's schematics?"

"Nope." He smiled at the ceiling as if to an old friend. "I'm reading Neuvième etiquette manuals."

"What the *fuck*?" Connor leant over him, fists clenched at his sides. For the first time in hours he looked like he was cracking. Too soon. Wait, *wait*, till there was someone here who needed hurting a damned sight more than Zack needed it. "I know how screwed we are without you bloody looking it up!"

"Don't think you do." Zack locked his hands under his head. "'Cause it doesn't matter how many times I read it, it stays the same. Weavers don't lie, Connor. Even to their targets, Neuvième Weavers *never* lie."

The lock creaked.

"Not me," Marcello said, backing away with both hands raised.

Thakar clapped his shoulder. "Never pass up on credit you could have taken."

Keep quiet.

Logan rolled to his feet in one move, staring at walls, ceiling, door. That hadn't been a voice in his ears, or even in his skull: it was a voice that ran all the way through him, head to heels, inescapable.

From the others' constipated expressions, they'd heard it too. Maybe not Galene. She was still sitting down near the door, staring at her boots, as she had since they'd been locked in here.

The guard is talking at the far corner. She thinks that what she can see is the door. Into Logan's mind, following the words, images danced: the familiar corridor, the strange Weaver woman twenty feet away. *Absolute silence. I don't want to have to kill her.*

The disembodied voice could want what it wished, but Logan was still armed, albeit with his own two hands: and he padded to the door, silent as death. Blood-rage rose in him again, till the world tinged red instead of green. The door swung open, quiet on well-oiled hinges, into a corridor scattered with broken bits of light fitting: Logan slid through and started right, towards the unsuspecting guard. Not absolutely silent, he was too angry for that, but with the alarm still roaring through the warehouses, it didn't matter as much as it should have done.

Invisible hands grabbed his collar and yanked him in the opposite direction. He bit his lip, stifling a cry. Blood, salty and warm, trickled into his mouth.

Better now? The voice again, this time more acid, and more like it was speaking down his ear. *When you've finished your idiocies, do join us. I promise you'll have your fill of slaughter – but in my good time, not yours.*

Logan rubbed at his collar. The barbell weighing him down vanished. Behind him, Marcello and Thakar were tiptoeing to the far corner and into the corridor that led towards the stock controller's office. He followed.

Zack, Galene and Pritie were already there. As Logan counted heads, Connor came up to his shoulder – just like him to be last out – and whispered to a patch of thin air, "What took so long?"

"I hitched in on an Ogre. Their hangars are at the far end of the 'port."

Neuvième accent: male voice. Out of the gloom, a man's figure swam into view – a man Connor's size, and maybe Connor's age. Blond hair bobbed in a tie at the nape of his neck. "I have some of your weapons. The rest are in the office." His eyes, glinting in the gloom, were on Logan, and he wasn't smiling.

No, and maybe he knew Logan without asking who he was, as Logan was damned certain he knew him. Like enough to Ellie – far more so than Calad, but Calad was only her half-brother – Michel Falavière.

"You knew what you were doing when you took up with Éloise." His voice was as hard as his face. "You knew she was a straight-laced little prig. When she has a job to do, she'll never let you stop her doing it any more than she would anyone else: the rules don't break, no matter who you are."

"But they bend." Connor shouldered past Logan, smiling broadly. "Nowhere in the rules did it say she couldn't send you to let us out immediately after having us locked up. But I suspect there's a bit more to this."

An answering smile flitted across Michel's lips. "As ever. But we need your gun arms. Do we have them?"

Words caught in Logan's throat. Fiery rage at Ellie, fanned rather than smothered by her brother's intervention: the old anger, street-anger, at anything that threatened to stop him living his life as he saw fit: fury at whoever'd conspired to create the antimagic generator, the men and women who'd ultimately set Ellie against him: impotent smouldering at Michel, who thought he'd the right to buy their services with their freedom. He'd a natural dose of curiosity about whatever these thrice-damned siblings were doing. But he was hardly likely to work out who he hated worst right now till he'd killed a few people, or a few dozen. Anything to clear that pulsing mist from the corners of his eyes.

"Give me a gun," he said in a voice that sounded thick even to him, "and let me aim."

Michel looked him up and down. "I won't allow you to hurt my sister."

"She's fucking gunshot-proof. Give." Without changing expression, Michel handed one over. Not a rifle, not anything he could use to tear into a man, just one of his handguns, but it'd do for now. He started past Michel, who caught his wrist. Logan kept walking.

"Wait." Logan ignored him. "*Wait.*" The grip tightened, vice-hard. He felt the tug on his collar again, but now also on his neck and legs. Outside, the fire alarm cut out. Michel's disembodied voice trickled back into his head: *You can knock down a few walls later. Hold it together for just a few minutes.* A warm hand gripped his shoulder, and he stared down into Michel's eyes – unafraid, and he wondered how often men were utterly unafraid of him. *Hate me if you want,* the voice bored into his skull. *Just do as I ask. Stay calm and quiet.* Michel looked back at the others, and Logan realised they could now all hear him. *We get into position.* Connor nodded before Logan could start to argue, and he and Michel led the others into the dark.

*

CHAPTER TWENTY-THREE

Connor followed Michel's ghost-pale figure through the warehouse corridors, listening, hoping. Still no sounds of pursuit behind them, though that wouldn't last. For now, he could hear a few mutterings and creakings up ahead, Logan's heavy breathing at his shoulder, faint patterings from Galene as she split off to climb to the rafters, fainter patterings from rats, a few vehicles outside.

He squeezed his pistol in his right hand. Still steady. How in hells he'd stayed this calm he didn't know. He hadn't scripted Éloise's betrayal, nor Logan's utter blindness, and nor, though it shamed him, Hendrix's competence. Circle Weavers never lied? No, but they hid the truth, dissembled, and simply didn't talk about things they didn't want to discuss. Connor's eyes drifted back to Michel. He was another puzzle: tucked beside them in back corridors – Hardblade's still – communicating like a merc would, with hand gestures and exaggerated facial expressions, as if his mind-reading powers were nothing.

No explanation, either, which grated, but in one respect it made life easier. If he didn't know what Michel and Éloise had plotted between them, he wouldn't need to feel guilty for spoiling it. Logan had been right about one thing at least: their first priority had to be getting those pallets into Sanctis Merovir's hands, no matter what the Falavières had planned. It was by far their best shot at survival.

The question was how best to do it, given that none of the Weavers – the Falavières or Hendrix's loyalists – seemed like they wanted to leave the warehouse. Start a fight, and hope they all killed each other? He couldn't exactly sneak out umpteen pallets of weed and powder without them noticing. The other option would be to slip off and sign the delivery docket while they were all still here, turning the extraction into Merovir's problem, but 'hostile Spellweavers are sitting on your goods' was likely to qualify as a material misstatement.

Ahead, the corridor ended at the back door of the stock controller's office. Michel stopped, stepped back and gestured for the others to go first – with his blond hair and pale skin, he was as good as a flag of surrender. Connor peered through the door's glass panel. Nobody inside, and the light was off: he clicked open the door and crept in.

Their remaining weapons, including Connor's assault rifle and Logan's assortment of grenades, were scattered on the desk. Connor holstered his pistol, rescued his rifle and, when Logan didn't make a move towards them, clipped a couple of the smoke bombs to his belt. The door to the main floor, beyond the desk and window, opened outwards. Connor ducked below window level, crawled to the door and eased down its handle. Not locked. He beckoned, and Thakar crawled past him to the far side of the doorway. Connor squeezed the handle again, this time opening the door.

Weed's faint woody smell seeped through the crack. Connor leant on the doorframe, seeing green glints in the shadows. Same smell as Sl'arani's warehouse: same conditions, near enough, in that he hadn't got enough guns and hadn't had enough sleep and had no clear comprehension of what he was doing.

Crack, click. Mutter. Connor withdrew into the office, eased to his feet beside the desk and peered through the window. He needn't have worried about crawling: full pallets blocked his view of the packing area. Just visible was the crown of a man's head, with nut-dark hair dancing as he worked. Alone? Looked like it. Connor crouched back down, pushed the door a few inches wider, and crept out sideways, keeping a pallet between him and the half-seen figure.

Silence, Michel had said. Connor drew up with his back to the pallet. Michel came up next to him, and Thakar led Pritie and Marcello off round the pallet's far side: where the fuck was Logan? Sulking in the office? Not late. Not *yet*.

Another crack, now definitely identifiable as splitting plastic. Half a curse, swallowed into a growl. Connor let his eyes drift up to the roof space overhead and to the right, looking for Galene, looking for the last piece of the pattern. Everything that had happened so far with the shipment came down to this. *Everything.*

"Looking for something?"

Connor froze. Beside him, Michel jerked and twisted round, staring up into the roof space on the far right of the warehouse. Connor turned round just in time to see Calad swing his legs off the topmost loading bay and drop down to the middle level.

His stomach fluttered. *Calad.* He looked more than two days older: different clothes, same pistol on his hip. Transcendent pity snaked across his face. That was new.

Connor hefted his rifle, tiptoed leftwards to the edge of the pallet furthest from Calad, and peered round. Myles Hendrix was standing alone in the middle of the packing area, the wreckage of six of Sl'arani's pallets scattered around him, every slat and box among them splintered, half the burlap packages mangled. Telempath or no, aware or unaware of armed enemies around him, he was staring up at Calad like he'd seen death transfigured.

Connor glanced back at the office. Zack was still in the doorway. Marcello, Thakar and Pritie were out of sight already. Still no Logan. Galene hadn't reached the roof space yet, as far as he could tell, and surely Éloise had figured somewhere in the setup. "We're early," he breathed, turning back towards Hendrix. Calad – he'd set the confrontation off early.

Hendrix made a move towards a weapon Connor couldn't see. "Uh-uh," Calad said, shaking his head. He raised his left hand. The antimagic generator glinted on his index finger. "I've used this before. You've more cause to fear it than I have." Hendrix's shoulders relaxed, and he spread out his hands away from his body.

The rear door banged open and two of Hendrix's Weaver squad dashed into the warehouse from the rear corridor. "They've escaped –" the young woman called, but she stopped, staring at Calad.

"Stand down, Jeanne," he called to her. "It's over. It's over, Myles," he said, harsher, to Hendrix. "You could only ever twist it so far."

The warehouse's pedestrian door creaked, and a third Weaver staggered in – the large man. The last of Hendrix's crew, aside from Éloise. "Stop!" the newcomer shouted, waving a hand at Calad. "He's got –"

"– the generator. They know. Especially Myles. Don't you?" Calad gestured to the wreckage around Hendrix's feet. "The blueprints aren't there, Myles. Connor Cardwain destroyed them when he hijacked the shipment three days ago. The *only* blueprints – as your buyer insisted." He held up his left hand again, generator still wrapped round its index finger. His right hand, Connor noted in increasing stupefaction, was close enough to his left for him to turn on the generator with minimal notice. "This is the only copy there is – unless the technician ignored your orders and made another generator, or kept a set of blueprints. Is he, or she, dead already? You were off the grid a few days before we started this. Sure, you might have been on assignment, but I doubt it." He shrugged. "And now you've killed Sl'arani too, and if he kept a blueprint set, I imagine he'll have locked it down so tightly that whoever succeeds him will abandon any attempt to crack into it. You win – or you will, as soon as the one solitary copy in the galaxy enters your possession."

No one spoke. The Weavers seemed too stunned to move. Connor tightened his grip on his gun. *Stay calm*, Michel had said. When a man stayed calm, he avoided alerting Weavers to his presence. He remembered Éloise, so adamant that only the worst kind of Circle Weaver would involve herself – or himself – in this kind of business. So naïve.

"And Delia," Calad pursued, leaning on the loading bay's rail, right hand playing over the antimagic ring. "Did you bring her in from the start? Or did she realise what you were doing, and decide to take a cut instead of turning you in? She's dead, I think," he added when Hendrix looked set to speak. "She drove off after a friend of mine, and as my friend's threads are still active, I assume she was the one who survived their encounter. I was angry with Delia at first, you know." He studied his left hand. "Not for attacking me, but for bringing the others into it. Otherwise it would have been just her life wasted: and yours, Myles. But Marius tells me Harlek died, and Rebekah." He sent a sad smile towards the massive Weaver man. "So. They're dead, Marius will never be hired again, Jeanne and Derrick are going to have an uncomfortable few years –" he indicated the man and woman who'd entered first – "and for what? What, Myles, made you *consider* it? I'm curious. And," he said, waving his left hand, "don't try to cloud our minds, or fob me off with nonsense about the Guild. You owe me the truth."

Hendrix rocked back on his heels. His hands gently rested on Connor's precious bales of weed. "Mentioning the Guild wouldn't be 'fobbing you off', Calad. The war never ended. It never will."

"And it has *nothing to do with this*."

"I'm curious how you can be so certain – but OK, OK." He jerked his head towards the spaceport. "The Guild isn't the only threat to the independent Circle worlds. I would include your sister's drug-running boyfriend in that –" Connor snorted under his breath – "but the serious issues lie further clockwise.

"The Circle Neuvième's surrounded by enemies far more insidious than the Federation and the Guild. Cinquième literalists, living under our protection, but murdering our people as witches and devils. Vingtième isolationists who paint us in the colours of our worst fanatics. Your mother's people – has Terra Nova ever forgiven Port Logis for the way it left the Union?" He laughed, a ghost of humour. "I've run an extermination squad: I've seen the hate in their eyes when we remind them what we are. They don't *want* a conscience: they want to be left alone to despoil the galaxy as they see fit." He spread his arms out wide. "We call them desecrators – isn't that what we are to them? We kill tens of thousands of their people at a time – and it makes them *angry*, not because of the deaths, but because they believe they deserve better.

"And I'll remind you that I'm speaking of *our closest ally*. The government that employs millions of our people, and allows them ethical dispensations that no other empire would ever consider, and stands by us against the Guild and the Federation. *They hate us*, Calad. They tolerate us only because there is no way to get rid of us. We need a foolproof way of protecting ourselves against the chance that they use Treizième-born Circle Weavers against us – people like your mother's family."

Calad didn't answer. He'd left too long a pause, Connor realised: long enough to make the others wonder if Hendrix might just have their people's interests, and their personal interests, at heart. Long enough to angle them back to his side. And Calad had antimagic, but unless he'd met up with Éloise already, he wasn't gunshot-proof.

Without conscious volition Connor slid his rifle onto his back and tiptoed one pallet away from Michel. He hadn't time to go further. "There was the other girl," he said, emerging into the pool of light in the packing area, six feet from Hendrix. Five heads fringed with coloured wings turned towards him. He raised his hands to show they were empty. "A Weaver woman, younger than me, guarding Sl'arani's warehouse. He didn't hire her. He told me so, before he died, but I knew as soon as I saw her that she didn't fit. She never fitted, in any way, unless you hired her, and told her to do what one of your people could never be known to have done: protect a drug runner." He allowed himself a sour smile. "Tell me, Hendrix, was it blackmail? Had she bitten your dick while she was sucking it?" For half a second he spied genuine hatred in Hendrix's eyes – and overhead he heard the tiny giveaway click of Galene loosening her safety catch in the roof space. "She's dead too, or I wouldn't be here talking to you. Rest assured she didn't live long enough to incriminate you. What was her name?"

Hendrix didn't speak. The woman Jeanne said, "Frizzy hair, electrokinetic, Circle tattoo on her forearm?"

"Yep."

"Her name was Melody."

"My condolences to her family." Connor inclined his head at Hendrix. "He hasn't done much work on the underside scene: I could tell that as soon as I met him. But any Weaver would know the risks of placing your pal Melody in a place where she was likely to get high. He'd know something always catches fire in those situations, and if she did get high, she wouldn't be able to inform on him later. I know it's illegal for your people to take drugs."

"He's a policeman," the big man, Marius, said. "He could have given her an indemnity form, in case she accidentally took anything in the course of business. Shall we go check his records?" His tone of voice indicated he didn't expect to find anything.

"All of you," Hendrix said, "need to stop overreacting and re-arrest that man." He pointed at Connor. No one moved. Connor bit his lip against a smile.

Behind Hendrix, to Calad's right, the warehouse's loading door creaked open. "Myles, what is going on?" a bored voice said from the doorway. Connor looked. A middle-aged man, dressed in Treizième clothes, or over-dressed in them: Knee-length pleated tunic over trousers rather than the straight-seamed, thigh-length version the Neuvième Weavers wore; long velvet-and-leather coat; elaborately ornamented holster at his hip. Connor looked him up and down, and felt his lip curl. He hadn't realised how similar the Neuvième folk were to Septième folk, physically: just looked at the differences – the extra height, the varying muscle, the wider range of skin tones from very fair to very dark. This newcomer wasn't fat, but he looked soft, with his pasty praline skin and slim hands. Hendrix's big man, Marius, was plump at the waist as much as he was muscled at the pectorals, but that just looked like it would enable him to knock a man down all the easier. Short hair on the newcomer, too. Connor couldn't remember when he'd seen short hair on a man in his middle life, barring accidents.

Hendrix closed his eyes for half a second too long. "Dariel. It will take me slightly longer than anticipated to produce the blueprints."

"Well, where's the prototype? My man needs the prototype."

Connor'd already half-lowered his hands: now he dropped them all the way. Behind 'Dariel', a little line of mercs trailed into the warehouse, and then another little line. It added up to a little *lot*. Foreign, again, by their dress, but with a familiar air of professional propensity to violence – and every one bore a familiar logo on his sleeve, Lionstooth's roaring cat.

Knuckles rapped on a wooden door. Connor glanced around. There wasn't a wooden door closer than the office's, twenty feet away. *It's me*, Michel's voice seeped back into his head. Connor visualised the Weaver knocking on a replica of his, Connor's, head made from wood. *Very funny. Dariel and three of the mercs are Weavers. Circle, but not Neuvième: they're Treizième. In theory they're bound by our rules. In practice, they'll pursue their own interests.* Connor bit his lip. Michel and Éloise – where in hells was she? – had probably counted on getting all the other Weavers on their side. *Where did you get that idea?* Michel didn't-say. *If Dariel wasn't going to join in with our idea of ethics, neither would his team. I familiarised myself with their abilities earlier. The odds are good, for everyone except you. You shouldn't have broken cover.* Connor rolled his eyes. As no one had bothered to warn him at the time, he'd have to live with it. And how had Michel known exactly what they were facing? *Because I flew in with them. Be quiet, now. I have to concentrate.* Connor blinked. That sounded like a cooler head than he'd met on the underside: hitching a ride with one's target…

"The prototype?" Hendrix said with a faint smile on his face. "He has it." He gestured up at Calad.

Dariel took half a step forward and peered up at Calad, on the gallery. Connor inched backwards. He couldn't afford to look for Galene. Michel must be able to work out how many of these mercs, if any, were shielded: at least they all knew Hendrix had shields. *Tell the others*, he thought as loudly as he could, but if Michel were still reading Connor's mind, he didn't give any sign that he'd taken the hint.

"Ah. Calad Falavière," Dariel said in a vague voice. "Gisele's son. I've met your grandfather several times. Pass it down, lad."

Calad stared down at him, still with that otherworldly look, as if he'd flown in from not another sector but another universe. "Myles," he said, "when you mentioned the Union and the Circle earlier – which side did you say you were on?"

"You've heard of the balance of terror. I employ you," Hendrix said, voice raised. He lifted a finger and wagged it at his other three Weavers. "I employ all of you. That generator has been bought and paid for. Calad, hand it over."

For a long moment no one moved. Calad's face was frozen, a masculine angel with no ability to condemn. Where in hells was Logan? And Éloise? They couldn't be fighting. They couldn't be fucking. Connor glanced towards the pallet where he'd last seen Michel hiding. No movement. He'd freed them so they could use their guns, hadn't he? Biting back a grimace, he let his hand brush his pistol's holster. Someone had to take a stand here, and he could only hope he wouldn't get killed doing it.

Calad pulled the antimagic generator from his finger. "Fine." He dropped it onto the warehouse floor ten feet beneath his feet. Hendrix started towards it.

A shot cracked out from the roof space, snaked over Hendrix's head and struck the generator square on.

For a few seconds all was silence: just the smell of Hendrix's singed hair, the stinging residue from Galene's sniper rifle, the gleam from the little puddle of molten metal on the floor. Dariel stared at the ruin of his employer's project, mouth slightly open, faint double chin beginning to wobble. Connor smothered an hysterical laugh. Thakar had wanted them to put a gun to it, hadn't he?

Dariel took a few paces forward. His watery eyes rose from the generator's detritus to Calad. "You." He lifted a hand and pointed at the boy Weaver. "You will pay." His shaking hand steadied, and the incredulity melted from his face, replaced by a look of vicious hatred. A petty man, who expected the world to conform to his wishes because it had always conformed to his wishes, who'd lived near wealth and power for so long that he believed that it could direct the world to its will no matter what stood in the way. And the petty man opened his fist, and flames arced out of his palm.

Connor backpedalled, looking for cover. Six of Dariel's gunmen knelt and another six took aim from behind them, half at Calad, half at Galene. Calad ducked back into cover on the high loading bay: Connor saw a couple of answering gunshots bark down from his approximate position.

More gunfire rippled from the far right. Zack and Pritie. One of Dariel's mercs fell, twitching. Connor pulled a smoke bomb from his belt, flung it at the crowd of mercs and, firing backwards into the fog, ran down the gap between two pallets. A shot hit a bale close to his head, and the stench of burning weed plumed up behind him. He covered his mouth and nose with his free hand, and skidded back behind the last row. Michel was where he'd left him, but was slumped on the ground with both hands on his head, shimmering like a glow-worm. No help *there*, at least not that he could see or touch.

Connor inhaled, tasting weed. Dariel and Hendrix, out there in the warehouse. Mercs stopped fighting when their paymasters died. *Take out the Weavers, and the rest will flee.*

Smoke flared beside him, higher than before. Connor froze. The closest pallet's plastic packaging crinkled, crumpled and burst into flame. He fell back, hand over his mouth again, and stumbled into Michel. The Weaver didn't react – too busy with whatever spell he was putting together. Connor pushed him to a prone position, tucked hands under his arms and dragged him across the floor, away from the fire.

Overhead the warehouse's fire alarm started blaring, and the sprinklers went off. Connor snorted as freezing water cascaded down his back. Crackles, in the air, smelt like Melody's spells had smelt, half a week and half a lifetime ago. He gritted his teeth. Fuck all magic.

Panting, dripping, he dragged Michel into another pallet's cover. "Why the fuck didn't you hide in the office?" he muttered. No response. Connor drew his pistol and peered round the corner.

Gunfire still clattered towards Galene's last position, and, across the far side of the warehouse, towards Calad up high and Pritie and Zack on the ground. Spells sizzled on the air, sporadic-seeming, a constant battle between offensive and defensive magics that only became visible in the few seconds where offence won out.

Defence. Galene, with a rain of gunfire falling on her, to no effect. No fresh yellow magic snaking in front of her – that meant she was wearing old shields. Sure, Éloise had shielded Logan out of affection, but *Galene*?

Galene, so silent earlier. She'd known what Éloise was going to do, and that could only have been because Éloise had warned her – her, no one else.

A click, and a tick. Connor jerked. Beside him, a tiny

grenade rolled across the floor, flashing. No sandbags. He tipped half a pallet of weed onto the thing, and backed away, tugging at Michel's arm.

Michel jerked awake, stared from side to side and raised one hand. Electricity arced from it into the weed pile. The grenade's ticking stopped.

Connor gripped the remains of the pallet. "What the fuck were you doing?" His voice was hoarse: too much smoke.

"Fighting Myles. He was trying to break your minds." Michel rolled to his knees and stopped, grimacing in pain. Connor bent and eased him to his feet. An overtone of raw desire hit him, as it had the one time he'd touched Calad, but this time he expected it, and fought it. They'd more important issues at hand.

"Where is Hendrix?"

"Looking for me." Michel's hand scrabbled for his neural jack. "I took his brain-print. Closest we'll get to a confession. Is the warehouse's uplink working yet? I need to copy this as soon as possible."

"I'll check." As soon as word of Sl'arani's death filtered to the main city, the relays would come online: a Septième requiem of inconsequence. Maybe word had got back already. He reached for his jack.

The warehouse lights flashed green. Connor shoved Michel to the floor as a gunshot went through the place where they had been standing. He rolled, and came up on one knee firing: but his gunshots ricocheted to each side, and he lowered his rifle and scrabbled backwards, looking for cover, any cover.

Stop that.

It was like a string pulling inside his head. He backed into the space between two pallets, hands fixed too far from his guns, staring at Hendrix, ten feet away down the row, and Michel, down on one knee with a nimbus of pale blue light playing around him. Pale pink light surrounded that, prying at its edges – the same colour as the wings sprouting up out of Hendrix's shoulders.

Connor swallowed, tasting vomit. That touch on his mind – more than Michel's businesslike communication, it seeped into him, controlling him, and he wondered if it had the option of convincing him it wasn't really there, and whether it had left him his self-awareness only to taunt him.

Maybe Hendrix had miscalculated. He had a pistol out, but couldn't seem to lift it: he was dragging on his hand like it weighed several tons. Michel, too, was scrabbling at his holster like a drunkard. If Connor had been able to laugh, he would have done: this looked like a mud-wrestling bout where neither opponent could outmanoeuvre the other.

"I'm bored," Michel whispered, a grating rasp that rattled Connor's back teeth. Great blue-silver wings burst from his back, and he forced himself to his feet. Lightning glittered in his hands like twin swords, an echo of the poor doomed girl Hendrix had sent into Sl'arani's warehouse.

Hendrix's gun hand snapped up. Between him and Michel, the air shimmered yellow, and Hendrix's gunshot ricocheted into the closest pallet. "I can't hold him," Marius called from the background in a strangled voice. "That's all. It's all."

Hendrix nodded. "Where possible, employ people you can defeat." He took a pace forward and tapped on the see-through yellow wall. "There's a way round everything, though."

"There is." Michel brought his glittering hands together. His silvery spell snapped up in an arc and flared over the barricade.

Hendrix flung up both his hands to cover his head, and a pale blue shield sprang into life over them. He staggered as Michel's spell hit him, but did not fall: as he lowered his hands, his eyes shifted to Connor. "Kill him."

The words echoed into his skull, *kill him*, and Connor felt his hand fall to his pistol. Kill Michel? With no uploaded record of Hendrix's guilt, that would leave them all as good as dead.

He should be able to fight it. All the legends said he should be able to overpower Hendrix's compulsion with the force of his own will. But Connor was no legendary hero, no Aelin Carrow or Jack Ellenson. However much he willed it, his hand and the gun in it kept moving upwards.

The pistol barrel stalled. Connor thought he felt Michel holding his hand. The serio-comic battle the two Weavers had had earlier, telepath versus telempath, reared up all the sharper. Over him? "Over my dead body," he croaked. Fat chance. Hendrix wouldn't let him turn the gun on himself till Michel was dead, even if Michel would let him shoot himself.

A shot spat from the direction of the office. His pistol vanished in a spurt of fire. The shock sent him sprawling – his shock, Hendrix's – and he cried out at sudden pain in his fingers. Broken in the impact. The gunshot slid off Marius's shield and glanced off Connor's left thigh. He collapsed, swearing, trying not to sob.

Hendrix had dropped him. He looked, through streaming eyes, back down the row. Thakar was sliding his pistol back into its holster. "Sorry," he said, shrugging. "Only out I could see."

"You'll do instead," Hendrix said, deathly quiet. Thakar went cross-eyed, and his hand, moving like a marionette's, fell back to his gun.

"Michel, help," he called.

"I'm trying –"

A pebble flashed down from the roof space and struck Hendrix on the temple. He stumbled and swore. Thakar stumbled too, hand flying away from his gun. Connor, fingers and leg throbbing, looked upwards. A tiny serious face stared down at him, then withdrew into shadow. Connor choked on a laugh. Didn't matter if Joshua just saw Thakar as a meal ticket, as long as it didn't affect his aim.

Michel rose, standing protectively over Connor with wings splayed. "There won't be a third time," he said. Silver fire licked up his arms. "Give in."

Hendrix half-laughed. "I can make sure no one believes you –"

Éloise cannoned into Hendrix from behind, flinging him against the Defence barrier. He grunted, in shock or pain, but squirmed round and drove a fist at her. He hit empty air and, staggering, thrust out his leg in a roundhouse kick.

She twisted his leg in hers, dropping him face down on concrete. Again he rose and struck out at her, a boxer's reaction, but she moved the quicker, and if her blows had less weight behind them than his, none of his were connecting.

Hendrix must have realised, for he wrong-footed *himself*

and barrelled full into her. She landed hard beneath him, grunting as the air burst from her lungs. He aimed a heavy punch at her forehead. His fist sank into a thick yellow mist around her, and he screamed, rolling away, his hand lacerated. She jabbed an elbow sideways and caught him in the neck.

"You cheated us," she said, and she rolled to her knees and reared over him. "You *employed* us, and you *cheated* us. No man cheats me twice." Hendrix pawed at his neck, fighting for air. Éloise punched him in the face. He shuddered and went still.

Connor collapsed back against the closest pallet, shivering, from cold or shock. Marius's shield faded. Michel retracted his wings, dismissed his silvery attack spells and went to his sister. She was still kneeling over Hendrix, and did not look up, but she lifted a hand, and Michel clasped it between his.

Thakar walked past Connor, touching his shoulder as he did so, and peered at Hendrix. "Hey," Éloise said, half a warning, an echo of Logan.

"Just checking." He looked back at Connor. "I could have done with breaking Logan's fingers instead of yours: you can't shoot left handed."

"I can point a pistol and pull its trigger. I'll take Hendrix's." His voice sounded strangled even to himself. Michel moved towards him, but he levered himself upright on his own, shucked off the now-useless assault rifle and staggered to Hendrix – very dead: Éloise had driven part of his skull into his brain. On the second try he caught hold of the Weaver's pistol. His thigh was on fire and his right hand was a mass of pain. Better to be very little use than no use.

Éloise got to her feet. She'd picked up a few bruises where her shields had caved in, and she was shivering, with exertion more than shock. "Use me as a firing platform."

Overhead, rafters screamed. Connor looked up. Galene had released the maintenance ladder, but couldn't get onto it for incoming fire. One of the bolts locking ladder to roof beams was already missing, and it dangled like a fraying rope. Éloise put out one hand on the closest pallet to steady herself. Pale yellow light danced around her: wings, unformed. She looked like she was about to be sick.

"*Arrête*," Michel said softly to her, tucking a hand round her waist.

"*Elle mourra.*"

"*Pas du tout.*" He clenched both hands into fists. Lightning burst from the rafters and cracked down towards the gunmen. Their barrage stopped. Galene finally shimmied down the ladder to the ground and sprinted into cover.

Familiar footsteps ran up to them from behind: Pritie and Marcello, with Zack puffing in the rear. "Why'd you quit covering our backs?" Thakar said.

"They're moving," Pritie said. "We need to shift." Zack nodded, looking the Weavers up and down. Connor grimaced. Éloise was staggering: Michel wasn't in much better shape. That was what gave men a *chance* against Weavers: tiredness, overwork and error, and above all, hubris. Otherwise, no man would survive long without a friendly Weaver to cover him.

The basis of the Circle as a merc corps: but maybe that was why someone had dreamt up a hand weapon – literally – that could neutralise Weavers at will…

Galene jogged up to them from the far side of the row, where Hendrix had ripped apart the shipment in a futile hunt for schematics that weren't there. Behind her followed the other Weaver woman, Jeanne. Tears streaked her face, maybe tears of anger: her mouth was set in a hard line, and she looked about as composed as Logan on a good day. As she passed Connor, she lowered one hand and touched his left leg. The pain in his thigh numbed at once.

"Thank you –"

"It's not healed: that was just a painkiller. Get it seen to later. Your trousers melted onto your skin: what in hells were you doing wearing artificial fibre to a gunfight? Derrick's dead," she said to Éloise without breaking stride. "Fucking psi-healer burnt his mind."

Michel's wings crackled, behind them. "I always enjoy pushing a lightning bolt down a psi-healer's throat. One can do it over and over again and never get bored."

"This one's mine," Jeanne said.

"Less talk," said Galene. She'd retracted her gun to a dimension more suitable for ground use, and was sighting down the scope. "Keep going." Michel nodded, picked up Connor's rifle and moved out into the lead with Jeanne and Thakar at his heels.

Connor followed more slowly. His mangled right hand throbbed, and the pistol, a Neuvième model, sat awkwardly in his left. But Thakar just ahead of him and Galene and Marcello just behind reminded him this was about more than just survival. He had to focus, on the consequences, on the *important* things –

– on where the *fuck* was Logan?

Pritie, gun high, headed up to the front to join Thakar. With Marcello and Zack playing rearguard, Connor found himself squeezed between Galene and Éloise. "I don't know how much fun you two had cooking this up," he said softly, "but I don't appreciate being the boy in the corner." Two stares frosted over him. He couldn't raise the energy to care. "When I say I want an explanation, I mean I fucking want one. Not later, now."

Éloise gave him another glare, but when he didn't blink, settled for an aggrieved sniff. "I had to warn one of you. Galene was the only one who wouldn't panic or give me away."

"Did you shield her from *Logan*?"

"Physically, yes. Mentally, from Hendrix," Galene said. She looked sideways at Éloise. "If he'd read my mind, he would have known Éloise was on to him, and he'd have overridden anything she tried to do."

Connor exhaled. He didn't like it, and yet could find few flaws in Éloise's logic, other than in the suggestion that he would have panicked. "You could have trusted me."

"I didn't want to have to trust Logan!"

Ahead, Michel and Jeanne stepped over the stricken defender, Marius. Pritie bent to examine him. From Connor's position five feet away he looked sick as a cat, breathing shallowly, olive skin gone sallow. "He's well enough," Jeanne hissed over her shoulder. Marius winced but did not contradict his compatriot.

Sporadic gunfire still spat just beyond the next pallet, a battle without a target. Someone trying to smoke out Calad? Michel, breathing carefully, stopped at the corner. *Eight mercs left*, his voice seeped back into Connor's mind, *plus the psi-healer, plus Dariel.* Connor frowned. Michel's mind-voice sounded like it was coming through a speaker with a malfunctioning volume control. Tired. They were all tired, and hurt, and too reliant on Defence magic for their survival.

Eight enemy gunhands, two enemy spellhands. They'd six gunhands and three spellhands, excluding Marius and Calad – for even if he could count Logan, he couldn't count himself. The odds were improving, but not quickly enough.

Éloise moved away from Connor, up to her brother, and covered his hand with hers. He kissed her forehead, and she nodded to him, gestured for the others to stay where they were, and walked round the corner. "Dariel," she called. "It's no use."

"Any defender has a weak point." That entitled voice, such a feeble type of man: but any man could be dangerous, and every Weaver was a killer. "All one has to do is fire enough shots." A gun went off, startlingly close. "The laws of physics," Dariel said in a chilly tone, "are immutable –"

His voice cut out in a squeal. Michel ran the last few steps to the corner. Connor caught him up just in time to see Éloise drop to one knee and slam both fists into the concrete floor. A yellow glittering curtain flared up in front of her, cutting the warehouse in two – and a dark shadow dropped from the highest loading bay straight into the closest knot of mercs.

Connor clutched Michel's shoulder. Behind him, he heard Marcello gasp. He couldn't look back: couldn't look away.

Pistol in one hand, knife in the other, golden magic wrapped round the knife, Calad was cutting into Dariel's remaining gunhands – seasoned pros, or Connor'd never met a merc – like they were defenceless children. Two lay dead already – killed on Calad's way down – and as Connor watched, he fired left at a third, slashed a fourth across the throat and barrelled into a fifth, taking her to the ground, just out of the blood-arc coming from his previous victim's throat. Éloise's shield mutated, as if an invisible monster were rising out of the floor, clothed in Defence magic: its limbs slashed down at the woman, and she lay still, head half-severed.

The man at the back hesitated for a fraction of a second, glancing at his boss. Calad rolled to his feet, knees bent, and fired at Éloise's shield. The shot ricocheted and took the merc through the head. A solid shield-tendril lashed round the seventh merc's throat and bore him to the ground, throttling him. The final merc dodged behind her Weaver buddy. "Wait," the purple-winged Weaver called.

"Why?" The golden fire around Calad's knife flared up and arced at the other Weaver, who flung up a purple-blue shield. Behind him, the last merc cried out and collapsed, clutching her head.

Fascinated, horrified, Connor tore his eyes from Calad and looked past him. He could hear that steady undercurrent of swearing from twenty feet away, hot raw fury, and as Dariel came floundering back into view thrusting punches and spells at a mobile shadow, Connor whispered into the silence inside his skull, *Éloise drew this weapon deliberately.*

The sprinklers went off again, over Dariel's head. Steam spurted off him. Out of the cloud, Logan rose like a dragon, a bent knife in his left hand and murder in his eyes. As Connor watched in something close to horror, Logan drove the knife into Dariel's abdomen. It crumpled on a shield.

He laughed, high and hysterical. "You can't kill me." He backed away towards the door. "You and the rest of this stinking slum. No more chances." He reached for the ring-key on his left hand.

Logan saw the move too, for he launched himself full-body at Dariel, bowling him to the ground. Heavy hands flew to Dariel's neck and tried to squeeze. Even from a dozen yards away Connor saw his brother's hands scrabbling inside a thick foam of magic, unable to catch hold.

Éloise was still on her knees: she half-reached for Logan, but doubled over, panting. Michel and Jeanne paid no attention, for they were locked in a frantic discussion in French. Connor understood a fraction of the words and none of the sentences.

He stared at Calad, now sparring physically with Dariel's psi-healer. Punches, kicks, the occasional tiny shaft of magic. Too tired? Too evenly matched in their magical skills? Too eager to toy with each other?

Jeanne broke away from Michel, bent over Éloise and shook her shoulder hard. "Drop the shield. I need to get out."

"*Je peux pas.*"

She swore, and looked up at Thakar. "Where's the back way out? We have to get round."

Thakar jerked his head towards the office. "Over there, chained up." Outside, Connor heard a hydrobike whining on approach, still a little way off. "How many did Dariel leave at the ship? Michel?" Michel was bending over his sister and did not answer.

A crack, and a high scream. Connor looked back to the far side of the warehouse. Unable to break Dariel's neck, Logan had found enough leverage to break his arm.

Push any man so far, but not too far. Dariel scrabbled away, kicking out like a man who'd never had to kick while in pain. Beneath him, beneath Logan, the floor started to steam, and to undulate, and to glow. Logan, startled out of his killing rage, scrambled to his feet. His boots were smoking. Liquid concrete flecked his legs.

"Too late," Dariel croaked, backing towards the door. His wings had melted into an amorphous red mist hanging around his neck and shoulders. Logan floundered after him, sinking inches at a time into the floor. Flames lapped at his ankles, trying to catch hold of his soaked trouser fabric. Dariel laughed again in sheer hysteria.

At Michel's feet, Éloise rose to her knees and grabbed her faint yellow shield with both hands. Maybe a credulous man would believe she was whispering magic words, but Connor recognised this snatch of French, and knew it for a string of obscenities.

The shield crumpled and caved in. Michel and Jeanne started forwards, maybe towards Calad, maybe towards Logan. That bike was getting louder and louder. Dariel's right arm was dangling useless at his side: his left hand groped for his ring-key and escape.

Engine squeals peaked, and a hydrobike fell into the doorway and ploughed into Dariel from behind. He had no time to scream. Logan flung himself sideways and threw up his arms to protect himself from bike and blood. Beneath him, the floor resolidified so quickly that he had to scramble away to avoid getting stuck in it.

"I surrender," the psi-healer shouted to Calad. He turned to Jeanne, hands raised in supplication. "I surrender!" She seemed likely to ignore him. Michel pushed past her, gun raised, and gestured for the man to sit down.

Calad wasn't paying any attention. He sheathed his knife and, fight forgotten, stared at the bike and the biker, gold-white wings quivering. "What in *hells* were you doing?" he said, voice rising.

"I?" It was a woman on the bike, hair spilling to her waist, and as she yanked off her helmet, Connor, incredibly, recognised her. It was Merovir's copper-headed dancer. She swung her legs off the bike and advanced on Calad, one finger wagging. "You send me after *one* and tackle the rest? You're a bloody imbecile –"

"I'm not the kind of card-carrying lunatic who'd immerse herself in –"

"I will *not* have that!"

Wings sprouted from the dancer's shoulders. Connor felt his jaw dropping. Not two, but *thirteen* colours snaked through them: she looked like a bird of paradise. "Harlequin," Marcello whispered, behind him.

Michel's gun was still up, Connor realised, and it was no longer pointing at Dariel's psi-healer. Jeanne, pistol raised, took half a step towards the young woman. "Don't," Thakar said, grabbing her gun barrel and forcing it to the ceiling.

"She's a Guild Weaver."

Thakar spat. "She's the Harlequin. Put up your gun."

Calad and the Harlequin were still shouting at each other, a few inches apart, hurling increasingly vicious invective in a couple of languages that Connor understood and several more that he didn't. Éloise struggled to her feet and ran past her half-brother, to Logan, who was still cracking dried concrete off his legs. She would have embraced him, but he grabbed her shoulders and held her away from him.

"I would have done *anything* for you." He shook her, fingernails digging into her pale skin. "You only *ever* have to tell me who or where or when to kill. Do you hear me?"

"It was the only way out!" She was crying, and maybe Logan was too, for his shoulders were shaking, and not with the effort of holding her up. "You big fool, you pushed me straight into a corner." She punched his shoulder, weakly, not like she wanted to avoid hurting him, but more like she'd run out of energy to do anything. "Tell me what else I could have done!"

Connor ran his left hand over his face. So damned easy when a man had hindsight: collate the facts, and calculate. But every mistake he'd made and every detail he'd misunderstood had led them all here. For the first time in an hour he wondered which way Hardblade would jump when she found out what had happened. Could Kylesdottir's death go without a sequel now that Hendrix was dead too? He didn't know. It was hard to care.

Outside, a few of the nearby engine noises split off from the rest and crescendoed. Thakar nudged Michel's shoulder, and pointed to Calad and the Harlequin. "Did they have backup stashed?"

"I have no idea." Michel didn't look at him, for he was too busy staring at the Harlequin. "I hoped Calad would stay out of sight till all this was over, and I didn't dare to fear she existed." In response, Thakar loosened his rifle and strode past the bickering children towards the door.

Connor limped after him. The pain block Jeanne had applied to his leg was wearing off. "You want to apologise for anything, you can start that spell going again," he said to her over his shoulder.

"It's still going."

"Could have fooled me." One car engine, several bikes. Underfoot the floor was wet with blood and scored from gunshots and spell-damage. Made it damnably difficult to walk. "Logan, put her down and get your arse over here."

"Fuck you." That wasn't Logan. Connor kept walking, right up to Thakar, and nudged him out of the doorway. This moment had to be his.

He stopped under the warehouse's eaves. Behind him, he half-heard and half-felt Thakar and Zack move to his shoulder, backup or tragedy clowns. The car landed outside the warehouse, amid the litter of bikes belonging to Dariel's dead crew, and its door, stencilled with a praying-mantis logo, popped open.

"Mister Cardwain, it's a pleasant surprise," Sanctis Merovir said, emerging behind his bodyguard. His Weaver, on a bike, landed beside the car, wearing a little satisfied smile. Must have told Merovir exactly when to move in.

"Whatever reports you had of my absence were premature." Connor clenched his screaming thigh muscles. Too damned old for this side of the game. "I can state categorically that Myles Hendrix is no longer a threat to your operations."

"Mine?" Merovir peered over Connor's shoulder – took some doing: either the gang lord had grown an inch or Connor was slouching – into the warehouse. His eyebrows rose. "Impressive casualty pile you have there. No, Hendrix is none of my concern." He turned back to Connor, with a faint smile playing across his lips. "Those pallets are the property of Haa'aa'tion, a rising star on the Dalish IV underside. She will be delighted to hear how well you protected her investment."

Connor took a deep breath. Now he was definitely swaying. "I'd like to direct you, Mister, to the five percent over/under delivery tolerance outlined in clause twelve of the contract you hold." Five percent. Half a pallet had gone up next to his head: maybe less than ninety-five percent had survived.

"Five percent." Merovir craned his neck past Connor again – further now: maybe he'd stood up straight without realising it. "Seeing as I also put a five percent over/under clause in my contract with Haa'aa'tion, we have nine and three quarter percent leeway."

"I'd say that meeting that appears plausible."

The Weaver came up to Merovir. "Mister, the girl..." he murmured.

Merovir switched his full attention past Connor's right shoulder. "Not the moment."

Connor looked: Jeanne, more mulish than angry; Marius, swaying like it had cost him too much to walk the fifty feet from where he had fallen; Calad and the Harlequin trying to push in front of each other like they both thought the other one needed a protector; Éloise, tears fresh on her cheeks and hair mussed, with Logan at her shoulder toting a stolen rifle like he'd been born with one of them in each hand.

"I'm aware of your professional interest in my business, Misters and Mistresses," Merovir said, and Connor wondered whether his Weaver had briefed him as well as he'd shielded him. "If you would like to pay a visit to Dalish IV to discuss the matter, I'm sure Haa'aa'tion would welcome you with open arms." No reference to their condition. No implication they would shy from a fight. No invitation to surrender.

"We aren't idiots –" began Jeanne.

Éloise batted a hand at her. "*Tais-toi.*" To Merovir she said, "Our employer is dead. Our contracts are void. You sold this shipment on the Septième, to stay on the Septième?" He nodded. "Then, m'sieur, we have no jurisdiction." Her eyes shifted to Connor, and her wings began to glitter, till it seemed not twilight but the dawn of an impossible day. "But if you *ever* put me in this position again, I will personally kill you. Drugs, slaves, whores: I will not compromise."

Logan laughed, gold eyes glittering, and swung the rifle off his shoulder. "That's my girl."

Éloise sniffed, but did not answer. Connor closed his eyes for a second. That hideous capacity for violence, switching on and off like a flashlight: and that was just Éloise. Did he have her on board along with Logan? The question of what she would charge for her services – aside from his sanity – rose and fell. He would worry about that later.

"Then," he said, surveying the little crowd of mercs and Weavers, "I'd say we're done here." But they weren't done. None of them were anywhere near done. He held out his right hand to Sanctis Merovir, broken fingers and all. "Mister Merovir, I trust this is the beginning of a profitable relationship."

Merovir smiled, like a cat. "I think it will be." And as he touched Connor's fingers, the bones in his skull shaded green. *I will outlive you,* Connor wanted to cry, but instead he stood his ground breathing polluted air and waiting, waiting, for the miracles he knew were to come.

*

CHAPTER TWENTY-FOUR

Calad hadn't known much about the underside before he came to the Septième, and he'd cautioned himself early on against romanticising the gangland lifestyle. From the outside it was easy to sigh at visions of noble pirates and smugglers eager to escape a corrupt officialdom in favour of free, open skies. Being here made it no easier, amid songs and stories lauding villains long dead. But Septième men grew up with the truth in their faces and up their nostrils: it was easier for them to face reality and smile.

What he couldn't have guessed without experiencing it was the sheer volume of bureaucracy involved in running an underside gang. As soon as Merovir's crew had hauled away the shipment, Connor and Galene had retreated to the offices to balance ledgers, record payments and, after waiting another fifteen minutes till the city learnt that Mister Sl'arani was permanently out of business, make overdue calls. Zack and Logan had waded in to the mess, while Marcello and Pritie re-checked the warehouse's remaining inventory and Thakar coaxed the little boy Joshua out of the rafters. Child labour was easier to reconcile with what Calad had imagined the Septième to be than was double-entry bookkeeping.

He wandered away from the office window towards the middle of the warehouse. Jeanne had wanted to call Myles's aunt, the head of his family, but Ella had sent her to attend to Connor's injured leg and had made the call herself. She was pacing backwards and forwards in the packing area, leaving bloody footprints behind her until it looked like she was the one who'd been stabbed, talking into her jack's tangler at the volume she would normally use for non-jack calls. At this rate June Hendrix Aldin would end up too deaf to be of much use to herself or anyone else until she got implants.

"How you dared to foist such a cretin on the rest of us entirely escapes me," Ella said with the bite of a Neuvième woman whose parents had been married. "Does the Hendrix family teach all its children that contract breach is acceptable? I wonder anyone employs any of you. No, I will not listen!"

Michel was outside the warehouse door, staring out into the night. Calad joined him. It had started to rain, a little stronger than drizzle, but it wasn't cold. Michel was smoking a cigarette. "That's new," Calad said, gesturing. "I thought you didn't."

"I don't, usually. Thakar gave me this one. I don't deny I needed it." He lifted the cigarette from his lips and studied it. "This isn't good grade tobacco. Cheap vape sticks on Terra Nova are made with better. I guess the worst stuff stays here." He inhaled another lungful of smoke. "Ella couldn't tell me much on the tangler. I had an enlightening conversation with Dariel on the way in: he thought I would run with him if he so much as asked." He brushed a strand of hair behind one ear. It was a wig, made from his own hair the day he joined the Union military. No Neuvième man would ever be seen in public with hair shorter than shoulder-length. After one more promotion he would be allowed to grow it out again. "I realised a lot of things were badly wrong – but I didn't expect to find you working with a Guild Weaver."

"She saved my life." Calad stared up to the night sky. Rain clouds and pollution blotted out the stars. "She didn't need to, but she saved my life –" had she needed to, after all? The generator would have killed Calad if he'd kept it on much longer, but it must have hurt her too. "And she stayed with me, and helped, despite not being part of this. I wouldn't even have got to Myles if she hadn't drawn off Delia." Michel was watching him, smoking and saying nothing. "I didn't know what Ella was doing –"

"She didn't want you involved."

"– but I knew Delia was the real danger because Myles trusted her. I had to get her out of the picture. Even if Ella'd realised what was going on, even if she'd confronted Myles, it wouldn't have gone well for her if Delia had been there."

"Maybe: maybe not." The cigarette had run down to the filter. Michel tossed it into a puddle and trod on it. "Yes, Atalanta helped. But it's a difficult situation. If Ella just had to twist contract regulations to the max to avoid having to kill her husband, what's your excuse for not shooting your redhead?"

Calad looked down at the drowning butt. An enemy was an enemy. All the stories, all the histories. Yes, it was an act of war for Guild to enter Circle space. But all of that went so deeply against what had actually happened. "I know. I guess – I just don't know." Michel held out an arm, and Calad leant into his embrace. He was tired. Bad food, injury, and too much time spent unconscious rather than asleep: he was young enough to shrug off exertion, but maybe not the rest.

Another arm slid round his waist from the other side, and he wrapped his free arm round his sister and hugged her tight to him. Her hair still smelt of combat, but when he looked down, she was smiling.

"Connor wanted bonuses," she said, "and I think we just got a bigger one than even he was expecting. Add that to the blood money the Dalishians were offering for Myles, and I think his starting capital has materialised."

"It'll make up for our contracts, too. At least we'll still get expenses." Calad thought about his ruined and stolen equipment, with a Dieusic hydrobike at the top of the list. *Considerable* expenses. "What happens about Dariel?"

Ella shrugged. "No comms at the time, so we can edit the camera images before they get transmitted: an underling came out here, and never went home. That's all anyone will know."

Michel spat into the rain. "I want them to know more. Some plutocrat's puppy threatens our civilisation, I want to get to the person behind it."

Calad sighed. He'd never felt so torn between Neuvième and Treizième. And Michel, born of the one, but employed by the other? Did the Union Fleet pay more than lip service to Circle ethics? He didn't know, and didn't want to find out.

But Ella had had her own troubles: all of the Neuvième, but with her heart on the Septième. Calad couldn't see her staying here, in among the dirt and smells, but she'd lived here for two years, long enough to understand.

"You were hard on his aunt."

Ella sighed, the exasperated sigh of an elder sister to a younger brother, and kissed his cheek. "They all had a choice, and a duty. I know you'll never disgrace us – just as we'll never allow you to disgrace yourself." She kissed him again and disentangled her arm from him. "I'm going to rescue Logan from that spreadsheet –" or rescue the spreadsheet from Logan – "and tell him the good news. What's Atalanta's surname?"

"I don't know."

"Well, find out. I've got her biometrics, but I need her full name for her chunk of the Hendrixes' money." She pattered back into the warehouse.

Calad stared after her, then at Michel. He hadn't heard of a Guild Weaver getting blood money from a Circle family before. He hadn't heard of a Guild Weaver teaming up with one Circle family against another before. Atalanta, whom he couldn't see or sense: "Where is she?"

Michel shrugged. "She headed into the city. Got nervy from being around all the nasty Circle Weavers." He slid his bike's ring-key off his left index finger and tossed it to Calad. "Take mine."

"Thank you."

Calad retreated to the rack and extracted Michel's bike. It was a military Loup T-4, a Union brand. The helmet was a size too big for him. As he adjusted the padding – military issue again – he realised any attempt to trap him between two cultures was bound to fail. He'd known what Ella meant, after all, when she spoke of duty, never mind that his mother was his father's second wife. A Treizième man would never consider his familial duty before acting. However hard Calad tried, he couldn't imagine abandoning his family, any more than he had ever believed himself abandoned by them.

He steered Michel's bike into the air, and drove away towards the city centre, putting the spaceport behind him. Overhead, ships beat down from exosphere into atmosphere, heading for the 'port to act as taxis, transports or traders. Around him, late-night visitants drove from city to city, native to alien, on business of their own, uncaring. As his bike passed over the warehousing's border and began to drift over the Pellite city, he saw gaudy booths being dismantled in lamplight, bunting being ripped down, a city spitting out something that did not belong. Drizzle sifted on the breeze.

Calad shivered. He could smell and taste nothing through the helmet, but he fancied the air felt harsher against his body than it had four days ago.

The human city, suburb and shanty town, began three hundred miles away to the north-east. Too many Circle Weavers, hence why Atalanta hadn't gone there in the first place, choosing instead to join the semi-permanent residents: bacteria on the edge of an unwelcoming ecosystem, tolerated like landfill flora.

He drove to her abandoned bedsit. She was not there. The external walls were spell-scored: not deep rents from Pyrokinesis or Telekinesis, but a telepath's lashes, destroying protections. When he doubled back to the cache in the deserted house, he saw no sign that the fight had passed that way, but neither had she disturbed the few tiny fragments she'd left there. Headed back to the 'port already, past him? If so, he'd never catch her, so he had to hope she hadn't.

Hoping got him nowhere. He returned to the bedsit, pulled off a glove and laid one bare hand on the wall. The Guild weave on the room ebbed over his fingers and washed away from him. It didn't matter: Atalanta, with her scattering trace, wasn't the one he was trying to find.

He slid his glove back on and accelerated, following the faint, fading touch of a Circle Weaver's Telepathy weft. Left, right, left again, under and around: a tangle, and a tale, the story of a pursuit and of a battle.

All at once he realised he was driving through thicker traces: some overlapping, and more that spoke of slow flying and two women trying to drive and shoot simultaneously. He decelerated, staring at gun-marks in mud brick and spell-scores on gantry metal. Weavers wouldn't be the most popular people in this bit of Pell Havasi for a long time.

Here the alleys narrowed into a morass of black tunnels dotted with lights so few in number that they seemed anomalous. Calad descended and raised his visor. The magic tasted thicker than ever. One of the shacks, at a street corner, had a hole in the roof, which had been covered by a clear plastic sheet recently enough that plastic and weights had not been stolen. Calad dropped to street level, beside a carved wooden door, and set the bike's lock.

He pulled off his helmet, pushed open the door, kicked his boots onto the rack just inside, splashed water onto his feet and slid past the chancel curtain in front of him into a tiny trignoscite temple. Some of its benches had been pulled to the sides, and fresh splinters studding the floor bore witness to the recent demise of several more.

Delia lay on a bier in the middle of the temple, eyes closed, black hair covered by a white veil. Calad knelt by her side. Tiny traces of her blood still darkened the cracks between each floor flag, beneath her resting place, and the candles burning beside her head played their light upon her shoulders till it seemed her wings had survived her.

Calad closed his eyes for a few seconds. Did he remember how to pray? The angel of Mercy's image floated in front of him: neither the simple little icon on the wall beside him nor the gentle saint in his mother's favourite monotarian shrine, but the ragged, bloodstained, triumphant martyr in the acre-wide trignoscite temple that crested Port Logis. "I forgive you," he said, and he meant it. None of this had been her fault. Forgiving Myles would take longer.

A dark figure who had been kneeling by the altars rose – a priest, middle-aged and thin, with prayer-beads still dangling from his hand. He nodded to Calad. "You knew her?"

Calad looked down at Delia's still face. "Not as well as I thought."

"That's the way of things." Running feet pattered down the alley outside, and the priest glanced at the doorway. "Children," he said, "scavengers. They want her body parts. It's as bad as cannibalism." It wasn't quite the same, Calad thought, circuitry and biocrete instead of organs and flesh, but he said nothing. Instead he looked up through the hole in the roof and the plastic sheet imperfectly covering it, and wondered about the nature of evil.

The priest followed his gaze. "She fell. I thought the bikes were too low, and then... she fell." His hand hovered near Delia's cheek. "I couldn't be sure – do you think... do you think she was already dead?"

"I think –" Calad hesitated. The priest's belt was black: a man of God by vocation, a firm believer, not like the jolly brown-belted hereditary priests who tended Port Logis's bleeding statues and who blurred the line between orthodoxy and apocrypha fast enough to make Calad's head swim. "I believe, when people fall from a height –" *human people: I know nothing about what happens to Ditans* – "they die of fright before the fall has a chance to kill them." *But not Delia. She would have fallen, and fought, and died as she hit the ground.*

The priest relaxed. "That's one blessing: I won't need to reconsecrate."

Calad looked at the roof again. "I know her family. They'll pay for the repairs." He rose from Delia's side, bowed to the priest, and headed out.

The bike was still in the alley where Calad had left it, but his boots had been stolen. With minor ingenuity he levered himself onto the bike without touching the alley floor, and kicked it into the air again.

She was where he'd guessed, on the closest high rooftop, staring down at the temple where Delia had died. Calad landed on the roof, dismounted and sat down beside her. He didn't say anything. He didn't know what to say. It had been a confusing few hours.

She surprised him by speaking first. "Has your sister left yet?"

"No. She'll take Logan home as soon as he's finished up here." He didn't know how he was to get back to the Treizième. He didn't know whether to go back to the Treizième, or to go to Port Logis and pray to a harsher God than he would find on Terra Nova. "What are you going to do?"

She shrugged. "Go home." Her gaze dropped from the temple to her feet, dangling off the roof edge. "I failed my assignment."

That stung. "Why?"

"The terms included not getting noticed by Circle Weavers. Trainee spies are meant to blend in, rather than succumbing to generous impulses."

Calad too looked down. He wanted to touch her hand. Below, he thought he saw a dead child in the alley, and wondered how to mourn. "I'm sorry."

"It was my decision. Besides, you would have found me in

the end anyway." He stared at her outline in the dim distant lamplight. She half-laughed. "Did you think I didn't know you'd realised I was here?"

"I would have been too dead to try to find you." Keeping his breath steady required concentration. "You didn't fail. You survived, didn't you?" She shrugged again, but didn't answer. "What did Ella say to you before you left?"

"Not a plea to join the Circle. Not a peace overture." She studied her hands, folded in her lap. "It may be worth a reprieve. I'll find out."

I hope so, Calad wanted to say, and he no longer cared about the endless conflict or any faction's rules or what happened to him, just what happened to her. "Ella needs to know your surname. She's getting some money for you – she can put it in a bank here, or wherever you want –"

"I don't need to be paid."

"It's not payment. It's an apology from Myles's family." After a few seconds' pause she nodded, as if she were trying to understand. "So, what's your surname?"

She stirred. "My given name's not Atalanta. That's a code name."

"Well, what's your name?"

She told him. Overhead, a breeze teased the clouds away from the moon.

*

EPILOGUE

Someone'd dotted flower boxes all over the spaceport concourse, in the holding zone between landing pads and front gate. A few floral creepers even ran up the black marble pillars propping up the roof. Logan gave up staring at them when he ran out of names for all the colours. "Why?" he muttered to Ellie.

"Why not?" She was dressed as brightly as a flower, in green-and-pink trousers tied at her waist below a flowing pink shawl embroidered with little birds. Her breasts were bare under the shawl. He knew, for he'd watched her get into it: she'd wrapped it twice round her chest and knotted it at the back of her neck in a few easy moves, though it was twice as long as he was tall. She slid her hand inside his jacket and pulled his spare knife back out from under it. "No concealed weapons. You could have bought another rocket launcher and walked in here with it, so long as you didn't try to conceal it."

"OK, OK." It made him itch. Everything made him itch, from the sight of the sea out of a sheer glass wall on their left to the precision polish job that had been done on every silver and white surface around them. The queues snaking past the customs staff were busy, crowded with Kriastans, humans and Sapilians, but it was easy to spot the locals. They all wore colours, not much black and no white, and they talked in loud voices about everything from their drug habits to their sex lives. Half had Weaver wings. Seeing that many glowing feathers in one place was just unnatural.

Logan fiddled with his neural jack. It had taken them twenty hours to fly in from Pell Havasi, and – following a few hours' sleep – he'd spent the time running through the translator programs on his jack and practising pronunciation till he could communicate, at least a little, in French. When they'd crossed the E-R Bridge, he'd stopped to listen to the magic's whisper, and it had seemed louder than ever before.

Ahead of them, the queue divided for the customs desks. A

Kriastan – massive: female – strolled past the closest free desk with a quip for the clerk. Sure, Logan'd always known they carried a lot of weapons, but he'd never guessed *how* many. Their turn next. Ellie tucked her arm into his and led him forward. The clerk smiled, and bobbed her glowing pink wing feathers. A few words for Ellie, too quick for him to catch them – "Enjoy our planet," for him, in faultless English – and she waved them past.

"That's it?" he muttered as soon as they were out of earshot.

In answer she pointed backwards. The customs clerk was bending over the man who'd been behind them in the queue, now on the ground with one dainty embroidered-shoed foot on his neck and his arm bent at a painful angle behind his back. "You're too used to trouble," Ellie murmured. "Don't provoke it, and it won't come."

Too used to a different setting, maybe. He trailed after her, staring at more sparklingly clean corridors, sea and mountains outside, flower troughs everywhere. It was too prettified, as unreal as Ellie's wings – but she was warm and real underneath: maybe this planet was real too. He looked back down at Ellie, and wondered when she would tell him that she was pregnant again.

A door slid open at the end of their corridor, into the arrival hall, acres across: fewer stores than at a Septième spaceport, more taxi stands, and a mass transit shuttle station of the kind Logan had seen twice in his life. Ellie fiddled with her shawl's knot at the back of her neck, adjusted the bag slung over her shoulder, and looked about herself, scanning the crowd.

"Maman! Maman!"

Ellie ran a few yards ahead of Logan and bent to embrace two tiny, black-haired, bouncing figures. Logan stopped, staring. A little boy and girl – the boy was the elder, Ellie'd said – clinging to her legs, chattering to her in French. Ellie kissed their foreheads, straightened and dropped a brief curtsy to the thin-faced peevish woman who'd been trailing the children.

"Enough is enough," the woman began, but Ellie cut her off in a stream of French too crude for Logan to follow. It didn't matter. The little girl, his little girl, was peering at him round Ellie's left leg, and as she saw him watching her, she smiled like the sun had risen. She let go of Ellie's leg and held out her arms.

THE END

Elsewhen Press

an independent publisher specialising in Speculative Fiction

Visit the Elsewhen Press website at elsewhen.co.uk for the latest information on all of our titles, authors and events; to read our blog; find out where to buy our books and ebooks; or to place an order.

Elsewhen Press

an independent publisher specialising in Speculative Fiction

GLASS SHORE
STEFAN JACKSON

What if 'Think Differently' was more than a campaign slogan? What if it was part of a mind control network geared towards advanced sciences, creating a vibrant, creative and competitive workforce? This is the world of *Glass Shore*, a dynamic existence featuring fierce vehicles, cruel weapons and serious body augmentation.

Manhattan, 2076. The fabled city of gold realised; a city of dazzling buildings and beautiful people; a city celebrated for converting an obsolete subway system into an adult playground. Manhattanite Nikki's life changes forever when she finds the files labelled 'Project Blue Book appendix 63-A'. The report contains a disc related to the Glass Shore, the horrendous nuclear event at Puget Sound in 2062. Disclosure of these files is not an option, so powerful people want Nikki dead. To protect her Nikki hires Apollo, her long-time friend and lover, who is magnificent at his job. He is also a clothes whore with an honest enthusiasm for life.

Nikki and Apollo are the hottest couple in Manhattan. Betrayed by friends at every turn, set upon by bounty hunters and other elements of security, law enforcement and civil protection, they utilise the best hotels, the sexy Underground and the glorious city of Manhattan as their shield.

Stefan Jackson was born in North Carolina beside the calm eddies of the Trent and Neuse rivers, but spent the latter part of his childhood in southern California. In 1994 he moved to Brooklyn looking for a change, drawn to the energetic confluence of the Hudson and East rivers of the Big Bright City. There he met a lovely woman who became his wife, and they have an enchanting daughter. And a cat.

He now lives in Queens, where he writes stories, plays drums, coaches pee-wee girl's basketball, works the cubicle life, cooks breakfast, rides the F line, laughs and rests his head in the land of jazz.

Stefan says "Cheers to the first fifty years. Hoping the next fifty are just as kind."

ISBN: 9781908168580 (epub, kindle)
ISBN: 9781908168481 (288pp paperback)

Visit bit.ly/GlassShore

Elsewhen Press

an independent publisher specialising in Speculative Fiction

ARTEESS: CONFLICT
JAMES STARLING

Arteess: Conflict is the first in a new science fiction series where much of the action takes place inside a game. But surviving the game is not child's play. We learn of science, betrayal, power and progress – from the perspective of innocent, but nevertheless accomplished gamers.

Created as an experiment into the nature of time itself, the virtual world of Arteess exists, in the near future, as a private digital realm. A full-body virtual reality experience where the talented, the shrewd and the lucky are invited to participate in an international war zone of nomadic factions. We are introduced into the world of Arteess alongside the Shard squad, a group of friends specialising in conflict arenas. Though each member possesses unique talents, they are ultimately defined by their personalities, their own personal battles and the moral choices they make in the consequence-free virtual environment.

Surrounded by sociopathic technicians, facetious pilots and a potentially insane commander, they must carve out a place for themselves while surviving the onslaught of rivals and the antics of the rest of their own faction.

James Starling is, by any definition of the word, a gamer. From the mean inhospitable streets of a lovely little community nestled deep within the Devon coastline, James finds himself caught between two distant generations. Dragged along with the modern and the technological, he revels in the virtual environments and endless community entertainment of this millennium's gaming scene. However you view it, he's certainly caught up in the rush of gaming to the point where it's become a bit of an obsession.

Bridging the chasm-like void between literature and gaming, James brings together both the disturbingly amusing black humour of the gaming community, and the focus, scope and monumental scale possible within modern literature. He's quite fond of the end result… *Arteess: Conflict* won the Silver Award in the Teenage Fiction category of the 2013 Wishing Shelf Independent Book Awards.

ISBN: 9781908168306 (epub, kindle)
ISBN: 9781908168207 (240pp, paperback)

Visit bit.ly/Arteess-Conflict

Elsewhen Press

an independent publisher specialising in Speculative Fiction

THE FIRST BOOK IN THE
INVERSE SHADOWS UNIVERSE

SUFFICIENTLY
ADVANCED
TECHNOLOGY
CHRISTOPHER NUTTALL

For the post-singularity Confederation, manipulating the quantum foam – the ability to alter the base code of the universe itself and achieve transcendence – is the holy grail of science. But it seems an impossible dream until their scouts encounter Darius, a lost colony world whose inhabitants have apparently discarded the technology that brought them to the planet in order to adopt a virtually feudal culture. On Darius, the ruling elite exhibits abilities that defy the accepted laws of physics. They can manipulate the quantum foam!

Desperate to understand what is happening on Darius, the Confederation dispatches a stealth team to infiltrate the planet's society and discover the truth behind their strange abilities. But they will soon realise that the people on Darius are not all the simple folk that they seem – and they are sitting on a secret that threatens the entire universe ...

Christopher Nuttall has been planning sci-fi books since he learned to read. Born and raised in Edinburgh, Chris created an alternate history website and eventually graduated to writing full-sized novels. Studying history independently allowed him to develop worlds that hung together and provided a base for storytelling. After graduating from university, Chris started writing full-time. As an indie author he has self-published a number of novels, but this is his fourth fantasy to be published by Elsewhen Press. *Sufficiently Advanced Technology* is his fourth novel to be published by Elsewhen Press, and the first in the Inverse Shadows universe. Chris is currently living in Borneo with his wife, muse, and critic Aisha.

ISBN: 9781908168344 (epub, kindle)
ISBN: 9781908168245 (336pp, paperback)

Visit bit.ly/SAT-Nuttall

Elsewhen Press

an independent publisher specialising in Speculative Fiction

ENTANGLEMENT
DOUGLAS THOMPSON

FINALLY, TRAVEL TO THE STARS IS HERE

In 2180, travel to neighbouring star systems has been mastered thanks to quantum teleportation using the 'entanglement' of sub-atomic matter; astronauts on earth can be duplicated on a remote world once the dupliport chamber has arrived there. In this way a variety of worlds can be explored, but what humanity discovers is both surprising and disturbing, enlightening and shocking. Each alternative to mankind that the astronauts find, sheds light on human shortcomings and potential while offering fresh perspectives of life on Earth. Meanwhile, at home, the lives of the astronauts and those in charge of the missions will never be the same again.

Best described as philosophical science fiction, *Entanglement* explores our assumptions about such constants as death, birth, sex and conflict, as the characters in the story explore distant worlds and the intelligent life that lives there. It is simultaneously a novel and a series of short stories: multiple worlds, each explored in a separate chapter, a separate story; every one another step on mankind's journey outwards to the stars and inwards to our own psyche. Yet the whole is much greater than the sum of the parts; the synergy of the episodes results in an overarching story arc that ultimately tells us more about ourselves than about the rest of the universe.

Douglas Thompson's short stories have appeared in a wide range of magazines and anthologies. He won the Grolsch/Herald Question of Style Award in 1989 and second prize in the Neil Gunn Writing Competition in 2007. His first book, *Ultrameta*, published in 2009, was nominated for the Edge Hill Prize, and shortlisted for the BFS Best Newcomer Award. *Entanglement* is his fifth novel.

ISBN: 9781908168153 (epub, kindle)
ISBN: 9781908168054 (336pp paperback)

Visit bit.ly/EntanglementBook

Elsewhen Press

an independent publisher specialising in Speculative Fiction

THE BLACK HOLE BAR

DAVE WEAVER

Simon, a traveller with time to kill, enters an inn on the outskirts of London. Inside he meets a motley crew competing to tell tales for their own amusement. So starts Dave Weaver's new novel, *The Black Hole Bar*, which has already been compared to Chaucer's *Canterbury Tales* and Boccaccio's *Decameron*.

Simon is an industrial journalist, on his way to yet another off-world assignment, a three month trip to Saturn's moon Titan to write a promotional piece about the harvesting of the Methane lakes on that forbidding world. But Simon is a troubled man. He's sure his wife is having an affair during his prolonged absences; he's bored with his job; and unsure where his life is going.

Simon has stumbled into what was supposed to be a closed session for the Black Hole Bar Writers' Group, their monthly short story competition. Simon writes stories too and begrudgingly they let him participate. The stories begin, and Simon starts taking the competition far more seriously than he intended.

Each of the bar's denizens tells two stories, variously strange, amusing and occasionally downright scary. The writers' own histories, lives crossed by tragedy and drama, come tumbling out one by one into the cramped little room and as they do so, we learn more about the background of this future world. A world recognisable as our possible future but also chilling in its recent past.

Ever since, as a boy, Dave Weaver first watched invading Daleks trundle across London Bridge in grainy BBC monochrome, thrilled to Doctor Quatermass' discovery of Martian corpses buried deep in the London Underground and read about mankind's tenuous grip on existence being almost wiped out by marauding Triffids, he has loved science fiction, particularly the British variety.

A graphic designer by day, Dave has been writing by night for over a decade. With numerous short stories published in anthologies and webzines, he has had two novels published by Elsewhen Press. Although much of his writing hovers on the shifting borders between fantasy and reality, science fiction has never been far away. After years of creating his own future-scapes of flawed space exploration, dystopian visions and time-warped analogies, Dave has his own tales to tell of future worlds and fantastic revelations. He firmly believes that the seeds of the future are all around us; it's not as far away or different as we might like to think.

ISBN: 9781908168597 (epub, kindle)
ISBN: 9781908168498 (256pp paperback)

Visit bit.ly/BlackHoleBar

Elsewhen Press

an independent publisher specialising in Speculative Fiction

THE BLUEPRINT TRILOGY
KATRINA MOUNTFORT

The *Blueprint* trilogy takes us to a future in which men and women are almost identical, and personal relationships are forbidden. Following a bio-terrorist attack, the population now lives within comfortable Citidomes. MindValues advocate acceptance and non-attachment. The BodyPerfect cult encourages a tall thin androgynous appearance, and looks are everything.

In *Future Perfect* we are introduced to Caia, an intelligent and highly educated young woman. In spite of severe governmental and societal strictures, Caia finds herself attracted to her co-worker, Mac, a rebel whose questioning of their so-called utopian society both adds to his allure and encourages her own questioning of the status quo. As Mac introduces her to illegal and subversive information she is drawn into a forbidden, dangerous world, alienated from her other co-workers and the companions with whom she shares her residence. In a society where every thought and action is controlled, informers are everywhere; whom can she trust? Katrina's story examines the enforcement of conformity through fear, the fostering of distorted and damaging attitudes towards forbidden love, manipulation of appearance and even the definition of beauty.

In *Forbidden Alliance* we return to Caia and Mac some sixteen years later in a story that poses questions of leadership, family loyalties and whether it is possible to justify the sacrifice of human lives for the greater good.

The *Blueprint* trilogy is a thought-provoking series with a dark undercurrent that will appeal to both an adult and young adult audience.

Katrina Mountfort was born in Leeds. After a degree in Biochemistry and a PhD in Food Science, she started work as a scientist. Since then, she's had a varied career having been a homeopath and forensic science researcher, and currently works as a freelance medical writer. She now lives in Saffron Walden with her husband and two dogs. When she hit forty, she decided it was time to fulfil her childhood dream of writing a novel!

Book 1: *Future Perfect*
ISBN: 9781908168559 (epub, kindle)
ISBN: 9781908168450 (288pp paperback)

Book 2: *Forbidden Alliance*
ISBN: 9781908168900 (epub, kindle)
ISBN: 9781908168801 (288pp paperback)

Visit bit.ly/BlueprintTrilogy

Elsewhen Press

an independent publisher specialising in Speculative Fiction

LiGa series

Sanem Ozdural

A thought-provoking series of books in an essentially contemporary setting, with elements of both science fiction and fantasy.

LiGa™

Book I

Literary science fiction, LiGa™ tells of a game in which the players are, literally, gambling with their lives. In the near-future a secretive organisation has developed technology to transfer the regenerative power of a body's cells from one person to another, conferring extended or even indefinite life expectancy. As a means of controlling who benefits from the technology, access is obtained by winning a tournament of chess or bridge to which only a select few are invited. At its core, the game is a test of a person's integrity, ability and resilience. Sanem's novel provides a fascinating insight into the motivation both of those characters who win and thus have the possibility of virtual immortality and of those who will effectively lose some of their life expectancy.

ISBN: 9781908168160 (epub, kindle)
ISBN: 9781908168061 (400pp paperback)

Visit bit.ly/BookLiGa

THE DARK SHALL DO WHAT LIGHT CANNOT

Book II

We find out more about the organisation behind LiGa as we travel with some of them to Pera, a place which lies beyond the Light Veil on the other side of reality. There are light trees there that eat sunlight and bear fruit that, in turn, lights up and energises (literally) the community of Pera. There are light birds that glitter in the night because they have eaten the seed of the lightberry. The House of Light and Dark, which is the domain of the Sun and her brother, Twilight, welcomes all creatures living in Pera. But in the midst of all the glitter, laughter and the songs, it must be remembered that the lightberry is poisonous to the non-Pera born, and the Land is afraid when the Sun retreats, for it is then that Twilight walks the streets…

ISBN: 9781908168740 (epub, kindle)
ISBN: 9781908168641 (400pp paperback)

Visit bit.ly/Darkshalldo

Elsewhen Press

an independent publisher specialising in Speculative Fiction

[Re]Awakenings

AN ANTHOLOGY OF NEW SPECULATIVE FICTION

● ALISON BUCK ● NEIL FAARID ● GINGERLILY ●

● ROBIN MORAN ● PR POPE ● ALEXANDER SKYE ●

● PETER WOLFE ●

[Re]Awakenings are the starting points for life-changing experiences; a new plane of existence, an alternate reality or cyber-reality. This genre-spanning anthology of new speculative fiction explores that theme with a spectrum of tales, from science fiction to fantasy to paranormal; in styles from clinically serious to joyfully silly. As you read through them all, and you must read all of them, you will discover along the way that stereo-typical distinctions between the genres within speculative fiction are often arbitrary and unhelpful. You will be taken on an emotional journey through a galaxy of sparkling fiction; you will laugh, you will cry; you will consider timeless truths and contemplate eternal questions.

All of life is within these pages, from birth to death (and in some cases beyond). In all of these stories, most of them specifically written for this anthology, the short story format has been used to great effect. If you haven't already heard of some of these authors, you soon will as they are undoubtedly destined to become future stars in the speculative fiction firmament. Remember, you read them here first!

[Re]Awakenings is a collection of short stories from exciting new voices in UK speculative fiction, compiled by guest editor PR Pope. It contains the following stories: Alison Buck: *Dreamers; Intervention; Mirror mirror; Podcast.* Neil Faarid: *The Adventures of Kit Brennan: Kidnapped!* Gingerlily: *The Dragon and the Rose.* Robin Moran: *The Merry Maiden Wails.* PR Pope: *Afterlife; Courtesy Bodies; On the Game.* Alexander Skye: *BlueWinter; Dreaming Mars; Exploring the Heavens; Worth it.* Peter Wolfe: *If you go into the woods today…*

ISBN: 9781908168108 (epub, kindle)
ISBN: 9781908168009 (288pp paperback)

Visit bit.ly/ReAwakenings

Elsewhen Press

an independent publisher specialising in Speculative Fiction

Queens of Antares
Bloodline returned
VOLUME 1 OF THE BLOODLINE TRILOGY

PR POPE

What would you do if you found out your dotty old Gran wasn't from Surrey after all, but from a planet six hundred light years away across the galaxy? Not only that, but she's really an exiled Princess from a Royal family that has been virtually wiped out by a tyrannical usurper. Would you believe it?

That's the question being asked by Caroline, Alex and Emily Wright, after moving in with Gran when their Father loses his job.

But you might find it easier to believe, if you were actually standing on that self-same planet looking into a sky with two suns.

That's the situation in which the three siblings find themselves when they accidentally get transported across the galaxy.

Would you join the fight for freedom against the tyrant, if that was the only way to get back home to Earth?

You now understand the dilemma facing Caroline, Alex and Emily.

What would you do?

Queens of Antares: Bloodline is a new trilogy for readers of all ages from 10 to 100. Already compared to CS Lewis and CJ Cherryh, PR Pope weaves an enchanting tale around three young people who are accidentally transported from their mundane lives to a new world, where they must find the strength to lead a revolution in order to make their way home. On the way they discover who they really are, where they belong and the enduring power of a bloodline.

ISBN: 9781908168115 (epub, kindle)
ISBN: 9781908168016 (224pp paperback)

Visit www.queensofantares.co.uk

Elsewhen Press

an independent publisher specialising in Speculative Fiction

A series of novels attempting to document the trials and tribulations of the **Transdimensional Authority**

Ira Nayman

If there were Alternate Realities, and in each there was a version of Earth (very similar, but perhaps significantly different in one particular regard, or divergent since one particular point in history) then imagine the problems that could be caused if someone, somewhere, managed to work out how to travel between them. Those problems would be ideal fodder for a News Service that could also span all the realities. Now you understand the reasoning behind the Alternate Reality News Service (ARNS). But you aren't the first. In fact, Canadian satirist and author Ira Nayman got there before you and has been the conduit for ARNS into our Reality for some years now, thanks to his website *Les Pages aux Folles.*

But also consider that if there were problems being caused by unregulated travel between realities, it's not just news but a perfect ~~excuse~~ reason to establish an Authority to oversee such travel and make sure that it is regulated. You probably thought jurisdictional issues are bad enough between competing national agencies of dubious acronym and even more dubious motivation, let alone between agencies from different nations. So imagine how each of them would cope with an Authority that has jurisdiction across the realities in different dimensions. Now, you understand the challenges for the investigators who work for the Transdimensional Authority (TA). But, perhaps more importantly, you can see the potential for humour. Again, Ira beat you to it.

Ira Nayman is the creator of *Les Pages aux Folles*, a Web site of political and social satire that is over 10 years old (that's positively Paleolithic in Internet years!). Five collections of Alternate Reality News Service (ARNS) stories which originally appeared on the Web site have been self-published in print. Ira's Web Goddess tells him he should make more of the fact that he won the 2010 Jonathan Swift Satire Writing Contest. So, Ira won the 2010 Jonathan Swift Satire Writing Contest.

Welcome to the Multiverse*
* Sorry for the inconvenience
Being the first
ISBN: 9781908168191 (epub, kindle)
ISBN: 9781908168092 (336pp paperback)

You Can't Kill the Multiverse*
* But You Can Mess With its Head
Being the second
ISBN: 9781908168399 (epub, kindle)
ISBN: 9781908168290 (320pp paperback)

Random Dingoes
Being the third
ISBN: 9781908168795 (epub, kindle)
ISBN: 9781908168696 (288pp paperback)

Visit bit.ly/TransdimensionalAuthority

Elsewhen Press

an independent publisher specialising in Speculative Fiction

TIMESTORM
STEVE HARRISON

In 1795 a convict ship leaves England for New South Wales in Australia. Nearing its destination, it encounters a savage storm but, miraculously, the battered ship stays afloat and limps into Sydney Harbour. The convicts rebel, overpower the crew and make their escape, destroying the ship in the process. Fleeing the sinking vessel with only the clothes on their backs, the survivors struggle ashore.

Among the escaped convicts, seething resentments fuel an appetite for brutal revenge against their former captors, while the crew attempts to track down and kill or recapture the escapees. However, it soon becomes apparent that both convicts and crew have more to concern them than shipwreck and a ruthless fight for survival; they have arrived in Sydney in 2017.

TimeStorm is a thrilling epic adventure story of revenge, survival and honour. In the literary footsteps of Hornblower, comes Lieutenant Christopher 'Kit' Blaney, an old-fashioned hero, a man of honour, duty and principle. But dragged into the 21st century... literally.

A great fan of the grand seafaring adventure fiction of CS Forester, Patrick O'Brien and Alexander Kent and modern action thriller writers like Lee Child, Steve Harrison combines several genres in his fast-paced debut novel as a group of desperate men from the 1700s clash in modern-day Sydney.

Steve Harrison was born in Yorkshire, England, grew up in Lancashire, migrated to New Zealand and eventually settled in Sydney, Australia, where he lives with his wife and daughter.

As he juggled careers in shipping, insurance, online gardening and the postal service, Steve wrote short stories, sports articles and a long running newspaper humour column called *HARRISCOPE: a mix of ancient wisdom and modern nonsense*. In recent years he has written a number of unproduced feature screenplays, although being unproduced was not the intention, and developed projects with producers in the US and UK. His script, *Sox*, was nominated for an Australian Writers' Guild 'Awgie' Award and he has written and produced three short films under his *Pronunciation Fillums* partnership. TimeStorm was Highly Commended in the Fellowship of Australian Writers (FAW) National Literary Awards for 2013.

ISBN: 9781908168542 (epub, kindle)
ISBN: 9781908168443 (368pp paperback)

Visit bit.ly/TimeStorm

Elsewhen Press
an independent publisher specialising in Speculative Fiction

Dandelion Trilogy
Mike French

Literary surrealism, contemporary fantasy, biting satire, dystopian science fiction. The Dandelion Trilogy by Mike French is all of these and more. Starting with *The Ascent of Isaac Steward*, this is literary surrealism at its most profound. A contemporary fantasy that follows one man's journey into his own mind as he struggles to come to terms with the trauma that has reshaped his life and starts to question his own existence. Moving forward to 2034 in *Blue Friday*, this biting satire warns of a Britain where overtime for married couples is banned, there is enforced viewing of family television (much of it repeats of old shows from the sixties and seventies), monitored family meal-times and a coming of age where twenty-five year-olds are automatically assigned a spouse by the state computer if they have failed to marry. Only the Overtime Underground network resists with the illicit Avodah drug to increase productivity. Finally *Convergence* delivers us into a truly dystopian future, where a covert military/governmental project uses prisoners on death row to explore what happens to people as they die, downloading the Convergence Point formed in the brain's memory at the point of death into clones. But when combined with Avodah they inadvertently trigger what may be the end of humanity – or a new beginning.

What does it have to do with dandelions? You'll have to read it to find out...

Mike French was the founder and senior editor of the prestigious literary magazine, *The View From Here*. His debut novel, *The Ascent of Isaac Steward* was published in 2011 and nominated for The Galaxy National Book Awards. He currently lives in Luton with his wife, three children and a growing number of pets.

Book 1: *The Ascent of Isaac Steward*
ISBN: 9781908168351 (epub, kindle)
ISBN: 9781908168252 (224pp paperback)

Book 2: *Blue Friday*
ISBN: 9781908168177 (epub, kindle)
ISBN: 9781908168078 (192pp paperback)

Book 3: *Convergence*
ISBN: 9781908168368 (epub, kindle)
ISBN: 9781908168269 (256pp paperback)

Visit bit.ly/DandelionTrilogy

Elsewhen Press

an independent publisher specialising in Speculative Fiction

MIKE FRENCH ~ KARL BROWN

A new way to combine art and prose in storytelling.

Your world is manipulated by computer coding, search engines and social networks.
It's just a matter of time before everything you watch, read and listen to
will be created by autonomous machines.

An Android Awakes : The struggle for survival and the fate of a story teller.

In the future some of us will become great writers, renowned artists, visionary filmmakers and talented photographers. Most of us though will just have more sex. Go forward a few more generations and none of us are creative save that of our procreation. Our culture is shaped by machines. The novel has become a mere 1000 words.

Android Writer PD121928 is part of the Android Publishing Programme. To replicate their idea of a writer's life, his partner has been forcibly removed and he lives in solitude with an allowance for drugs and prostitutes. He also has just had his novel *The Eating of Citizen Kane* rejected. He has 14 more attempts to get a novel accepted for the humans by the Programme or he will be deactivated.

Can one of his characters and their story save him?

Featuring Absolute Zero (the coolest spaceship ever built – literally), an ocean in the sky, sub-atomic particles, a Märchen zoo, android communion, naked angels and mockingbirds, *An Android Awakes* hurtles towards the shocking conclusion of Android Writer PD121928's fate.

Writer: Mike French
Artist: Karl Brown
Colour on Digital Edition: Vicky Delfosse
Logo Design & Cover Design: Craig Nash
Design Consultant: Sophie Carpenter
Visual & Script Consultant: Josh Hodson

ISBN: 9781908168733 (epub, kindle)
ISBN: 9781908168634 (208pp paperback)

Visit bit.ly/AnAndroidAwakes

About the Author

Zoë Sumra was born in London, but spent her later childhood living in Lancashire, where she started writing novels at the age of twelve due to extreme boredom. After completing the obligatory epic fantasy trilogy in her teens, she spent four years at the University of St Andrews, where she learnt to fence both foil and sabre and cemented her passion for space opera. She now lives in London with her husband and a collection of swords. When she's not writing or fencing, Zoë works as a print controller for an advertising company.